PRAISE FOR

Foxglove

A #1 *New York Times* Bestseller

An Indie Bestseller

A *Wall Street Journal* Bestseller

A *Cosmopolitan* Best Young Adult Book

"The gothic romance *Belladonna* gets a worthy sequel in *Foxglove*, bringing fans back to a mesmerizing world where Signa and Death go head-to-head with Fate."
—*Cosmopolitan*

"A seductive tale of love and vengeance. . . . This immersive gothic fantasy blends mystery and magic into a morally complex world where Death and Fate are brothers."
—Barnes & Noble Reads

"Complex, rich, and full of unexpected consequences that play out from invents in the first book, this series remains a winner."
—*Paste*

PRAISE FOR

Belladonna

A *New York Times* Bestseller

A *USA Today* Bestseller

An Indie Bestseller

"A deliciously deadly Gothic romance."

—Stephanie Garber, #1 *New York Times* bestselling author of *Once Upon a Broken Heart*

"Decadently atmospheric."

—Kerri Maniscalco, #1 *New York Times* bestselling author of the Kingdom of the Wicked series

"The kind of wicked fairy tale I've loved for most of my life. Grace's world is vivid and sexy."

—Renée Ahdieh, #1 *New York Times* bestselling author of *The Wrath & the Dawn*

"A perfect, addicting escape."

—Adrienne Young, *New York Times* bestselling author of *Fable*

"A Gothic-infused masterpiece sure to become YA's new obsession. Utterly original and completely addictive, *Belladonna* is a fantasy to die for."

—Rachel Griffin, *New York Times* bestselling author of *The Nature of Witches*

"This book is a true pleasure to read from beginning to end."
—Jennifer L. Armentrout, *New York Times* bestselling author of *From Blood & Ash*

"With... an absolutely spellbinding mix of mystery and romance, this is YA fantasy at its finest."
—Jessica Olson, author of *A Forgery of Roses*

"Equal parts sensuous and sinister."
—Astrid Scholte, author of *Four Dead Queens*

"With exquisite pacing, luscious details, and impeccable prose, Grace's latest is a standout."
—BuzzFeed

"The Gothic novel of your *Bridgerton* and *Jane Eyre* dreams."
—*Teen Vogue*

"Highly imaginative and excitingly original... lush evocative writing, magical world-building and a gripping, well-crafted storyline."
—The Nerd Daily

FOXGLOVE

FOXG

LOVE

ADALYN GRACE

LB
LITTLE, BROWN AND COMPANY
New York Boston

This book is a work of fiction. Names, characters, places, and incidents are the product of the author's imagination or are used fictitiously. Any resemblance to actual events, locales, or persons, living or dead, is coincidental.

Copyright © 2023 by Adalyn Grace, Inc.
Excerpt from *Wisteria* copyright © 2024 by Adalyn Grace, Inc.

Cover art copyright © 2023 by Elena Masci. Cover design by Jenny Kimura.
Cover copyright © 2023 by Hachette Book Group, Inc.
Watercolor foxgloves © Inna Sinano/Shutterstock.com; ornament © L Studio Design/Shutterstock.com; black wall texture © Ton Photographer/Shutterstock.com.
Interior design by Jenny Kimura and Carla Weise.

Hachette Book Group supports the right to free expression and the value of copyright. The purpose of copyright is to encourage writers and artists to produce the creative works that enrich our culture.

The scanning, uploading, and distribution of this book without permission is a theft of the author's intellectual property. If you would like permission to use material from the book (other than for review purposes), please contact permissions@hbgusa.com. Thank you for your support of the author's rights.

Little, Brown and Company
Hachette Book Group
1290 Avenue of the Americas, New York, NY 10104
Visit us at LBYR.com

Originally published in hardcover and ebook by Little, Brown and Company in August 2023
First Trade Paperback Edition: July 2024

Little, Brown and Company is a division of Hachette Book Group, Inc.
The Little, Brown name and logo are registered trademarks of Hachette Book Group, Inc.

The publisher is not responsible for websites (or their content) that are not owned by the publisher.

Little, Brown and Company books may be purchased in bulk for business, educational, or promotional use. For information, please contact your local bookseller or the Hachette Book Group Special Markets Department at special.markets@hbgusa.com.

The Library of Congress has cataloged the hardcover edition as follows:
Names: Grace, Adalyn, author.
Title: Foxglove / Adalyn Grace.
Description: First edition. | New York : Little, Brown and Company, 2023. | Series: Belladonna; 2 | Audience: Ages 14 and up. | Summary: "Nineteen-year-old Signa Farrow must solve a duke's murder and contend with a seemingly all-powerful deity, Fate." —Provided by publisher
Identifiers: LCCN 2022058878 | ISBN 9780316162500 (hardcover) | ISBN 9780316158541 (ebook)
Subjects: CYAC: Fate and fatalism—Fiction. | Death—Fiction. | Supernatural—Fiction. | Mystery and detective stories. | LCGFT: Paranormal fiction. | Detective and mystery fiction. | Novels.
Classification: LCC PZ7.1.G6993 Fo 2023 | DDC [Fic]—dc23
LC record available at https://lccn.loc.gov/2022058878

ISBNs: 978-0-316-16243-2 (paperback), 978-0-316-15854-1 (ebook), 978-0-316-57989-6 (B&N special edition paperback)

Printed in the United States of America

CCR

10 9 8 7 6 5 4 3 2 1

I have a friend who was asked,
"What gets you out of bed in the morning?"
during a job interview.
She answered: "My alarm clock."

This book is for her—for always being my first reader, the best travel partner, an A+ stalker, and for making me laugh even when she doesn't mean to.

PART ONE

PROLOGUE

It had taken Fate a millennium to learn the songs of the threads, and even longer to discover how to weave them.

He sat on the floor of a cellar lit by a waning candle, hunched over a bare tapestry draped across his lap. Above it, a needle glinted between nimble fingers, the color threaded through it ever changing as Fate crafted yet another lifetime.

The first color was always the same—a hymn of white that signified new life. He promptly followed it with a calming hum of blue threaded across the canvas, fueled by the music that thrummed in his veins. Passionate riffs of red and a wailing of yellow came next, the colors exploding over the tapestry like a sunburst as Fate allowed himself to be consumed by the life of a wealthy aristocrat who would one day become so devastatingly beautiful that she'd inspire the most wondrous art. Paintings and sculptures, music and poetry—none of which would ever fully capture her beauty. Her life was a series of torrid affairs, each of them spun from gossamer threads as fragile as they were exquisite. With each new lover she took and every twist he foretold, Fate grew more frantic, tearing through her life as he followed a crescendo only he could hear.

Anyone who saw him work would assume Fate was more a musician than an artist—the needle his bow and the tapestry his violin as he strummed life across a canvas. With every slice of his needle, he hurried to capture an entire lifetime that came to him in seconds, spinning songs into colors. He wove with such haste that he did not think. Did not breathe. So lost was he to the story that when the strike of a minor chord sounded and the thread of his needle turned black to mark the end of the tapestry, there came a second where Fate did not remember who he was, let alone what he was crafting.

Fate remembered himself eventually, though, when he looked about the empty room with its bare gray walls and recalled that such vibrant colors no longer belonged to him but to those whose stories he foretold. For while Fate's tapestry had once shone a brilliant and pure gold, the final thread had been marred by a new color for centuries—a quiet, perfect silver that he couldn't bring himself to look upon, for it signified all that had been taken from him. All that *Death* had taken from him.

As he blew out the candle, the walls surrounding him morphed into rows of tapestries that hung from moving lines stretched endlessly ahead. The moment a clear space revealed itself, Fate stilled the line long enough to hang the newest addition. He brushed his finger across its whorls of rich crimson—his favorite of all the colors, for love and passion that strong always made the most gripping stories. The tapestry continued onward as he drew back his hand, and onward it would continue until all the threads had unwoven and it returned on the next line, blank and ready to craft a new tale.

Golden eyes had slid to his next canvas when a sound from behind drew his attention. It was unlike any he'd heard before, one as soft as harp song and yet as arresting as Death's minor chord. It drowned out all other noise, and while Fate made it a rule to never revisit the tapestries he'd already hung—for why alter a masterpiece?—he could not resist its call.

Fate moved between the rows, ducking and sidestepping as he made his way toward it. The line stilled as he approached, and Fate saw that the song did not come from one tapestry but two.

The first was perhaps the ugliest that Fate had ever woven, for too much of it was gray, and purpled like a bruise. And yet it was one that Fate had taken his time with, every thread sewed with precision as he crafted this cruel gift for his brother: a woman Death would love but could never have. Only now, Fate frowned as he looked upon the tapestry, for somehow his creation had been altered. The gray shifted into lines of black that merged into red and gold. Yellow. Blue. And then more black—not just a single line of it but thousands of threads that continued to stitch themselves even as Fate took the marred creation in his fists.

The second tapestry was no better than the first. Swirls of faded rose and icy blues were struck out by thick lines of black and white, over and over like the keys of a piano. He bent to listen to its song—the darkest, quietest hymn in which each note struck like a punch—and drew away with a sharp breath. Its beauty was undeniable, and yet it was *wrong.*

Fetching a needle he'd tucked behind his ear, Fate stuck it through the second tapestry to see what might happen when he tried to weave in the final black thread of death. To his surprise, the tapestry spit the needle back into his palm. He clenched his fist around it.

Whatever these monstrosities were, he had not created them. The sight of them soured his stomach, and he yanked both tapestries from their lines. Even as Fate hauled them over his shoulder, they continued to grow, black and white stitches waterfalling down his back, brushing over each lip of the stairs he stomped up while trying not to trip. He hurried to a crackling stone hearth that cast an amber glow across yet another bare room, this one dressed with nothing more than a single leather armchair that faced the roaring flames.

Fate tossed the striped tapestry into the flames and took a seat in his chair, eager to watch it burn. Yet the flames sizzled out the moment the fire was fed, bringing an all too familiar chill into the room. It felt like ice sinking through his bones, seizing hold of his body and sending tremors down his spine.

Fate lurched to a stand and yanked the tapestry out, scowling as the hearth reignited. Anger stirring, he took the hideously bruised tapestry this time and thrust it into flames that coughed embers up at his face. Fate stumbled back, shielding himself. When he'd glared down at the fire, it was neither red nor orange but a color he thought he'd never see again.

Color leached from his face as he latched trembling fingers around the tapestry, not caring that the heat scorched his palms as he freed it from the flames. He pushed the chair to the edge of the room so that he could spread the tapestry before him on the floor. He fell to his knees, staring, searching—and there they were, glinting like stars: silver threads. Perfect, impossible silver threads. Until he blinked, and they were no more.

His breath grew strained. Likely, what he saw was little more than a product of his loneliness. A delirium brought on by too much work. Because after all this time searching... could he have found her at last?

As delicate as a lover, Fate brushed his hand across the threads to behold exactly who this tapestry belonged to—a girl he'd crafted out of spite, made to tempt Death just enough to ruin the man when it turned out they could no longer be together. And yet her fate had somehow continued to spiral onward, no longer in his control.

The second tapestry was similar, belonging to a girl who had defied Fate not once, not twice, but three times over. Death had often warned him that he was too cavalier with the fates he wove—that there was no such thing as a perfect creation and that, someday, someone would overcome the future he had bestowed upon them and beat Fate at his own game. Until now, he had never believed that could be true.

He needed to know. Needed to see this girl with threads of silver, this Signa Farrow, for himself. And so Fate grabbed his hat and gloves, and he went to crash a party.

ONE

IT'S SAID THAT FOXGLOVE IS MOST LETHAL JUST BEFORE THE SEEDS ripen.

Signa Farrow could not help but think of that alluringly toxic flower, and her family's manor that shared its namesake, as she stared down at the corpse of the once Duke of Berness. Lord Julius Wakefield.

All her life she'd heard the stories of how her parents had died in that manor, their breath stolen by poison. Signa had found wrinkled newspaper clippings detailing the incident buried in her grandmother's attic when she was a child, and she remembered thinking what a beautifully tragic evening it must have been. She'd envisioned bodies dancing beneath a buttery haze of lights while satin gowns twirled about the ballroom floor, and Signa thought of how lovely it must have been in those final moments before Death arrived. She'd taken comfort knowing that her mother had died in a ball gown, doing what she'd loved most.

Never had Signa allowed herself to imagine the tragedy of such a death or stopped to consider the shattering glasses and earsplitting screams like those that reverberated through Thorn Grove's ballroom. Until her cousin Blythe stumbled forward as someone shoved past her, Signa hadn't given any thought to how a person would have to mind their hands and toes to avoid being trampled by those who hurried past the body lying dead at their feet and rushed toward an exit.

This death was not the beautiful, peaceful one that she had dreamed for her parents.

This death was merciless.

Everett Wakefield sank to his knees beside his father. He wilted over the corpse, showing no awareness of the mounting chaos even as his cousin Eliza Wakefield gripped him by one shoulder. Her face was green as lichen. Gathering one long look at her dead uncle, she clutched her stomach and heaved her dinner onto the marble floor. Everett didn't so much as flinch as her sickness spilled onto his boots.

Moments before, the Duke of Berness had been all smiles as he'd prepared to partner with the Hawthornes on their esteemed business, Grey's Gentleman's Club. The arrangement had been the town's most notable gossip for weeks and a venture that Elijah Hawthorne, Signa's former guardian, had been preening about for even longer. Yet as he stood behind the corpse of that almost-partner with a flute of water trembling in his hands, Elijah Hawthorne no longer preened. He'd gone so white that his skin was like marble, veins of blue corded beneath his eyes.

"Who did this to me?" Lord Wakefield's spirit hovered over his

body, his translucent feet not quite touching the ground as he twisted to face Death and Signa—the only ones who could see him.

Signa was asking herself the very same question, though with the restless crowd surrounding them, she couldn't very well answer Lord Wakefield aloud. She waited to see if more bodies would fall, wondering all the while if this was how it had been at Foxglove the night of her parents' deaths. If it had felt too bright and too glittery for the sickness that marred the air—and if her mother's sweat-soiled gown and coiled hair had felt as heavy then as Signa's did now.

So lost in her thoughts and her panic was Signa that she flinched when Death whispered beside her, "Easy, Little Bird. No one else will die tonight."

If that was meant to reassure her, he'd need to try harder.

Everett held his father's limp hand, his tears falling in a bone-chilling silence as his father's spirit sank to his knees before him.

"Is there a way to reverse this?" Lord Wakefield surveyed Signa with such severity—such hope—that her shoulders caved inward. God, what she wouldn't give to be able to tell him yes.

As it was, she had to pretend not to hear him, for her focus had been stolen by a man who stood opposite the corpse, watching Signa's every move. His presence alone had her drawing back, every hair on her body standing on end.

Never had she seen this man, yet she knew who he was the moment his molten stare pressed into her. With his gaze, the haze of lights dimmed, and the panicked screams of partygoers dulled, ebbing away until they were little more than a distant hum. While Death's grip on her tightened, Signa found that she could not turn to look at him. The man who called himself Fate consumed her, and by the slice of a smile on his lips, he knew it.

"It's a pleasure, Miss Farrow." His voice was as rich as honey, though it held none of its sweetness. "I've been searching for you for a very long time."

He was taller than Death in his human form but slender and corded with delicate muscle. Where Death was fair skinned and sharpened by a cut jawline and hollow cheekbones, Fate sported deceptively charming dimples upon bronze skin. Where Death was dark intrigue, Fate shimmered as if a beacon for all the world's light.

"Why are you here?" It was Death who spoke in a tone of bitter ice, for Signa's lips were numb, useless things.

Fate tipped his head to look at Death's hand on Signa's shoulder, only a slip of fabric between their touch. "I wanted to meet the young woman who had stolen my brother's heart."

Signa's attention halted. *Brother.* Death hadn't mentioned having one, and from the tension in the air, she wasn't certain whether she should believe it. Never had she felt such lethality from Death, whose shadows pooled beneath him. She yearned to draw back and find solace in their protection, but no matter how much she begged her body to move, it was as though her feet were nailed to the floor. Signa felt like little more than a bug beneath Fate's glare, half expecting him to lift his boot to squash her. Instead, he drew two steps forward and took Signa's face in a hand so startlingly soft that she flinched—*a noble's hand,* she thought. He bent to her level, his touch scorching her skin.

"Let her go." Death's shadows spiraled forward, halting at the back of Fate's neck when the man brushed his thumb across Signa's throat.

"We'll have none of that." Fate didn't so much as look up to acknowledge Death's threat. "You may have reign over the dead and dying, but let's not forget that it's my hand that controls the fates of the living. For as long as she breathes, this one is mine."

The cold snapped from the room as Death stilled. Signa struggled against Fate's grasp, but the man held tight. He bent, nearly nose to nose as he inspected her. And while no words were spoken, a searching look lurked within his ancient eyes. Something so dark and fevered that she bit her tongue, not daring to make a move against this man who had stilled even Death.

In a whisper, Fate asked, "Miss Farrow, have you any idea who I am?"

Looking at him was like gazing into the sun. The longer Signa stared, the hazier the world became, streaks of sunlight bursting across her vision. His voice was going misty, too, the words soft as cream as they clotted together.

Signa's temples pulsed with a blossoming headache. "Only by name," she managed, nearly gasping the words. From his touch to his voice, everything about this man was scalding.

Fate's grip on her face tightened, holding her focus. "Think harder."

"There's nothing to think of, sir." If she didn't get away from him quickly, her head was going to split open. "I've never seen you a day in my life."

"Is that so?" Fate released his grip. Though his severity was plain, there was something familiar about his rage. Something that reminded Signa of the helpless fledgling she'd held in her hands months ago, or of the wounded animals she'd come across in the woods. As Fate rolled his shoulders back and dusted off his cravat, Death swept in, shadows swathing Signa. He eased her against his chest, curling a hand around her waist.

"What did he say to you?" Death's shadows were colder than usual, flickering and irate. Signa tried to tell him, to soothe him, but every time she opened her mouth to speak Fate's question aloud, it bolted shut. She tried three times before she understood it was not shock or the pulsating headache that prevented her from speaking, and she turned to glare at Fate.

Death said nothing as he slipped past her. Darkness seeped from him with every step, leaching color from the gilded walls and splintering across the marble pillars. Signa breathed easier, no longer having to squint as Death stood toe to toe with Fate in his human form, his voice that of a reaper found only in the most terrifying nightmares. "Lay another finger on her, and it will be the last thing you ever do."

Fate wielded his amusement like a weapon, expertly crafted and honed to perfection. "Look at you, all grown up. What a fierce protector you've become." He snapped his fingers, and the world surged into motion. Muted screams became shrill in Signa's ears. The press of rushing bodies more intense. The scent of bitter almond wafting from the dead body beneath them more obvious by the second. "You are not the only one who can make threats, brother. Shall I make one of my own?"

It was impossible to say how much time had passed or whether any had at all, but soon Elijah was rushing a constable into the ballroom to inspect the body. Fate no longer stood before them, now amid the small crowd that had remained. Though Signa could not hear the words he whispered into a woman's ear, she didn't care one bit for the horror that crept over the woman's face. Fevered, she whispered to the man beside her, who in turn spread whatever was said to his husband. Soon the entire ballroom was ablaze in gossip and heated glances cast toward Elijah and his brother, Byron, who stood beside him, his rosewood walking stick trembling in his hand. The guests kept a wide berth from Blythe as well, as though the Hawthornes were a blight that would infect all those who dared get too close.

Though Elijah faced the crowd's sudden wariness with his head held high, the roaring whispers had Blythe sinking in on herself. Her narrowed eyes sharpened as they swept the room—which suddenly felt much too large and far too bright—toward faces that didn't dare hold her stare.

Familiar with this feeling and how deeply it could tear at a person, Signa whirled to those who were watching. "Have you no shame? A man has just died, and yet you behave like this is a theater. Leave, and let the constable do his work." Though several of the guests turned up their noses, they made little haste to leave, especially as Fate stepped through the crowd and approached the constable. Signa started toward him to stop whatever Fate might have been up to, but Death caught her elbow and drew her back.

Not yet, Death warned with words that rang through her head. *Until we know what he wants, we shouldn't make a move.* Signa balled her fists at her sides and had to do everything in her power not to give in to the temptation.

In an act so effortlessly performed that he ought to have sold tickets, Fate made a show of pointing one slender finger toward the Hawthorne brothers.

"It was him," Fate announced, standing taller among the gasps. Signa hadn't even a moment to react to the fact that, unlike Death, Fate was now fully visible to those in the room. "It was Elijah Hawthorne who handed Lord Wakefield a drink. I saw it with my own eyes!" There were murmurs of agreement. Low, quiet rumblings of people convincing themselves that they, too, had seen exactly what this man spoke of.

The constable's face hardened as he stooped beside the body and picked up a shard of the shattered champagne flute. When he lifted it to smell the residue, his nose wrinkled. "Cyanide," he said flatly, and Signa had to remind herself to look surprised. The constable shared none of the crowd's astonishment, and Signa wondered whether his equanimity had to do with what she'd been reading in the papers for the past several months.

Poison—cyanide in particular—was growing unnervingly popular. Nearly undetectable, it was a clever way to commit a murder. Some had gone as far as to call it a woman's weapon, for it required little effort and no brute force—though Signa could have done without that label.

Her eyes fell to Everett and Eliza Wakefield. Eliza was still turned away from the body, clutching her stomach while silent tremors rattled Everett.

Fate drew a small step forward to rest a hand on Everett's shoulder. Crouching to Everett's level, Fate asked him, "You saw Elijah Hawthorne hand that glass to your father, did you not?"

Everett's head wrenched up. His eyes had hollowed out, their light sucked away. "Both of them," he said, rising to his feet, a fire raging in his voice. "Byron was near them, too. I want both the Hawthorne men taken into custody!"

Signa's chest burned when she saw a faint shimmer of gold at Fate's fingertips. He moved them ever so slowly, and when she squinted, Signa could have sworn that there were threads as thin as spiderwebs glistening between them.

"Listen here, boy," Byron began. He stopped only when Elijah grabbed hold of his brother's arm and said, "We'd be happy to tell you anything we know. I assure you that we want to find the truth as much as you do."

Signa was more grateful than ever for Elijah's newfound sobriety. She didn't dare imagine how he might have responded months ago, back when he was delirious from heartbreak over the death of his wife and the illness of his daughter, Blythe. He likely would have found humor in the irony of the situation. Now, though, she was relieved to see that his mouth was set in a grim line.

There was no knowing what game Fate was playing, but surely Elijah and Byron would have no trouble with the constable. He escorted the Hawthorne brothers through the ballroom, allowing them only a moment to stop beside Blythe and Signa.

Elijah took Blythe's face in both hands and pressed a kiss to her forehead. "This is nothing to fret over, all right? We'll have everything sorted out by morning."

Elijah embraced Signa then, and her body warmed from head to foot as he kissed her forehead, just as he had kissed his own daughter. Perhaps it was because both she and Blythe were on the verge of tears—each of the girls holding the other's hand—that Elijah looked so calm. Like a man on his way to tea, rather than one publicly accused of murder.

"Do not trouble your mind, my girls." He set a hand upon their shoulders. "I'll see you soon."

And then both Elijah and Byron were gone, escorted out of Thorn Grove like the gentlemen they were. Signa stared down the hall even after they'd disappeared, blinking back her tears so that Fate wouldn't be allowed the satisfaction of seeing her cry.

Elijah would be fine. There would be a few questions, and then the alleged involvement of the Hawthorne brothers in this death would be put to rest before a coroner even arrived to retrieve the body.

Signa squeezed Blythe's hand to signal as much, though her cousin wasn't looking at her, or even at her departing father. Instead, Fate was the sole focus of Blythe's rage. Before either she or Death could stop her, Blythe slipped her hand from Signa's and marched across the ballroom, clutching her skirts so tightly that it seemed she might tear the fabric.

"You saw no such thing tonight, neither from my father nor my uncle!" Even in heels, Blythe was a good deal shorter than Fate, though that didn't stop Blythe from getting as close as physically possible and stabbing her finger into his stomach like it was a weapon. "I don't know what you want from my family, but I'll be damned before I ever allow you to have it." Blythe shoved past him without concern for who might have been watching and started toward Thorn Grove's butler, Charles Warwick. Fate scoffed but did not spare her another glance before he turned back toward Death and Signa.

"It's your move, brother," he said. "Make it a good one."

As quickly as he had appeared, Fate was gone again, leaving only chaos in his wake.

TWO

An hour later, the halls of Thorn Grove were eerie in their stillness.

Signa kept close to the shadows, her fingers curling into the banister's gnarled wood as she took her time descending the stairs with cautious steps. When the iron bolts locked behind the last of the gossipmongers and Warwick had retired to his quarters, Signa became overly aware of every groan and creak of the wood that echoed through the foyer.

Her nose tickled from the smoke of too many hastily blown-out candles, which cast the manor into such darkness that Signa shouldn't have been able to see her own two hands before her. Yet she may as well have been in a summer glade, for the glow of a spirit seeped beneath the ballroom's threshold and illuminated an effortless path toward the double doors. She expected that Death must still be in there preparing the late duke, and she was trying to peer discreetly inside when the hairs along the back of her neck rose and a voice sounded behind her.

"He's asked for a few minutes alone with his son."

Signa stumbled back, having been ready to abandon her own skin before she realized that the low, resonant voice belonged to Death. She checked behind her, ensuring that no one was lurking on the stairwell before she waved him down the hall. The last thing the Hawthornes needed was to find her alone in the darkness, talking to herself moments after a murder.

Death had returned to the form of his shadow self, gliding across the walls behind Signa, who tried not to shiver from his nearness. A million questions plagued her mind, but the first that slipped out as she sealed the parlor doors shut was: "When were you going to tell me that you have a *brother*?"

Death's sigh came as a soft brush of wind that blew wisps of hair from Signa's face as he took her hands into his own. Had she not been gloved, his touch would have been enough to still her heart and bring out the powers of the reaper that lay dormant within her. But because of those gloves, Signa remained entirely human as she curled her fingers around his.

"I've not spoken to him in several hundred years," Death answered at last, his shadows gentle as they tucked a strand of hair behind her ear with great care not to touch her skin. "Were it not impossible for us to die, I wouldn't even be certain I still had a brother."

Signa recalled the way he'd shrunk in Fate's presence and the tension in his grip as he'd held her. Even now, alone and pressed against the bookcases in a corner of the room, Death kept his voice low. She tried not to grind her teeth, hating to see him so anxious. Death was not meant to cower. He was not meant to *fear*. Who was Fate, exactly, to sweep in and make his brother respond in such a way?

"He's toying with us," Signa said. Her skin itched, and she was more unnerved than she cared to admit. She eased only when Death pulled her close, her heart fluttering as his thumb stroked a soothing line down the length of one glove.

"Of course he is. Fate controls the lives of his creations—what they see, what they say, how they move... Their paths and actions are all foretold by his hand. My brother is dangerous, and whatever his reason for being here, we can be sure that he has no good intentions."

Signa didn't care much for being referred to as one of Fate's "creations." After all she'd overcome, boiling her choices down to Fate made her success feel unearned. Like he somehow had a hand in all her hardest decisions and her biggest triumphs.

"He certainly didn't treat you like a brother." Signa pressed her thumb softly into Death's palms, wanting only to pry her gloves off so that she might feel more of him.

"For the longest time, the two of us had only each other," Death said. "We came to view ourselves as brothers, though that title means little these days. Fate hates me more than any person in this world ever has." Signa didn't have the opportunity to press for more before Death stole his hand away to take hold of her chin, tipping it toward him. As dark as it was in the parlor, Signa could still see the cut of his jaw among the ever-shifting shadows. The tension in her shoulders eased as he touched her bare skin for the first time that night. Coolness flooded through her body, and Signa tipped her head against him, savoring the touch.

"Tell me the truth." Death's lips brushed her ear, and her knees buckled. "Did he hurt you, Little Bird?"

Signa cursed her traitorous heart. She wanted more information, for only in that moment was she beginning to realize there was so much left to learn about this man she'd believed she understood. But the longer Death held her, the more Signa felt herself melting beneath his touch as, beat by beat, her heart stilled.

How long had it been since he'd held her like this? Days? Weeks? For them to see each other, someone nearby had to be dead or dying, and ever since Blythe had recovered from belladonna poisoning, such circumstances were rare. Signa was glad for that, of course, for she could use some stability and a bit less death in her life. Still, she'd spent too many nights remembering the burn of Death's lips against hers and how it felt when his shadows glided across her skin. For too long she'd been able to communicate with him only through her thoughts, but with him physically present, her control wavered. Her mind may have wanted answers, but her body wanted *him*.

"Are you trying to distract me?" she asked as she peeled off her gloves and discarded them onto the floor.

The deep rumble of Death's laughter had heat stirring in her lower belly. Signa's blood burned with desire as he asked, "Is it working?"

"Too well." Signa trailed a hand down his arm, watching as the shadows melted beneath her fingertips and gave way to skin. To hair that was white as bone, and a frame as tall as a willow and broad as an oak. To eyes as dark as galaxies, which shone as they looked upon her with the very same hunger that pulsed deep within her core. "But not enough to keep me from asking what your life was like before I met you. I want to know everything, Death. The good and the bad."

Endless was the silence that stretched between them, the only response that of a branch scraping against the window, the sound sharp and staggered in the spring breeze. Then Death whispered, "What might you think when you discover that the bad outweighs the good?"

Signa tried to commit this feeling of his skin beneath hers to memory, savoring it while she still could. "I will think that everything you've gone through has made you the man who stands before me today. And I quite like that man."

Death's arm snaked around her waist, his fingers curling into the folds of her dress. "How is it that you always know the right thing to say?"

Melting into the contours of his body, she laughed. "I seem to recall you accusing me of the opposite a few months back. Or have you already forgotten?"

"I couldn't forget that clever tongue of yours even if I wanted to, Little Bird. And I will tell you whatever you want to know about me. But first, I believe we have some catching up to do."

Death settled a hand on each of Signa's hips as his shadows swept behind her, scattering checker pieces to the floor as he laid her upon the table where she and Elijah had played several months prior. Signa had a fleeting, humorous thought of how she'd hated Death so passionately then. Yet here she was months later with her legs locked around him and her skirts lifted as she kissed him fully. She tasted his lips and thought of nothing but how much she wanted them to consume her. Signa kept herself gripped around him, and when they'd had enough of the table, they moved to the chaise, where he came down over her, one knee settled between her legs.

Death's lips savored her neck, her collarbones, the tender flesh just above her corset. "I have thought of you every day." His voice was a rushing stream, pulling her into the depths of its current and devouring her whole. "I have thought of *this,* and all the ways I would make my absence up to you."

There were not enough words in this world to describe the ways Death's touch made her feel. One day, when she was old and her human life had run its course, there would come a time when the cold would call to her and not let go. Signa wasn't eager for that day, but she wasn't afraid of it, either. She had learned to appreciate the cold that seized her veins; to revel in its power, for it was part of who she was meant to be. And so she guided Death closer, placing his hands on the laces of her corset.

Except, rather than release his hands, Signa stilled as she recognized the chaise they were settled upon as the one that Blythe and Percy had used to watch Signa's early etiquette lessons. Her eyes darted to the thick Persian rug that she'd tripped on when Percy had been helping teach her to dance. Signa pushed away from

Death, clutching her chest as she thought of the last time she'd seen her cousin—in a burning garden, made the meal of a hungry hellhound.

"Signa?" Lost in her haze of memories, Signa barely heard the reaper's call. She didn't regret her decision; if she'd made any other, Blythe would be dead. Still, she couldn't stop hearing Percy's laughter. Couldn't stop seeing his smile in her mind's eye and remembering how red his nose had turned whenever they'd ventured into the snow.

"This is where I learned to dance." She curled her fingers into the cushions, nails dragging across the fabric. "Percy helped teach me."

That was all Death needed to understand, adjusting his position so that he could scoop her into his arms. Signa sat between his thighs, cradled against the pleasant coolness of his chest. "You are not responsible for what happened to your cousin."

She appreciated him saying so, but that didn't make it true.

"I was given a choice," she whispered, "and I made it."

With his chin resting on her head, Signa felt Death's gentle hum before she heard it. "Are you saying that if you were in that position again, you'd choose a different path?"

She wouldn't, and that's what terrified her more than anything. What kept her up at night wasn't that she'd given the command to trade Percy's life for Blythe's, but that she'd do it again. She had begun to love Percy, truly. But it'd been almost too easy to let him die. Perhaps she was already more of a reaper than she'd let herself believe.

"I will not lie to you and say that this is an easy existence." Death's touch was tender, one hand snaking around her waist as she tipped her head against his shoulder. "Perhaps it was wrong for me to ask you to make that choice, but there was no easy answer. I didn't want you to lose both of them."

"You cannot protect me from who I am." As she said it, the realization of those words sank in. Already Signa had accepted the dark power within her. Still, there would always be that whisper. The one that she had grown up with, that had made her believe everything about her was wrong.

When someone cleared their throat at the doorway, Signa threw herself from Death and spun to look at who had silently entered the room, not having heard the door open. Fortunately, it remained shut; it was Lord Wakefield's spirit who stared at them from the threshold.

"It's no wonder you weren't more interested in my son." He folded his hands behind his back, not bothering to conceal the judgment in his voice or how the corners of his eyes creased as he assessed Signa, then turned to Death. *"No matter how I try to avoid thinking about what might come next, it seems that I keep finding myself gravitating back to you."*

Death extended his hand to the duke. "That's a good thing. It means you're ready to join me and leave this place behind."

The duke didn't draw forward but instead asked, *"Does it hurt to pass on?"*

Death's gentle smile was a brilliant sight. "Not in the slightest."

It melted Signa's heart to hear how tenderly he spoke, and she was glad that all the years had not hardened him. The tension in the duke's fists eased, and he stretched a hand toward Death's only to pull it away the moment before they touched.

"My son will have to take over my duties," said Lord Wakefield, the words tumbling out. *"I'm not sure I've prepared him."*

Again, Death stretched his hand forward. "You've done the job you were meant to do. Your son will be fine."

"The duties are demanding," he argued. *"Perhaps I should stay and watch over him. He won't rest until my murderer is found."*

"I know," Signa told him. Given how the last spirit she'd been near had possessed her, she fought every instinct in her body that told her to run when Lord Wakefield's attention whipped toward her. Although she didn't know Everett well, she had seen his face as he'd held his father. "I'm sure you're right about Everett, and I have every intention of helping him find your killer, my lord." Whether Signa wanted to, Fate had ensured that this was her task to deal with.

It took a moment for the duke to bow his head, out of excuses. His eyes fell to Death's hand, and this time he took it.

"Take care of him." The duke's voice cracked as Death's shadows wound around him. But before they left, Death cast Signa one final look.

I do not know when or how, he told her, the words little more than a whisper in her mind, *but I will find my way back to you soon.*

Signa forced a smile, wishing she could easily accept those words. Doubt and loneliness were meant to be things of her past. Yet as the shadows consumed Death and the duke whole, she realized that perhaps this was only their beginning.

As breath settled back into her lungs, Signa adjusted her skirts and slipped on her gloves. The moment she started toward the doors, however, her returning heartbeat fluttered. She stumbled, gripping the edge of a tea table to keep herself upright.

This was far from Signa's first time tempting death, but this time... Something was different. This time, Signa choked as her breath returned, coughing into her gloves as a fit overcame her. She dug her nails into the wood; it felt as though she'd swallowed shards of glass that were trying to slice their way through her.

Minutes passed before she was able to catch her breath. And when she peeled her hands away from her mouth, breathless and shaking, Signa's white gloves shone crimson with blood.

THREE

Blythe

The sky was pale with an arriving dawn, and still Blythe had not heard a word on the status of her father and uncle. She paced the floor of her sitting room, fretting across a thick Persian rug that she couldn't help but to stomp upon with extra vigor, for its beauty felt noticeably out of place for a night as severe as this one.

Blythe had not yet changed out of her gown, which shimmered as it trailed behind her. How happy she'd been to put it on, finally having an occasion to wear something luxurious. Now, she scowled as it wound around her legs with every twist and turn.

She kept waiting for the click of the doorknob. For Warwick or Signa or *someone* to arrive with news that her father had returned and that it had all been a misunderstanding. Perhaps it wasn't cyanide at all, but a heart attack with phenomenally poor timing. She could only pray and hope, because of all the places a man might drop dead, why on God's green earth did it have to be at Thorn Grove?

And why did that man have to be a *duke*? Blythe had only just begun to feel well enough to venture back into society, and already she was exhausted by the stares and the gossip surrounding her home and family. Her mind swirled with the memory of the shocked faces that had watched Lord Wakefield fall—the faces that had turned their attention to her father as the cause.

Blythe's hands balled into fists. Nothing would please her more than to stuff socks into every bystander's mouth to stop such ludicrous gossip. Yes, her family had suffered great tragedies of late. And yes, she supposed Thorn Grove *was* a little strange with its odd decor and general dreariness, but there was nothing supernatural about any of it.

At least...she certainly hoped there wasn't. Little by little, though, Blythe had to admit that a sliver of doubt had begun to fill the darkest crevices of her mind with wild, impossible ideas. Inklings that perhaps there was more to this situation than she could see on the surface, for there had lately been too many nights when she awoke at the witching hour to memories of knocking on death's door.

She remembered little about those feverish moments months ago when it had felt like a veil had been cast over reality, distancing her from real life. But her dreams did not have the same haze over those memories. In them, she remembered how her father had held her hair back as she lost what little remained in her stomach. She remembered how he'd blamed the governess, Marjorie, and how Signa had been speaking with someone—a faceless, shapeless figure that no one else seemed able to see.

In her dreams, Blythe remembered something strange stirring

inside her, something light and warm that pulsed every time she'd been meant to die. She'd felt it days before Signa had arrived, and again on the night Percy had disappeared from Thorn Grove. Even now a tight, hot coil squeezed in the center of her chest, tightening and tightening until it felt as though she could barely breathe around it. It was nice sometimes—a balmy, pleasant reminder of all she'd overcome. Other times, like there in her sitting room, it blazed within her and made settling impossible.

Thinking of the man who'd accused her father only made it worse. Never in her life had Blythe seen the man with golden-brown skin and eyes as blinding as the sun, though she supposed that meant little, considering she'd been ill for nearly a full year and hadn't the faintest clue who a great deal of people were these days.

He had the appearance and self-righteousness of a noble, but whether he was a prince or a duke or God himself come down from the heavens to smite them all, the man was a fool to come into her home and accuse her father. For all she knew, *he* could have been the killer, and she intended to make that point known to anyone who would listen.

Only when the sun had officially ascended did Blythe force herself to try to settle, flitting from the table to the bed, then back out into the sitting room to find whichever chair might best help with that effort. Having refused the help of her maid earlier in the evening, Blythe was left to claw at whatever parts of her corset she could reach, trying to give herself room to breathe. She eventually fell upon a chaise and kicked her boots onto the table before her. It felt like hours passed as she stared thoughtlessly up at the ceiling, and she practically leaped to her feet when a knock sounded at the door. Her hair was certain to be a mess, and surely the bare hint of rouge she'd worn on her lips and face had smudged. Yet she made no effort to make herself presentable because there was only one thing that mattered.

"Father?" She tried to conceal the severity of her disappointment when it turned out to be Elaine Bartley, her lady's maid, who stood at the threshold.

"There's no word of him yet, miss." Elaine made her way into the sitting room, observing Blythe's state with a solemn frown.

Though Blythe would have preferred news above all else, her longing could not be disguised when she caught sight of the tray of tea and pastries Elaine set on the table.

"I thought you might still be up. Miss Farrow is, too. And Mr. Warwick. Breakfast will be ready in another two hours, though I thought you might be hungry since I doubt you've slept a wink."

Blythe *was* hungry. Ravenously so. But before she could pour herself a cup of tea, Elaine added, "How about we get you into something more comfortable? I don't imagine a ball gown is ideal for either sleeping or eating." Despite the daylight peeking in from behind the curtains, Elaine acquired a nightgown and helped Blythe change into it. It was only then, so close to Elaine, that Blythe saw how red rimmed and squinty the woman's eyes were. Elaine pressed a hand to her forehead, looking unsteady on her feet.

"Are you ill?" Blythe asked, holding her breath a little just in case. Only having just gotten back on her feet, the last thing she wanted was to catch a sickness that could ruin her progress.

Elaine's cheeks flushed. "On and off, miss, though I expect it's nothing more than the ragweed. The pollen gets the best of me every year." Elaine stepped away so that Blythe could smooth out her nightgown. It was far more comfortable than her previous attire, as light as air. She looked toward a freestanding mirror to see how horrid a state she was in, yet it was Elaine's reflection that captured Blythe's attention.

Cold terror raced through her, seizing hold of Blythe as she stared at a reflection with purple bags under her eyes and a withering, skeletal frame. The Elaine in the mirror was little more than flesh clinging to bone, and Blythe's throat thickened around a scream she couldn't summon. She couldn't stop shaking, nor could she look away as the gaunt face twisted toward her, every facial bone and the outline of each tooth visible through paper-thin skin as Elaine asked, "Have you caught a chill?"

Her voice was the scratch of branches against a windowpane, so abrasive that Blythe fell back as the familiar weight of sickness seized her. Perhaps she had fallen asleep, and this was all a dream—for what else was there to explain the wisps of shadows that seeped into Elaine's skin and spread through her like a blight?

Blythe tore her gaze away, breathing so heavily that the maid took Blythe's hands to steady her. Every inch of Blythe's body went cold.

"Miss?" Elaine whispered. "Miss Hawthorne, are you well?"

This time Blythe did scream, her heart lodged in her throat as she spun away from the woman's skeletal touch. Except . . . there was nothing skeletal about it. The Elaine who stood before her was the one Blythe had always known. Even when Blythe glanced from the maid to the mirror once more, the reflected Elaine was full-bodied and—aside from the red-rimmed and glossy eyes—appeared to be in perfect health.

Blythe swallowed. If she wasn't dreaming, then perhaps she was delirious from lack of sleep? She looked pointedly away from Elaine, trying to settle her stomach before her sickness spilled onto the floor and she gave Elaine a reason to remain in her room even a second longer.

"A break would do you some good." Blythe's voice trembled with every forced word as she tried to cast away the oddity of what she'd just witnessed. "You ought to take the day off."

The last time Blythe had seen hallucinations... No. She couldn't be getting poisoned again. She refused to even consider it.

"That's kind of you, but I wouldn't dream of it," Elaine said. "What kind of person would I be if I were to leave you and your cousin now?" As Blythe sat down, Elaine crouched to help work off her long white gloves. It took everything in Blythe not to flinch as Elaine's fingers grazed her bare skin.

Cold. Elaine's fingers were so, so cold.

Elaine, fortunately, made quick work of the task and rose to her feet. "I'm not much of a fan of idle time anyways. Especially these days." She spoke those last words so ominously that Blythe understood at once that she was referring to all that had happened within Thorn Grove as of late. The rumors of spirits or ghosts or whatever one wanted to call them, and the strange string of murders.

Only... after what she'd just seen in the mirror, Blythe hesitated to call them rumors. She looked to Elaine once more, squinting.

No longer could she see a sickly pallor, or the stirrings of a blight. Elaine's voice, too, was back to normal. It was as though Blythe had imagined the whole thing.

"Thank you for your help," Blythe said in a tone of sharp dismissal. She turned away and tapped her fingers against one hip just to have something else to focus on. Surely, her mind was playing tricks on her. She'd had champagne at the party, and the day had been long and exhausting. That had to be all it was. "I'll see you at breakfast."

Elaine curtsied before seeing herself out, and the moment the door shut behind her, a deep fatigue settled into Blythe's bones.

Perhaps the party had been too much too soon after her illness. She couldn't make it to the bed, but instead reached for her tea and a cranberry scone, too sweet for her liking, to shove into her mouth. As she chewed, she hoped that by the time she rose for breakfast, her father would be safely back at Thorn Grove, all would be well, and the unfortunate day would forever be a thing of the past.

FOUR

Signa had little idea how many people were left at Thorn Grove these days. Elijah had culled the majority of the staff after Blythe's illness, leaving only those he trusted most and those the girls vouched for personally, like Elaine. A few new staff had been hired, of course, as they still needed help to tend to the horses and to clean the sprawling manor. But as Signa walked the dreary halls in the still-gray hours of the morning, passing looming portraits of long-deceased Hawthornes, she couldn't help but think that the manor felt eerily similar to a graveyard with so many memories of its past residents imbued into the walls and not a single living soul in sight. Signa wouldn't have been surprised if, after Lord Wakefield's death, the staff had packed their belongings and headed elsewhere to find new employment.

There was at least one silver lining—whatever illness Signa had succumbed to the night prior seemed to have passed quickly. She'd buried her bloodied gloves in the yard and cast them from her mind. She couldn't die, after all, and had been under insurmountable stress lately. Perhaps it was a passing illness. Perhaps it was poison. Or perhaps it was something that would require more thought than she was ready to give it.

As Signa made her way down the stairs for breakfast, she was relieved to see that the table had been set for her, meaning that someone else was, in fact, still at the manor. Perhaps alerted by the noise of her chair sliding against the wood as she took her seat, Warwick emerged from the kitchen wearing spectacles low on the bridge of his nose. Behind them were haunted, bloodshot eyes. Signa was certain the only reason her own eyes did not mirror his heavily shadowed ones was because, for her, none of the recent events felt new or surprising. She might not have anticipated Fate's arrival, but she should have known her life would never be *easy*. Perhaps she should change her way of thinking to instead always anticipate the worst, and to be pleasantly surprised if nothing horrible happened.

"Good morning, Miss Farrow." When the words came out in a croak, Warwick cleared his throat and tried again. "Shall I fetch your breakfast?"

Signa glanced around at the empty chairs, unsettled by the unnerving quiet. "Why don't you eat with me, Warwick?" she asked despite knowing there were probably more than a hundred silly societal rules about the inappropriateness of such a suggestion. "Has there been word of Byron or Elijah?"

The black, bushy mustache upon Warwick's upper lip straightened over the top of what Signa could only assume was a frown. He gave no verbal answer to her request to dine with him but instead remained standing. "Not yet, I'm afraid."

She steadied a hand on her nervous stomach. Nothing good could come from a visit with the constable taking so long. "What of Miss Hawthorne? How is she faring?"

He opened his mouth to speak when a feminine voice from behind swept in. "Obviously, she has seen better days." Blythe all but dragged herself into the dining room, looking worse than either of them. Her icy-blond hair hadn't been brushed and was still dented from where pins had fastened the waves. Fine hairs were strewn about her head, ratted tendrils falling over bony shoulders. The remnants of powder still clung to the creases of her face, rouge smeared across her lips. Like her father had done so many times before, Blythe wore only green velvet slippers and a robe over a loose ivory nightgown. Though Warwick startled at her appearance, Signa didn't hesitate to embrace her cousin, having needed the reassurance of seeing Blythe unharmed more than she'd realized. Blythe squeezed her back once before she took her seat beside Signa and grabbed the newspaper across from them.

Flopping it open, she skimmed the pages quickly, until, with a relieved breath, she said, "There doesn't appear to be any mention of Lord Wakefield's death."

"Perhaps Everett is paying them off," Signa said, uncertain whether she should feel worry or relief. "I imagine such news would make headlines otherwise."

Still reading, Blythe asked, "They'll be announcing Everett as the duke now, won't they?"

"I would expect so."

Folding the paper shut and tossing it to the side, Blythe turned to Warwick. "Does the offer of breakfast extend to me, as well?"

He pushed up his spectacles, quick to rectify himself. Signa supposed he ought to have been familiar with such oddities, given that he worked directly with Elijah. Seeing Blythe mirror her father's actions, however, appeared to be a first for him. Those actions were perhaps not the most reassuring sign of the young woman's state of mind, but Signa still admired Blythe's complete lack of regard for societal expectations—envied it, too, considering that she herself had risen early to get dressed for the day. Given all that had happened the night prior, such a thing felt ridiculous.

Warwick disappeared only to return minutes later to set out porridge, sliced ham, scones, kippers, eggs, and toast on platters before them. Elaine worked beside him, rosy cheeked and humming as she poured tea into their cups and set the pot on the table.

Blythe took hold of her unsweetened tea, her winter-sharp eyes fixed on the maid who fluttered out of the room with a small curtsy.

"Does Elaine seem ill to you?" Blythe asked, leaning in with a conspiring whisper. "Does she seem feverish? Phlegmy?"

Odd though the question was, Signa obliged with a simple reply. "I don't believe so, though I don't remember ever hearing her hum before."

"That's precisely what I mean!" Blythe drew her steaming cup to her lips. "Today of all days."

Given her own relationship with the deceased, Signa couldn't fault any person's way of mourning or dealing with troubling times. Still, Elaine had always erred on the side of propriety, and such behavior was most certainly odd. "It's all very strange. I don't understand why the constable is taking so long."

"I don't understand any of it." Blythe lifted her feet to sit cross-legged in her chair as she turned fully toward Signa. "What could make them believe that my father would want to kill the duke? He wanted out of Grey's more than anything."

That much was true, and though Signa felt no desire to be the one to break this news to her cousin, she felt it her obligation to say in an apologetic voice, "He *was* the one who offered Lord Wakefield a drink." Then, before Blythe could tear her head from her neck, Signa grabbed her hand and hurried to add, "*I* know that doesn't make him a killer, but it does give the constable reason for suspicion."

"What about that man from last night?" Blythe ripped into her toast. "The one who made the accusation against my father. Have you ever seen him before?"

There was the question, again. The same one that Fate had asked her the night prior.

"I have not." Signa slathered a mountain of butter onto her lemon scone and tried to ignore the bitterness festering within her. While the words were her truth, Signa couldn't help but feel that she was lying. She'd come to view Blythe as a sister, and day by day the need to share what she was and everything she was capable of was becoming impossible to ignore. But how exactly did you tell someone who had no experience with the paranormal that not only was Death a sentient being who had helped Signa hunt down Blythe's murderer—who just so happened to be the brother that Blythe still believed was alive—but also that the man responsible for accusing her father was Death's brother, Fate?

If that wasn't convoluted enough, there was also the fact that Signa and Death were intimate, and that she had the powers of a reaper. It would be a lot for anyone to take in, surely, and was a conversation Signa wasn't convinced even *could* be broached.

And so, rather than say anything more, she filled her plate with ham and eggs and slathered more butter onto another lemon scone. When everything went to hell, at least she could always count on scones.

"Whoever he is, he certainly has some nerve," Blythe pressed, sipping her tea with a ferocity Signa had not known possible. "Or perhaps an ulterior motive. I intend to find him and see which it is."

The very thought had Signa so distracted that she burned her tongue on the tea, forgetting to blow on it. "Do not forget that you are a Hawthorne," she said carefully, stirring in a third spoonful of sugar. "Your family is bound to have enemies, be it for reasons of jealousy or bitterness. Perhaps your father refused someone's entry into the club. Perhaps it has nothing to do with Elijah at all, but with Lord Wakefield. If someone wants his title, Everett could be the next victim. We can't dive into this situation without thinking it through."

Blythe leaned back in her seat, stabbing her fork into a chunk of ham. "Then what do you propose we do? I cannot be expected to sit idly by."

Signa hated that such a question made her skin buzz and some tiny part of her spark to life. Uncovering Blythe's murderer was not something Signa wished to ever relive, but for the Hawthornes, she wouldn't hesitate. Still, it was unnerving how quickly her mind latched on to the idea of a new puzzle dangling before her. Already she found herself trying to sort out the scattered pieces.

"I think that, for now, we wait and see what happens with Elijah."

It was not an answer that Blythe appreciated, though some small part of her must have realized it was their best option.

"I must warn you that my patience is limited, cousin," Blythe said.

"And I must warn *you* that, were you to venture out into the world right now, looking as you do and behaving as boorishly as you are, you would only further the belief that there's something strange about the Hawthornes." Signa smiled when Blythe cut her a look, though the jest was short-lived as a heavy *clunk-clunk-clunk*ing echoed outside the dining room doors. So familiar was the sound that Signa and Blythe shared a look before bolting to their feet as the double doors opened and Byron Hawthorne stepped inside.

His shoulders were bowed, and his gaunt cheeks and neck were shadowed with dark stubble. Signa looked behind him, to where Warwick stood alone, and clutched the back of her chair to support herself.

Blythe noticed Warwick at the same time, and the smile melted from her face. "Where is my father?"

"I did everything I could." Byron fisted his cane tight and looked his niece in the eye. "I'm sorry, Blythe, but I'm afraid that Elijah is being detained for the murder of Lord Wakefield."

FIVE

As well acquainted with death as Signa was, she'd met very few murderers in her lifetime. There was Percy, of course. And she supposed herself, though she tried not to stew on that. Still, she didn't need more experience to understand that Elijah Hawthorne was no murderer.

"What possible motive do they think he had?" Signa demanded as the puzzle pieces scattered in her mind's eye. "He wanted to be done with Grey's!"

"Lord Wakefield had already made a sizable payment to secure his future in the business." Byron looked as though he'd aged twenty years overnight as he peeled off his gloves and tossed them onto the table. "They're theorizing that Grey's was bordering on financial ruin due to Elijah's neglect and that he needed the money but didn't want to give up full ownership."

His forehead was perspiring, and Warwick was quick to fetch

him a glass of water and a stool as Byron took a seat and propped up his bad knee.

"That's preposterous!" As fair skinned as she was, Blythe's face and neck were flushed with rage. Byron nodded at her, then did a double take when he noticed his niece's state of dress.

"What in God's name are you... Oh, never mind. Despite what the truth may be, it was Elijah who gave Lord Wakefield the drink. The fool admitted it himself."

Blythe's indignant huff was enough to suggest she thought her father was ridiculous for admitting to such a thing. Signa agreed, especially given the circumstances. She knew from experience how awful it was to have people believe you were the reason for someone's death. But to have people believe you killed a *duke*? It would soon be in every paper throughout the country, ruining the Hawthornes' reputation and that of Grey's with it.

"If he was trying to save Grey's from financial ruin," Signa said, "then why would he kill a duke and soil its reputation? Where's the logic in that?"

Byron's eyes narrowed, and Signa tried not to show her offense at his surprise. Byron was by far the most traditional member of the Hawthorne family; in her months at Thorn Grove, she'd come to learn that when Elijah had initially taken over the family business, Byron was filled with such jealousy that, rather than working alongside Elijah, he went into the service to make himself scarce. According to Elijah, Byron had ascended high into the rankings before an injury sent him home with a bad knee. He had little choice but to partake in the family business soon after, though military training had made him more rigid than ever.

Byron operated under the belief that there was a proper order to all things—that women had their place and men had theirs. Signa was a little surprised he was even entertaining this conversation. Perhaps the past few months had had some positive influence on him after all.

"You're right." Byron set down his water glass. "It's not logical at all. Unfortunately, after the past year, no one is *expecting* Elijah to think rationally."

"He no longer indulges," Blythe argued. "Not even a little."

The thin skin around Byron's eyes creased in genuine apology. "Once you earn a reputation for yourself, it's difficult to change the way others perceive you. I'm afraid your father is facing a long and arduous uphill climb."

"But you believe him," Blythe pressed, "don't you?" Signa's belly churned when Byron looked away. She was glad that Blythe couldn't see the shadows that darkened his expression. "It's not for me to decide," he said.

Signa thought of all the people who had shown up for the party the night prior. She thought of their painted-on grins and their pretty words, congratulating Elijah one moment only to condemn him the next. How quickly everyone had turned on him. How quickly they would turn on *anyone*. For too many years she'd been willing to fight tooth and nail for a place in society, and she hated herself for it. Hated how hard she had tried to mold and shape herself into something worse than any poison she'd ever tasted.

"Surely my father got the drink from the true killer," Blythe suggested.

Byron's seat gave a low creak as he leaned back, shut his eyes, and began to massage his temples. "He claims he got it off a serving tray and doesn't remember who from."

Signa went to take a sip of her tea only to find she'd already drunk it all. Her mind had been too busy processing this new information to notice, for it made little sense. No one else at the party had been sick, so how was it that someone had managed to poison a single drink on a serving tray and ensure it landed on its right mark. Unless, perhaps...

"Do you think it possible that Lord Wakefield wasn't the intended victim?" she asked, thinking of Percy and how the tea he'd poisoned had been meant for his birth mother, Marjorie.

Blythe went rigid. "You think the poison was for my father?"

"It's a possibility." Signa drummed her fingers on the table as she worked through the idea. "It could have been meant for anyone, really. If it *had* been meant for Elijah, the person behind this was unaware that he's no longer drinking."

"We can theorize all day." Byron seemed ready to fall asleep in his seat, should they let him. "All that matters right now is that the authorities believe Elijah is the murderer. And if they don't find a more obvious culprit by the time of his trial..."

He didn't need to say the rest; the truth of it already hung heavy around them. The punishment for murder was execution. If they didn't find the true culprit, Elijah would be hanged.

Blythe hadn't taken a bite of food since Byron walked in, yet she still clutched her fork so tightly that her knuckles were bone white.

"We cannot leave this up to a constable," Signa said. With Fate involved, that option would only end in loss. However, it wasn't as though she could say that aloud, and Byron hadn't changed enough to stop himself from fixing Signa with an incredulous stare.

"I know there's something strange about you, Miss Farrow," he began, not unkindly. Or at least not unkindly for *him*. "I know that, with this strangeness, you have helped my family once already. But you are no Hawthorne, and this is not something any young lady should get herself involved with. No one would fault you if you were to return to Foxglove early."

Signa hadn't realized those words would feel like a bludgeon until they struck.

Beside her, Blythe threw her fork onto the table with a clatter. "To *Foxglove*?" she demanded. "Why on earth would she go there?"

"Because that is her home, Blythe. To be frank, the last thing we need is to give anyone another reason to scrutinize our family, and Signa is a beacon of unfavorable attention."

There was no time for Signa to form her own thoughts before Blythe sat up straighter, fuming. "How do you think it would look if she left us now? People would think we frightened her off!"

As much as Signa could both hear and acknowledge the argument surrounding her, she could hardly pay it any mind. Her heart had lurched from her chest to her throat, hammering so fiercely that she worried she might be sick.

Foxglove.

For months that manor had been looming over her. When she'd

turned twenty and inherited her parents' fortune, Elijah had given her all the help she might need to pursue getting the manor set up for her arrival. He'd given her recommendations, contact information for a newspaper that would put out ads for staff, and had even offered to purchase her a ticket for the train. Eventually, though, as ledgers of his notes and advice began to pile up with dust in her sitting room, Elijah stopped discussing Foxglove altogether. Ages ago he'd told Signa that she could remain at Thorn Grove for as long as she liked, and it seemed he'd meant it.

Signa knew she'd be expected to leave eventually, but the thought of returning to Foxglove felt like stepping into a past that Signa had long since left behind. Here at Thorn Grove, she finally had a family. And as Blythe slid her hand into Signa's beneath the table and squeezed tight, all Signa could think about was how much she wanted to keep that family close.

"She's not leaving." It was Blythe who decided, unfaltering beneath Byron's glower.

Both girls ignored the way he pinched the bridge of his nose. "If she stays, she'll need to help us." His eyes were severe as they flicked to Signa, searching her face. He frowned, not seeming to favor what he saw. "Can you do that, Miss Farrow?"

Signa had to fight to find her voice as she asked, "What would I need to do?"

"You and Blythe will do what all ladies your age are meant to." Signa's skin prickled at his words. Still, when Byron leaned in, so did she. "Focus on bolstering the name of this family. Or, at the very least, maintaining our reputation. God knows Elijah could use the help. If you're going to stay, we cannot have you sulking about inside. You must be out and about, proving that you are confident in this family's innocence. It will only fan the flames if people believe that we have holed ourselves up out of fear."

To her surprise, Signa had no argument. When she had first walked into the room, she'd thought about how silly it had seemed to have breakfast and to go on pretending that everything was normal. But perhaps putting on a good face and maintaining a charade that all was well would ease the gossip. Not to mention that if it meant remaining at Thorn Grove with Blythe and Elijah, Signa was willing to do anything.

Byron pried himself from his chair, ready to make his exit, when the dining room's double doors swung open and a raven-haired maid Signa had seen only in passing hurried in with a letter set upon a silver tray. She curtsied—something Signa was still getting used to—then extended the tray to Signa, who took one look at the golden envelope and tasted acid.

She knew without looking who it was from, for the shade itself was too similar to Fate's burnished eyes to be coincidence. Blythe's curiosity prickled at Signa's skin as she took the envelope from the tray.

"Open it," Blythe urged, leaning in to catch a glimpse of the written words. Byron was observing them, too, and since there was no way out of it, Signa tore open the envelope. Inside there was no letter but an invitation written in gilded script.

To the ineffable Miss Signa Farrow,

She already wanted to burn Fate alive for his ridiculous greeting alone.

Your presence has been requested to join
His Majesty Prince Aris Dryden of Verena
at Wisteria Gardens
this Saturday evening at six o'clock
for a grand ball to celebrate his arrival to Celadon.

Signa barely managed to refrain from crumbling the invitation in her hands. A *prince*! How ridiculous this man was to think he could waltz in with such a grand facade. She had every intention of tearing the parchment apart until Blythe—reading over her shoulder with gleaming eyes—plucked the invitation from her fingers.

"Signa." Her cousin's voice was breathy with wonder, and Signa realized that whatever game Fate was playing, she'd already lost. "We must go! If we can impress a prince, perhaps he might help us clear my father's name."

The truth seared a hole in Signa's tongue, though it wasn't as though she could admit to knowing that this man was no prince.

"Blythe is right." Byron plucked the invitation from his niece's hands. Such a bad habit must have run in the family. "This is the perfect opportunity. At the very least, you must attend and demonstrate to everyone your confidence in this family. You may not be a Hawthorne by blood, but perhaps that's to our benefit. Others may be more likely to believe you."

Signa tried not to scrunch up her nose. She would do it, of

course, even if the last thing she wanted was to throw herself back into society's clutches during the season. She made it a point not to look too closely at Byron or Blythe, staring instead at the hands she folded against her lap.

As quiet as the night, Blythe whispered, "My father is innocent. I know he is. Please say that you'll help him."

Signa steeled herself, shoulders back, and gathered every ounce of courage within her. If she had to play Fate's game, then so be it. She was a reaper—a shadow of the night with a lethal touch. She would protect her family. Her *home*. And when she was through with him, Signa would ensure that Fate regretted the day he'd ever challenged her.

"Of course I will," Signa promised, staring firmly into her cousin's eyes. "I'll go to the party or woo the prince, or whatever it takes. We will save your father, Blythe. Of that, I'm certain."

SIX

It was to her suite that Signa soon retired, Fate's invitation clutched in her hand. If she was going to beat Fate at his own game, then she needed more information. Signa locked the heavy oak door behind her, then contemplated dragging over her dresser to further block entry before deciding that would only draw *more* attention. The lock alone would have to suffice.

Gundry watched from the foot of her bed, yawning from behind the billowing canopy as Signa pressed her ear to the door. She moved to the nightstand only when she was certain no one was wandering the halls, then opened the top drawer and withdrew a small bundle of silk cloth. Cradling it close to her chest, Signa took the bundle to her bed and spread it over the linen, revealing a handful of berries so dark they were nearly black.

Belladonna.

Behind her, Gundry growled deep in his throat. The hellhound had been with her for the past several months, sent by Death as a companion. Mostly, he spent his days lazing away near a hearth or, when the weather permitted, flitting through burnished leaves in the yard. Signa had told everyone he was a stray she'd picked up during a trek through the woods, and though it took some convincing, Elijah had agreed to let him stay.

No one who met Gundry would think the hound much of a protector, but sometimes, as Signa watched him stir during the witching hours, she'd remember the shadows that had dripped from his open jaws and how he'd clamped those jaws around Percy with a single command.

"Hush," she told him, bopping the beast on his wet snout. "I may regret this, but I need your help." When Signa was in her reaper form, it was only Death who could either see or hear her. She could perhaps show that she was near with a sudden gust, or windows slamming shut on a mild day. But if she hoped to communicate with Elijah, she'd need assistance.

"Ready yourself, Gundry. We're going on an adventure."

Gundry's ears flattened. He looked from her to the berries with a whine that Signa paid little mind as she drew the curtains shut and scrawled a hurried note onto a piece of tea-stained parchment. The ink was still wet when she folded the sheet and reached forward to scratch Gundry under his chin, slipping the note beneath his collar.

"We'll be fine," she told him. "I promise."

There weren't many berries left—perhaps fifteen or so—and it would be several more months until the belladonna near Thorn

Grove was back in bloom. All she had remaining were dried and shriveled berries from last autumn's stash, which would likely taste as rotten as they looked. Still, they should do the trick. It'd take at least five berries to produce the results she needed, and so it was precisely five berries that she scooped into her palms before bundling the cloth and setting it aside.

Signa took a seat on the bed and pressed all five berries upon her tongue. They were crunchy and bitter, their rot soiling her mouth. Yet she swallowed them down all the same and curled her fingers in Gundry's soft coat as she waited for the effects to take hold.

Signa shut her eyes as her vision swam and sipped slow breaths through her lips until she could take in no more. Only then did she crack an eye open as the belladonna claimed her, the reaper's power spreading through her veins. She greeted it like a lover, embracing the cold and the darkness that wisped around her fingertips.

"Hello, you," she whispered to the shadows that swathed her hands. Gundry still lay with his chin on her lap, though he was changed. There were shadows where his eyes had once been, and more that oozed like smoke from his maw. The last time he'd been in this form, it had been too dark to notice that Gundry's ribs protruded from his skin, or that his hollowed-out insides were visible through a gaping hole in his belly that swirled with darkness. Gundry looked every bit like a beast that had crawled its way out of the depths of hell, with elongated canines and massive paws that were twice the size of her face. And yet he was still the same Gundry, whining and nudging his wet nose against Signa's hip.

"I'm all right," she said, slipping from the bed. "Come, we should hurry."

Signa steeled her nerves. Death had once said that her powers were about intention—want something, then take it. Facing the barest wall in her suite, she focused on Elijah's face as she imagined a portal of shadows that would take her to see him. It was certainly possible; Death had done something similar the night he'd taken her to see the bridge of souls. Still, just because something *could* be done, it didn't mean that she knew how to do it. She was having trouble focusing as slivers of sunlight cut through the windows. Her powers felt out of place in the daylight, perhaps even forbidden. Only under the cover of night could she stop thinking about how odd it was to not be able to feel the press of the springtime heat against her skin.

It was thoughts like that, however, that would get Signa into trouble. There was no choice but to cast aside her doubts, and to step into the shadows that built upon the wall. Unfortunately, Signa smacked face-first into the wall the moment she tried and rocked back, cursing the blasted space as though it had reached out and attacked her.

The ground rumbled suddenly with a deep, smoky laugh. Signa squeezed her eyes shut, refusing to turn and look at Death from where he waited on her bed.

"How long have you been watching?"

"Long enough." He sounded smug, but Signa didn't spare him a glance to confirm that he looked it, too. "What are you up to, Little Bird?"

Her poor nose felt as though she'd just taken a brick to the face, and she tried to rub away its aching. "What does it look like I'm up to? I'm trying to use these beastly powers." Only when he chuckled again did she shoot him a glare so scathing that Death's lips promptly uncurled. He tried his best to look inconspicuous, though there was no denying the amusement glittering in his eyes.

"What for?" he asked. "I thought we agreed that you'd only use those berries in an emergency."

She glanced to her reserve of belladonna—ten berries left. If she wanted to avoid having to take more, there was no time to stand around chatting.

"Your brother is on an expedited mission to ruin my family. If that's not an emergency, I don't know what is." A surge of panic shot through her, and Signa clutched her chest as the heart within it fluttered. Death was behind her in an instant, his hands on her shoulders. She settled against his body as her heart stilled once more, and lifted her hand to his.

"I let myself get too worked up," she said. "It won't happen again—"

"Your body is acclimating to the belladonna." Death swept a strand of hair from her face and tucked it behind one ear. "You shouldn't be using it."

"Elijah is in *prison*." Death's eyes were filled with such concern that Signa had to keep her eyes trained on his chest. "We'll discuss this later."

Only then did he ease his hold on her, though to help maintain her current state, he didn't let go entirely. "Very well." He waved his free hand at the wall, where fervent shadows swarmed. "Is this what you wanted?"

She kept her chin high. "It is."

"Wonderful. I quite like your face, and I'm not sure that it could handle another one of your attempts." Slipping his hand from her shoulder and down to hold hers, he pulled her toward the writhing shadows. "Whenever you're ready."

At her heels, Gundry gave a low whine. Signa cast a cursory glance at the parchment beneath his collar—ensuring it was still secure—before she gave his head a gentle pat and stepped forward.

It was a familiar feeling to let the shadows pull her from one place to another, like slipping through a lake and emerging dry. Strange and a little unsettling, but also deceptively peaceful, given where they'd ended up.

No longer were they in Signa's bedchamber but in a too-small room with such little light that, at first, Signa thought her sight had been spirited away. Only because she was a reaper did her vision normalize, the darkness soon giving way to reveal the outline of a small cot. A chamber pot. And, eventually, a man huddled on the cold stone floor, knees drawn into his chest.

Signa started toward him before Death's grip tightened. "Remember that you are a reaper right now. Mind your touch."

Signa backed toward a wall with her arms wound tight around herself. "Are we in the prison?" She was glad she wasn't human in that moment, for the stone splitting from the ground was caked with so much dust that she feared for her ability to breathe. It felt like one wrong move was all it would take for this place to come shattering down upon them.

"Yes." Death spoke in the placating tone he'd used with Lord Wakefield and other restless spirits, and though Signa recognized the tactic, she also appreciated it. "No light is allowed in the cells. The idea is to blind the prisoners—to never let them see each other or their surroundings, so that they might feel entirely alone. I've picked up far too many people from rooms just like this one, driven to madness from the isolation."

As she looked at Elijah, Death's words cut deep. "Go to him," Signa whispered, summoning the hound to her side. Gundry took one look at her before he bowed his head and padded the few short steps toward Elijah. The shadows swirling around his protruding ribs slipped from him with every step, shedding from his skin until his body filled out and he was nothing but a common hound with a gentle whimper.

Elijah startled at the sound, jerking his face toward it. The left side of his face was bruised and swollen. His hands and clothing were covered in the grime of the room, stained a sooty gray. Signa covered her mouth, scrutinizing the cut along his brow, to the bone and begging for an infection.

"Who is that?" he croaked, trying to squint through the darkness. "Is someone there?"

Signa squeezed Death's hand, keeping herself grounded. She could only watch as Gundry nudged Elijah's leg, still and calm even as Elijah pulled away. "Gundry? Can this truly be you?"

Gundry pressed his snout into Elijah's leg, and with trembling hands Elijah reached out to pet the beast. The moment his fingers curled into Gundry's fur, Elijah's voice croaked with a hoarse laugh. "It seems I have gone delusional." He stroked down Gundry's back and then back up again, stopping when his fingertips brushed the slip of paper tucked beneath the hound's collar. Elijah stilled at the sound, glancing at the door once before he tugged the note from Gundry's collar.

He held it up, though there wasn't enough light to read it, especially where some of the letters had smudged. His hands shook as, ever so slowly, he scooted toward the cell door and held the note up to the keyhole in the iron lock, squinting to read one letter at a time with only the barest hint of light.

Is there a suspect?

It took such a painfully long time that Signa had half a mind to go back and fetch him a lighter. But the idea had hardly formed in her head before the cell door rattled. Elijah shoved the note into his mouth and swallowed as the door swung open, nearly hitting him. Elijah's eyes flew at once to Gundry, but the hound was nowhere in sight, already back at Death and Signa's side and concealed in the shadows.

Hideous was the only way to describe the man who stepped inside the cell. His face was too small for his body, round and oily, and he wore a gruesome grin that Signa longed to wipe from his chapped lips. She looked at once to his knuckles—scabbed, which answered the question of what had happened to Elijah's face.

"Get up, Hawthorne. This ain't a gentleman's club."

Signa hadn't realized how tightly Death was holding her back until he squeezed her hand.

Steady, Little Bird. The words were a gentle buzz in her mind. *Steady.*

If not for Death's presence, such a thing would have felt impossible as the man gripped Elijah by the collar and hauled him to his feet. As awful as it was to watch, Signa was glad that Elijah didn't fight back. Who knew what might happen if he dared to make a move against these men.

The guard threw Elijah a mask that looked like little more than a sack with slits for eyes. Elijah put it on without protest, though a moment before he slid the monstrosity down his face, his eyes trailed to the back of the cramped cell, right to where Signa stood pressed against Death. She stiffened, though as he continued to search, it became clear that he couldn't see her.

"Byron did not speak on my behalf." Elijah's words were so quiet that the prison guard cupped an ear.

"What was that, Hawthorne?" The hideous man stepped forward, yanking the mask the rest of the way onto Elijah's face. "You got something to say?"

Signa could hardly see the pleading eyes that searched for her, but she knew enough to understand. Elijah said nothing more as the guard hauled him out of the cell, though his message was loud and clear: Byron Hawthorne had lied when he said he'd done everything he could to protect Elijah.

Which meant that Signa had a prime suspect in Lord Wakefield's murder.

SEVEN

Signa barely sensed the shift as Death drew her from Elijah's cell, through the shadows that leached any returning warmth from her skin and back to the safety of her suite at Thorn Grove. Her mind was a deluge of thoughts, all of them about Byron. She tried to steady herself against the edge of the vanity only to forget what form she was in, stumbling as her hand slipped through it.

Why might Byron be involved in this? Did he still want Grey's? Was he capable of murdering for it? She'd believed that he'd finally come to terms with separating himself from the business, as he'd taken quite an interest in eligible women this season. It had seemed that he would find a wife and settle down.

Signa held her stomach, fighting the sickness that gripped her every time she pictured Elijah's bloodied, beaten face. She could kill the man that did that to him and thought of the way she might do it. She could return to the prison. Follow him out into the dark of the night and wrap her hands around his throat. He'd be dead in an instant, and as for his soul... Oh, how she wished to destroy it. To form her shadows into a scythe and slice through the man until his very essence was wiped from the earth.

As if able to sense the bitter thoughts festering within her, Death drew Signa close, smoothing his hands down her arms. "I understand what you're feeling and have acted on that impulse more times than I can count. Rarely is it worth it, Little Bird. Awful as that man may be, he has a family. One he does not treat so poorly, and who rely on him. If there's one thing I've learned, it's that we do not get to play God. We do not get to tamper with Fate, especially when he is breathing down our necks."

Signa wished that Death had not spoken, and that those few words alone weren't enough to plant the idea of that man's family in her mind. It was for them that she shut her eyes and willed her mind to ease away from such vicious thoughts of death.

God, what was happening to her?

"Byron told us that he tried everything," Signa whispered, forcing her mind elsewhere. Onto a new puzzle in need of solving.

"Then we'll have to find out why he lied." The more Signa let the fire within her fizzle out, the more Death's grip eased. "In the meantime, I'll ensure no one lays another finger on Elijah."

Signa watched as Gundry padded toward her sitting room, shuffling in circles a few times before he settled beside her writing desk. "Elijah must believe himself mad for the things he saw today. Using Gundry was the only way I knew how to communicate with him."

"Elijah is no fool," Death told her. "He deserves more credit than you give him. He suspected the supernatural with his wife's spirit, just as I believe he's always suspected it of you."

This made her still, a surge of fear tightening her throat. "You think Elijah knows about me?"

"He knows that you were able to communicate with Lillian. And I believe he's always known that you are more than you appear." His finger grazed the bare skin of her neck, and as it slid down, the coil of tension in her body eased. "Relax your mind, Little Bird. We will solve this."

She tried to let those words hit her. Tried to wrap them around her soul and find comfort within them. This wouldn't always be her life; they would save Elijah, and then the nightmare would be over.

One more time. One more mystery. And then she could finally—*finally*—have the peaceful life she'd always wanted. No more murders. No more mysteries that kept her mind churning at all hours of the night. Just a peaceful life with the Hawthornes, and the man that she loved.

Signa rolled some of the tension from her shoulders as Death cupped the side of her face and bent to kiss her with lips that tasted sweet as nectar and felt as all-consuming as winter. She tipped her head back as he peppered kisses across her skin, and though she wanted to let him continue—wanted the distraction of his deft fingers undoing the silk laces of her dress and to feel his shadows along her thighs—she forced herself to peel away.

"We have things to discuss." Signa cleared her throat, each word forced and awkward. She would love nothing more than to back onto the bed and pull him over her. To let his body become her greatest distraction and to let it ease her worries until she finally fell asleep for the first time in over twenty-four hours. But there was still the matter of Fate, and until she knew more about who they were up against, her mind would allow no distractions. "Primarily, your brother."

Death's jaw tightened. "I will deal with my brother. You don't need to concern yourself with—" His eyes fell past her to the golden envelope on her nightstand. As if instinctively, Death dropped his hand from her to stalk toward it, and Signa shuddered at the immediate warmth that consumed her body in his absence. She clamped her eyes shut, fighting the wave of nausea that ripped through her.

"Death," Signa called, reaching out for him.

"What is this?" He picked up the envelope and tore the note free, scoffing as he read the gilded words. "Who does he think he is, waltzing in here like damned royalty—"

"Death!" Signa called again, but it was too late. She doubled over as breath crashed back into her lungs. Her stomach lurched, and Signa fell to her knees beside a wastebasket seconds before she threw up once, twice, and then a third time. Finally, she was able to sit back, the neck of her gown dampened with sweat. Her vision was a haze, Death's shadows swaying in and out of it as he crouched beside her.

"I'm fine," she whispered through chattering teeth, straining not to lose sight of him. It was a futile effort; it'd be only moments before the belladonna was entirely out of her system.

You most certainly are not fine. Death's voice once again filled the space of her mind, and Signa couldn't help her resentful scowl. She wanted him to stay with her. To hear his voice spoken aloud. To hold him. *The reek of death clings to your skin, Signa. What's going on?*

She lowered her face to stare at the floor. "It's nothing. Merely a fever." The chattering of her teeth was lessening with each word, and slowly she was beginning to feel more herself.

This is no fever. His shadows twisted behind her, drawing from the bed a blanket that he carefully wrapped over her shoulders. It did little to calm the shivers racking through her. *Why are you not surprised by this?*

Signa gripped a corner of the blanket with one hand. Though she had a theory about what was happening, she had no desire to speak the truth into existence. Unfortunately, Death was nothing if not a patient man. It wasn't as though she could be rid of him, either, considering he could speak quite literally into her mind. She had little choice but to tell him the truth.

"Now isn't the first time something like this has happened."

There was a long beat in which Death did not respond, and in that moment, Signa's heart raced. Would he leave? Had he already left? She was about to call for him but then heard his voice once more, clipped and firm as he asked, *When?*

"Last night," she whispered, feeling herself shatter with each word. She knew already what he would think, just as she also knew that there could be no more secrets between them. "After you left with Lord Wakefield, I began coughing up blood."

There was a shift in the room, and Signa could sense that Death had moved farther from her. *After you crossed the veil back into life,* he said. *I knew those berries were a bad idea. If stepping in and out of the veil is what's causing you to be sick, then you must stop taking them.*

She clenched her free hand against the floor, nails grating against the wood planks. She couldn't just *stop.* Couldn't just not see him. But saying that would do her no good, so instead she asked, "How else am I to defend myself against your brother?"

I told you already that Fate is my responsibility. His voice sounded even more distant, and she knew from the trail of it that he was backing toward the window. *Should he even dream of touching you, I will be there. If you must use the berries, do so in emergencies only. Promise me, this time. Swear it. This sickness is surely Fate's doing.*

Signa glanced to where Fate's note lay on the table, golden and gleaming. Perhaps their animosity had started as a feud between two brothers, but the moment that Fate involved the Hawthornes, it became Signa's war. And so, she did not answer him, knowing that she had every intention of going to that party and confronting Fate face-to-face. Instead, she asked, "Why is he doing this? What happened between you two?"

As much as I wish I could tell you it was all a misunderstanding, I'm afraid my brother has every right to hate me. The response was quiet at first, as though she were listening to him through water-clogged ears. Signa had to strain her focus to hear him when he said, *I have not seen him since the year 1346, when I killed the only woman that Fate has ever loved.*

Signa clung to the end of that sentence, waiting for more. And yet the silence dragged on, first for a minute, then for two.

"Death?" Signa hauled herself to her feet, clutching the blanket.

There was a stillness in her mind that she'd not had in a long while, one so heavy that she at once understood something was wrong.

"Death!" she called again, dread burning her throat. She could still feel his presence in the air that had gone frigid with his nearness, and knew he was still there from the goose bumps that spiked along her skin.

But she could not see him. Could not touch him. And now, with a growing panic rising in her chest, Signa realized that she could no longer hear him.

EIGHT

SIGNA SEARCHED FOR DEATH EVERYWHERE. SOMETIMES, WHEN THE temperature plummeted or she felt the caress of a particularly gentle breeze across her cheek, she would imagine that he was there beside her. She took her morning walks when the springtime sky was still a dreary gray and the lawn sparkled with the morning dew, ensuring she was alone as she spoke to a man who she couldn't be certain was even there, giving him the updates of her investigation.

Nearly a week had passed since the day Elijah had been taken. Nearly a week of tailing Byron as he puttered around Thorn Grove, busying himself with hiring staff and assigning duties, inspecting all work with a critical eye. With the deal for Grey's Gentleman's Club having fallen through, he often took to Elijah's study from sunrise to sunset to go over ledgers and paperwork.

There was little else Signa could do while he was in there, and thus she took to spending many afternoons pricking a needle into her finger, watching the blood swell and then stop seconds later without any sickness. Her powers still worked; it seemed it was only when she crossed the veil and had full access to them that she took ill. Though she knew little of Fate's abilities, she guessed this situation was somehow his doing. If she didn't already have enough of a reason to want to beat him at his own game, she certainly did now.

Blythe, too, had put on her detective's cap, and unlike Signa, she was less distracted with worries of Fate and the image of Elijah hunched and beaten in his cell. However, she also didn't have all the information, and Signa had no idea how to broach that conversation. *Good morning, Blythe. I am a grim reaper who used my powers to visit your father in his cell. He suggested that I investigate your uncle. Would you like to join me in my continued mission of tearing your family apart?*

No. If it meant sparing Blythe the pain of such knowledge, Signa would bear the burden of it forever. Just as she intended to do with the truth about Percy.

Blythe spent her mornings and afternoons in the library, reading about poisons and poring over whatever news clippings she could find for murders involving cyanide. She'd spent the first few evenings since Elijah was imprisoned at the dinner table, sharing the details of her findings with whoever would listen. Once Byron realized that she had no intention of discussing more dinner-friendly topics, he instructed the two girls to take their suppers elsewhere so he could have some peace, which meant that evenings quickly turned into Signa cutting into a piece of roast as Blythe discussed—in extraordinary detail—the latest murder she'd read about.

By the time Fate's soiree rolled around—or rather Prince Aris's soiree, as that was the name he'd been going by—the day felt as much of a mental reprieve as it did a chance to confront the man face-to-face. Every time Signa read the name and saw those gilded letters, another crinkle marred the invitation.

Elaine had helped Signa ready herself that afternoon, practically glowing as she laced her into a gorgeous satin gown the color of ripe autumn moss and adorned with golden embroidery. The dress was perhaps a few shades too dark for both this year's style and the season, yet Signa loved the way it reflected back at her in the mirror. It felt rich against her skin and fit her like a glove—tight around the waist and narrowly avoiding a scandal at the bust. As she was unmarried, her hair had been pulled back from her face, twisted and pinned into elegant curls. She loosened a few of them as she inspected herself, wishing that Death would be there to see her. Maybe he would be. Maybe he was already here and trying to warn her not to attend the soiree; with their communication halted, it wasn't as if she'd know.

"If you don't have a hundred handsome men asking for your hand by the season's end, then surely there is no hope for any of us." Elaine lowered her hands to her hips as she looked Signa over. She was the single rose among the aptly named Thorn Grove these days, and Signa wondered if perhaps it was for her and Blythe's benefit that Elaine's cheeks were so rosy and her smile so bright, to make up for the foulness that plagued the manor. But the more time that passed, the more genuine it seemed. When Signa had first met Elaine, the young woman had been quiet and reserved. Now she hummed when she strolled the halls and shared stories of happy news whenever she delivered tea. Though her cheerfulness was sometimes odd, such grim circumstances made it that much more appreciated.

As for the comment about the men... Signa smoothed out her long white kid gloves, never having realized they could be so interesting. Her wealth was no secret, and with the Hawthornes feeding her as well as they had been, Signa had filled out in a lovely way. Her skin was suppler than when she'd first arrived at the manor, and though there were some who still considered her eyes with great skepticism—for one was a winter's blue and the other a melted gold—Signa knew she was pretty enough to draw interest. However, knowing that she couldn't summon Death whenever she wanted had her yearning for him even more, and seeking the attention of others less than ever.

"Oh, don't make such a face," Elaine chided, looking at Signa's reflection in the mirror in front of them. "If this is about Mr. Everett Wakefield, even I know he's keen on you. I'm certain that once Mr. Hawthorne is proved innocent, all will be well. Though, if you ask me, I say why not go for the prince, instead? Especially if he's handsome."

Signa didn't care one bit for the playfulness of Elaine's voice or the way she wagged her brows. More than anything, though, she hated the suggestion that a man as despicable as Fate could ever be thought of as *handsome.* He was ghastlier than anyone she'd ever laid eyes on—which was saying a lot, considering she had grown up seeing all sorts of strange spirits with parts of their bodies stabbed or rotted or blown away in old wars.

Signa didn't have the heart to shoo Elaine away when her lady's maid pinched some color into her cheeks and ushered her out the door. "You best be on your way, miss. Your uncle will be meeting you in the carriage."

While the idea of being escorted by Byron for an entire evening once would have stalled Signa's steps, she was eager to get him out of Thorn Grove and away from Elijah's study. Fate wasn't the only one to be wary of; she needed to see how Byron behaved in the public eye. Whom would he approach or find himself in conversation with? What might his mannerisms be? Whatever he did, she'd be there to track his every move.

Skirts in one hand, Signa held the other above her eyes, blocking out the beaming sunlight as she hurried to a polished carriage led by two stallions with slick black coats and thick muscle. The wiry groom who opened the door was decidedly not Death's human charade, Sylas Thorly, and Signa felt a little pang in her chest as the young man helped her up.

To Signa's surprise, it wasn't Byron who waited for her inside.

"Hello, cousin!" Blythe's voice was more cheerful than it had any right to be, and Signa fixed her with the most vicious glare to signal as much. "Oh, don't give me that look. Surely, you knew I was going to come."

"I expected you would consider it, though I had hoped you'd see reason." Signa halted at the door, debating the merits of dragging Blythe out by the skirts when the driver cleared his throat.

"Hurry and take your seat," Blythe scolded. "We're already late." She wore a shade of blue so pale it could almost pass for white and kept her hair as loose as possible while still maintaining societal rules. There was a healthy flush to her cheeks, and Signa hated that there was such a glimmer of determination in her eyes, for she had no idea how she might possibly manage to convince Blythe to stay home.

"Where is Byron?" Signa asked.

"He'll follow us in the next carriage," Blythe answered. "With our gowns, there wouldn't have been room for him to stretch his legs."

Again, the driver cleared his throat. Recognizing that she'd lost this round, Signa sighed and slid onto the velvet seat across from Blythe. Her cousin folded her hands on her lap and inspected the sapphire jewel upon her gloved finger, not meeting Signa's eyes.

"You shouldn't have come."

"Of course I should have." Blythe was dismissive, as though that fact was the most obvious thing in the world. "Look at me. I couldn't let this dress go to waste."

"I'm being serious, Blythe—"

"So am I." Only then did Blythe look up with a dark severity in her icy eyes. "My father's life is at stake. I do not care if the prince is sixty years old or the most boorish man that has ever walked this earth. There is power to being a pretty girl in a pretty dress, and if I have any chance of getting him on our side, I intend to do so. Now, will you help me or not?" She stretched out a hand, and—against her better judgment—Signa let her fingers slip through Blythe's.

Even through the gloves Signa could feel every bone in Blythe's fingers. She was still so thin; still so frail. Though Blythe tried not to show it, she was clearly still recovering, and the last thing in the world that Signa wanted was for her to get sucked into Fate's games any more than the Hawthorne family had already been.

"I will always help you." Signa squeezed Blythe's hand in both of her own. "But, given the current state of the Hawthornes and that it's my name on the invitation, perhaps it would be prudent if I spoke to the prince first."

"Perhaps." Blythe shrugged her delicate shoulders. "Though Uncle says the invitation was likely for the family. I understand your concern, but I've been to hell and back in this past year. I believed that I would never again attend a ball, let alone ride in another carriage. Yet here I am. A prince does not frighten me, cousin. Especially not one who doesn't even have the decency to properly invite me to his soiree."

Signa had little choice but to lean back in her seat and settle her hands into her lap. How much simpler it would have been if only Blythe knew the truth. Step-by-step, she was veering closer to the web that Fate had spun for them. But if Blythe wouldn't protect herself, then so be it. Signa would work twice as hard to keep the Hawthornes safe, and away from his ensnarement.

No matter what happened that evening, she would not allow Fate to win.

NINE

THEY'D BEEN RIDING FOR WHAT FELT LIKE HOURS, JOURNEYING through twisting brambly roads and hills so precarious that both Signa and Blythe had to squint their eyes shut for fear of falling. Eventually, though, forest gave way to sprawling hills cast a burnished orange by the setting sun as the first sign of Wisteria Gardens emerged.

The palace sat upon acres of grass so ripe a green that it reminded Signa of illustrated pages from old fairy tales. It was situated on a vast mountainside, massive enough that Thorn Grove felt like little more than a farmer's cottage in comparison.

Both Signa and Blythe pressed their faces to the windows as their carriage continued past iron gates strung with ivy and half green with lichen. Before them was a line of at least a dozen more carriages that rolled through a courtyard paved with pristine white stones. Grass nearly the color of Signa's dress sprouted between them, so meticulously clipped that it made the walkway look ready for a life-size game of chess. It was upon those stones that the young women were dropped off, Signa's heart fluttering in spite of itself as she stepped out of the carriage.

Wisteria Gardens was almost eerie in its beauty. The setting sun burned behind the palace, and the breeze was so gentle and lulling that Signa was almost tricked into believing the place was little more than the innocent countryside home of a prince. She looked to her right, where ripe green hills rolled down a mountainside full of grazing horses and bleating sheep. It was odd, though, how the sounds they made seemed to repeat themselves as if on a loop, and how there was no scent of them in the air. She smelled only the wisteria and looked past the courtyard to see the blooming trees that were the palace's namesake, purple blossoms dangling from the branches and crawling up the side of the palace. There was even a wisteria-laden archway along the walking path, exquisitely maintained.

"This place is incredible." Awe laced Blythe's voice as she stepped forward and hooked her arm through Signa's. "How strange that I've never been here before. I wasn't aware it existed."

Signa bit her tongue. How Fate intended to stroll into Celadon with a palace that had appeared out of thin air and call himself a prince, Signa hadn't the faintest idea. And yet no one seemed to question it; not even Blythe, who pulled Signa along while Byron eased himself out of the next carriage and hurried to catch up. Blythe led them toward a towering marble fountain of a woman in a gown of ivy and flowers that split at her midthigh and twisted around her ankles. Water poured from the chalice she tipped precariously in her hands. Live lotus flowers and lily pads drifted at her feet.

There were other fountains, too. Smaller, but each of them as extravagant as the next and surrounded by short spiraling hedges or adorned by the most bizarre flowers that once again reminded Signa of a fairy tale—ancient and magical things that seemed out of place in the real world. All around them towered wisteria trees in full bloom, their rich petals dangling overhead like the most glorious canopy. Everyone was gaping in delight as they stretched their hands toward petals that were somehow always just out of reach. Yet as beautiful as it was, the courtyard dulled in comparison to the palace itself.

Never had Signa seen anything so massive. Where Thorn Grove was dark, Wisteria's exterior was a spotless white, adorned with gilded carvings and more windows than Signa could count, each of them sporting marvelous stained glass. There was a long stone walkway leading up to the palace, with a pond on either side. Sculptures loomed from the water, some of them of gorgeous women or powerfully built men, while others were of beastly creatures that could come from only the wildest of imaginations. They appeared to be made from marble, some of them blanketed with moss and creeping fig, and each as excessive as the next. Signa stretched her fingers out to draw them across their damp stone, then turned toward Byron at the tapping sound of his walking stick coming up the path.

"I want you both on your best behavior," he warned, fighting the same slack-jawed awe that everyone at Wisteria wore. "This prince could be our key to clearing Elijah's name."

Signa very much doubted that.

Blythe squeezed Signa's arm, her footsteps hastening as they followed a trail of bustling crinoline toward the palace. There were whispers, too. A few of them sounded excited, but the majority were low and prickled at Signa's skin. She turned to catch the eyes of too many strangers staring at them with dagger-sharp glances and spiteful rumors searing their tongues.

Though Signa was used to such behavior, it never stung any less, especially considering that she'd believed herself finally free of it. Blythe, too, kept her jaw tipped high and her expression flat, refusing to mark herself as prey before ravenous vultures. It was she who had warned Signa all those months ago of just how willing society was to pluck the skin from one's bones to worsen any wound. And if there was one thing that Signa had learned about society, it was that people loved little more than watching those above them fall from grace.

"Come." Signa steered her cousin forward. "I'd like to see the inside. I imagine it must be even more grand."

Oh, how right she was. If the exterior of Wisteria was opulent, the interior was decadently lavish. Like the exterior, the walls inside Wisteria were bright and pristine, decorated with extravagant ivory wallpaper and gold flourishes. It would seem Fate had a taste for the color, for the mirrors and paintings were also plated in a matching gold.

"Oh, it's magnificent!" Blythe craned her neck to gaze three stories up to the ceiling—which was painted a brilliant shade of red—and beheld the most intricate floral designs swirled throughout. Ahead were two grand staircases that met in the middle of the second story. They were covered in a thick red-and-gold rug, and the girls followed suit as guests climbed the stairs. They slowed their steps for Byron, and Signa used the time to take in every inch of the decor.

Strung along the walls were the wildest assortment of oil paintings, each one depicting strange and nonsensical things. One showcased a garden full of fairies that danced around overgrown mushrooms, while another portrayed two women dancing in a candlelit ballroom, their dresses igniting into flames behind them. Tucked into every corner were the most elaborately carved vases or sculptures. Most were tame, while others elicited blushes and concerned gasps, such as the statue of three people in the heat of passion, and another of a man brushing his hand along his lover's cheek with more tenderness than Signa knew was possible to impart into a piece of stone.

Each painting conveyed a story with such richness that the art felt alive. She wasn't convinced that, if she glanced away, they wouldn't spring to life and continue their stories.

"His lordship is quite the collector," said someone ahead, and Signa recognized the sharp voice as belonging to Diana Blackwater, a mousy and uncivilized girl who could often be found attached to the hip of Eliza Wakefield. She was perhaps one of the worst vultures Signa had met thus far, and Signa made sure to stay quiet, trying to keep from Diana's view.

"A collector, indeed." Byron's scowl grew in severity with every piece of art they passed. "At the very least, they should have had these pieces temporarily moved. Avert your eyes, girls. You shouldn't see such atrocities."

Arms still linked, Blythe leaned toward her cousin and whispered, "It would seem he hasn't the faintest idea what's in half the books that end up on our nightstands."

Signa pressed her lips together to keep from laughing. Though she ducked her head and pretended to follow Byron's instructions, her eyes remained lifted to inspect every inch of the palace and its art.

As much as she hated to admit it, Wisteria was beautiful. Even so, there was a sense of oddness to the palace. A looming heaviness that permeated the air and had her wishing that Death could be at her side. Signa's palms ached with the absence of his touch as she forced herself up every step, feeling as though she were treading water. When she squinted, a strange golden haze blanketed everything. Yet no one else said a word about it, and soon enough, they were at the top floor, in what was, regrettably, the most gorgeous ballroom she had ever seen.

Unlike the rest of the palace, the ballroom was not bright and crisp but made up of ornate panels backed with gold leaf. There was no part of the walls that went bare; all were either mirrored or featured gilded carvings of foxes climbing trees or rolling among the flowers, lit by sconces that set the room ablaze in warm, rich amber.

"What I wouldn't give to live here." Blythe's words were breathy and wondrous. Everyone seemed to agree with her; the guests were all chattering and whispering, twirling around the room to take in its extravagance. While the rest of the palace was decorated with art, this exquisite room *was* the art.

Byron straightened beneath the amber glow and whispered to the girls, "Tonight is not the night to overindulge. Mingle, but keep your wits sharp and your tongues soft, understood?"

"Understood," Blythe echoed dismissively. "But I daresay, Uncle, that Signa and I won't ever manage to draw the prince's eye with you looming over us. Surely we may walk about the room ourselves?"

Byron opened his mouth to speak, though his lips sealed as he scanned the crowd. Alerted at once, Signa tried to follow his gaze to who had drawn his attention, though there were far too many bodies to decipher which guest had caught his eye.

"Very well," Byron huffed as he adjusted his cravat. "Be mindful about how you present yourselves. And do let me know if either of you finds this evening's host."

Signa could only hope that she would be the first to hunt Fate down, though it was going to be difficult, given that she needed to keep an eye on Byron, too.

Gently, she unlinked her arm from Blythe's. "We'll have a better chance at finding the prince if we split up. Will you manage?" The decision could very well come back to bite her, though Signa needed some space if she was going to tail Byron.

Blythe tossed her hair back with a sharp "Of course I will" and disappeared into the throng of guests. It wasn't long until Signa jumped, feeling a hand on her shoulder.

"Miss Farrow?"

She bit down her groan, for the voice was the same grating one she'd heard while climbing the staircase.

"Miss Blackwater." Signa attempted her most curt smile as she turned toward Diana, though it barely touched her cheeks. It was fortunate the room was so dark. "How lovely it is to see you."

"Likewise." There was a gleam in Diana's eyes that made Signa feel as though she were a mouse, and Diana the hungriest feline. "I must admit that I didn't expect you out so soon, given the scandal."

It would seem they were getting right to the point, then. Very well. If there was one thing Signa had learned by then, it was that a person could not cower when targeted by a vulture, for such a scavenger would only continue to circle. To peck and wear its prey down until it was ripe for the feast.

Signa Farrow was many things, but she was not prey. Having no intention of letting Diana continue her pecking, Signa made herself tall and relied on a skill that every proper lady had been forced to utilize at one point in time or another, whether for the benefit of herself or a man whose ego she was expected to stroke: feigning ignorance.

"The scandal?" Signa pressed a hand to her chest. "I can only assume you're referring to the tragedy that befell Lord Wakefield? The man was murdered in cold blood, Miss Blackwater. Heavens, I dare not reduce what happened to him as a mere scandal." Oh, how good it felt to watch Diana's cheeks flare crimson. "I'm glad that Mr. Hawthorne has been so willing to help with the investigation of such a tragedy." Signa put a little sigh into her voice, quite proud of her performance. It was a shame that Blythe was not nearby to watch; it would have delighted her.

"Of course not." Diana's mouth was small and shrewd, and she held her lips together in a line so thin they looked almost nonexistent. "Though it does you no good to be associated with that family. You were doing so well for yourself with Everett, though I can't imagine he'll be interested in you now."

Signa's merciless smile remained unwavering. "How *is* Lord Wakefield?" she asked, referring to Everett. His new title was strange upon her lips, especially given the circumstances.

"Ask Eliza." Diana fluffed out a long white fan and waved it against herself as she nodded toward the throng. "It seems that despite the circumstances, she could not refuse an invitation from the prince."

Signa followed Diana's gaze. Sure enough, Eliza was not at home, mourning the loss of her uncle. She hadn't even donned traditional mourning wear but was instead dressed in a beautiful lavender gown. Still, there was a pallor to Eliza's skin and haunted shadows beneath her eyes as Signa surveyed her conversing with a small crowd expressing condolences. She was surprised to see that one of the men nearest to Eliza was Byron.

"What a time to be flirting one's way through a ball." Diana gave her fan a little flutter that didn't hide her cruel smile. "I suppose she must not have loved her uncle as much as she wanted us to believe."

There hadn't been much in Signa's old etiquette books about the particulars of dealing with royalty, especially when a familial relation had just passed. Though Eliza's presence at the ball did seem unusual, Signa doubted that it was easy for someone to pass up a direct invitation from a prince. Still... It was remarkably odd, especially considering that she was chatting with Byron.

"Miss Wakefield is doing the best that she can." It was another voice that spoke; one that normally would have soothed Signa but at that moment made her skin prickle—Charlotte Killinger. Signa's oldest childhood friend and the only person who had seen her follow Percy into the garden the night they all believed he'd vanished from Thorn Grove. Signa had done her best to avoid Charlotte and her prying eyes, but that was certain to be more difficult with Fate forcing her back into the throes of society.

"We all are." Signa hated that she tensed when Charlotte laid a hand on her shoulder. Hated that guilt welled up in her and threatened to leak like a rusted faucet.

She didn't regret what she'd done or the choice she'd made to end Percy's life in favor of Blythe's. But she also didn't want anyone else knowing about it. Not ever.

"How are you faring?" Charlotte asked, and Signa immediately wished her friend were less kind. That she was as sharp and guarded as she'd been when Signa had first arrived at Thorn Grove last autumn.

"We're all eager to learn the truth," Signa said by way of answer, despising the heaviness in her chest. "How is Everett?"

"Still grappling with the gravity of the situation, I think. He's barely spoken a word since that night."

Signa may not have been able to remember her parents, but she remembered her grandmother, whom she had loved deeply. She also remembered the pain of losing her, and never again wanted to relive the emotions she knew Everett was enduring.

"The duke's killer will be found." Signa filled her voice with such confidence that both Charlotte and Diana straightened as if reproached. Signa didn't care, for it was the only way to convince herself. She had found a murderer before. Now, she only needed to do it once more. Watching Byron fill out Eliza's dance card, Signa wondered if Elijah had already set her on the right path.

TEN

Blythe

Blythe knew when she wasn't wanted. Mostly because it was an entirely different experience than the ripe smiles and too-cheerful voices that she was accustomed to. All around her were faces she'd known her entire life, yet not a single person asked how she or her family were faring.

But to be concerned about it would be silly, for being the subject of gossip always had an expiration date and the vultures would move on the moment the next scandal reared its ugly head. And when they decided to welcome her again—when they tried to get on her good side and exchange gossip like it was gold—ha! She would eat them alive. Because Blythe Hawthorne was not nearly as forgiving as her cousin, and she had no desire to be.

She was glad, though, that Signa had agreed to stay at Thorn Grove. Even if she was acting stranger by the day—which was saying a lot, given Signa's perpetual oddness—Blythe wasn't certain how she'd manage without her. Selfish though it was, she hoped that Signa would remain with her at Thorn Grove forever, for so long as she had one person on her side, Blythe refused to give a rat's ass about what anyone else thought. Her feelings about society were akin to her father's: It was there whenever someone was in need of entertainment, and while it was important to at least make an effort to keep one's name from the scandal sheets, it mattered little in the grand scheme. So long as she had money and status, the vultures would return to shove their greedy little beaks into her pockets soon enough.

And that was a fine way of things. Blythe didn't need pity, nor did she need anyone's protection. For too long she'd been treated like some fragile heirloom meant to sit on a shelf, too precious to be taken out into the world. But she was no delicate artifact, nor the soft doll that her family seemed to think her.

Perhaps that was why when Blythe bit, she bit hard. She was small and still frail from sickness, and because of her blond hair, fair skin, and lips as pink and pretty as a rose, people often dismissed the cleverness of her mind or her ability to handle herself. But high society had been her domain since birth, and she more than knew how to navigate it in whatever way she saw fit. She just... could never quite get herself to care.

Seeing that Signa was distracted—and having realized the prince was not yet in attendance—Blythe had made her escape from the amber ballroom and the whispers. Wisteria Gardens was far brighter than Thorn Grove, and Blythe found herself unable to look away, mesmerized by its boldness. It was lavish, and perhaps even a little gaudy with its extravagance, but everywhere she turned there was something magnificent to catch her eye. Intricate busts carved from marble. Rich oil paintings made from the brightest cobalt and a gold so striking that she could only imagine how much each would cost an eager collector. There was no theme to any of it; every picture and every statue was thoroughly different from all others.

The voices behind her faded as she followed the art down an endless hallway, passing delicate sculptures of butterflies and pottery so ancient it looked as though it belonged to another time. She stopped at the end of the hall, beneath a towering painting of a woman so beautiful that Blythe lost her breath. Like the figure in the courtyard fountain, the woman stood waist-deep in a pond filled with lotus flowers. She tenderly cupped one and stared down at it with such fondness that Blythe felt compelled to step forward to investigate further.

The woman's hair was pale as snow and fell to her hips in elegant waves, the ends of it sweeping into the pond. She wore a thin white gown that billowed in the water, the fabric so sheer that her figure beneath it skimmed the edge of visibility. Foxes crept in the grass behind her, their golden eyes watching through towering ferns. The image felt like a moment captured in time, so real that Blythe kept waiting for the woman to look up. Kept waiting to see whether her eyes were brown or blue or green...

"They're silver."

Blythe nearly tripped into the portrait at the voice behind her—brisk, deep, and decidedly masculine. She turned at once, and, given the man's height, the first thing she noticed was not his face but that he wore a coat of ivory and gold, with fitted trousers to match. From the quality and color of the material alone, Blythe understood at once whom she was speaking with and dropped into a practiced curtsy.

"Your Highness." She dipped her head, heart in her throat. For while she may have found society and all its customs to be silly, she could behave long enough to impress a prince.

"You were trying to look at her eyes, weren't you?" the prince asked. "They're silver."

Ever so slowly Blythe straightened, eyes trailing up and over the beautiful stitching of his coat, then toward a ruffled white cravat that climbed so high on his neck it appeared to be strangling him. And then she looked even higher, to his face, and her breath caught.

Two familiar amber eyes looked past her to the painting, sparing no concern for Blythe, whose mouth had fallen slack. The man before her was the very one she'd cursed in her bedroom several nights prior. The same one she'd planned to give a piece of her mind the next time she saw him. The man who had condemned her father was the very same prince she was meant to charm, yet the thought of sparing him a single kind word made Blythe want to cut off her own tongue.

"You." The word slipped from Blythe before her mind could catch up with her mouth. She had to clutch her skirts to keep her hands from shaking. "*You're* Prince Aris?"

She couldn't be certain whether he recognized her, for the

prince made only a low grunt beneath his breath and stepped toward the painting. His face was expressionless as he inspected it. "What do you think of her?"

So jarred was she by the question that Blythe turned and followed his gaze to the painting, giving her mind a moment to process the fact that it would be in her best interest to excuse herself before she said something she'd regret. She sucked in every foul word burning her tongue; she knew she'd already made a piss-poor first impression by practically shoving herself into the man and condemning him at Thorn Grove. Just as she knew that someone like him could change the fate of her family with a single word.

"She is the most beautiful woman I've ever seen," Blythe answered truthfully, steadying her temper.

The man grunted again but didn't turn away. "Is that all?"

So that he wouldn't see her annoyance, Blythe stepped in front of the prince as she tried to look at the painting not as a consumer impressed with it on the surface but as an artist.

"She is gentle," Blythe said, "but sad. There is a weight to her smile, and creases near her eyes that make her seem older than she appears. She has much love for wherever this place is, though she's very tired. Perhaps from standing too long in a frigid pond that smells like duck droppings and dead fish?"

When she drew back, a sly grin on her face, Blythe found that the prince was no longer staring at the painting but at her. She'd hoped that he'd have at least a smidgen of humor somewhere beneath his rigid demeanor, yet his expression remained surly. He kept his hands behind his back, and with even more of a bite, said, "You are the girl who threw herself at me like a wild boar."

Blythe had to press her lips together to keep from saying the first thing that came to mind; calling him a bitter and resentful brute who had potentially ruined her life would only get her so far. Still, she couldn't help biting back. "And you are the man who publicly condemned my father to prison with no proof."

He clicked his tongue, and Blythe hated that she couldn't for the life of her decipher the vague look on his face. Boredom? Intrigue?

"Your father was the one to give Lord Wakefield that drink, was he not?" The way he phrased the question made it sound so enragingly simple that Blythe clenched her skirts tighter.

"My father would never have killed Lord Wakefield. He was wrongly accused."

"Was he now?" Aris brushed a hand over his cravat as if smoothing away an invisible speck of dust. "Then answer the question. Did your father give Lord Wakefield the drink that killed him, or didn't he?"

Blythe had been born into this life of high society. She had spent years playing by its rules and learning that wordplay was no less dangerous than wielding a sword. Even so, it was Signa who was better at this dance of wits, or elegantly twisting out of a situation she did not wish to be in.

Blythe had inherited too much of her father's temperament and was getting far worse about managing her annoyance with every year she grew older. She had such little patience for the game that she drew a breath from her nose and exhaled it through her mouth so that she did not say anything foul. Not because he didn't deserve it but because she needed him. Unfortunately.

"My father is an innocent man." Her words were sharper, daring him to challenge her.

Aris's vague expression gave way to the smallest hint of a smirk. "If that's the case, then I'm certain justice will prevail. It sounds like your father will be a free man in no time."

He certainly would be if Blythe had anything to say about it. The prince's comment sounded so much like something Byron would say, however, that she had to stop herself from making a face.

"It would appear, sir," Blythe began, trying her best to imitate her cousin's forced niceties, "that you give yourself too little credit. A man of your title must be aware of how much sway you have over society."

Aris gloated a little at this, and if Blythe didn't hate him already, she certainly would have then.

Already, Blythe had lost her mother, and her brother had fled Thorn Grove without a word. If someone wanted to take her father away, they would have to pry him from her cold, dead fingers. As pompous as this prince was, he was quite possibly her father's best hope. She just had to play her cards right.

"Do forgive me for my outburst the other night, Your Highness." Her smile was so forced and pinched that her eyes creased. "Understandably, I am not accustomed to death, let alone a murder within my own home. Though I do wonder why you attended the ball that night dressed as a commoner? I had no idea you were a prince."

Aris regarded her shrewdly, and Blythe got the sense that he was weighing whether she was worth his time. To her surprise, he leaned toward her. "I plan to remain in this town for some time, and I wanted to meet its people without all the pretenses."

"And where is it you hail from?" She took a step back. "I must admit, I knew nothing of this palace's existence. It's so beautiful that it seems a shame to tuck it away for all this time. The art alone is enough to open a museum."

"You enjoy the art?" He seemed pleased by this, and Blythe locked onto that crumb at once.

"I find most of it to be phenomenal. Are you a collector?"

He opened his mouth to speak, snapped it shut, then repeated this pattern once more and asked, " 'Most of it'?"

Blythe's heart spiked with dread, but before she could offer any excuse to save herself, Aris waved a dismissive hand and said, "I'm a consumer of art in all forms. Paintings, music, books, sculptures—everything but poetry. I've never cared for poetry. Too pretentious."

Too pretentious, said the prince while wandering the halls of his enormous, gilded palace. Blythe forced herself to find something else to focus on before she could laugh at the absurdity.

"And what about her?" She motioned to the towering painting of the woman. "It's the same woman I saw in the courtyard, isn't it? She's lovely."

"She is." The blazing light in Aris's eyes dimmed. "And she's the most priceless artifact in this palace."

"She's certainly the largest." Blythe tipped her head back. She couldn't imagine how long it must have taken someone to paint such a magnificent piece. It was at least three times her height and twice as wide, taking up the entire expanse of a wall. "Given that she's so priceless, it's fortunate that you don't need to worry about someone sneaking off with the portrait. It would require a small army to move."

"At least," he agreed, the severity of his tone easing some. "Though I doubt anyone would attempt to steal from Wisteria if they wish to keep their head."

As he stared at the painting once more, Blythe took note of the oddness of his eyes. They reminded her of Signa's, only his were an even richer shade of gold. Perhaps the color was genetic. Not that she'd seen any other members of his royal family to know. She hadn't the faintest clue what they might look like or even who else there was. If she was to use this man, then she first needed to find out more about him. And if not him, then perhaps there was a queen who would listen to her plead her father's case.

"Why are you out prowling the halls rather than enjoying the ball?" Blythe asked, trying to draw his attention away from the painting. "You're the host. Shouldn't you be busy getting harassed by every mama and affluent businessman by now?"

He scrunched his nose, and for a split second Aris looked boyish enough to appear *almost* approachable. "I suppose they'll be looking for me, won't they? It is the season, after all."

"Is that not why you've invited us? To find yourself a princess to carry on such a proud lineage?"

"I don't recall inviting *you* at all." There was a tic in his jaw as he watched her, and it took everything in Blythe not to show her embarrassment. He truly had avoided inviting her, then. She supposed it was only to be expected, given all that had happened with the Hawthornes, but it hurt more than she cared to admit to be scorned so thoroughly.

"I apologize if my presence offends you," she said with every ounce of bitterness she had to spare. "I was recently sick and confined to my bed for some time. Now that I am well again, the excitement of seeing my cousin's invitation got the better of me."

Had she been looking up, Blythe might have noticed the heat in his stare. She might have seen the millions of gossamer threads that surrounded them. There were even some attached to her, and Fate studied them with great interest.

"You," he said at last, "are the girl who defied death."

Blythe stilled at the odd phrasing. She didn't need to ask how he knew that; this whole town reeked of gossip. Still, it was jarring to hear it said aloud, and she didn't care to give that time of her life any more attention. "I am a woman," she corrected. "But yes, I very likely should have died several times over. It is a miracle that I did not."

"A miracle indeed." She wondered whether she was imagining that Aris's voice had cooled significantly, or that he seemed to have taken a renewed interest in her. "I am glad that you came, Miss . . ."

"Hawthorne," she said. "My name is—"

"Blythe!"

Blythe spun toward the urgent voice that called to her from across the hall. Signa's skin was flushed and her curls disheveled as though she'd been running. Rather than look at her cousin, however, Signa had her eyes trained on the prince. Blythe tried to gather

Signa's attention and warn her that this man was the one they'd been searching for. *This* was whom they needed to impress. Yet her cousin didn't once turn toward her. It took Blythe drawing a step closer to realize that Signa's eyes were even stranger than usual, wide with alarm.

"Blythe," Signa repeated with the gentleness of an ox, "we should get back to the ball. Byron's bound to notice your absence."

Once again Blythe tried to send her cousin a message with her eyes, but if Signa understood it, she paid it no mind as Aris slid past Blythe and closed the gap between them. "Ah, Miss Farrow," he said. Blythe could have sworn his voice was lighter, a sudden pep in his step that had not been there seconds before. "I was hoping you'd come."

Signa inched closer, nearly knocking into one of the strange sculptures. Her eyes never strayed from Aris. She was behaving like a skittish fawn staring down the barrel of a rifle.

"My cousin and I were just heading in to enjoy the ball," she said, sidestepping and grabbing hold of her cousin's arm with such vigor that Blythe winced. "Our uncle will be looking for us."

"Signa, behave yourself." Blythe kept her words low, spitting them through a smile. "This is the *prince*." She'd hoped that the news would relax Signa. That she'd stand up straight and stop behaving so boorishly. But it seemed that Blythe would have to be twice the lady to compensate for Signa, who didn't so much as flinch.

"Miss Farrow is right." Blythe smiled with each word, her heart hammering. For her father's sake, she needed to make a good impression. "Someone might get the wrong idea if they caught us out here alone. We'd be happy to have an escort back to the ballroom, however. I find myself in need of a partner for my first dance."

"I don't think that's a good—" Signa lurched forward just as Prince Aris offered his arm. His eyes glinted as gold as the gilded panels around them.

"Of course, Miss Hawthorne." He smiled as Blythe slid her hand over his forearm. "I would be delighted."

ELEVEN

If looks could kill, Signa aimed to obliterate Fate as he strolled onto the dance floor with Blythe on his arm. One corner of his lip quirked when he caught Signa glaring. From the placement of his hands to the smug gleam that lit his face, it seemed Fate was making every effort to get under Signa's skin. Unfortunately for her, it was working.

"Is that Blythe Hawthorne on the arm of a *prince*?" Bodies pressed in behind Signa, falling into a tizzy of whispers that had her digging her heels into the marble. She'd been a fool to let Blythe out of her sight, too distracted by Byron and Eliza, who even then fought to steal her attention. The pair no longer stood near the dance floor but had excused themselves to a corner of the room. Eliza spared no glance at Byron; in fact, she held her fan out to cover her mouth. Every so often Signa would catch a glimpse of Eliza's lips and see that they were moving. Byron stood close enough to listen, and though he hid it well, he was speaking, too.

Signa longed to get closer, sensing with everything in her that she was missing something important. But if Fate had made one thing clear, it was that he intended to allow Signa no reprieve. She'd been enough of a fool already to allow Blythe to fall into his hands; she wouldn't make the same mistake again by allowing him anything more than a single dance with her cousin.

The ballroom fell quiet as Fate bowed to Blythe, who returned the formality with a curtsy. Though she would have heard the whispers by now, Blythe was light on her feet and held herself with the grace of a queen as she placed one delicate hand atop Fate's arm and allowed his other to settle upon her waist. The swell of a waltz filled the ballroom, and with every step the couple took, Signa's pulse throbbed in her neck.

How was it that Fate had managed to convince everyone that he was royalty? He had only to appear and already ladies were fawning while men straightened their vests. Signa thought to ask some of those men for more information—where the prince allegedly came from, or where his parents, the queen and king, were—yet the moment her mouth formed the words, their eyes went glossy and stared blankly back at her. They watched her as though swept into a dream, never hearing the questions.

No one else noticed it. But Signa did, just as she noticed that while the voices had quieted, they wielded their whispers like finely honed blades and flocked around Blythe like wolves circling for the kill. She wished again that Death were present, if only to feel his comforting chill against her bones as she watched her cousin with increasing dread in her stomach. On her own, Signa's abilities were not yet a match against Fate's. She thumbed at the belladonna she kept tucked in her dress regardless, just in case. Whether Fate intended it or not, he was broadening the target on Blythe's back, and one of these days someone was bound to take aim. Signa wished only that she could be Blythe's shield.

Fate set his hand on the small of Blythe's back, a small gesture but one that was far from innocent. Like every other unmarried woman in the crowd, Signa readied herself to pounce the moment the song was over, unwilling to watch her cousin continue this parade of tossing her hair back and smiling in some ridiculous attempt to sway a man she undoubtedly hated.

"Look at them," Charlotte whispered dreamily, leaning her head against Signa's shoulder. "They make quite the pair, don't they? Their children would look like little sunbursts."

"He knows that her father's been accused of murder, doesn't he?" Diana flapped her fan against the heat of the ballroom, and for once Signa found herself wishing she had one of her own. Why was it that these events always looked so much more glamorous on the outside than they truly were?

It was a challenge to stand idly by as Fate and Blythe danced. Though, given all the eyes on Signa, she had little choice but to force a smile onto her lips. She needed to get onto that dance floor, which meant that she needed to make herself look approachable at the very least. Already Charlotte and Diana were being swept away with invitations, names filling their dance cards. Eliza Wakefield, too, had rejoined the others on the floor. Though her dress dazzled as she spun and twirled in the arms of a man Signa had never seen, her smile was frayed at the ends, and her gaze kept flickering toward the corner where Byron stood watching, the sconces cutting grim shadows across his face.

Signa nearly cursed when she realized what she was doing. How much easier it would have been if she'd been honest with Death about her intent to come and had him watching over Byron. As it was, she had to make a choice—there would be time for Byron later. But first, getting Blythe as far from Fate as possible took precedence.

She accepted a dance from the first man to ask her and took her place across from him in a row of other women. Down the row her eyes wandered, searching for Blythe. It wasn't until she turned her attention back to her partner that Signa noticed the man who stood before her was not the same one who'd invited her to dance. It was Fate himself, silent but for the gleam in his eyes that spoke louder than laughter. There was no time to retreat before the song began.

"Is there something I can help you with, Miss Farrow? I could feel your eyes boring into me from across the ballroom." Fate stepped forward, the burnished amber of the walls casting a glow on the floor that reminded Signa of a late autumn sunset, almost as though they were dancing upon fallen maple leaves. Yet there was no gentle crunch beneath her footsteps; no settling of her mind and easing of her chest that came from autumn's stillness. Signa mirrored her partner as he lifted one hand to the air, their palms nearly touching as they circled each other as if on either side of a looking glass.

Heat seared between the open space of their palms, jolts of static prickling her fingertips. Signa kept a straight face despite it all. From the low swell of music to the sunset lighting, everything about Fate was a performance she refused to acknowledge. "Whatever your issue is with me, my cousin has no part of this."

"On the contrary," he said, and Signa noticed for the first time that there was the hint of an accent in his voice. It wasn't like any she'd heard before, but something old and strange and almost guttural. "Because of your insistence that she live, your cousin has now defied her fate three times over. Three times, she was meant to die."

Signa's throat squeezed tight as she realized that the room's chattering had ceased. Gone was the low sweep of autumn as winter's silent chill leached in. There were no whispers or laughter, nor even the soft tinking of glassware. While those around her continued to dance, their movements had sharpened, every one of them as precise as the next and perfectly coordinated. Pretty faces smiled at no one, their unblinking eyes filling with tears that streaked down their cheeks and onto grinning lips. They were little more than puppets and Fate their puppeteer, twisting and twirling and bending them to his every whim.

Everywhere Signa looked there were signs of Fate's power. From the palace and the golden threads spun around it, to his control over so many beings at once. It was an effortless power—one he didn't even seem to consider as he spun Signa across the dance floor.

"Free them." While her command was firm, Signa was careful not to let emotion slip in. It wouldn't do to give Fate anything more to hold over her, though something in his gleaming eyes told her that he already knew how deeply his power bothered her.

"You must have many questions for me," he said. "Promise me another dance, and I'll answer whatever you wish me to."

She had to stop her brows from shooting up. Fate was baiting her, yes, but if there was even a possibility that he was being sincere . . .

"Anything?" she pressed, scrutinizing his every movement.

"Within reason. Though you must first promise to stop your glaring."

She forced her gaze away from him.

"And your scowling."

"Very well." It was Blythe that Signa thought of as she blocked out the image of hollow faces spinning beside her. "I agree to one more dance."

Dazzling was the only word to describe the smile that spread slowly across Fate's lips. He made the tiniest motion with his free hand, fingers barely shifting, and suddenly laughter filled the air. There were whispers again, and chatter all around as the dance ended and partners separated in search of the next name on their dance cards. All the while, Fate kept a firm hold of Signa.

He was so indiscreet that Signa could only hope her cheeks did not flush as quiet gasps and tittering laughter rose behind her. First Blythe, and now her. She could only imagine what Byron must be thinking, though wasn't it he who had suggested that Marjorie sleep with Elijah to stop him mourning his late wife? Perhaps he believed this was exactly the sort of play that Signa should be making.

"Thank you for that," she admonished, earning only a grin from Fate as music reverberated through the ballroom once more. It wasn't a proper waltz but rather an old tune that sounded like something from another time. Something that made her feel as though they should be dancing barefoot in a forest glade rather than a dimly lit ballroom.

Fate was close enough that Signa smelled the wisteria on his clothing, mild and sweet. He drew the first step, leading her through the dance with practiced grace.

"You were right. I do have questions, *many* of them," she said, trying to sound less anxious than she felt.

To her surprise, Fate's touch was firm but careful, and he watched Signa's face as though she were a puzzle in need of solving. She suspected that her own face looked the same.

"So long as there's music and we are dancing, you may ask them." His voice was gentler than she expected.

"Why is it that no one is questioning a palace that has appeared out of nowhere?" Signa demanded, wasting no time. "No one seems to recognize you as the man who accused my uncle. They only see you as a prince." Her steps were rigid as she counted from one to three in her head. Signa would be damned if she allowed herself to blunder a simple dance before Fate.

"Human minds are easy to placate." Again, the golden threads around them glistened. "I can control what they see, what they do... If necessary, I could have everyone forget that Elijah's imprisonment ever happened."

Fate braced her when she missed a step, as if he'd anticipated her doing so. Only then did Signa allow herself to truly look at this man. She didn't care for the heat of Fate's body, or that touching him made her hands clammy. Still, she appreciated that he was gentle with her, and that he handed his information over easily. It didn't hurt that feigning the role of a prince didn't feel out of reach for him, either. His face was one that belonged on the pages of newspapers throughout the world, broad and chiseled in all the right places, with a proud square jaw. He was strong, too, his body firm beneath her fingers. And she couldn't forget the cleverness in those eyes—always a little squinted, as though he was in a constant state of assessment and perpetually dissatisfied with his findings.

Signa could have sworn she'd seen that look before, though she couldn't place where.

"Why are you here?" she asked as he spun her.

His answer was too simple. Too relaxed. "I'm here to meet you, Miss Farrow."

She missed another step, though Fate took her by the elbow and corrected her before anyone could notice.

Signa scowled, trying not to let herself linger too long on his words. It would seem, with increasing evidence, that the man was a true and proper rake with a tongue of silver. "What about your brother? Are you not here for him?"

Fate leaned forward, a mere breath away from starting a new scandal. "I no longer have a brother. I told you already, I'm here for you."

Signa trained her eyes on his chest, hating herself when she felt her cheeks warm.

The light in Fate's eyes dimmed when he was unable to catch her gaze. "This song will only play for so long. Aren't you going to ask *why* I'm here for you?"

"No." She had no intention of falling for his tricks, and certainly not when there were more pressing matters. "I want you to leave Blythe alone. The price for her life has already been paid."

"Yes, by a man who had ten more years left on this earth. Believe me, I'm aware." Fate's grip tightened, and though he didn't show it, she could feel a storm raging inside him. "There is a ripple effect when you toy with a person's fate. Why don't you take a guess who's left to deal with the repercussions."

Signa's skin burned beneath his sweltering touch. "I promise you that she's worth our effort. Mine and yours."

He puffed an amused breath from deep in his chest. "No one is worth that much."

"I don't believe you mean that." She gave no thought to what she was saying, the words pouring from her even as Fate's expression went taut. "You can't tell me that there's never been someone you would do anything for. That there was never anyone you believed was worth it."

The music crashed to a halt. All around her, bodies slumped forward, bent at the waist like puppets with their strings cut. The walls flickered, the facade splintering to reveal glimpses of bare gray stone webbed and cracking. Signa shot a panicked look through the crowd in search of Blythe, but her cousin was nowhere in sight.

Fate took a breath, then tightened his hold on Signa as the music started once more. Immediately, the crumbling stone disappeared, replaced once more by gilded amber as bodies snapped upright like tin soldiers and twirled without any sign that they'd ever stopped.

"What exactly did Death tell you?"

"Only that you once loved a woman," she said in a rush, staring at the walls as they flickered from gray to gilded, "and that he had to take her."

"Well, that's a start." Fate's laugh was the grate of carriage chains dragging over cobblestone. "But I'm afraid that barely scratches the surface, *Little Bird*."

Chills rippled through her, and Signa had to fight every instinct telling her to pull away. "Don't you dare call me that. He was about to tell me more, but *you* took away his ability to speak with me. Didn't you?"

With his square jaw shadowed by flickering candles, Fate's princely face broke with the smallest crack of pain. There one moment and gone when she next blinked, just like the palace.

"Death doesn't deserve happiness." The music was coming to a crescendo, and Fate hastened their dancing until they were moving so quickly that Signa's vision began to blur.

"What of me?" she demanded. "Does my happiness mean nothing?"

"On the contrary, Miss Farrow, it means everything."

Signa was panting for air by the time the music stopped, sweat beading her temples and gliding down her back. Fate didn't have a hair out of place.

"It's my turn to ask a question," he said at last, so quiet she had to strain to hear him. "When you heard that song just now, did you recognize it?"

She riffled through her mind, hoping to find something there to appease him. The answer he wanted was clear, and with so much at stake, she wanted little more than to give it to him. But no matter how much she strained—no matter how much she looked upon him or let his skin sear hers—nothing about this man was familiar.

"I've heard many songs in my life. I can't be expected to remember them all."

Fate ran his palms down his face, groaning into them. Only when his shoulders eased and his anger ebbed did he extend a hand. "Please." It was a plea, gentle as a lullaby. "Take it and we'll try it again. I need you to remember. I need you to *listen,* and to remember who I am."

Signa drew back, tucking her hands close to her sides. "Who you are?" Perhaps her initial impression of Fate wasn't as far off the mark as she'd thought. "I would know if I'd met you before."

Fate didn't withdraw his hand but instead pressed it forward as his stare bore into her. "No, Miss Farrow, you might not. Not if we met in another lifetime."

TWELVE

It didn't feel appropriate to laugh. Not at the situation, nor at the man who had bared his soul to her and seemed terrified of what she might do with it. And so Signa didn't laugh despite how it bubbled nervously within her, for this was one of the most preposterous things she'd ever heard.

"You're not saying anything." Fate's jaw flexed. "Please, say something."

Signa opened her mouth, only for the words to curdle like cream upon her tongue. He was Fate—he knew how a person's life would play out, just as he must have known who was behind Lord Wakefield's murder and how they might save Elijah. Signa may not have been the person he wanted her to be, but she also couldn't afford to have this man as her enemy.

"You think I'm... what? Your reincarnated lover?" Her mouth felt as raw as if she'd swallowed glass as Fate closed the space between them. "Why on earth would you think it's *me*?"

“For every human life, there is a tapestry that defines their fate,” he said. “On yours were threads of silver that I did not sew. My threads are gold while Death’s are black. And yours... yours have always been silver.”

She didn’t look at him as he spoke, but at the glistening gold threads around them. They were *everywhere*. He had stilled every body in the room. Had brought time to a standstill. And yet, even with all that, there wasn’t so much as a bead of sweat on his brow.

She’d always known that Death was powerful, though his abilities often came in large, sudden bursts—sharp wind, or a deadly touch. Fate’s power felt more consuming. It was infinite and terrifying, and all Signa could do was ease her hand toward the belladonna berries she carried with her.

“There are not enough colors in this world for every person to have their own,” she whispered. “So why do I?”

Signa stilled as Fate took her chin between two fingers and tipped her head back so that she could look only at him. “Because you’re not a regular human, and you’re not a reaper, either. You are Life, and you have no idea how long I’ve been looking for you.” He had a look in his eyes that almost made Signa draw back when she realized what it was—hunger. Like he was a starved man, and she was a feast laid before him.

Life.

Life.

This time, Signa could not control the laugh that escaped her. She threw both hands over her mouth, smothering the sound, but it was too late. He thought she was *Life*? Good God, where had he been these past several months?

Fate's eyes narrowed, deep lines knitting between his brows. "You do not feel a pull toward Death because you are a *reaper*, Miss Farrow. You feel a pull toward him because he's the one who took you from me. In another time, you were *my* wife."

Another laugh bubbled in her throat, though she fought this one down. His *wife*! The very idea was ludicrous, for this man had clearly never witnessed her deathly powers in action.

"It's your brother that I love." Signa spoke low and soft, as though placating a skittish fawn. "I'm not who you think I am, but I'll help you look for her. We can find Life together."

From the way Fate drew back, one might think she'd struck the man across the face. The gold in his eyes burned molten, and behind him all of Wisteria quivered. For a sliver of a moment Signa once again saw the palace for what it truly was—bare gray walls and cracked slate floors. Empty, hollow, and as lifeless as his marionettes that swayed as the ground beneath them trembled, kept on their feet only by their golden threads. Then they were back in the amber ballroom and surrounded by the laughter of guests, the transition so fast that Signa had to convince herself it wasn't her imagination.

"My tapestries do not lie." Fate was no longer reserved nor coy. His movements were erratic as he took her by the shoulders, bending to capture her gaze. "I am not a man who begs, but I am begging now for you to listen to me. I am begging you to *think*, Miss Farrow. To think about what it is that you want. Are you happy to spend the rest of your life surrounded by death? By pain and grief?"

Signa didn't realize she was shaking until she reached up to knock him away from her. "It's not so gruesome as that," she whispered, recalling the night she'd first seen a soul, or the night Death had taken her to the bridge into the afterlife. "Death is simply the way of things."

"'The way of things'?" Fate scoffed. "What if those hands of yours *could* do more than kill? I could show you how. I could teach you. You'd want that, wouldn't you?"

She didn't.

She *couldn't.*

Signa had only recently accepted the darkness within her, and found the beauty in it, and yet... There was that whisper, again. The one that warned if she was so hesitant to admit to Blythe what she was and the things she could do, then perhaps she was an abomination.

She didn't want Blythe to be afraid of her. She didn't want *anyone* she loved to fear her. But if they knew the truth... how could they not? There wasn't a soul alive who would welcome a reaper with open arms.

Only for that reason did Signa feel a pull toward Fate's promise, though there was no world in which she could entertain his help. If not because of how it would affect Death, then because she'd only recently started to feel comfortable in her own skin, and the idea of once again opening herself up for exploration was terrifying. And so Signa did not answer the question about her powers. Instead, she told Fate, "No matter what you say or what you might think, I love your brother. I will not leave him, nor is it fair to keep me away from him."

Fate's smile thinned, a darkness stirring in his eyes. "They say that all is fair in love and war. I have built my trench and brought my rifles, and I have no intention of retreating. I will pursue you until you remember who you are. If that means I need to court you, Signa Farrow, I will. Flowers, promenades, even poetry if that's what you want. Whatever it is you enjoy, I will learn, and eventually you'll remember the life we once had."

This wasn't going at all how Signa had expected. She could feel the prickle of nerves along her chest and had to step away to take the fan from Diana's frozen hand, flipping it open in a desperate attempt to cool herself.

Fate had to be wrong. She wasn't Life. She couldn't be. She had killed her aunt Magda. She'd *stolen* lives, not given them. Fate was a foolishly hopeful man. But perhaps there was a way to use that to her advantage.

"Make a deal with me." There was hardly time to consider her words before she spoke them aloud, stilling her fan.

"A *deal?*" he echoed. "I'm not certain that you understand the magnitude of making a deal with me."

Of course she didn't. A bargain with Fate felt every bit as dangerous as one with Death, and yet Signa could not seem to stop herself. If this was her one opportunity, she had to seize it. "I do not have to stand idly by while you throw flowers at me or show up at my doorstep. But if you restore my ability to communicate with Death, then I will entertain this fantasy of yours."

Fate's jaw clenched, and Wisteria Gardens felt like a furnace against her skin, the air stifling and oppressive. Though she wanted little more than to retreat to a window and escape the heat of his severity, Signa kept her shoulders squared and her chin held high until Fate's expression turned sour.

"I have conditions. First, your communication with Death will only be restored during the evenings after you and I meet."

When she opened her mouth to argue, his lifted brows halted her protest. It seemed this deal was as good as it was going to get. "And you swear to honor this bargain?"

"Of course I do." Each word was clipped. "It matters little in the grand scheme of things. Eventually you will remember me, and when you do you'll decide to stop communication with him on your own. *That* will be better than any revenge I could imagine."

Signa's breath burned her throat. He was too confident. Too calculated. But what choice did she have? "Very well. Count tonight as our first outing, and I accept." She spoke so quietly that she wouldn't have been certain she'd said the words aloud if not for the sight of Fate's grin. While she'd thought he was enigmatic before, it was like she'd flipped a switch with those last two words. He was practically glowing.

"Deals with Fate are binding, Miss Farrow. When I wish to collect, you must be ready." He spoke as though he was savoring every word.

Signa had read enough fairy stories to know not to agree so easily. "Three events or outings are all you get. And after that, you'll restore my ability to communicate with Death in full."

His laugh had shivers rolling up her spine. "A month," he corrected, "during which I may call upon you multiple times."

It was less time than she'd expected, though still long enough that Signa did not have to fake her frustration. "Very well," she agreed, "but I have one more question you must answer first—who killed Lord Wakefield?"

To her surprise, Fate's grin never wavered. "There is no more music, and we are no longer dancing." All at once bodies twisted toward the doors, the guests marching like soldiers down the stairs. "I hope that your evening was as lovely as mine. I will see you again soon, Miss Farrow."

She did not linger or allow herself to spend so much as a second reconsidering the situation she'd gotten herself into. As the rest of the guests filed out of the ballroom, Signa gathered her skirts and fled Wisteria Gardens.

THIRTEEN

Signa found Blythe slumped in the carriage, looking like she'd been to hell and back—they both did.

"Where were you?" Signa demanded as she slammed the carriage door shut, much to the surprise of the driver, who had leaned forward to do the same thing.

Blythe blinked. Once, and then again. "I... dancing, I think? It was so warm that I must have come out here for air." She took her time with each word, piecing them together like a puzzle.

She didn't remember. Of *course* she didn't remember.

Signa's head fell back against the seat as she tried to decide whether to be angry or relieved. Eventually she huffed, "It felt like we were dancing in the devil's armpit," hoping to placate Blythe's unease. "Byron is already in the carriage behind us. Everyone's leaving."

"So early?" Blythe frowned, mental wheels still turning. She glanced out the window to a sky as black as pitch. "Where on earth has the time gone?"

Only when the driver snapped the reins and the horses began their descent down the mountain did Signa allow herself a proper breath. Blythe, however, fretted at her fingernails, absently picking at the cuticles.

While they'd both taken great care with their appearance that morning, Blythe's pale blond hair looked as though she'd been hunted through the woods. A halo of stray baby hairs were strewn around her face at every angle, and her fair cheeks were deeply flushed. For her part, Signa could feel that every square inch of her skin was sticky, and she imagined any powders or rouge she'd bothered with that morning had probably all but melted away.

"Did you learn anything?" Blythe asked as she tipped her head against the window. Signa pressed against the window, too, trying to catch one last look at the fountain in the courtyard. The sculpture of a woman who looked so unlike herself that Signa scratched at her arms and tried to dispel the possibility from her mind.

It wasn't her. It couldn't be.

"Only more rumors," Signa answered. "Charlotte was there. Eliza, too."

"Not even in her mourning wear," Blythe noted. "Odd, don't you think? She couldn't keep her eyes off Aris, even while she danced with Lord Bainbridge all evening."

Signa's blood froze. *"Aris?* Don't you mean the prince?"

"Must I be formal around you, too, cousin?" Blythe admonished.

Signa had to bite the inside of her cheek to keep from making a retort. Blythe was clever; if she thought Signa was withholding information, she'd sniff out the truth like a bloodhound. It was a relief when Blythe continued, with only a slight edge in her voice, "I'm surprised Eliza came at all. If she keeps it up, it won't be long before the vultures descend on her."

Though Signa was no fan of Eliza—the young woman had always been the worst of the gossips, and perhaps the most judgmental of any of the ladies Signa had met thus far—she understood better than most that grief could make a person do unfathomable things.

"I assure you it's the season that's changing her behavior, not her grief," Blythe added, as though she could read Signa's thoughts plainly upon her face. "The moment she heard that a prince was entering the fray, she turned as eager as a mama. Did you see her neckline?"

"Have you seen mine?" Signa motioned toward the bodice of her dress, and Blythe reached forward to grip Signa by the knee.

"Precisely my point! Your atrocious behavior aside, we came here with every intention of seducing a prince, and so did she. Or that viscount, at the very least. It seems a strange thing to be focused on with her uncle's death, doesn't it? He was the closest thing to a father that Eliza had."

It *was* a little peculiar, just as it was peculiar that she'd spent so much time near Byron whenever she wasn't dancing. Still, even before Lord Wakefield's death, Signa had witnessed Eliza's change in demeanor the moment she'd debuted into society. She'd wanted a match her first year out, which wasn't something Signa could hold against her. After all, hadn't Signa hoped that for herself once, too?

"It's worth keeping an eye on her," Signa agreed. "Though I don't see what motive she would have to kill the duke."

Blythe sighed and slipped on her gloves. "No, I suppose she wouldn't have one. She did rather enjoy parading through town on his arm. He always bought her the prettiest dresses."

Perhaps there was a motive to find, though it seemed like a stretch. *Every* suspect seemed like a stretch. Finding the killer felt like little more than a wild-goose chase, and while Byron was at the top of her list, the pieces weren't fitting together. She wanted to tell Blythe what she'd noticed between him and Eliza Wakefield, but Blythe had been through enough when it came to her family; Signa didn't want her to feel betrayed by her uncle, too.

The road beneath their carriage had smoothed as they journeyed down the mountainside. When the conversation lulled, Blythe rested her head against the window and shut her eyes. After a few moments she was breathing deeply. Signa leaned back, sprawling her legs beneath the dress and then frowning, for the action reminded her of when she'd first started speaking to Death—to Sylas. The two of them had been in a train car when he'd spread his obscenely long legs, as rude as could be.

God, how she wished he could be with her now.

Gazing out the window, she caught glimpses of a beautiful blue moon through towering alder trees. Staring at it brought back memories of autumn. Of riding horseback beneath the stars with Sylas by her side. The breeze had nipped at her skin, and she could still recall the wry grin on his face as he'd tipped his head back to the sky and howled with Gundry.

She hadn't wanted him to know about her escapades at Wisteria Gardens, especially considering he'd begged her not to go. But she missed him, and there was no saying how long Fate's agreement would last. Signa didn't want to wait until she was back at Thorn Grove before she spoke with Death; like Blythe, she tipped her own head against the carriage window and shut her eyes.

Do you intend to tell me the rest of the story about your brother? she asked. *Or shall I sit and ponder the ending for all of eternity?*

Signa waited, stilling her foot when she noticed its nervous tapping. Perhaps this was all for nothing. Perhaps Death still wouldn't be able to hear her, and this was little more than Fate's cruel joke. It seemed an eternity had passed before Signa's eyes prickled with tears as she felt his attention home in on her. She hadn't always been able to tell when Death was there listening, but ever since shared thoughts had become their most frequent form of communication, Signa had learned to sense his small subtleties—a quiet hum in her body. A prickling of her senses, suddenly more attuned to his.

Oh, Little Bird, how I've missed you. Though he may not have been with her in person, Death's voice was a balm that soothed Signa all the same. She was glad Blythe was asleep, for there was no masking her grin. She swiped at her eyes, savoring the moment.

Fate was a fool if he thought that she would ever leave Death. She loved him like the winter, resolute and all-consuming. Loved him with summer's steadiness, and with the ferocity of nature itself.

I've missed you, too, she told him while she still had the chance. *And there are a million other things I'd rather talk to you about, but I don't know how long we have.*

She heard Death's sigh as though he were beside her and willed herself to pretend that he was. That if she only reached out, the icy chill of his body would creep into hers. *I take it you've spoken with my brother?*

I need you to tell me who Life is, Signa said by way of an answer, hoping to bypass any argument they had no time for. *I need you to tell me everything.*

For a long moment there was only silence. Signa hesitated, wondering if Fate's side of the agreement had already hit its time limit. But when she focused, she could feel Death still lurking in the corners of her mind, biding his time before he answered, *Fate was all I had for many ages. Our relationship was not perfect—he has always felt that I should interfere with the human world less, while I have always suggested that he interfere more. That he listen to the requests of the souls whose lives he weaves, and take them into account. But Fate believes himself to be the perfect artist. Once a story is woven, he moves on to the next and doesn't look back. We didn't always agree on each other's methods, but at the end of the day we were all each other had. Until, one day, we weren't.* It was here that Death paused, seemingly to gather his thoughts. Each subsequent word felt raw, as though this memory was costing him something great.

There was a woman like us, he continued. *One who had always been in this world in one form or another. Her name was Life, and she was radiant. Fate was immediately taken with her, and they fell in love before my eyes. Life would create a soul, and Fate would give it purpose. He would weave their story before her. They were kinder stories then. Woven with more care because Life wanted her souls to thrive, and Fate wanted her to be happy. For her to smile. She had a beautiful smile.*

Signa's shoulders stiffened a little, and Death at once clarified, *I loved her very much, Little Bird. But it was not romantic. The older we became, the more I began to realize that Life was not like me or Fate. Although he and I were ageless, lines creased her eyes and mouth. She began to tire, and there came a time when the new souls she could generate were few and far between.*

One day, she pulled me aside to tell me that it was time for her to go. She told me that life was not meant to be infinite, and that she would return to us in a new form soon enough. For there is no life without experiencing death. She asked me to take her, but first, she wanted one more day with Fate. One more day to say goodbye.

Of course Fate realized what was happening, Death continued, each word seeming to stick to his teeth like gristle. *He demanded that I refuse her request. He made it clear that if I didn't, he would never speak to me again. He couldn't see that I was mourning, too, and in that mourning…I was susceptible.*

When Life came to me the next day, I refused her, and it was the most selfish thing I have ever done. For Life was stronger than any of us, and she knew it was her time to go. She would reincarnate, but none of us knew where or what form she would assume—nor did we know how long it would take for her to find us again. We'd spent a great deal of our existence without her already, and neither Fate nor I wanted to risk that again. But it's as I said already—one way or another, it was her time.

The more I resisted it, the worse the situation became. Signa kept still, hardly breathing as she clung to his every word. *I heard the call of her death. I knew it was time. Still, I resisted until it was pent up inside me and burst, and I gave her the worst imaginable death possible.*

The plague, Signa. The Black Death. I was trying so selfishly to keep her alive until I couldn't manage any longer. She was the first victim, and then it spread and spread—and, God, how it spread. Do you know how many people died because of my selfishness? Do you know how many innocent lives were taken because of my mistake?

She wished that he was there beside her. That she could take his hand and hold him while he shared this story that was so much worse than she'd expected.

Twenty-five million, he said at last, and Signa felt the severity of such a number like a blow to her stomach. *In four years, I claimed twenty-five million innocent lives. All because I was unwilling to let her go.*

You loved her, Signa told him, hating that they could speak only through this strange bond that existed between them. *We all do ridiculous things for the ones we love.* It was why she'd protected Blythe. Why she'd made this deal with Fate, just to have the chance to speak with Death.

It was more than ridiculous, Signa. It was selfish and cruel. I have not seen Life since, and neither has my brother. Perhaps this is our punishment, or perhaps she doesn't remember us. It's hard to be certain of anything, but I haven't been able to find Life since the day I watched her die.

Signa wanted to tell Death everything Fate had told her. She wanted him to laugh and agree that it was absurd to believe that she could be the woman they'd spent so long searching for. But the words clotted in her throat, for she was terrified of what he might think.

If it was true that she was someone else—if there was even a small chance that she was *Life,* the woman he had killed and the one whom his brother had loved so deeply—would he feel differently about her?

Now it's my turn to ask a question. Was your visit with my brother eventful?

Signa homed in on each syllable Death spoke, scouring his voice for any sense of just how angry he might be. It was unnervingly difficult to tell.

The ball was pointless. She curled her fingers into the carriage seat. *I feel no closer to stopping Fate or discovering Lord Wakefield's murderer than I did last week. I'm worried about Elijah. And Blythe, too, if we can't find a way to clear his name. Can't you get into the constable's head and convince him of Elijah's innocence, as you did with Thorn Grove's staff when Percy disappeared?*

Death's silence weighed on her for a long while as he considered her request. *If I did that, Fate would only retaliate with something worse. He won't let us disappear this.*

At this point, Signa deserved an award for resisting the mounting urge to throw her head back and scream. Sensing her worry, Death said in a voice as smooth as silk, *Do not lose faith. We already have a list of suspects in everyone who was at Thorn Grove the night of the murder.*

That wasn't nearly as reassuring as he seemed to think. *Half of the town was at Thorn Grove that night.*

Perhaps, but this is a start, which is more than you had the last time you solved a murder.

Signa supposed it was true, given that she hadn't known a single soul when she'd first come to Thorn Grove. Still, she'd known

Blythe's would-be murderer would have had frequent access to Thorn Grove, which... wasn't much more to go on than she had for Lord Wakefield's killer.

Why does it feel so much harder this time? She wanted to sound confident; to believe that she would solve this case. But she couldn't manage the facade. Not with Death.

My brother wasn't breathing down your neck last time, out for revenge and making light of the situation. And you didn't love the Hawthornes as you do now. Not at first.

She did love them, immensely so. Which was why she needed to get her head on straight and figure this out. Death was right; even if it wasn't a great lead, she had someone to start with—Byron.

I don't yet know how to help you, Death continued, his words as lulling as the spring breeze, *but I will speak to my brother. And in the meantime, I want you to stay away from him. Truly, this time. Can you promise me that?*

It would be an impossible promise, given Fate's intentions with her. But Signa didn't think Death needed to know the full details of that. At least not until she deciphered her own feelings, first. *I promise to do what I can, and that I will use discretion.* It was the best she could offer, and though he sighed her name, Death seemed to know better than to protest.

Has anyone ever told you how immensely stubborn you are?

She was surprised by the grin that split her lips. *Would you have me any other way?*

His pause was enough of an answer. *Keep it up, Little Bird, and we'll see if you're still as stubborn the next time I get my hands on you.*

The mental image of that promise sent her into an imaginative spiral. She shifted, suddenly uncomfortably warm in what felt like the mountains of fabric she wore. *And just what will you do? Describe it to me in detail.*

Death's voice was a low growl, yet Signa never managed to hear his reply. Instead, her body jolted to attention as a voice that was decidedly *not* Death's asked, "What on earth has you grinning like that?"

Signa's eyes flew open as Blythe took her by the shoulder, leaning forward to inspect her cousin. She pressed the back of her hand to Signa's cheeks, her forehead wrinkling. "You're flushed from the neck up! Do you think you're coming down with something?"

Blythe's hand was hot against her skin, though Signa had only a moment to notice it before she jerked back in surprise. "I'm perfectly well!"

She must have flushed even deeper, for Blythe narrowed her eyes for a long moment before her face lit with delight. "Oh my God, you were dreaming about a man, weren't you? Who was it? You must tell me!"

Death's low, rumbling laughter sounded in the back of Signa's mind. *Go on,* he taunted, *tell her.*

"It was no one—"

"Don't give me that." Blythe scoffed. "Did you meet someone at the ball? Given that you did not so much as blink in his presence, it surely wasn't the prince."

As much as she would have loved to say she'd met someone, Signa was so flustered that it was a struggle to even recall her own name, let alone that of anyone else at the soiree. Knowing Blythe, handing over a name would be like granting her permission to stalk the poor man and figure out every last detail about him, his family, his deepest secrets, and his worthiness of Signa. And so, without giving it too much thought, she said the first name that came to her mind.

"It was of Everett Wakefield."

Blythe's mouth slammed shut. She folded her hands pleasantly in her lap, doing a poor job of appearing at ease. "Well he's . . . I mean, I suppose he *is* eligible. But goodness, Signa, the timing. I wondered if you still might be interested in him after everything. It seemed your attention diverted from him over the past months, though I didn't want to pry. God only knows he could use some company, with everything he's going through—though have you seen the way Charlotte looks at him? I wonder what she might think if the two of you were to make a match."

"I suppose I'll have to ask." As the towering spires and iron gates of Thorn Grove came into view, Signa breathed a sigh of relief so heavy it fogged the window. The sooner she could get out of the carriage, the better.

Death, after all, was waiting for her.

FOURTEEN

Blythe didn't bother to knock when she arrived at Signa's room early that next morning, flushed and breathless as her body bowed to the weight of the floral arrangement she carried. It was nearly half as large as she was, with wisteria that draped over beautiful greenery.

"Dare I ask what feminine wiles you worked to earn the prince's affection so quickly?" Blythe set the arrangement on Signa's tea table, trying not to trip over the flowers that skirted the floor.

It was barely sunrise, though Signa was already wide awake, seated at the desk in her sitting room and poring over the list of names of those who had received an invitation to Thorn Grove the night of Lord Wakefield's murder. Several of them seemed to have been crossed out while she'd been sleeping, and it took her a solid ten minutes of staring at the parchment before she realized that this update could have been done only by Death. The realization had her scouring the table until she found a letter he'd left for her folded into the list of names. Wildflowers were pressed into the page, and Signa's heart practically burst at the sight of it.

Fate may have been able to stop them from speaking, but he couldn't stop this. She'd just unfolded the letter, which detailed all the things they'd do once this was over and all the places they'd see, when Blythe burst through the door, leaving Signa to shove the letter down her bodice as she pushed up from her chair. Crossing the room, she inspected the flowers with a frown.

"They're beautiful," Blythe said between stretches, trying to soothe her back from the weight of the arrangement. "Given the way you spoke to him and how you daydream of Lord Wakefield now, I had thought they were for me until I saw your name on the letter. I've no idea how you managed to tame such a beastly man, but I'm impressed."

Signa bent to see that Blythe was right—in the middle of the arrangement was a gilded envelope addressed to her. She pried it from the flowers, knocking a few petals to the table in her haste.

"I thought you didn't care for the prince," Blythe pushed, her eyes narrowing as she drew several steps closer to examine the envelope.

"For someone who also did not care for him, you certainly seem interested in what he sent," Signa bit back. She didn't mean to come across as antagonistic as she did, but Blythe's prying ate at her nerves, and whatever this letter said, she preferred that Blythe not see it.

"Is it so wrong to be curious?" Blythe swept the fallen petals away. "Rest assured, I despise the man enough that he should have sent *me* flowers as an apology for burdening me with his existence. They're quite lovely."

They were, unfortunately. They appeared expensive, too, which meant that anyone who saw them delivered would immediately understand the prince's intent. Signa could only imagine the ways in which Byron's mind was already scheming.

"Aren't you going to read the letter?" Blythe tipped onto her toes, trying once more to look over Signa's shoulder. "If you've won the prince's favor then you must respond!"

Signa bit back her groan as she tore the envelope open, angling her body away from Blythe, who further encroached by the second. Signa didn't *want* to know what Fate had to say, but she didn't doubt that he would realize what she'd done if she simply threw the letter into the hearth. And blast it if she wasn't a little curious herself.

With fretting fingers, Signa pried the slip of parchment within it free. There was but a simple sentence written in elegant script:

Give me the chance, and I shall show you that I am not the villain here, Miss Farrow.

Signa felt faint.

"What does it say?" Blythe asked as Signa tucked the note against her chest and out of sight.

"Nothing. It's only a note to thank me for dancing with him."

There was a tart pucker to Blythe's lips. "I danced with him, too. Let me see that—"

Signa dodged out of the way when Blythe made to grab the letter, then recalled what Elijah had done with his slip of paper back in the prison cell and crumbled it. When Blythe extended her palm expectantly, Signa popped the paper into her mouth.

Only, it was much thicker than the small slip of paper she'd brought Elijah, and she choked.

Blythe's mouth hung ajar. "What on earth are you thinking?" With or without the letter preventing her from speaking, Signa couldn't respond.

Fortunately, there was no need, as she was rescued by a knock upon the door and Elaine hurrying inside a moment later.

"Miss Farrow!" cried the maid. "You must ready yourself at once!"

"What is it, Elaine?" It was Blythe who asked, allowing Signa a moment to spit out the wad of parchment and scrub her tongue clean. She hurried to rip the damp paper and toss its remains into her wastebasket when no one was looking. "Has something happened?"

"He's *here*, miss." Elaine's voice quaked with anticipation, and Signa's blood froze as she prayed that the woman meant Elijah. Perhaps Fate's letter meant that he'd decided to help them after all. But then Elaine continued, "Everett Wakefield is here to see you. Mr. Hawthorne is with him in the parlor."

Blythe made a noise of appreciation in the back of her throat. "First the prince and now the duke. *Someone* had an eventful evening."

Signa slumped back in her chair. "Lord Wakefield is here to see *me*? But I'm not receiving today." The words sounded absurd even to her own ears, for surely he wouldn't be calling on her without good reason given all that was going on, especially not at such an early hour. Still, curiosity had Signa back on her feet, knocking Blythe gently on the shoulder when she noticed her smug grin. "Very well. We mustn't keep him waiting."

Elaine hurried to help Signa out of her dressing gown and into a beautiful cream housedress with a high neckline and long sleeves adorned with lace around the wrists. Signa quickly pulled on her gloves herself, cognizant of how Elaine fussed, ensuring that every strand of hair was in place. It felt ridiculous for anyone to be concerned with her appearance when Everett's father had recently died, but she didn't argue.

"It seems like you made quite the impression on the prince," Elaine said. "You should see all the arrangements he's sent for you."

Good God, there were more.

Blythe swept the hem of her nightgown into the air, bowing low. "Shall I curtsy when I address you from now on, cousin? I wouldn't want to offend a princess."

"Since when has a title stopped you from offending anyone?" Signa's words cut off in a gasp as Elaine tightened the laces of her corset so severely that Signa worried her ribs might crack. Readying oneself in the morning truly was an arduous affair, and by the time she was dressed and ready, Elaine was sweating and Signa was breathless and a little sore, while Blythe watched from a chair in the corner.

"Did Lord Wakefield give any word of why he is here?" Signa asked as she slipped into her shoes, already starting out the door.

Elaine followed behind her. She was shorter than Signa and had to hustle to keep up. "Only that he came to speak with you."

Signa had wondered every day for the past two weeks how Everett was faring. Unlike his cousin Eliza, he'd kept a low profile, never once leaving his estate. If he had, Signa would have heard the gossip. So why was it that the first time he left, he'd chosen to come to Thorn Grove of all places?

"Wait!" Blythe hissed as she followed them. She was still dressed in her robe and nightgown, hair undone as she bounded down the hallway. "I'm coming, too!"

Elaine spun to face her with a horrified gasp. "You most certainly are not! We'd need to get you dressed appropriately, and there's no time—"

Blythe waved her away. "He's not going to *see* me. I'm just going to listen. Speak loudly, cousin. Enunciate."

Though Signa would have loved nothing more than to tell Blythe just how silly and nosy she sounded, there was no time to argue. They'd reached the top of the stairs, and Blythe at once drew a step back, ducking into a corner of the landing. Elaine remained there as well, leaving Signa to descend by herself.

The lady's maid had been right—there were flowers everywhere. Giant arrangements of peonies and roses. Lilacs. Endless wisteria draping from massive marble vases. Saying that it was excessive was an understatement. Signa tried her best to ignore everything as she made her way toward the parlor, taking a moment to assess the situation while still unnoticed.

Byron and Everett sat across from each other, a tray of tea and untouched pastries between them. Everett was dressed from head to toe in mourning black, and he held his hat in his lap. His warm brown skin had gone ashy, and there were fine lines Signa had never noticed carved upon his forehead.

Though his every movement was sluggish, Everett made polite conversation and Byron was every bit as proper as Percy had once been, sticking to easy subjects and trying not to pry, though Signa was certain he wanted to. She didn't hear any mention of Elijah's name, nor the duke's—and soon enough curiosity bested her. At the threshold to the parlor, she cleared her throat.

The two men rose to their feet. "Miss Farrow!" Everett drew the tiniest of steps forward, glancing discreetly at the flowers behind her. "Forgive me for once again arriving unannounced. I promise I will not make a habit of it. I would have sent a letter detailing my arrival, but..."

He didn't need to say anything more. People were little more than piranhas these days, waiting for Everett to emerge so that they might tear into him. She stepped into the parlor, going immediately to his side. Improper though it was, she took one of Everett's hands in her own. "There are no apologies necessary. Please, let us sit. I am sorry about your father, and while I know it's not a fair question, I can't help but to ask it.... How are you faring?"

"Miss Killinger has been most gracious with her time," he said as he sat, drawing her down beside him. "She's been helping me arrange everything. The funeral, the burial... the ceremony for my title. Truthfully, that's why I'm here. I wanted to invite you and your family, and to apologize for my behavior that night. I've no idea what came over me when I said what I did about your uncles." His gaze slid sideways to Byron, who nodded but watched Everett with keen eyes. It seemed they'd already had a discussion of their own.

"I wasn't in my right mind," Everett continued. "I want you to know that I spoke with the constable as soon as I got my wits back, and that I spoke on Elijah's behalf."

Signa straightened, ignoring a quiet thunk from the stairway, where Blythe was listening. "Are you saying that he'll be released?"

The long delay before Everett spoke again was enough of an answer. Gently, he eased his hand from hers. "I don't believe that your uncle had any reason to poison my father—but Mr. Hawthorne confessed to being the one to hand him the drink, and the constable believes he had a reason to want my father dead. They're keeping him regardless of what I say. I just thought you should know that I never meant for this to happen."

Were she in Everett's shoes and the situation reversed, Signa probably would have hated him. The tactical side of her mind ventured at once to thoughts of potential motives. But then she remembered the letter from Fate that signaled his intent to prove himself. Could Everett's reversal be a gift from *him*? The apology in Everett's eyes was sincere enough that she could almost allow her body to be at ease. *Almost* but not quite, given that there was no telling whether Everett had come of his own volition or Fate had planted the seed in his mind.

"You speaking on his behalf at all is a great help," she managed to say at last. "What happened to your father was horrible, Everett. The fact that you're even thinking of my uncle right now is deeply appreciated, but you must take care of yourself. If there's anything I can do for you, please let me know."

"There is something, actually." He leaned away just enough to reach into his coat and withdraw a letter. "As I've said, I must formally take my place as the Duke of Berness, and it would mean the world to me if you and your family attended the investiture."

When he pressed the letter into her palm, Signa stilled. What he was asking was no small thing, and if not for Fate, Signa doubted that Everett would even ask. Though, without Fate, she didn't believe that Elijah would have been accused in the first place. Still, if she and her family showed up to the investiture with an invitation in hand from the man who had named her uncle a culprit... Well, what could be a better step for clearing Elijah's name?

"I made a hasty accusation that night." Everett brushed a hand over his hair, Adam's apple bobbing in his throat. "For that, I apologize. I figure this is the least I can do to help repair the damage I've caused to your family." Byron cleared his throat, and Signa looked at him just long enough to see him nod once.

She set the invitation in her lap and flashed Everett a smile. "We'll be there." She hadn't realized he was so tense until his shoulders eased upon hearing her answer.

"Wonderful," he said, and she knew that even if Fate had orchestrated this whole thing, Everett still meant every word. He was a kinder person than she was—than most people were, really. Deeply, wonderfully kind.

Everett stood then, and both Byron and Signa followed suit. "I should go before anyone sees my carriage out front. But I apologize again, to your entire family, and I look forward to seeing you all at the ceremony."

"You are going to make a fine duke," Byron told him. "Your father would be proud."

Those five words alone were enough to steal Everett's breath and snatch any remaining light from his eyes. Signa stared at the pale press of his lips, guilt swelling within her as she watched him try to rectify himself. "Thank you." His voice was flat, though he'd forced himself to smile. "I certainly hope so. Now, if you'll excuse me." Perhaps unable to feign stability any longer, Everett set his hat atop his head and hurried off to his carriage.

The moment the door shut behind him, Blythe practically flew down the staircase. Her gown trailed behind her until it became wedged between two floral arrangements, and she had to stop to pry the hem out. "Do you think he was being genuine?" she asked when she'd caught her breath.

"He seemed sincere," Signa admitted. "Though it's hard to say."

"This is precisely the sort of attention we need." Byron scanned beyond the open door to where the servants were still gathering Fate's gifts. "We'll have to tread carefully. One wrong move, Miss Farrow, and everything shatters. When is the investiture?"

Signa pried open the envelope and removed the invitation, skimming down the elegant script until she saw the date. "The twentieth of April."

"Less than a week. Not much time to plan." Byron ran a hand down the length of his jaw, and when he looked once more at Signa, it was not with concern but rather the same consideration that one might give when inspecting a horse prior to the races. "This is going better than I anticipated. Keep it up, and we may have Elijah back sooner than we could have hoped."

Whether he *did* hope, however, was the question. And it was time that Signa finally got an answer.

FIFTEEN

THE BELLADONNA BERRIES WERE PRUNED AND SHRIVELED AS SIGNA unfurled them from their wrapping. Only ten berries remained, and as she stared at them, she imagined Death's voice in her head, telling her not to take this risk. That they would find another way.

For two weeks Byron had done nothing to prove himself the culprit, but if he was, then there was no time to waste. She'd waited hours for him to leave Elijah's study, and there was no telling when he might be back. Byron had barely left the room even to sleep, and when he did, he never left it unlocked. If Signa wanted to know what he spent his days doing in there, this was her chance to figure it out.

As the temperature of her bedroom plummeted, Signa knew that while she may not have been able to see him, Death was there with her, watching as she palmed five of the remaining berries. The windows ripped open, frost icing their edges as a breeze tore into the room and knocked one of the berries from her palms. She glared behind her at where she hoped Death stood before she picked it back up and steadied her trembling hands, not wanting him to see just how afraid she was.

Something strange was going on with her powers, but Fate wouldn't let her take ill enough to die if he suspected she might be Life. It wasn't a comforting thought, but it gave her the confidence to move forward with her plan. She popped the berries into her mouth before she could change her mind and chewed, grimacing at the rot that soiled her tongue. She knelt against the bed frame after that, waiting for the familiar effects to overcome her. It took longer than usual, the berries less potent. She would need to move quickly to avoid getting stuck on the other side of the study door.

Eventually, when the world had spun into a haze of gray and her body turned cold, Signa opened her eyes. She didn't need to turn to know where Death stood, for his shadows had already curled around her, bringing her to his chest. He hugged her so fiercely that Signa wondered whether he'd ever let go.

She settled into the familiar rush of power that coursed through her in this form, tipping her head against him as she summoned the night. Shadows swept to her, gliding up her feet and swathing her fingertips until they blanketed her skin like armor. Signa's hands flexed as she welcomed them. The power felt so natural that she pitied Fate and his hope.

"Hello, Little Bird." Death's voice cut through the night, a cool burn against her skin.

God, it was good to hear his voice. Not just in her head but sweeping through the room like a glorious storm. She leaned away so that she could look at him—not a human, but shadows cast in the shape of a man, face and skin masked by darkness.

"Don't be angry with me," she whispered, and though she would have loved nothing more than to let herself fall back into his arms and feel him there against her, Signa feared she'd have less time than ever to remain in this state with the berries as old as they were. "There isn't time."

"There's never any time these days. And it's no use being angry; I have resigned myself to the understanding that you will forever ignore my wishes and will do whatever you want." Though he kept his voice light as he followed her out the door, he hovered within arm's reach, observing her every move. They kept to the walls, close to the portraits of the Hawthorne lineage, which Death inspected as they walked. "There really are a lot of them, aren't there?" He took a few more steps, stopping at another portrait of a woman with flat eyes and an angry mouth. "I remember the day I picked this one up. She wouldn't stop screaming and told me that if she was dead, then I needed to take her husband, too. He was perfectly healthy."

Signa smiled and let her hand slide into his, savoring the moment while it lasted. She'd journeyed down these halls with Sylas before, sleuthing for clues about Lillian Hawthorne's murder. She knew she shouldn't feel nearly as giddy as she did, but Signa's life had never been normal, and sneaking into the study to investigate her uncle with Death at her side felt like her own personal brand of courtship.

"This is the one." Signa paused to listen for any footsteps or signs of life from inside. When only silence answered, Signa shuddered as she slipped through the door.

Elijah's study was as she remembered—an expansive room with leather chairs as rich as caramel and sleek, polished furniture. It had a masculine essence, warm and sophisticated and smelling of pine. The hundreds of books shelved across the walls were pristine and untouched, though the desk was another story. It was a mess of tea-stained papers and journals filled with notes on every page.

Death joined Signa as she prowled around the desk, commanding her shadows to slide the chair out of the way so she didn't have to stand in the middle of a piece of furniture and feel like a true ghost. He laughed, low and pleased, as he watched her. "I didn't expect you would have such control already."

"Of course I do." She summoned the shadows around her again, their tendrils turning the pages she could not touch in her spirit form. "I'm a reaper, after all."

The words were as much for her own benefit as his, though she stumbled on them. When she was in this form, being able to command the shadows made her feel more powerful than anything in this world. She liked that she and Death were so similar. Liked that there was a side to her that only he understood.

But as much as she craved the thrum of this power coursing through her, Fate's suspicions still beat against the back of her mind. If he was right—if her hands really could bring life instead of death—then shouldn't *that* be the power she craved?

She didn't want to believe it could be true, and yet the idea had burrowed too deeply into her mind, a constant itch she couldn't scratch. She had to distract herself from it by sorting through the pages and clippings scattered on the desk. The first that drew her eye featured a story of the garden fire.

Signa's throat tightened. So lost in her thoughts was she that she tried to reach for the paper herself, only for her ghostly hand to slip through it. Death stepped beside her, inspecting the pages from over her shoulder. And then he spoke aloud the truth that filled Signa with such dread—"Byron is investigating Percy's disappearance."

There weren't just notes in the ledgers but also the names of vendors and friends. Charlotte Killinger's name was underlined, and Signa noticed with great distaste that her own name had been circled. Elijah's, too.

Behind them was a map that Death turned and inspected in grim silence. Signa turned to it as well, though she immediately wished she hadn't. There were towns struck through with an *X*, and only one still circled—Amestris. She returned to the desk to find the same name on the ledgers, with the address of every inn and pub in Amestris noted.

"Byron's searching for him," Signa whispered. Her guilt was acidic, burning through her. It seemed Byron had searched nearly half the country by now. Page by page his notes lost their elegance, until nearly illegible writing was scrawled across the journal. Some of it was so difficult to read that she nearly missed a word at the top the most recent page: *Murder?*

The shadows evaporated from her like smoke as Signa stumbled backward. Death gripped her by the shoulders, steadying her.

"He knows." Had Signa been in her mortal form, she would have been sick. As it was, she settled a hand over her stomach and tried to quell the burning guilt. "He knows Percy is dead. He knows someone killed him. My name is on those papers, Death. He must think it was me. He must know—"

"He knows nothing." Death's fingers curled into her skin. "We left no trace behind. Byron can suspect all he wants, but he doesn't know a thing. I promise you, I took care of it."

Perhaps. Yet all she could see were the maps with cities crossed out and the dozens of scattered notes written by a wild hand. Outwardly, Byron was maintaining his composure. But inwardly...

"He loved Percy." Signa's lips numbed at the words. "He loved him, and he'll never see him again. He doesn't even know what happened." She felt as though she were a forgotten doll, held together by threads that were fraying at the seams. As cruel as Percy was in the end, did his family not deserve answers? She had hoped to spare them such a painful truth, yet there was nothing she could say without them knowing she was responsible for his death. If that happened... she would lose the Hawthornes forever.

"Signa." Death's grip on her tightened. Her body was flickering in and out of its spirit form, visible one second and translucent the next. Shadows wisped around her, frenzied. "If it wasn't Percy they had to mourn, it would be Blythe—" He cut off sharply as the handle of the door wiggled.

Death threw his shadows around them. Though Byron wouldn't be able to see or hear them, both Signa and Death kept as still as could be, feeding off each other's anxiety.

Only, it wasn't Byron who entered the study. It was Blythe, and as Signa stood there, invisible in her reaper form, she felt rather silly for not having first asked her cousin about the key to this room. She'd been walking on eggshells around Blythe when it came to her suspicions about Byron, yet she should have known that her cousin would be as suspicious of him as she was. Signa should have known that while she was avoiding her, Blythe was doing her own sleuthing.

Blythe was as quiet as the dead as she made her way to the desk, though not nearly as careful as Signa had been as she riffled through the papers. She didn't always close journals to the page they'd been opened to, nor was she careful about keeping everything organized. So that Byron wouldn't realize they'd been there, Signa took care to reorganize things every time Blythe looked away and moved on to the next parchment. They were to be little more than ghosts passing through, just as Sylas had told her all those seasons ago.

Blythe dug deeper than Signa had, prying her way through the desk until she happened upon a tiny velvet box in one of the drawers. She stilled, and Signa gripped Death's shoulder. Even without looking inside, the contents of the box were undeniable. Still, Blythe pulled the top open to reveal a stunning emerald stone set on a gold band.

That's Elijah's desk. She threw the words at Death as his shadows stirred, seeming unnerved.

Byron's been using it for a week. The ring could belong to either of them.

The ring likely wasn't Elijah's, given how he was only just beginning to spend his days without losing himself to thoughts of his late wife. Byron, on the other hand, had been far more invested in this season than ever.

She thought back to how odd his behavior had been at Fate's soiree, and how he and Eliza had stood beside each other on more than one occasion. Surely, there couldn't have been anything going on between them . . . could there?

Blythe snapped the box shut, dropping the ring back into the drawer with a deep frown. She shifted her focus to the desk, eyes more critical now as she lifted several of the clippings to skim through once more. It took a beat longer for the realization to hit Blythe than it had Signa. It wasn't until she noticed the article about the fire that she dropped the news clippings, face turning bone white as she pored over Byron's theory. Not that Percy was gone but that he, too, had been murdered. Blythe was stiff as she read over the words too many times. Then she scooped up the papers and placed them back where she found them. She gripped the desk by the edges, unaware that Signa was beside her, watching as her cousin sorted through the names on Byron's list. Watching as she saw Elijah's name. Signa's.

"No," Blythe whispered, and oh how Signa wanted to take her cousin's hand and tell her everything. But Blythe would never forgive her. And why should she?

Signa had told herself that she wasn't keeping this secret for her own sake but for Blythe's. But as guilt pressed against her, Signa realized how deeply she'd been lying to herself. She wanted to spare Blythe, of course. More than anything, though, Signa was terrified of losing her. She was terrified of returning alone to Foxglove, once again left behind by those she loved. Had Death not been gripping her, she would have reverted into human form, if only to reach out to her cousin. To apologize for everything she'd had to do to save Blythe's life that night in the woods.

Fate's words rattled in her head, over and over again: *What if those hands of yours could do more than kill? You'd want that, wouldn't you?*

In that moment, she did. If it meant never again being the one responsible for the tears of someone she loved, then God did she want it.

The world spiraled around her, too warm. No. Not warm. Hot. Blazing, scorching, like something was burning her alive. She clutched her head, sinking to her knees.

This was not the cooling comfort of death but a blazing fire that tore its way through her as thick vines erupted from the wooden planks beneath her feet. It was like that night in the woods, back when Gundry had stood at her side and Signa had raised the dead garden to ensnare Percy. Only this was no dead bramble rising from the earth, but thriving ivy that clawed its way up through the floor like wildfire.

What's happening? Signa demanded, panicked as thick lichen devoured the legs of Elijah's desk and wisteria wove itself between splinters of wood. Death careened backward, hissing as he clawed at the vines that somehow ensnared his shadows.

Blythe threw herself from the desk and away from the growing earth with a squeal, kicking at moss that worked its way up her boots. She rubbed at her watering eyes as if trying to disillusion herself, though when she lowered her hands, ripe green stems stretched from the wall and curled around her fingers. This time Blythe screamed as she stumbled over a chair.

We should leave. Death grabbed a fistful of the ivy that had ensnared Signa's hands. Thorns dug into her skin, drawing wisps of darkness rather than blood. She couldn't see straight enough to get them off herself, and she was shaking as Death ripped them free and hurried her out of the study. They didn't stop once on their way back to Signa's suite. Not to speak. Not to ask questions. Not for anything. But the moment they *were* back, the flowering vines fell away from their bodies, swept aside by the shadows that Death let drip from him as he returned to his human form. Only then could Signa see the pointedness of his gaze and how he set about watching her as though he'd never seen her before.

"I'm sorry," she rasped. "I swear I didn't mean to. I—I didn't know it was true. I didn't... I didn't think—" Her chest was tight as breath swept back into her lungs. The blood in her veins burned, and her body flickered in and out of view. But she wasn't sick yet. She wasn't coughing blood or throwing up, and she clung to that victory.

"Say something," Signa all but whimpered when she finally got the courage to address Death. Usually, he did a fine job at playing human, but in that moment he'd forgotten to blink as he stared at her. Signa tried to ground herself. Tried to stay steady and calm any way she could, since it would do neither of them any good if she started sprouting things again.

Death's fingers curled one by one around hers and he shut his eyes. "You grew that, Signa."

"I know. I didn't mean—"

"You're not listening to me." He squeezed her hand tight, and Signa's fear surged. It couldn't have been true.

It couldn't have. She'd killed Percy. She'd killed Magda. Her hands were *lethal.* Poisonous and deadly, because she was a reaper.

She was a *reaper.*

But one look into Death's gray eyes, and her entire world shifted.

"You *grew* something." There was a perilous calm to Death's words as he bent to capture her stare. "You didn't claim a life. You didn't take anyone or anything away. You *created* something. There is only one person in this world with the powers to do such a thing."

Signa would have given up her entire fortune to stop him from speaking. To hit the clock and still time forever, because although she understood the words that were to come and that some deep, secret part of her *wanted* to hear them, there was nothing to prepare her for the weight of what they meant as Death said, "Signa. You used Life's powers."

This time there was no denying it. She had seen the thorns and the vines sprout from beneath her own feet. Had watched as they'd climbed up the shadows and crept along her skin. Still, it seemed impossible. Because if she had Life's powers... If she could *give* life...

All her life those around Signa had treated her like she was evil incarnate. Over the years she had grown to lean in to the oddities of who she was and what she could do—and she finally felt comfortable in her own skin.

And yet... For years Signa had internalized this hatred for

herself. Though she thought she'd managed to put it behind her, it seemed that change did not come so easily. There was no switch she could simply press that would allow her to forget how much she had hated herself. The memories were as lashing as the sea, threatening to drown her in the self-loathing that consumed her.

All this time, her life never had to be this way.

"Did you know?" Death's voice was a scythe that cleaved through her chest. "Did you know that this was why my brother came here?"

She held firmly to his hand, for in the back of her mind a voice warned her not to let go. That if she did, everything would be different. "I was afraid to believe it could be true."

Death's grip tensed. "But it *is* true, Signa. All this time I have been nothing but a fool to believe that you and I were made for each other. That if Fate had his counterpart, then surely I might have one as well. I thought it was a sign that I could touch you without killing you, but now I know why—"

"This is precisely why I was afraid!" Signa's mind was a flurry of thoughts that had turned her words sharp. "Don't you dare get philosophical on me. Don't you dare think for even a moment that this changes anything between us. You told me before that you were the one to reap Life's soul. How did you do it?"

Death stilled. "The same way I always do."

"Through touching her, right?" Signa was so relieved when Death nodded, she had to choke back a laugh. "Then don't you see? I don't know what I am, but I cannot be her. I don't die when you touch me, Death. I am not *her*."

"But you have her powers," he said. "Which means that your options are limitless, Little Bird. You no longer need to be consumed so thoroughly by all that's dead or dying."

"You don't get to make that decision for me." She would wage war on this hill if doing so would make him come to his senses. "You don't get to tell me what I should do, and you don't get to pull away from me. Not now."

He seemed to recognize the intensity of the emotion pouring through her before she did, for his lips brushed the back of her hand as he drew her close. "I would never dream of it. You mean more to me than you will ever understand, and I will not willingly leave. But if we're going to be together, then I want it to be by *choice*. Don't shut out this other side of you simply because you're afraid of how I might feel. If you're who I think you are . . . you deserve to explore that. You deserve to know what it means."

Perhaps, though there were no words for how deeply the idea unsettled her. These powers were no soft thing. They were wildfire upon her skin and felt as if they would burn her whole if she allowed them to.

"Whatever you decide, I will be here," Death promised. "Until the moment you tell me to leave, I will be by your side."

Signa leaned her head against his chest, trying to fill the ache in her heart. "What of Fate? If it's true that I may be who he's looking for, then where does he fit into our picture?"

She was glad for the sudden tightness in Death's face. Glad when he wound himself around her and pulled her in close. "Whatever you are and whatever you can do, you are not who Fate expects you to be. You are still Signa Farrow, and I am not a good enough man to allow my brother to take you from me."

Those were the words she wanted—that she *needed*—and she could only hope that Death meant them. Because Signa Farrow had another secret—one that she didn't dare admit aloud. And it was that while the vines tore through the floor and the burn of Life's powers lanced through her, Signa had heard the song that she and Fate had danced to.

She had heard the song he'd asked her to remember.

SIXTEEN

Blythe

SURELY, BLYTHE WAS BEING POISONED AGAIN, FOR WHAT ELSE COULD explain what she'd seen in her father's study?

She had never run faster than she did the moment she was able to free herself from the ivy, and it had taken hours of pacing and fretting and convincing herself that she must be seeing things before she'd gathered enough nerve to return to the study, only to find that no plants waited inside. Every floorboard was unscathed, and the desk and its papers were free from even a bit of earth.

It was then that Blythe realized she was losing her mind.

She refused to linger in the study, sucking in thin breaths as she hurried not to her room but down the stairs and out of Thorn Grove altogether, trying not to scream and alert the entire manor to her ailment.

It'd been a long while since she'd left Thorn Grove in anything but a carriage. Worried about a relapse in her health, Elijah had kept a cautious eye on her, ensuring that Blythe had little physical exertion and that the staff doted on her. But her body was trembling too fiercely for her to hole up alone in her room, and so Blythe took to stomping around the yard for the good part of an hour, soaking up the springtime warmth into her bones as she debated whether she should tell Signa what had happened.

In the end Blythe decided she wanted more time. More time to see if this was only a temporary relapse. More time to feel at least a little normal, without everyone treating her like a fragile crystal heirloom. And so she ventured to the stables instead, where a groom she'd never seen crouched in the hay with a small foal curled beside him. The poor thing was quivering, its eyes unopened and its breaths heavy. A beautiful golden mare poked its head over from the next stall, watching. Blythe's gut clenched as she realized that it was her mother's horse, Mitra.

The groom sang as he stroked his fingers through the foal's coat, and though it took a minute for her to recognize the tune, Blythe's laugh was the softest breath when she realized he was singing an entirely inappropriate song about a bonny lass who worked on a farm, his voice tired and thick with a lilting brogue.

Blythe's eyes trailed from him to the foal, and very quietly she asked, "Will it be all right?"

The groom bolted upright. "Miss Hawthorne! Oh, God. Forgive me, I'd no idea I was in the presence of a lady." His eyes were round and wide, and he was failing spectacularly at not tripping over himself. "Is there something I can help you with?"

"The foal. Will it be all right?"

His face softened. "Only time will tell, miss. All there is to do now is make him comfortable and pray for the best."

Blythe's chest tightened to a point where she could barely breathe, and she hated that she followed her first instinct of turning away from the newborn. It was too difficult to look at the dead or the dying these days; the reminder of how much time she'd spent at that threshold was still too awful to bear.

She forced her attention back to the task at hand. Her father would rage if he knew she'd even made the trek to the stables in the first place, let alone that she wanted to ride horseback. Fortunately for her, the groom was new to the job, hired by Byron only a week prior.

"I'd like to take Mitra out." Blythe folded her hands behind her back and tried to look confident. The groom glanced past her, the tiniest crease knitting between his brows when he saw she was alone.

"Will you be needing an escort?"

It was a sincere question. An honest and expected one that any proper groom would think to ask. Still, it had Blythe bristling, for there was a time when something like riding horseback had been so easy for her that his question would have been laughable. Now she was too unfamiliar with her new stamina to know when she might tire, and she wasn't so foolish as to allow the possibility of getting stuck unaccompanied in the woods. And so Blythe bit her tongue and told him, "That would be much appreciated, Mr...."

"Crepsley. William Crepsley." He had hands calloused from hard work, a broad frame, and suntanned skin that did not belong to a man of high society. He couldn't have been much older than Blythe, and she noted his kind round face and earnestness. Given how new he was, he would undoubtedly wish to make a good impression, which meant that he'd be far too easy to take advantage of.

"Will the foal be all right alone?"

"It won't be alone," William promised. "The examiner will be here soon, and Mr. Haysworth will care for it in the interim."

Blythe nodded, though she didn't have the faintest clue who Mr. Haysworth was. For twenty years she'd lived within the walls of Thorn Grove, and yet it was becoming more unfamiliar to her by the day. It would take ages to learn the names and faces of the new staff members.

"Very well. Then I would appreciate an escort to the Killinger estate, Mr. Crepsley. I'm happy to lead the way."

As William nodded and set off to ready the horses, Blythe found herself more grateful than he would ever know. Not because he was kind or so fresh to this job that he didn't realize she wasn't meant to be here, but because if the earth began to sprout moss and thorns once again, at least this time she wouldn't be alone.

William was slower than he ought to have been, though Blythe gave him no trouble. She was certain he was triple-checking his work, likely because he'd not had the opportunity to prep a horse for a proper ride since he'd started at Thorn Grove. But she kept her patience, and soon the groom returned with Mitra and another saddled white mare.

Mitra approached with her head low and her tail swishing, snorting a pleasant greeting at Blythe, who pressed a palm to the horse's forehead and curled her fingers into the beautiful golden mane. It'd been ages since she'd seen the horse. Ages since her mother had been alive and well enough to go on rides with her nearly every afternoon. Blythe could almost hear the echo of her mother's laughter as they rode. Could almost see her windblown hair shining like a sunburst against the sky.

For too long she'd avoided the memories of her mother, desperate not to follow in her path. But now, standing on the other side of death's door, Blythe ached with nostalgia that had her longing for any remnants of her mother that were still left on this earth.

"Here you are, miss." William steadied Mitra as Blythe slipped her foot into the stirrup and hoisted herself onto the saddle. Her throat tightened the moment she felt the steady lull of Mitra's breathing beneath her. How long had it been since she'd had the strength to pull herself up without thinking anything of it? Blythe turned away from the groom as tears pricked her eyes.

Perhaps her subconscious had known all along that this was what she needed. She must have been more on edge than she'd realized to find so much solace in the stables. Still, Blythe's heart couldn't quite settle its discontented pounding. Not after what she'd seen in her father's study, or what she'd read in those journals.

Blythe tightened her grip on the reins, determined to find the truth.

Charlotte Killinger had run into Signa the night of Percy's disappearance. She was the one who'd alerted Elijah that the garden was on fire. Blythe had talked to her once already, months ago. But perhaps there was more information to be gleaned; if anyone could tell her more about what happened that night in the woods, it was Charlotte.

Blythe led the charge through the softened soil and into woods so achingly familiar that she felt like a child once more. She didn't see just trees of ripe green bending toward them like a wanting mouth, but saw the ghost of her mother weaving through spindly branches, never letting them tear the hem of her white dress as they so often did with Blythe's. Birds knocked their greetings upon the trunks of towering oaks or sang sweet spring pleasantries. Blythe heard her brother's laughter within them. Heard him scolding her for letting herself get so soiled and calling after their mother to help Blythe fish her snared hair from greedy branches.

The farther they ventured into the woods the more Blythe's nose stung and her eyes watered. She was glad, at least, that time had not dulled her familiarity with the land. She'd grown up on this soil, snatching plump berries from the bushes and trailing after Percy just long enough to see his ever so gentlemanly self sneak into a thicket of trees with different ladies over the years when he thought no one was paying attention. She nearly laughed at the memory; she'd be sure to tease Percy about it once they managed to find him.

Blythe didn't need a path to know where she was going. She could make her way through the woods by the bend of the branches or by which trees browned with each waning season. The woods had always been a part of her, more entrenched in her soul than she'd ever realized.

Blythe would have given anything to close her eyes and let herself turn left, down the forgotten path to her mother's garden, where the scent of lilies would caress her. She wanted to let herself believe that her mother would be waiting for her, watching the lotus flowers cascade through the pond or sitting on her favorite bench and reading a book that Blythe would later steal for herself.

But all that awaited her in the garden were ashes and the ghost of too-sweet memories. And so, Blythe turned right, away from the garden and toward the home of Charlotte Killinger.

It took less than twenty minutes to reach the estate that sat nestled at the base of the woods, sheltered by a fortress of towering elms. It wasn't nearly as large as Thorn Grove, though its charm was unrivaled. Where Thorn Grove was grim, even the gray smoke pluming from the chimney of the Killinger estate somehow felt lovely. Creeping vines snaked around the estate's dark stone, fighting to consume a front door that also seemed to be at war with the shrubbery growing against it. If someone tore out the image of a fairy-tale cottage and magicked it to life, Blythe imagined it would look like Charlotte's home. The lawn upon which the home sat was a rich and vibrant green, surrounded by goose plums and a single elderberry tree. Moss crept up the iron fence around the property, and through its slats Blythe saw that Charlotte was already outside.

She was not, however, alone.

Everett Wakefield sat beside Charlotte, sporting a boyish grin. Charlotte was laughing, squeezing his hands in hers as they spoke in low, happy whispers. There was no sign of any escort, and Blythe felt every bit a voyeur as Everett stole a kiss that Charlotte was all too happy to return.

Flushed from the neck up, Blythe turned toward William and said, louder than she had any right to, "Would you look at that, Mr. Crepsley, it seems we've arrived sooner than expected!"

Charlotte shoved Everett away from her, the two of them whispering in a rush of words Blythe couldn't decipher. She pretended to be looking elsewhere and entirely unaware of Everett as he scurried out of sight.

Blythe had always known that Charlotte was interested in Everett; she just hadn't known whether her interest was reciprocated. How curious that neither of them had said anything of their relationship.

Only after adjusting her dress and ensuring her hair was in place did Charlotte hurry toward them.

"Look at you!" She gasped. "It's been so long since I've seen you atop a horse!"

Ignoring the weariness of her bones and everything she had just witnessed, Blythe tipped her chin upward and said, "I fear the world is not prepared for the power I wield now that my strength has returned."

Charlotte rolled her eyes. "And just like that, I've seen enough." She tried to inconspicuously rub away a grass stain on her skirt as William dropped from his mare and took hold of Mitra's reigns so that Blythe could dismount. She hadn't realized how winded she was, for while her strength had greatly recovered in the past few months, every now and then that familiar exhaustion would catch up with her, prickling her vision or tightening her chest. A reminder not to overexert herself.

As keen as she was, Charlotte must have been able to sense her friend's fatigue. She looped her arm through Blythe's in a silent offer of support.

"Is it just the two of you?" Charlotte looked toward the forest, likely searching for Signa. "Why don't we have a seat? Mr. Pembrooke?" Charlotte turned to a tall, heavyset man in a suit just as he emerged from the house. "Please show Miss Hawthorne's groom to the stables and see that he is given whatever he desires."

"At once, my lady." Mr. Pembrooke nodded, and the two men were on their way across the field and to the stables a moment later.

"Forgive my spontaneity," Blythe said once they were alone. "I know you don't typically receive visitors today, but I felt it best if I got away from Thorn Grove for a while."

Momentarily, the light in Charlotte's expression winked out. "It's a wonder you don't get out more often, with everything they say about that place."

Had Charlotte said such a thing the day before, Blythe might have been offended. But after what she'd witnessed in the study, she could no longer be certain that the rumors of Thorn Grove's hauntings weren't true.

"I've managed this long," Blythe replied. There was a blueberry bush behind them, sad and dying despite the warming weather. She looked to the bush as she spoke, skimming her fingers over its bare twigs. "Though there is something I'd like to speak with you about."

Blythe had never seen anyone swallow a frog, but she imagined that if she had, they would look like Charlotte did in that moment. "Oh?" Her eyes strayed toward the direction in which Everett had hurried off. While Blythe would have loved nothing more than to ask about what she'd witnessed between them, Charlotte was far too proper to be comfortable knowing that anyone had been privy to such a moment of fondness.

"I'd like for you to walk me through everything you saw the night of my brother's disappearance."

Charlotte's relief was so intense that Blythe could almost feel it easing her own tired muscles. "No good can come of this conversation, Blythe. We've been over this already."

They had been. Still, Blythe pressed, "Oblige me once more. I promise this will be the last time I ask."

Charlotte sighed as she led Blythe to a nearby bench beneath the shade of a great maple tree, away from prying ears. "I've told you everything I know. I saw Percy briefly in the woods, heading toward your mother's garden. He hardly acknowledged me when I said hello, and—"

"How did he seem?" Blythe interrupted, squinting hard at the ground to visualize the scene in her mind. "Was he in a hurry? Was he walking slowly?"

Charlotte's dark eyes cut to her with alarming severity. "He seemed like everyone who runs out of Thorn Grove talking of ghosts. If you want me to be frank with you, he sounded half mad. He told me he was headed to the garden—that's it. Our conversation was brief." She told Blythe then of how Signa had gone after him, and how Charlotte herself had made haste to Thorn Grove to warn Elijah.

"And then the smoke started, right?" Blythe asked. "We must be missing something! Percy wouldn't just run off into the forest. He wouldn't just disappear like that, especially not when—"

"When you were sick?" Charlotte didn't wait to see Blythe's face fall before she scooted close and laid a hand on her lap. "If he truly left of his own accord, then there must have been a good reason for it."

It was the same story that Blythe had heard a thousand times over. The same one that Signa had shared. Percy was paranoid that someone was after him after being poisoned at the Christmas ball. Because Elijah had made it clear that Percy would never take over Grey's, he had no reason to remain at Thorn Grove. He fled for his safety. The story, in every respect, fit.

Except for one thing—why had Percy never tried to contact them? Not for money, not to share his whereabouts, and most painfully, not to check on Blythe's health and ensure she was still alive. Perhaps he was worried that contacting anyone would endanger him, but... wouldn't he have at least *tried*?

Perhaps Percy truly had started a life under a different name, someplace where their family wasn't a constant target. Blythe, however, couldn't ignore Byron's notes or the crossed-off maps. The Hawthornes' resources were infinite.

Charlotte was tentative when she next spoke, her words low. "If Percy moved elsewhere, they should have been able to find him."

"What do you mean, 'if'?" Blythe pressed, her mind unable to stray from that single word. "If he didn't leave on his own accord, then what do you think happened?"

Charlotte glanced over her shoulder, as if to ensure no one was approaching. "It's not my place to speculate."

"Of course I want you to speculate! That's why I'm here—"

This time when Blythe's words cut off, it was because Charlotte pressed her hand over Blythe's mouth, smothering any sound.

"You are glossing over an important part of what came next, Blythe. The part where I ran into your cousin. It's hardly me that you should be asking these questions—I wasn't the one who ran *toward* the fire that night."

Blythe tore herself from Charlotte, wiping her mouth. "You think *Signa* is the reason for Percy's disappearance?" Blythe's laughter was a harsh, cleaving sound that had Charlotte sitting stiffly upright. "What do you think she could have done to him? Run him out of town? Do you think she's strong enough to have killed him?"

Blythe was a coiled snake ready to strike the hand feeding her. She knew full well that she had no business behaving like this at Charlotte's own home, and yet she couldn't withhold the anger that festered within her. She was used to people backing away when she bit; it was how she protected herself from whatever she didn't care to face. So when Charlotte sat tall and unflinching, it was Blythe who began to shrivel, panic settling in.

"I knew Signa when we were only children," Charlotte insisted. "She was my closest friend because I *liked* that she was a little strange, and that she spent her days in the woods like I did. People would say things about her, but I never listened. There are rumors, though. Rumors about why she's been passed from family to family, and why all her guardians have died.

"People always said that she was cursed, though I didn't believe it until her uncle died," Charlotte continued, each word quieter than the previous. "And then my own mother followed. My father and I fled, and for years I thought it was silly. Signa couldn't have been the reason my mother and her uncle contracted the disease that killed them. I was glad to see her again, but ever since that night in the garden I can't help but wonder . . . why did she run *toward* the fire?"

Blythe didn't need to think about the answer; she knew it in her bones. "She was looking for Percy."

"Perhaps." Charlotte's fingers clenched the edge of the bench. "Again, it's not my place to speculate."

Blythe wished suddenly that she'd never come to Charlotte's. Because Signa had *saved* her life. She had been there when no one else had. She was Blythe's *person,* which was all Blythe could think of as she flagged William and summoned their horses. She mounted wordlessly while Charlotte looked on, her expression hostile.

"Everett wants to keep his eye on her, you know," she called as Blythe gathered the reins in her hand. "Why do you think he's invited you all to the investiture? Surely, you can't believe it's because he still cares for her."

Blythe paused then, only for a moment and only because she had never heard such malice seep from Charlotte's tongue. Even Miss Killinger seemed to quickly recognize her slipup, for her eyes went wide as she covered her mouth.

And though Blythe knew better—though she hadn't wanted to say a word about it—she felt such a protective fire for Signa that she could not help but reply. "Given what I just witnessed between you and Everett, it never crossed my mind that he did. When you go back to him, do tell him hello for me, would you?"

Charlotte drew back, and Blythe hated that she'd hit her mark. One word from Blythe, and Charlotte's reputation would be ruined.

Blythe wouldn't say anything, of course, and she hated herself for even letting Charlotte believe that she might. Without another breath between them, Charlotte hurried inside while Blythe snapped the reins and set off atop Mitra, William keeping pace beside her.

"There was a man hiding in the stables," he whispered. "He was squatting behind a hay bale."

The look that Blythe cut him was indignant. "No, there was not."

This time, as she gave Mitra a gentle kick and hurried into the forest's embrace, it wasn't her mother that Blythe thought of as branches clawed her hair and snagged her dress. She was instead reminded of the ladies of this season, who would claw at anyone they could to get ahead; Charlotte's competitiveness had her behaving no better than the others.

Yet that wasn't why, in that moment, Blythe hated Charlotte more than anyone in the world. Rather, it was because Charlotte had planted a seed inside her mind. And no matter how hard Blythe tried to be rid of it, the idea was a weed within her thoughts, burying itself deep and spreading its roots.

There was no way that Signa would have ever harmed Percy. She loved him, just as she loved Blythe....

...Didn't she?

SEVENTEEN

There had been a time at the start of the season when hopeful men called on the ladies of Thorn Grove every Monday and Thursday. They'd come with lavish gifts and sweet sentiments, only to be met with Blythe's easy dismissal and Signa's apologies. Those men had trickled out over the weeks, disappearing entirely after Lord Wakefield's death. While this had irritated Byron so much that he never once turned the page of the paper he'd been pretending to read, Signa was now thankful for the time it allowed her to spend with Blythe, curled upon a chaise in the drawing room and sharing their theories and hunting for Lord Wakefield's murderer while Byron likely suspected they were gossiping about men.

Blythe had been quiet since the previous day's incident in the study, though, and often Signa would catch her cousin's eyes wandering to her, scrutinizing Signa in a way she never had before. Surely, she couldn't have known that Signa had anything to do with what had happened, and yet...

"What about Charlotte?" Blythe whispered, her legs drawn beneath her as a cup of tea steamed her face. "In books the killer is always the quiet one."

"The only thing Charlotte wants is a good match this season." Signa was grateful that despite the abysmal turnout they were having on their visiting day, Byron still insisted on having fresh scones and hot tea readily available. Since summoning the reaper's powers the day prior, an inexplicable tiredness had settled over Signa's body, making her thoughts fuzzy and her body ache. She slathered a scone with lemon curd and hoped that the sugar might revive her. "What are your thoughts of Everett?"

Blythe's face contorted, though she gave Signa no time to question the strange expression before she smoothed it away and answered, "I imagine he wants to find the killer as much as we do. Not to mention I've never even heard the man raise his voice."

"Nor have I," Signa agreed. "Though gaining the duke's title *does* give him a motive."

"Perhaps, but what benefit would that have to him now? He was always set to inherit, and it's not as though he's lacking money or status."

"At least none that we know of," Signa countered though it was a weak argument. There was always a chance that the murder had been random, though in all Signa's years surrounded by the dead, when it came to murder, it tended to be those closest to the victim who were responsible.

It would be unwise to rule out Everett, even if all she could think of was his sheer devastation and the hollowness of his eyes as he wilted over his father's corpse. Lord Wakefield's relatives were not the only suspects in question, however.

Though Signa felt the prickling of anxiety along her skin, she forced out the next words in a whisper: "Byron has a motive, too, you know." She slid him a sidelong look, ensuring he was still distracted by the newspaper. "He's always wanted Grey's."

To Signa's surprise, Blythe took the theory in stride.

"I know. But cold as Byron can be, he loves his family. Still... it would be silly not to consider it, which is why I sneaked into his study."

Never—not even in the presence of Death—had Signa's blood gone so cold. "Did you find anything interesting?"

Footsteps sounded down the hall just as Blythe grabbed Signa's hand and opened her mouth to speak. Byron straightened as a maid came into the parlor with a single calling card set in the middle of a silver tray. His eyes flashed toward the girls.

"Right yourselves at once," he hissed. "It's the prince."

Never had Signa imagined that she could feel so relieved by Fate's arrival.

Blythe practically flew to the piano bench near the back of the room, but not before tugging at Signa's bodice. She tried her best to lower it until Signa swatted her hand away and readjusted herself in time to hear the snap of Fate's boots as he made his grand entrance.

He looked just as he did the last time Signa had seen him, which was to say that he was handsome by a majority vote, dignified, and as confidently pretentious as could be. Though the parlor itself brightened with his presence, Signa's prospects for the day grew drearier by the second.

"A pleasure, Mr. Hawthorne." Fate bowed his head, his hands too full of more ridiculous flowers to properly shake Byron's.

"Prince Aris, the pleasure is all ours." Byron ushered him forward. "Please, have a seat and let us get you some tea." The girls shared a look. Never had either of them heard Byron be so . . . accommodating. "Blythe, why don't you give your cousin some privacy?"

"I'm quite fine where I am, thank you," Blythe said from her spot on the piano bench, close enough to listen to any conversation if she really strained. "I do think Mr. Worthington has his eye on me, and I wouldn't want to offend him if he shows up today." She didn't turn to see Byron's scowl and instead pressed her fingers to the piano keys, beginning a beautiful piece that Signa noticed was too soft, as though Blythe was not fully pressing down.

It truly was astounding how nosy she was.

Fate crossed the floor to take a seat beside Signa, wisteria once again draping from a bouquet in his hands. "Hello, Miss Farrow." When he tried to hand it to her, she checked to see if Byron was watching. Given that he was, she accepted the bouquet, her knuckles white as she clutched it to her chest.

"Hello, Your *Highness.* To what do I owe this unexpected pleasure?"

"Is it truly so unexpected?" The room's temperature had plummeted by the time Fate approached. Though Signa knew from the chill that Death was near, Fate didn't betray where his brother stood with so much as a glance as he asked, "Do you like the flowers?"

She sniffed, feeling a sneeze coming on as she set them on a side table.

"You certainly do have a penchant for your favorite things, don't you?" Signa hadn't noticed before just how much his nose tended to scrunch up with his distaste.

"They're *your* favorites," he corrected. "Or at least they were." Fate stilled as Signa adjusted herself so that she was angled between him and Blythe. His attention shifted between the two of them before he unfastened the buttons of his waistcoat and took a seat.

"I've no intention of harming your cousin."

"Why should I believe you?" Signa challenged in her fiercest whisper. "You've already imprisoned one Hawthorne."

His teeth snapped together with an audible click. "Your uncle would have been imprisoned whether I was there or not." Each word was a hiss of breath, low enough for it to be impossible for Blythe to hear no matter how slow or how quiet her piano playing became.

"But you *were* there, weren't you?" For Byron's benefit, Signa spat the words through a bracing smile. "I can't believe a word that you're telling me."

He assumed a tired, withered expression. "I know that we are still getting to know each other, Miss Farrow, so you have little reason to believe me. But I make it a point to never lie." Finally, his eyes skimmed up and over her shoulder. It was little more than a fleeting glance, yet it was enough for Signa to know exactly where Death lingered. The very act of envisioning him there had the pressure in her chest deflating, for she knew that no matter what happened, he would keep Blythe safe.

As quickly as Fate had sat down, he was on his feet again. "If you wouldn't mind, Mr. Hawthorne, I would love for Miss Farrow to accompany me for a promenade around the grounds of Thorn Grove. Do you find that agreeable?" The question was more for her benefit than Byron's, for as the gold of Fate's eyes glinted and the threads around him glimmered like the morning dew, Byron's face became drawn and his eyes hollow. Though propriety called for them to be accompanied by an escort, Byron's only response was a slow nod. Blythe remained staring down at the piano, repeatedly striking the same three chords in succession.

Signa's spine pulled taut as a bow, and she threw a look toward where Death stood. "I can handle myself. Stay with Blythe, please."

"You heard the lady." Fate offered his arm, and Signa could only imagine what Death's face must have looked like as she took it.

She was glad in that moment that she could not see Death, for she despised how deeply this would affect him. Had the situation been reversed, such a sight would have Signa wallowing in her misery, especially given her newfound abilities. Yet she hoped that he understood this was not for Fate's benefit, for Signa cared only for two things—getting Elijah out of that cell and keeping Fate away from any other Hawthornes.

And so Signa followed Fate and the path he carved through the manor, out the front doors of Thorn Grove, and into the fields of blooming wildflowers that stretched endlessly ahead. She had to rely on Fate's arm for support more than she would have liked, each of her steps slow and calculated, her body far weaker than she gave it credit for.

So weak, in fact, that Fate took notice.

"You used the reaper's powers," he noted without inflection. "Didn't you?"

Refusing to grant him the satisfaction of a scowl, Signa coiled her anger tightly within her belly. "There was something I needed to do."

He hummed under his breath, his arm tensing beneath her grip. "Are the consequences worth it?"

Given everything that had happened and everything she'd learned, it was impossible to answer. On one hand, she was glad to have the information. On the other, Signa still remembered the searing of her body and that music stirring in the depths of her mind as she'd watched Blythe flee from Elijah's study.

Taking great interest in her boots, she answered, "I'd rather not discuss that."

Fate's laugh was not like Death's. It was not midnight's seductive call that shuddered down her spine with dark promises. Rather, it was warm and crisp, like the summer dawn. "Very well," he said, trying not to crush the wildflowers beneath his boots as he led Signa down a path she and Blythe had walked a hundred times before.

Late spring was far from Signa's favorite time of year. There was something about the heat that made her temper flare; it sapped the energy straight from her bones, leaving her wilted and burnt and unquenchable for the rest of the day. *Oppressive* was the only word to describe the air around them, so thick and damp that she was already beginning to perspire beneath the many layers of her dress. The finer hairs around her face began to curl, stray wisps escaping their elegant confines every minute that Signa spent outdoors, the overgrown grass scratching her ankles.

Rather than promenade, there was a large picnic blanket spread beneath the bend of an oak tree, and Signa frowned as Fate motioned for her to sit upon it. She couldn't look away from a slug that was sliding up the length of the blanket's edge, searching for somewhere dark and cool to escape to. She had never related more to a slug in her life.

Never, not in a million years, could Signa envision Death seated here before her, the two of them withering in the sunlight while trying to sip tea and make merry as the heat glared down on them. She didn't care to be a sunflower, unfurling her petals in the daylight for all to see. She would rather be an adorable little mushroom, thriving in the dark crevices where few ventured to look.

"Well?" Fate was setting out the most beautiful porcelain trays before her, taking great care to lay each one just so. "Do you like it?" There was such hopefulness in his voice that, rather than take another jab at him, Signa stilled. She looked to the slug, as though it might help her find the right words, when he set the picnic basket beside him and started to stand.

"It's fine if you don't," he said hurriedly. "We can attend a ballet this evening. We could take an actual promenade, perhaps around the park—"

Signa reached out to take hold of his hand, jolting at how still he went. Never in her life had she felt such command over someone, not even Death. In that moment she felt every bit of the tension wound within Fate, ready to break free and spring from his skin. He was a desperate man, and more susceptible than Signa had expected. One day she might use that to her advantage. But in that moment she could think only of how sad it was. How sad and how broken *he* was.

"This is very nice," she told Fate, guilt churning within her belly as his shoulders relaxed. She thought of Death's pleasant chill against her skin, craving it more than ever in the unbearable heat. And yet she would rather suffer there in the heat than be seen publicly with *Prince* Aris.

"You always used to love the spring," Fate whispered as he took his seat, looking pained to draw away from her, "but summer was your favorite. We would spend our days just like this, enjoying meals by the sea or exploring old cities that felt new. I'd hoped that a picnic might spark some sort of memory."

Signa frowned, the music she'd remembered playing on a loop in her head. Perhaps it was only a fluke—nothing more than her memory of dancing with Fate back at Wisteria Gardens getting the better of her. She was more curious about him than she had any right to be, and while it was true that in his presence she felt a strange and undeniable pull, there was nothing romantic between them.

"I hate summer." Signa didn't mean for it to be cruel, and she hated that those words had Fate shrinking in on himself, his frown severe. "I'm not very partial to the spring, either. I prefer the colder seasons."

His jaw was tense, hands flexing as he gripped the basket. "Of course. My apologies." He didn't look at her as he doled out a platter of cold meats, then sandwiches that had been cut with the utmost precision. Even the cups he filled with fresh lemon juice and sugar syrup were both meticulously filled to the same point, not so low as to be unsatisfying but not so high that she'd spill it when she sipped. Delicate lavender petals floated atop it.

"Did you make all of this yourself?" Signa took the drink gratefully, trying to spy what else was in the basket. There were pastries, including some sort of glazed tart that looked as though it had been baked by an expert hand.

"Are you surprised?" he asked by way of answer, and the small smile he tried to hide was enough to confirm her suspicion that he had. Glancing down at her lemonade, she took a cautious sip to see whether it tasted half as good as it looked—it was even better.

Signa truly looked at Fate then, as he filled a plate for her and then for himself. Unlike Death, this man was made for the sun. He practically glowed beneath it, as though it was a part of him. He seemed comfortable in a fitted white shirt he'd loosened at the collar and trousers cut at the ankles, exposing them as he leaned back to watch her.

"They'll be the fashion one day," he noted when he caught her staring. "It'll be a while until they catch on, but I've wanted to try them ever since I crafted the fate of a woman who thought them up."

Signa drew the plate he'd made for her into her lap, taking a hesitant bite of a cold cut that was so rich she began to salivate.

"Dear God." She had to look down at what she was eating just to confirm it wasn't somehow a manifestation of her hunger. "Do you always eat like this?"

Fate's laugh was proud and warm. "Of course. I know the finest cooks and artisans in the world, Miss Farrow. Why would you settle for average when everything upon your tongue could taste of ambrosia?"

He and Death truly could not have been more different, and Signa found herself pondering what an eternity spent with Fate's powers would be like. Though there was a chance that every day might feel rich and exciting, she wondered if everything else seemed to dull in comparison. How unsatisfying every day must have felt when you were always on the hunt for something more beautiful or more luxurious than the last. "What of the art in Wisteria Gardens?" she found herself asking. "How do you come to collect it?"

"Some pieces are from the most talented artists I've ever come across, most of them unrecognized. The majority of the art, however, is mine." There was an ease to the way Fate spoke, a casualness in his voice and posture that Signa was uncertain what to do with. She wanted to hate Fate, truly. Yet while his methods needed vast improvement, she also understood them, for she would do anything to help Elijah. Already she had killed for Blythe. And should Death ever be in such a position... Signa shuddered to think about the lengths she'd go to save him.

She was no better than Fate, really. And while she could not give him what he wanted, she had to admit that being with him didn't feel as bad as she'd expected.

"So you spend your days drinking the finest wine and eating the most delicious food you can find?" she teased. "It sounds exhausting."

The barest hint of a smile cracked his lips. "It's not so luxurious as that, I'm afraid. Mostly I work."

"By weaving tapestries," she specified as she plucked the slug from the blanket and tucked it into the soil at the base of the oak. She may have been doomed to burn in the sunlight, but at least the slug didn't have to.

"By weaving tapestries," he echoed. "Yes. Though you make it sound so simple."

"Is it not?" She thought of her own abilities as the reaper and how natural they felt. Her powers of Life, however... As much as she was drawn to exploring them, using them had felt like tearing herself apart from the inside out. Signa clung to his words, desperate to understand. There would be some relief, she imagined, if she knew someone else who struggled with their own unusual abilities.

Fate leaned forward, and so bright was his smile that Signa's heart stuttered. "I could show you if you'd like?"

Curiosity festered within her, yet she could only imagine the ideas Fate would get if she agreed. She had no desire to let this man continue believing there was a chance of anything between them, no matter how tempting the idea of watching him work might have been.

"You said that you wouldn't hurt Blythe." Signa set aside her plate and cup, both empty. "And you said that you make it a point not to lie, so will you vow that to me, then? That no matter what happens between us, you will bring her no harm? That you will not warp her mind, or turn her into one of your puppets?"

"My puppets?" He snorted, finishing off his drink before reaching into his pocket and brandishing a silver sewing needle. Without a moment's hesitation, Fate pricked the tip of it into his finger. Upon it, a single bead of blood shone gold. "Very well. If this is what it takes to ease your mind, then I will make you the most binding promise of all. Give me your hand."

She did, so used to pricking her own finger when she'd been testing out her abilities that she didn't blink when he pierced the needle into her skin. The moment her blood welled up, he pressed his against it.

"For as long as I exist, I vow to never bring harm to Blythe Hawthorne." Fate's blood seared against her skin, and Signa gritted through the pain with a hiss.

Before he could pull away, she gripped his hand tighter. "And what of Death?" Though she knew she was pressing her luck when he tried to withdraw his hand, Signa held on. "Will you also vow not to hurt him?"

Fate stopped trying to pull away and instead allowed his eyes to meet hers as he said coolly, "He will not be extended the same courtesy."

Signa jerked away, her blood pulsing a manic rhythm. Rationally she could understand Fate's anger. Given who it was toward, however, she accepted none of it.

"I expect my communication with him to be restored immediately," she demanded as Fate wiped their smeared blood onto a handkerchief he'd produced from his pocket. He was a shell of the man he'd been moments ago, scowling so deeply it looked as though someone had taken a chisel and carved it upon his face.

"You'll be able to speak with him this evening." Fate stood, stomping across the blanket before he grabbed the basket, the tart still inside. If only she'd waited another five minutes before picking this fight, she might have been able to try it. "Rest well, Miss Farrow. I'll be seeing you soon."

That, Signa was sure, she could count on.

EIGHTEEN

When Signa returned to her rooms that evening, Death was waiting.

Though she could not see him, his oppressiveness weighed upon her the moment she stepped over the threshold. It felt as though she were wading through gelatin as she forced one foot after the other, her excitement stifled by the instinct to turn back.

Her eyes darted around the room, and she wished she could catch a glimpse of him. But all she saw was Gundry curled by the fire, his paws sprawled near the hearth as he slept, seemingly without a care in the world even as every hair along Signa's neck rose.

"What is it?" she whispered, though she already knew the source of Death's anger before his words filled her thoughts.

Tell me I'm mistaken. For once Death's voice was no balm to her soul but a blizzard that chilled every inch of her. *Tell me that you are no fool, Little Bird, and that you did not make a bargain with my brother.*

"I did not make a bargain with your brother." Signa shut the door behind her and turned the lock, worried someone might stroll by and see her breath pluming the air. "I made *two.* And I understand if you're frustrated, but—"

Frustrated? The fire in the hearth flickered, rousing Gundry from his slumber. The hound lifted his head and growled low in his throat. *You haven't the faintest idea what you've gotten yourself into. Fate is not someone you* bargain *with, Signa.*

The last time Signa could remember hearing him this angry was after she'd first met Eliza Wakefield and the other girls for tea months earlier. He'd hated how Signa had stifled herself around them, pretending to be someone she wasn't solely to appease them. This time, though, there wasn't just anger in his tone, but something else that Signa couldn't place.

"What other choice did I have?" she asked. "It was either a bargain with him or never getting to see or speak with you again. Besides, it was my idea, not his."

Death's laugh was the most intoxicating poison, and even amid her mounting annoyance, Signa found herself wanting little more than to drown herself in it.

This is what he wanted to happen. He spat each word, as if he could not get them past his lips fast enough. *It was Fate who laid out this game and placed its pieces precisely where he wanted them. And you fell for the trap.*

There was a storm brewing in Signa's chest, rage heating her cheeks and palms. This was *her* idea, not Fate's. *She* had come up with it. *She* had approached him, ensuring that every word was spoken with intention so that she could get precisely what she wanted out of the deal.

She was in control... wasn't she?

These are not decisions you have to make alone, Death told her, and Signa knew he must have been close from the way frost brushed across her lips. *And yet you have done so.*

His last few words were spoken pointedly enough that Signa took note. She braced herself against her desk, squeezing the edge of it. "What exactly are you trying to say?"

Death's answer did not come with storm-sharpened wind but with a sigh that eased much of the pressure in the room. *I would understand if you wanted to make the deal, Signa. So much has been thrown at you, and you have options now that you didn't have before. It makes sense if you're curious, though I must warn you—*

"I have no need for your warnings." Signa realized then what the strange tension was in Death's voice: fear.

He thought she was *interested* in Fate. The very idea was absurd, yet no laugh bubbled in her throat. Instead, she followed Gundry's eyes to where Death stood and gave herself no time to contemplate before she stalked toward him. She ripped off a glove at the last second and managed to find a bare slice of his skin before Death had the chance to pull away.

Immediately, Signa's heartbeat slowed, only this time her shift into the reaper was far from peaceful. She fell to her knees as her lungs collapsed, head swimming as her body fought for breaths that refused to come. She gripped her throat, clawing at it until all she saw was white. There was no saying how long she was like that before irate shadows slipped into her vision, seizing hold of her. Even in his rage Death was tender, and Signa leaned into his embrace.

"My foolish girl," he whispered, drawing her into powerful arms that wound tight around her. "What were you thinking?"

That was the problem—when it came to those Signa loved, she often wasn't thinking at all. She leaned back, cupping his face.

"You're the fool," she told him. "When I made that deal, it's because I wanted *you,* not your ridiculous brother. Why are you so afraid of him?"

Death set his hands atop hers, and though he offered a smile for Signa's benefit, it didn't reach his eyes. "It's not him I'm afraid of, Signa."

"Who, then?" she pressed, searching his eyes, which hardened as he looked at her. "Who are you afraid of?"

There was no reading his stare. No deciphering the tension in his jaw as he stepped back and extended a hand to her. "Come," he whispered, and Signa wished she could disappear into that honeyed tone. "I'll show you."

Wisteria Gardens was almost unrecognizable as Death led Signa through its once-illustrious courtyard. If not for the marble fountain and the thriving wisteria draped over them from the canopy above, she wouldn't have had the faintest idea where he'd taken her. As it was, she hesitated as they approached a palace that looked nothing like the one she'd ventured into only a few nights prior.

"We'll need to be quick," Death said. "There's no saying when Fate will return." He held Signa's hand as they cut across the lawn to the dilapidated stone building. It was the very same one she'd glimpsed in the moment that Fate's powers had slipped during his soiree. Able to see it fully in the glow of the setting sun, Signa took in the ancient gray stones that looked one door slam away from crumbling. If not for the fact that she was in her reaper form, Signa might not have dared approach it for fear of it toppling upon her.

"Why does it look like this?" She frowned at the withering grass beneath her feet, missing the verdant green fields from the days prior. There were no animals, either, she noticed. No bleating sheep or hoofbeats to fill the air. The palace was eerily silent—a resting dreamworld awaiting the return of its dreamer.

"My brother created this home ages ago." Death cast a look around them before he pulled Signa through the front wall. "It is a part of him and has always reflected who he is and what he's feeling internally."

Where there was once a grand entryway and a gorgeous parlor with a roaring hearth, now the entry coughed thick plumes of gray smoke from dying embers. The interior walls were every bit as bare and ruined as the palace's exterior, and though much of the art was still on display, the colors had dulled to blend in with the gray stone. Gone was any hint of the extravagance Fate had made such a show of.

"It doesn't even look like the same place," Signa whispered, taking one step up the staircase. It was so rickety that she had no doubt the planks would have snapped beneath her feet were she not gliding across them.

"It used to be every bit as luxurious as you last saw it, forever changing with his whims or to suit wherever he traveled." Death kept his shadows near Signa as they made their way toward the highest story.

"What happened to it?" She folded her hands and pressed them against her chest, resisting the urge to touch anything as she and Death made their way past the ballroom. Signa poked her head inside, her heart falling when she found that all the beautiful amber paneling had vanished.

Rather than answer right away, Death led her farther down the hall to the portrait where Signa had seen Blythe and Fate speaking. She hadn't gotten a chance to look closely at it then but now saw that the woman depicted was the loveliest she'd ever seen, with hair as pale as bone and a softness she couldn't look away from.

"That's Life," she whispered, somehow recognizing the woman. "Isn't it?"

Sorrow plagued Death's eyes. "Wisteria began to deteriorate the moment my brother lost her. I let myself believe that he'd get better with time, but this place is worse now than I've ever seen it."

Life's painting, Signa noticed, was the only thing in the palace that was still in full color. She had to stand several lengths away and tip her head back to see it fully, for it took up the length of an entire wall. She tilted her head, trying to catch a glimpse of the woman's eyes as Death eased her away.

"You asked me who I was afraid of." He stretched his hand out, brushing fingers across the portrait's frame. "My brother may be a nuisance, but I do not fear him. I do, however, fear you, Signa. I fear that someday you will break my heart."

His sincerity tore through her, bowing her spine. "It seems that even Death has irrational fears," she whispered. Death, however, did not seem convinced.

"There is only one person in this world who ever held the power you used the night in Elijah's study," he said. "So long as my brother believes that you and she are one and the same, he won't leave you be. Having seen the two of them together, I can understand why.

"When I look around this place, I see my brother for what he is," Death continued. "A desperate man who has spent hundreds of years unable to move on from the woman who laid claim to his heart. He will not know peace until he finds her. To make a deal with him, you need to understand the stakes. You need to see him for who he is. None of us would want to spend a single lifetime in such despair, let alone the eternity my brother will endure."

Signa couldn't tear her eyes from the portrait. The woman in it was different from her in every way, and yet Signa felt drawn to Life in a manner that words could not describe.

Fate presented himself as a confident and assured man, but if what Death said was true and Wisteria Gardens was truly a reflection of his inner self, then Fate was on the precipice of breaking beyond repair. She tried to swallow down the pity knotting her throat, turning away from the portrait.

"There's more to see." Death reached for the frame again, keeping one hand on Signa to ensure she remained in her reaper form. It took him a moment before he found a small latch, a soft click sounding as he pressed it.

The portrait swung open, revealing a massive room of tapestries. "Watch your head," Death warned as they stepped inside, and she ducked just in time for a tapestry to swing over her head, its threads unraveling into an assortment of colors, each of which landed in a separate basket.

Signa couldn't look away. It didn't make sense how the lines of tapestries continued to move, let alone how threads and needles wove without any hand to guide them, yet the room reminded Signa of a factory all the same. She was enthralled by the process, tempted to disappear down the line and explore when Death squeezed her hand.

"To you and me, these will only ever look like tapestries. But to Fate, a single thread is the difference between life and death. That is his power, Signa. If ever you believe that you are the one in control—if ever he tries to strike another deal—I want you to think of this room."

Signa shivered. She may not have understood this place in its entirety, but there was no denying its raw magic. Perhaps Death was right—Signa may not have been as clever with her deal as she'd believed.

"My brother will use every bit of his power to steal you away." Death's hand slid to her hip, backing her against the stone wall as a dark possessiveness worked its way into his voice. "And unless you decide that you *want* to go, I will use every bit of mine and more to keep you here with me. There are to be no more bargains. Do you understand?" He tipped her chin up, speaking the words against her lips.

His voice muddled her thoughts, not a single one of them tame as she arched her back and pressed deeper into Death's touch. She was helpless against him, craving him against her skin.

"No more bargains," she repeated, pleasure shooting through her as she captured his lips. Death groaned softly as he hooked his arms around her, hiking her up so that she could wrap her legs around his waist.

"Very good." His hand slipped beneath her skirts then, snaking up her thigh.

She gave no thought to where they were as she tipped her head against the stone, urging his hand higher. Yet Death stilled as a noise sounded from the first floor, easing his hand back and pressing it instead to Signa's lips.

Easy, Death's voice whispered through her mind. *My brother cannot see us in this state.*

Perhaps not, though he *could* see that the door had been left ajar. Ever so slowly, Death slid his shadows toward the portrait, though the moment he went to press it shut, it gave a quiet squeak that made the rest of the palace still, as if holding its breath. Fate, too, was quiet for a long moment before Signa heard the stomp of Fate's boots hurrying up the steps.

Signa curled her fingers into Death's shoulders. *Brilliant work. Very "ghosts passing through" of you,* she hissed, tensing with Fate's every step. Death ignored her as the shadows surged forward, shutting the door with a click so loud that she nearly groaned.

Death smirked at her then, pressing one last kiss to Signa's mouth before he leaned forward and whispered in her ear, "Hold on tight."

She did, and the second the door swung open and Fate stalked inside, Death threw the shadows around them and transported them back to Thorn Grove.

NINETEEN

As much as she'd read about garden parties, Signa had never had the pleasure of attending one, especially not one thrown by a queen.

Covington Palace was made up of five hundred and seventy-five rooms and looked every bit as astounding as that number from the moment Signa walked through its opulent doors. Columns of white marble lorded over the entry, adorned with gilded bronze capitals. One by one people were welcomed inside and herded onto an endless red rug so plush that Signa wondered what it might feel like beneath bare toes. Of course she wouldn't dare try to see, given the company she was in. It seemed there wasn't a single nose not tilted haughtily into the air, nor a lone man who did not walk as though his chest had been stung and swollen by a hive of wasps.

Guests were shepherded into a room with ivory walls, where a matching chandelier the size of Thorn Grove's parlor dripped with crystals so thick that a single one was all it would take to make a poor man rich. Signa found her place beside Blythe and Byron. They didn't dare speak, for the room felt too sumptuous to spoil with words.

At the head of the room sat a gold-and-crimson throne, and all heads bowed as the queen emerged. Signa had met her only once, when she was presented for the season, and had been so full of nerves that her ankles nearly gave out during her curtsy. Now, though, she managed to hold one as a beautiful woman with rich brown skin took her place on the throne. She was plump and middle-aged, dressed in a silk rose-colored gown with a collar of Honiton lace, and a small crown of diamonds on her head. The queen's gaze softened only when Everett Wakefield entered the room and was brought before her.

He'd been fitted into a handsome ensemble made of black silk chenille and trimmed in fur. His waistcoat was heavily decorated with silver threads and metallic buttons, with his family's crest—a gray wolf prowling around a silver-and-white shield—displayed proudly above his heart.

Everett wasn't the only one who Signa's roaming eyes wandered to. Among a crowd buzzing with excitement, she stilled when she spotted Fate's eyes on her. It'd been several days since he'd nearly caught her and Death at Wisteria, and pity still made her throat thick.

More flowers had come from him that very morning—this time paired with chocolates, which Blythe had happily taken off her hands—and every day Signa tried her best to ignore the offerings and the giggling maids. As much sympathy as she felt for him, there was Death and his fears to consider, too. For that reason alone she despised Fate's gifts; she didn't want the pressure of his false hope, or for him to have any additional motive to take his frustrations out on Death or the Hawthornes.

Signa couldn't say exactly when the feeling had started—perhaps it had always been there to some extent—but the pressure of so many expectations was rapidly mounting: Blythe expected Signa to be a good cousin, a *normal* cousin, while Byron wanted her to be a prim and proper lady aiding the restoration of the family name. Fate expected her to be another woman entirely, one with powers that Signa would have once given the world for.

As for herself... Well, Signa needed to solve a murder, protect everyone she loved, and get to the root of who she was and what she could do.

It was exhausting.

Everett knelt before the queen, and Signa fixed her attention on him as the title of duke was bestowed. The queen dipped a scepter onto Everett's right shoulder, then his left. Signa joined in the clapping as he rose to his feet, putting on her most polite and demure behavior for the several glaring eyes and haughty faces cast toward her family. Everyone had begun to head outside for the party, and Byron nudged her leg with his walking stick, silently commanding that Signa do the same.

"He's a fine boy, that one," Byron murmured loud enough for the eavesdroppers around them to hear. "He'll make a wonderful duke."

Though Signa agreed on both counts, she made no comment. It felt too odd to look at Everett in his formal wear and see anything but the tears in his eyes as he'd held the hand of his father's corpse only weeks before.

"Signa?" Blythe's voice cut her thoughts. "You look as though you're in a daze. Come, let's get to the party." She looped their arms together.

Blythe had been skittish since the incident in the study, and too often Signa saw her restless eyes scanning the corners of every room. She'd also noticed the glow of candlelight beneath Blythe's door late the evening before while her cousin should have been sleeping. Signa had tried to get Blythe's mind off it by bringing her newspaper clippings of recent crimes when they took tea in the afternoons, but Blythe's interest in them was tight and forced.

Signa had hoped that the day's outing would do her some good. Though people sent them scornful looks, gossip would be kept to a minimum within the queen's presence, which was a welcomed reprieve. Scanning the crowd, Signa caught a glimpse of Everett as she was ushered to the garden, her chest warming when he waved.

She started to wave back when she noticed with quick embarrassment that he was waving at Charlotte Killinger, who stood only steps behind them. Charlotte's smile was bright as a harvest moon as she placed her hands on both Signa's and Blythe's shoulders. "You both look lovely."

Signa wished she could say the same, but *lovely* was an understatement for Charlotte. Dressed in a pale mauve gown and a matching feathered hat, Charlotte was lovely enough that all eyes seemed to follow her. She was also so perfectly proper that Signa found herself straightening her spine, intimidated by such polish. Blythe, on the other hand, stiffened and clutched Signa tight.

"I think it feels like a funeral procession," Blythe noted bleakly, not looking at Charlotte. "You feel it, don't you, Signa? There's a heaviness in the air."

Given that Signa's experience with the dead was much more pronounced, she didn't feel anything of the sort. She understood the sentiment though, and nodded her agreement.

"How is Lord Wakefield holding up?" This, Signa directed at Charlotte. "I hear you've been a big help to him."

"He's faring better than I expected, all things considered." Though Signa hadn't a clue what might have happened between the two, Charlotte appeared fully aware of Blythe's hesitation as she eased away and unfurled her fan, motions soft and gentle. "I didn't expect the Wakefields to seek me out, given all that happened, though I'm glad they did. That family could use some support."

Signa ignored Blythe's quiet snort and instead asked, " 'All that happened'?"

Charlotte's hand stilled with the fan covering her mouth. While most of her expression was concealed, Signa still noticed that Charlotte's eyes widened a little, as if realizing she'd misspoken. Only then did Blythe's attention stray toward her, lips pursed.

"It's nothing of note." Charlotte snapped her fan shut, trying to dismiss the question. "Regardless, Eliza was worried for her cousin and asked me to stay with them for the first few days after the duke's death. Everett was sick every time he ate—he couldn't keep so much as bread down. I think he's only just beginning to realize that his father is truly gone. He's not well, but he's coming to terms with the loss as well as one can."

Blythe must have felt every bit as suspicious as Signa at Charlotte's quick dismissal on the matter, for she slid her cousin a look. Unfortunately, Blythe's interest was soon lost as she drew a sharp breath while looking at the right side of Signa's head. Her voice was harsh as she grabbed Signa by the wrist and leaned in. "What on earth have you got in your hair?"

Signa's stomach lurched, praying to God that it wasn't some awful crawling thing. "Get it out!" She tried to look but was unable to see anything until Blythe tugged free several strands that had been tucked behind Signa's ear.

They were as silver as starlight.

"Fix it." Signa's words were little more than an urgent breath. "Tear it out if you must, but make sure no one can see."

"Have you lost your mind? I'm not going to rip out your hair!"

Oh, how Signa could curse Fate. She'd wanted to believe that she'd gotten away with nothing more than tiredness from last using her reaper powers, but it seemed he was right about those consequences after all.

Blythe's frown was severe as she carefully tucked the silver strands away just in time for Charlotte to look over with a lift to her brow. Signa straightened, smiling despite the thundering of her heart.

A duke was dead, Fate had stopped her from communicating with Death, her childhood friend was a potential suspect in a murder, and now her hair was turning silver as though she'd aged overnight.

What else could possibly go wrong?

Signa tried to pull herself back into reality, not wishing to focus on her hair so much that she alerted other people to her predicament. She shifted her attention back to Everett, who was greeting lovely women in pale tea dresses with twirling parasols to block out sunlight that was doing its best to burn Signa where she stood. Everett didn't *look* like a man capable of murder... but she'd been wrong before.

Eliza was nearby as well, and Signa noticed after a second look that the dark-haired man who spoke to her was none other than Byron. When Charlotte caught her looking, she hummed under her breath.

"Miss Wakefield always did want to marry a Hawthorne," Charlotte mused. "I just thought it would be Percy. They were so close before he left."

The sound Blythe made was unintelligible. "Eliza and my *uncle*? Your mind is far more apt to storytelling than I would have imagined."

Charlotte waved her fan harder, cutting Blythe a scathing look. "They've been seeing each other for some time. He's a good match, unmarried and affluent. I daresay he might have asked for her hand by now, if not for the scandal with your father. Or maybe he has, and they're biding their time until your family's name is cleared."

As much as Signa disliked the idea of Eliza being welcomed into the family, it certainly helped make sense of the ring they'd found in Elijah's study.

Blythe wrapped her hands around her stomach, likely thinking the same thing. "It seems more happened while I was stuck in bed than I realized."

"Or perhaps you've been far too concerned with yourself to consider what everyone else is doing."

"Now, now, enough of that," Signa said, alarmed. Whatever had happened between Charlotte and Blythe, there would be time to settle it later, in private. "We're all friends here…" Her voice trailed off when she caught sight of a golden head of hair making its way through the throng. An angry heat festered in her stomach, thinking of her silver hair and their argument from when they last spoke. There was so much happening; so many thoughts to parse that she wasn't sure how she could handle anything else. Fortunately, Fate turned at the last moment, headed not toward her but to Everett.

"I swear I can't keep pace with you these days," Blythe huffed under her breath. "First you're dreaming of a duke, and now you lose your thoughts in the presence of a prince."

"You've been dreaming of Everett?" There was tension in Charlotte's jaw, though Signa couldn't find it in her to answer. Fate's presence was all-consuming. Though they were here to bolster Elijah's name and make a good impression on the guests, Signa very much doubted anyone would remember that she and the Hawthorne family had attended when there was someone far more interesting to think about.

"I can't believe he's visiting all the way from Verena." Signa turned to see that the voice came from a small group of ladies she recognized from other social events this season. Diana Blackwater was among them, flapping her fan so fiercely that her white bonnet bobbed upon her small head. "It's such a lovely place, right on the water. My father took me there for a visit when I was young. The prince and I became quite close."

One of the younger girls gasped. "Do you think he came all this way for you?"

Diana, bless her, was positively preening. How silly it was to watch her and the entire town play into Fate's trap.

"Do tell us about him," one girl said with prying hopefulness. "Is he charming?"

"He is *quite* the gentleman," Diana said with a practiced swoon. It seemed everyone was an actor, these days. "He's well-mannered and incredibly attentive. If you thought Wisteria Gardens was beautiful, you would perish upon seeing his family's royal palace."

Ha. Well-mannered, indeed.

"I must admit that I was pleased to see Aris—forgive me, I do mean *Prince* Dryden—visiting the year of my debut," Diana continued. "I've always had such a fondness for Verena, and always imagined myself ending up there one day."

She wasn't worth it. She *wasn't.* And yet Signa's hands twitched with annoyance. Diana and her lies didn't mean anything in the grand scheme of things, but there was something about her that irked Signa so much that she spun to face the girl.

"It must be fate," Signa mused, smile so wide that her eyes squinted halfway shut.

Diana returned a thin smile, fanning herself with a touch more aggression. "I daresay you're right, Miss Farrow."

"I couldn't agree more. Fate is a very powerful thing." It was the alleged prince himself who spoke as he and Everett approached. Diana and the rest of the ladies fell silent as he and the freshly minted duke dipped their heads in greeting. Fate's eyes, however, lifted to watch Signa from beneath long lashes, and that strange heat in her belly was back.

"Prince Aris," she said with as much revulsion as publicly acceptable. "You're still in town?"

"*Still?* Did you intend on leaving?" It was Everett who asked, setting a hand on Fate's shoulder as though they were good friends. Signa couldn't help but fixate on that touch, glaring, for why was it that Fate could manage to not just be seen but also *touched,* when Death couldn't manage either? "I expected you'd be here through the season."

"I will be," Fate said coolly enough to prickle Signa's skin. "Miss Farrow must have misunderstood. I have every intention of remaining here until she agrees to accept my proposal."

The words were so casual that everyone within hearing distance stilled, looking at one another to ensure they'd heard the same thing. Signa's cheeks burned.

"Surely, you mean until *someone* accepts your proposal." She tried to smile. To make light of his comment.

Fortunately, Fate bowed his head and obliged her with a small, amused smirk. "Of course, Miss Farrow. Do forgive me for misspeaking."

Oh, how Signa wished that she could summon her shadows and claim Fate where he stood. She hated that he sounded so charming, and that there was a dimple in his cheek that made him look entirely too friendly. When she decided she could no longer bear to entertain him, Signa diverted her attention onto Everett.

"Congratulations, Lord Wakefield," she said at last, hoping to create some diversion from whatever game Fate was playing.

"Yes, congratulations." Charlotte took a squeaky breath when Everett approached. "You look very respectable in that sash. Your father would be proud."

Everett looked so bashful as he adjusted his waistcoat that Signa sought Blythe's eyes to share a look. Her cousin, however, was fixated on the ground.

"Thank you, Miss Killinger," he said. "That's truly appreciated."

Charlotte shyly glanced away as she pushed a fallen curl from her shoulder. It seemed they might mill about each other all day if someone didn't do something to rouse them from their stupor. And though Signa opened her mouth to relieve her friend, Fate beat her to it.

"The day is far too perfect for us to continue standing around chatting." He tipped his head toward the garden. "How would you all fancy a game of croquet?"

TWENTY

THE PALACE GARDEN WAS THE OPPOSITE OF WISTERIA'S IN EVERY way, understated in its beauty with elegant rosebushes and shady oaks that lined trim pathways. Servants passed by with trays of dainty sandwiches and savories, which guests ate as they gossiped together in the shade. As she and Blythe made the trek across the lawn, Signa found herself wishing that she could be one of those guests, soaking in the garden's beauty while stuffing her face with food.

Instead, she found herself continually looking at Everett, examining the smile that didn't quite reach his eyes as he greeted others. Might he have had a motive to kill his father? Could his face be that of a killer?

Charlotte was at his side, speaking to him in low and happy tones. Signa watched them all the while, trying purposely to keep her focus from Fate. Blythe must have been doing the same, for she whistled quietly under her breath. "Perhaps it's time to turn your attention toward being a princess, after all. They seem to be forming quite the pair." Blythe spoke as if testing Signa's feelings about the matter.

"And yet neither one has spoken a word about an attachment," Signa replied, and nudged Blythe toward where Everett was bowing to more ladies and eager mothers that approached as Charlotte watched, her expression more vacant with each new face.

It felt like they were stopped every few feet as Fate led the way across a seemingly endless lawn of the most perfect grass—truly, not a single blade was browning, and all seemed cut to precisely the same length. When Fate caught Signa stealing a look at him, he offered his arm with a gloating puff of his chest. Blythe practically shoved her forward, and Signa shot her a withering glare before she begrudgingly took Fate's arm and allowed him to pull her ahead.

"What do you say to a game, Miss Farrow?" he asked. Though the question was teasing, it was easy to see the vulnerability he was masking.

"I would say no," she answered honestly, "but do I have a choice?"

Fate took the jab in stride. "Would your answer change if I said we can consider it part of our courting?"

She nearly missed a step. Before so many eyes, the last thing she wanted was to be seen courted by Fate, nor did she wish to fan the flames of his interest when he refused to promise he would not harm Death. But even if she refused, she doubted Fate would leave. Not to mention that Signa would give just about anything to hear Death's voice again.

"Give him to me for a full day." Signa sidestepped a little closer toward Fate, trying to keep her voice low. Blythe, she was sure, was likely trying her best to listen in. "Starting now."

Fate walked with strong, confident strides, yet somehow still managed to look elegant. Almost like he was floating, with no scuffs on his leather boots. "I will not change the terms of our agreement."

She made certain to kick the grass a little harder with her next step, hoping to send some mud onto his boots. Somehow, it didn't land. "Very well. But no cheating. I don't like men who play dirty."

He laughed. "If playing dirty is what it takes to get you to remember all that you have lost, then I will be the filthiest bastard you've ever met, Signa Farrow. You'll have your time with Death after our game."

Signa had not anticipated the warmth that flared within her. Her throat was too tight to swallow, and she dared not look Fate in the eye.

The field was empty apart from the wickets and stakes meant for the game, and whether that was because everyone else was smart enough to enjoy palace food while they could or because of Fate's hand, Signa had to wonder. She was glad for a few seconds of reprieve when he left her side to scoop up two of the mallets, one of which he handed to her.

"What do you say, ladies? Up for a game?" There was a spark in Everett's eyes, and after all he had undergone these past few weeks, Signa's foul mood eased at the welcomed sight.

"I'd rather watch," Charlotte answered with a small smile that immediately had Everett grinning back. Signa couldn't believe her eyes—just when had this fire between them begun?

"You'll stay nearby?" he inquired.

"Of course." Charlotte walked a few short feet away, stopping beneath the shady bend of a tree. "I'll be right here, rooting for both teams!"

"If that's the case, then my team will be me and my cousin," Signa said, not about to allow herself or Blythe to be stuck on a team with Fate.

While she expected him to be annoyed by her declaration, his amusement seemed only to grow. "Very well, though you should know that in Verena we play for prizes."

Dread crept into Signa's stomach. She should have known there would be a catch.

"What's the prize?" Blythe asked as she tested the weight of her mallet.

"Whatever you'd like it to be." Fate kicked over two balls for each team. Both of Signa's had a stripe of purple around them to match her mallet. "For us, perhaps a song written and sung in our praise? A favor? Or maybe even a kiss from a lovely lady?"

Everett straightened a little, glancing toward Charlotte. "I don't think that—"

"Oh, come now, Everett." Fate laughed. "It's only a kiss."

The refusal was upon the tip of Signa's tongue, and yet Blythe jumped in.

"We can have anything?" she asked.

The trap had been sprung, and Signa wasn't convinced that Fate could look any more gloating than he did then. "Anything that's in my power to give."

Blythe didn't pause to consider her request, though she at least had the sense to lower her voice when she said, "If we win, then the prince must put in a good word for my father." Before either man could say anything more, she added, "And I want to see him. Immediately."

Everett lowered his mallet, his face severe. "Miss Hawthorne, that's not possible—"

"Consider it done." Fate's lack of hesitation gave Everett pause. He blinked, seeming to question in that moment just how much power a prince might have. "I accept those terms."

Signa's mind worked through the request, threading through his choice of words for any hidden meanings. But before she could get her thoughts together, Blythe swung her mallet over her shoulder and started toward the field.

"Wonderful." She batted away a blond curl that had escaped her wide-brimmed ivory hat. "You'd best prepare yourself, princeling. I've no intention of letting you kiss me."

"*Letting* me?" Fate's laugh was far too genuine. "You're not to my taste, love."

"So it seems there is a God." Blythe clapped her hands together and looked to the sky as if praying. "It only took looking at your art for me to understand how terrible your taste is."

Fate's grip tightened on his mallet, and Everett and Signa shared a look. At least there were two people here behaving appropriately, though both Fate and Blythe reeked so thoroughly of determination that convincing them to play without stakes wasn't an option, even if there was a second when Signa considered wringing Blythe's neck.

How did one beat Fate in his own game? Couldn't he change the outcome? Twist everything to his favor? She wanted to win as much as Blythe, yet it wasn't until a chill tore through the air around her shoulders that Signa believed they might have a chance.

Signa gripped the handle of her mallet and tried to capture her fleeing breath. At once she turned to Fate, who had given himself away by looking directly at the spot next to Signa—where, she now realized, Death stood. Though she could neither see nor hear him, the mallet pressed harder into her palms, as if to say that he was there with her. That he would help.

"Ladies first," Fate offered with an edge of annoyance. It was the only thing that revealed just how he felt about Death's arrival.

Blythe positioned herself as though she'd played a thousand times before, squaring herself to the ball and striking it straight on. The ball hurtled through the first wicket, and Fate's smile twitched downward. He stole a look at Blythe, then at Death, but as far as Signa had been able to tell, that hit was all her own.

Blythe flashed Fate a wicked grin as she strode up to the ball, earning a second turn from scoring a point. Her next strike had the ball across the field, more than halfway toward the next wicket. She inspected her work with a satisfied little nod before strolling back to them. "I suppose that will do."

It was Everett's turn next, and Signa felt the chill wash toward him. Fate, too, took a subtle step closer to Everett. Golden threads glistened, drawing the mallet back, but it seemed that something got hold of the ball the moment the mallet struck—Death. He at least had the decency to scoot the ball forward a few inches for Everett's sake, though it was a crooked shot away from the first wicket that left Everett scratching his head.

"I'm usually not such a horrendous shot." He glanced above him, as if checking whether the wind itself was his offender.

"You'll get it next time." Blythe's voice was automatic, as though she'd had to tell players that too many times before. "Perhaps the prince will make up for it on his turn."

"I intend to," Fate bit back, glowering when Blythe never dropped her smile.

"It sounds like someone underestimated us." She stretched her gloved hand before her, inspecting it for any sign of dirt. "I used to make my brother play with me every Sunday."

Signa could have sworn that there was the tiniest hitch in Blythe's voice, and that her icy blue eyes were suddenly much sharper as she shared a look with Charlotte. There was little time to think about it though, for as Blythe reminded her, "It's your turn, Signa."

Everything Signa knew about croquet she had learned from watching Blythe approximately two minutes prior. She approached the ball just as her cousin had, squaring herself to it and doing her best to appear as though this were second nature, and that she'd swung a mallet a thousand times before. Really, though, she was pleading with Death under her breath.

Fortunately, he seemed to know exactly what to do. She couldn't say whether her mallet had even struck before the ball was rocketing through the next wicket. Everett whistled low behind them, but when Signa glanced back toward her cousin with a victorious grin, she was surprised to find that Blythe's smug expression had been wiped clean, her pale brows creased.

It was possible she was overly focused. With such a prize on the line, how could she not have been? Still, Blythe looked between Signa and the ball with such skepticism that Signa's palms began to sweat through her gloves. She gave her hands a shake before fisting the mallet for her second turn. Once again she felt the familiar breeze of Death's shadows as he jumped into action, gliding the ball along the path and straight through the next wicket.

"I daresay we've been played, Your Highness," Everett mused, glancing back at Charlotte every so often to see whether she was enjoying herself. "Perhaps we should quit while we're ahead."

Fate scoffed as he stalked toward his team's ball. "Nonsense. We have time to redeem ourselves." The threads around him blazed an intense gold, winding around his mallet. But Death's shadows must have intertwined with them, for the mallet was slower than it ought to have been on the swing. Even so, the ball slid through the wicket.

"I do enjoy a nice, *fair* game." Fate repositioned himself for his second strike, bending at the hips. The second he did, he whispered at the ground, "I do not make a habit of cheating, brother. But if you continue to, then so will I." Then he struck, and this time the ball was off, not quite reaching the wicket. He glared at it, lips curled as though the ball had personally offended him.

Blythe was already preparing herself as Fate made his way back to them. He stopped to watch her, while Death, it seemed, could not help himself from one last interference. As Blythe raised her mallet back, it swung from her grip and struck Fate between the legs.

Blythe careened backward, mirroring Signa as she covered her mouth with both hands. A gust of wind tore around them, hard enough to knock off the hats of a few affronted ladies in the distance. Signa glared hard at the spot where Death must have stood.

It was like watching a scene play out in slow motion as Fate stumbled, lips pressed so tight they were bone white as he dropped to his knees.

Behind them, Charlotte covered her squealing mouth.

Blythe rushed toward Fate, stopped, stepped back, then continued toward him again, as if unable to figure out whether he'd want her apology or her head on a platter. Eventually she settled on the apology. Her cheeks were red as a cherry tart.

"Your Highness! Are you all right? I'm so sorry, is there anything—"

Everett took her by the shoulder and drew her back, his expression grave. "Perhaps some space, Miss Hawthorne. You don't need to be involved in such a delicate situation."

Signa bit the inside of her cheek, hard. "Was that really necessary?" she hissed at Death. "He already wants to kill you!"

It was an accident, Little Bird. They really ought to put a better grip on those mallets. I didn't expect it to hit *him.*

Signa's chest felt as though it swelled three sizes when she heard Death's voice in her head. It seemed the pain of Fate's accident must have temporarily caused his powers to slip, and though she knew that couldn't have been a good thing, her stomach fluttered all the same. How nice it was to hear him again, if only for a few seconds.

"Are you all right?" Blythe demanded. "Shall I see if there's a doctor to examine you?"

"There's no need for a doctor, Miss Hawthorne," Fate seethed. "And I certainly do not need an examination. Just... give me a moment."

"Sit the rest of the game out," Everett suggested through a wince. "I'll represent our team. Miss Farrow and Miss Hawthorne can choose a player to represent theirs."

"Let's not make a fuss over nothing." Even through a wince, Fate managed to sound convincing.

Nothing? Death echoed with mirth. *I wouldn't admit that so freely, brother.*

Had Signa been able to see him, Death certainly would have gotten her most insidious glare. She never knew that brothers could be so infuriating. Was he *trying* to bring Fate's wrath upon them?

Fate rolled his shoulders back, ignoring Death as he eased to a stand. "There's little harm done. I'm fit enough to play."

Though Blythe appeared skeptical, she didn't dare wound his pride by arguing. Neither did Everett, and soon enough they fell back into the game, feigning that nothing had happened.

The game lasted around two hours, during which Death's voice faded away. Turn after turn both Everett and Signa tried their best—without Death's influence—though Everett bounced several balls from the wickets, and Signa kept missing the ball altogether. Only

Blythe and Fate were scoring any points for their respective teams, and the tension between them grew so thick that the other two gave them a wide berth.

Blythe was spectacular, so focused on the game that she did not so much as smile each time the ball passed through a wicket. Her gaze was cool and level, mind unwavering from the task at hand.

Fate was just as well practiced. As he ought to have been, Signa supposed, considering how long he'd been alive. He didn't need to rely on his magic to aid him, and remained true to his word about avoiding it even as he kept up with Blythe. Soon enough, just as Signa's back had begun to ache and she had half a mind to lie on the fine grass, Blythe's shot knocked Fate's ball from its position near the last wicket, and she took the final point.

Only then did she throw her mallet down and spin toward Fate. Her eyes were gleaming with constrained satisfaction. Signa had no doubt that if they were alone, she'd be celebrating her victory with nothing short of a battle cry.

"I want to see my father tomorrow." Blythe kept her voice even, and though Fate wore the face of a man scorned, he nodded.

"I keep my promises, Miss Hawthorne. Consider it done."

The hours had slipped away while they'd played. It wasn't so late that the sun had fully set, though it was late enough that guests had started to disperse and all food and drink service had ended. Though the game wasn't particularly strenuous, the sun had been sweltering, and Everett dabbed perspiration from his forehead with a handkerchief. It'd been nice to play a game with him; to see him jest and smile and pretend that they were normal people with normal lives—people not surrounded by death and disaster, if only for a few hours.

Everett turned to the cousins and Charlotte, who had rejoined them and was stealing sideways glances at Blythe. "Shall I walk you ladies to your carriage?" he asked. "It's later than I realized."

"I think that would be wise." There was something wrong about Blythe's tone. A tension that only a knowledgeable ear would pick up. Signa straightened at the sound.

It was unlike her cousin not to take her arm as they walked, nor to revel in her victory. Signa slid a look at Charlotte, though the girl swiftly turned away as she and Everett bid the cousins a farewell.

"It was a good match, Miss Hawthorne," Fate admitted as Blythe and Signa stood beside their carriage. "Arrive to the prison before sunrise tomorrow. I'll see what can be done."

Blythe nodded, and while it seemed she was not *trying* to be harsh, she was quick to turn from Fate and throw the carriage door open.

"Let's get going," she demanded. And though Signa's entire body itched with the knowledge that something was horribly, desperately wrong, she followed her cousin inside.

TWENTY-ONE

Blythe

Blythe's chest felt frightfully close to bursting as she pressed herself against the carriage and as far from Signa as space allowed. She settled clammy fingers against her throat, focusing on her beating pulse and counting each of her breaths to try to bring herself back into some semblance of calm.

She couldn't stop looking at Signa, who wasn't so foolish as to not notice. Like Blythe, Signa kept herself pressed to the opposite side of the carriage, making herself small in the cramped space.

People always said that she was cursed. No matter how hard Blythe tried, she couldn't shake Charlotte's warning. *Why did she run* toward *the fire?*

From the moment they'd met, Blythe had known there was something strange about Signa. She'd considered others' nervousness toward her a misunderstanding and social bias, as Signa's skin was eerily pale and her eyes large and knowing. But when Signa had arrived at Thorn Grove, Blythe's life had improved tenfold. It had been *fun*.

There'd been someone to fill her in on all the gossip and scandals she'd missed. Someone who didn't just treat her like the fragile sick girl. Not to mention that her life had been spared thanks to Signa. And beyond that, she'd also met a wonderful friend. A sister, really.

At least, she thought she had.

Blythe curled her hands into fists, letting her fingernails dig into her skin as though the pain might somehow clear her head, which hadn't stopped spinning since the game of croquet.

There were no words for what she'd seen—gauzy, hazy glimpses of shadows that hovered behind Signa. Shadows that Signa had spoken to when she thought no one was listening, and that had helped guide her mallet.

It was positively ridiculous and impossible and preposterous, and yet... Blythe had seen those shadows before. When she had been breaths away from dying, they had shared a room with her. She hadn't wanted to give thought to those dark times and dredge up such bitter memories, but she was certain that Signa had seen those shadows, too; had spoken with them.

As close as she had been to death, the memory itself was fuzzy. No matter how hard Blythe tried, she couldn't sharpen her mind's eye or bring that scene into focus. But there were other oddities, too. Ones that she *did* remember, like when Elaine's reflection had shown a sickly, dying body. Or when thorny vines had erupted from beneath the floorboards to tear into her.

Blythe could see the shadows even then, fainter than they'd been but still lingering around Signa like a gray haze. She squinted, ensuring it wasn't a trick of the light.

"What is it?" Signa asked with a hitch of nerves that immediately made Blythe's stomach flip with guilt. "Have I grown a third arm?"

"No, but you *are* sprouting silver hair." Blythe's mouth was painfully dry. It was a struggle to even form the words, for she hated these thoughts. Hated that she could even be considering Signa in this way. But Charlotte's seedling about suspecting Signa in Percy's disappearance had taken root and was growing into a full conspiracy, and the events of the day had further convinced her that something *was not right*.

"What happened today?" Each word tore at Blythe's throat, and though she'd asked the question, she didn't know if she was ready for the answer.

Signa tensed. "Do you mean with the prince?" She sounded so genuine that Blythe again wondered whether she might have been hallucinating these strange horrors. Perhaps this was a strange side effect of being so close to death one too many times, and Signa knew nothing about the darkness that followed her. Perhaps these horrors were all in Blythe's head.

But there was no way that Signa didn't know *something* about Percy, and so Blythe forced herself to press on. "I want you to tell me I'm wrong. I want you to tell me I need to lie down and that I'm seeing things, because the rooms you walk into get *cold*, Signa. Your hair is losing its color, and there is a darkness that follows you even now. A darkness that I've seen you *speak* to.

"You haven't played a game of croquet in your life," Blythe continued. It was a guess, but she must have been right, given that Signa did not argue. "Something was helping you, or *someone.* I need you to explain it to me because I feel like I'm losing my mind."

Signa opened her mouth, presumably to argue, but to her credit promptly shut it once more.

Blythe knew then—knew with everything in her, no matter how much she wished she could play dumb—that Charlotte had been onto something, and that perhaps there was more merit to the rumors about Signa than she and her family had ever acknowledged.

Her cousin was quiet, and Blythe instinctively wrapped her hand around the carriage's handle in case she needed to throw herself out. It looked like Signa was having some sort of mental conversation with herself, and Blythe wondered whether she'd try to come up with a story. Whether she would try to get out of this.

Instead, Signa reached forward to take Blythe's free hand, and all Blythe could do was squeeze it tight, praying that her uneasiness was a mistake. That Signa would tell her that she was being paranoid.

Instead, Signa said, "There's something I need to show you," and Blythe felt her world shatter.

TWENTY-TWO

With every breath Signa prayed that her lungs would give out. That they would turn to lead or temporarily shut off and spare her from the next moments.

Are you certain you want to do this? Death's voice was in her head, and God how she wished she could lose herself within it. It was too much—Everett, Byron, Charlotte, Elijah... and now Blythe asking questions Signa wished she wouldn't. Her chest was so tight that it felt like one wrong move was all it would take for her to explode.

She needed to tell Blythe. She *had* to.

Blythe was already leaning as far from Signa as she could manage, arms wound around herself. Signa had to tamp down her pain and press on, for in that moment Blythe was watching her with eyes no different from everyone else's. Like she was convinced that Signa might suddenly leap to attack her. Like she was a beast. A monster.

And maybe she was. Perhaps she deserved that fear. After all, she'd committed atrocities from which there was no turning back.

Still, she loved Blythe and owed her the truth. But one could not simply admit to being a reaper in love with Death and be believed. She needed to prove it.

They arrived at Thorn Grove, and it didn't take long before Byron dismissed them, stretching his back and eager to slip into evening attire. Signa didn't afford Blythe the same luxury. She immediately took her cousin by the hand and led her outside, toward the stables, flexing her fingers when Blythe snatched her grip away.

I can speak to her in her sleep, Death urged. *I'll tell her that her brother left. To stop looking. You don't have to do this.*

I do was all Signa told him. If Blythe was too strong-willed for Death's whispers the first time he'd tried to convince all of Thorn Grove not to try to find Percy, there was no chance she'd fall for them now. Besides, twisting Blythe's mind would make them no better than Fate. He may have toyed with humans like they were his playthings, but Signa would make no such marionettes. She didn't want to live her life continuing to keep Blythe in the dark.

"What are we doing here?" Blythe's body was tensed, like she was readying herself to sprint away as Signa led them to the stables, toward the stall where the newborn foal lay curled on the hay. William Crepsley was seated beside it once again, stroking the foal's chestnut hair. Its breaths were little more than rasps, and the poor thing trembled with each one. No matter how much anyone wanted to believe he'd pull through, Signa knew the foal wouldn't make it through the night.

William stood when he noticed them, removing his working cap and holding it over his chest with both hands. "I wasn't expecting anyone tonight. Is there something I can do for you?"

"You could give us a few minutes of privacy," Signa told him with icy calm. "We'd like to sit with the foal."

"Of course, Miss Farrow." His face went tender, and he nodded before opening the stall door and slipping out. Blythe followed Signa inside with hesitant steps, sinking to her knees into the hay opposite her cousin. She looked behind her, ensuring that William was gone before she set her hand tenderly on the foal's neck and whispered to Signa, "You're scaring me. What are we doing here?"

Signa pried her gloves off in silence and set them to the side. If she spoke, she feared she'd lose all nerve. Tentatively, Signa drew the last of her pruned belladonna berries from her pocket and pressed them to her tongue.

"Signa!" Blythe tried to smack them away from her, but Signa leaned out of reach. "What's gotten into you? Spit those out!"

"Don't touch me." Signa made her voice as lethal as everyone thought her to be. Blythe fell back with wild eyes, looking like a startled deer ready to bolt. More calmly, only when she was certain that Blythe had been frightened enough to keep her distance, Signa added, "I'll be all right." She hoped it was true. She'd never quite used her powers in this way before, but Death had once told her that they were built on intention. Want it, take it.

What she wanted now was to allow herself to still be seen by Blythe, even in her reaper form. She needed to prove to her cousin that she could truly do the things she was about to claim, and so that's what she focused on as the nausea took over and the poison leached through her.

Death was beside her at once, tense and ranting about how foolish she was for consuming the last of the berries. For a moment Signa swore that Blythe looked at him, or at least near him. Blythe shuddered from the sudden rush of cold and pushed herself against the side of the stall. Signa wouldn't blame her if she fled. She'd be glad for it. But she knew Blythe well enough to know that she wasn't going anywhere.

"You have to throw that up right now." Blythe's voice trembled, but she made no move forward. "You need to get the poison out of you."

Signa shut her eyes, uncertain whether it was right for her to feel so relieved. "You can see me?"

Blythe stiffened. "Of course I can see you. Stop talking nonsense!"

Her plan may have worked, but Signa's body shook from the effort of keeping herself visible, the shadows around her too pale. Too gray. Death was at her side at once, pressing his hands against her bare skin, cursing himself as he helped solidify her place on his side of the veil.

"That shouldn't be possible." Death's voice was breathless. "Not while she's still alive."

Something must have happened when we saved her, she told him. *She avoided dying three separate times. Perhaps there's more of a price to that than we thought.*

Signa hovered close to the foal, mindful of even the barest hint of her touch. "Tell it you're here," Signa whispered to Blythe. "Give it whatever comfort you can. It's not long for this world."

"Mr. Crepsley said it could make a recovery." Blythe's bottom lip quivered, but still she drew the foal's head to her lap and stroked its neck. "Try to relax, angel. You'll be all right." Her voice was soft as snowfall.

Signa told herself that it was a mercy to end the foal's life. It had struggled enough, and she knew as she stretched her bare fingers toward it that she could give it the peaceful, easy rest it deserved.

"Whatever you do," Signa warned, "do not touch me. No matter what you see, no matter what you think, don't you dare touch me." Only when Blythe had bobbed her head in a fraction of a nod did Signa slip her fingers through the foal's dark mane, pressing them against the velvety skin of its neck. There was no need to summon the reaper's powers; they leached through her entire being, shadows dripping from her fingertips as the bitter cold took control.

And in that moment, as the foal's heartbeat stilled beneath her touch and Blythe covered her mouth with tears in her eyes, Signa hated herself for having these powers. With just a single touch, the foal shuddered once before releasing the quietest exhale.

It was dead within the second. Signa had *killed* it within a second.

No one moved an inch until Blythe finally stared up at her. She clutched the foal close, arms wrapping around its thick neck. "W-we should call for William. He might be able to revive—"

Signa curled her fingers in the straw. "There's no reviving the dead, Blythe. He's gone."

Signa didn't anticipate the severity with which her cousin's eyes would pin her. They were red rimmed and repulsed.

Signa had seen those same eyes too many times before. On different faces, perhaps, but always with that same stare. She'd seen it when the Killingers had fled after her uncle's death. Had seen it when she'd left her aunt Magda's house half a year ago, and it seemed everyone in the entire town had shown up to cross themselves as they watched her go.

It was the look of contempt.

Hate.

Fear.

And it hurt all the worse that, this time, it came from Blythe.

"You killed it." It wasn't a question. It was a whispered chant she repeated over and over again as she cradled the dead foal closer. "Why, Signa? Why would you do that?" The moment that question passed Blythe's lips, something within Signa shattered.

Perhaps she was never meant for this life. Never meant to have friends or living, breathing people who cared for her. Because at one point or another, they would always look at her as Blythe did now.

Would it be different, she wondered, if she leaned into her other powers? If she pushed aside the siren song of the reaper and instead leaned into Life's burning magic? Could that make her happy, or would she be no different than the girl she had been last autumn, focused solely on pleasing everyone else?

"Bring him back." Blythe's words were like poison, lethal and so searing that Signa's throat tightened. "Bring him back right now."

"I can't do that—"

"Now, Signa! I want him back *now*!"

Guilt swelled within her, and there was the heat again, stirring deep in her belly as she tried to give Blythe what she wanted. Tried to give her cousin a version of herself that was worthy of the love

Blythe had to offer. It burned through her, so hot that Signa worried her skin would melt. She refused to shy away from it, though, curling her fingers into the foal's mane even when the tears came and a scream tore through her throat.

It took seconds that felt like years of agony; like Signa herself was in the depths of hell, eaten alive by the flames. Distantly she heard Death calling to her, though she couldn't make out the words. It hurt too much to listen. To focus. To do anything at all... until suddenly it didn't.

All at once the heat disappeared, and beneath Signa's hands the foal's chest rose and fell, stronger this time. It pushed from Blythe's grip, eyes clear of the fog that had been weighing it down since birth.

In and out its chest moved. Signa couldn't pull her focus away, counting every breath.

One. She had done that...

Two. She had done *that.*

Three... Signa turned at once toward Death, but with the belladonna purged from her body and her heart racing once more, he'd disappeared from sight.

"I brought him back." Signa stared at the foal. Her hands felt like they were on fire, and she had to touch her lips to confirm they hadn't melted away. She nearly spun to Blythe, and though she wasn't sure what she was expecting, it wasn't to see Blythe push up onto shaky feet and back away as though Signa was the devil himself.

Because this was what she'd asked for.

This was what she'd *wanted.*

And yet, with words so vicious that each of them felt worse than death, Blythe choked, "I wasn't talking about the *horse*."

Ice flooded through Signa once more, removing all traces of the aching heat. For the first time she found no comfort in it. The girls watched each other, Blythe a predator and Signa the wounded prey.

"I can explain—" Signa began, but Blythe didn't let her say another word.

"I need you to tell me one thing." As quietly as Blythe spoke, her voice was the only sound in the world that Signa could hear right then. "I need you to tell me if my brother really left Thorn Grove the night of the fire."

What Signa wouldn't have done to have had these abilities earlier. If she'd had them a few months prior, she could have saved Blythe herself. She could have found a different way to deal with Percy.

Why now, of all possible times? Why now, when it was too late to go back?

She bowed her head, and though she knew it would doom her, said, "No."

Blythe's hand flew to her mouth, barely covering the sob that racked her body. Through it she forced out each word, "Is my brother alive?"

"Blythe—"

"It's yes or no!" The sharpness in Blythe's voice was intended not to wound but to kill. "Is Percy alive?"

Signa had known this question would come. All along she'd known that, one day, she'd have to admit the truth of what she had done to this family. She wished only that it hadn't come so fast. That she'd had more time with Blythe before losing her forever.

But she had been warned that there was a price for toying with Fate and playing God, and it seemed her payment was finally due.

"No," Signa whispered, knowing that every day for the rest of her existence she would wish to forget this moment. "No, he's not."

Blythe did not blink. Did not breathe or even twitch her lips. The only sign that she'd heard Signa was in the shaking hand she wound around her stomach, as if holding herself in. And when Blythe finally did speak, exhaling unsteadily, she became winter incarnate, each word raging with the force of a tempest.

"I want you gone from Thorn Grove by morning."

Nine words, Blythe had whispered. Nine words, and Signa felt any remaining happiness she had slip from her grasp.

Without leaving any room for rebuttal, Blythe gathered her skirts and fled the stables. All Signa could do was sit, numb and hollow, as she watched the foal bend to eat its hay.

TWENTY-THREE

Signa gave little thought to what she did next. Thinking would require feeling, and she had no desire to suffer through anything of the sort. Not yet.

Moments after Blythe had fled, William returned in a panic to find Signa hugging her knees, unblinking as she watched the foal.

"Miss Farrow?" Fear edged his voice.

Had she been able to see herself, Signa might have understood why he drew a step back as she stood to face him. She would have seen the wildness in her eyes and the straw in her hair. Would have seen the way she flexed her fingers as though her nails were claws, and the pain that cracked her expression like a porcelain cup. One wrong word, one wrong move, and she would shatter.

"Leave me alone."

"It's getting late," William whispered. "I've come to accompany you back to the manor."

She cut him a look so scathing that his mouth snapped closed. Only after a long moment of staring down at the foal did he step inside and scoop it into his arms. "Stay as long as you'd like, then. But I'm putting the foal with his mother." William said it like a question, so Signa nodded. It would be better that way, if she didn't have to look at the foal—at proof of what she was, and the impossibility of what she'd done.

She waited for William to disappear. For the noise around her to settle into swishing tails and softly stamping hooves before she tilted her head up at the ceiling, shut her eyes, and asked, "You're still here, aren't you?"

Signa was met by a wave of icy air, and a voice that slipped through her mind like the finest velvet. *Of course I am.*

"I brought a foal back to life."

You brought a foal back to life, Death repeated without a hint of emotion to betray his thoughts. *The silver in your hair is gone, as well. How are you feeling?*

The question was so ridiculous that she couldn't contain her bitter laughter. How was she feeling? God, she couldn't even begin to process it.

Tell me how I can help, Little Bird. Signa knew he pressed closer when her fingertips numbed from the chill of his body. *Tell me how to make this better.*

That was just it—there *was* no making it better, and the reality of that was sinking in too quickly to process.

"I feel like I'm being pulled in a thousand directions." The admission was quiet, whispered from her most fragile depths. "I'm tired of people being afraid of me. I'm tired of feeling like I'm not enough. No matter what I do, I'm disappointing someone. But the one I truly feel most disappointed in is myself, because I hate feeling like this, Death. I thought I was done."

Death's voice came as easy as the autumn breeze, sweeping in and lulling her into its comfort. *If people are afraid,* he said, *then let them be afraid. Your shoulders were not meant to bear the weight of their expectations, Signa. You were not made to please others.*

He was right. Despite the result, Signa did not regret telling her cousin the truth and unburdening herself of this secret.

Signa had tried to please Blythe; she had made herself feel as though she were burning from the inside out to bring the foal back to life. Yet doing so hadn't mattered at all. *None* of it mattered. Signa had made her choices, and now it was time for her to own them.

Still, she would mourn all that she would miss, like sneaking into Blythe's room for gossip at all hours of the night, listening to ridiculous family banter over dinner, laughing with her about whatever ridiculous thing Diana said or did at tea. There would be no more rides with Mitra, or seeing Lillian's garden once it healed from the fire and managed to bloom again. She wouldn't even have Death's voice in her head to help ease the transition if Fate continued to keep him from her.

Signa would be fully and utterly alone.

"You asked me what I want," Signa said at last, fingertips curling in the hay, "and it's to know that you're not going to leave me, too. No matter what I am or am not. No matter what your brother tries; tell me that you'll be by my side."

She stilled when she felt the pressure of him against her gloved hand as he pressed a kiss to the back of it, as fragile as a wish.

You have me. It was a promise that Signa wound around herself, hoarding it. Protecting it. *So long as you want me, you will always have me.*

"What if I want you now?" Signa was on her knees in the hay, following the sound of his voice and hoping, as she lifted her head, that she was looking at the space where he crouched, invisible to her eyes.

Perhaps it was silly, but throughout her life, Death had been her one constant. He, more than anyone else in this world, had helped her feel comfortable in her own skin. As everything and everyone was working to tear that apart, telling her who she was and what she should be, it made sense that she needed him more than anything else.

Death made no sound as he weighed her words, and when his answer came it was as gentle as the patter of raindrops after a storm. *I don't want to hurt you, Signa. I won't risk your life.*

She knew that, of course. She didn't want to risk it, either. Without a clue how these new powers of hers worked, or how far Fate was willing to go to keep her from Death, the gamble wasn't worth it. Yet when he lifted a hand to her cheek and she could feel the leather of his gloves brush her bottom lip, she had an idea. A way to defy the constraints around them and to still have exactly what she wanted—him.

Signa captured his hand in hers by touch alone, smoothing circles into his palm. There was nothing in front of her as far as she could see. No hand she was holding. No eyes she was looking into. She *felt* him, though. And that counted for something.

Signa . . . Death's voice was low and tentative as she skimmed her fingers up his arm, following the shape of him over his shoulder and down his chest. Down and down until he jerked away. *Careful. Your skin almost touched mine.*

She was so tired of needing to be careful. She'd discarded her gloves when she'd used her abilities on the foal, and they still lay half buried in the hay. She rose to fetch them and slipped the satin over her fingers.

"It's only a problem if our skin touches, isn't it? Then we won't let that happen." Her lips ached, desperately wanting to pull his face into hers and kiss him. To *see* him. But for now, this was the next best thing. She took his hand then, guiding it beneath her dress and petticoat, to one ankle, then slowly up the length of her stockings. She leaned into the corner of the stall, lifting her skirts to her knees. The low, appreciative sound Death made in the back of his throat was the most intoxicating music. She didn't need to guide his hand; he seemed to have taken off his gloves as he undid her boots, tossing them to the side as he brushed his thumb against her ankle. Her calves. Farther and farther up, tracing patterns along her inner thigh.

Warmth flooded her, her lower belly stirring with anticipation as she shut her eyes and focused on the heat of her skin beneath his touch. On the shivers that rolled through her spine.

I love it when you make that face, he teased, one thumb sweeping up to skim beneath her eyes, where her cheeks were undoubtedly flushed. *I so rarely get to see it. Usually when we're like this . . .*

"I'm dead?" Signa offered with a breathy laugh. "Only temporarily."

It was different to experience him like this, still alive with her blood pulsing. Her breaths came faster as Death gripped her by the hips and pulled her onto his knee, and faster still as her body sparked with electricity and she straddled his thigh. With one hand Death braced her from behind, while the other hand curved up her thigh, gripping her close as Signa pressed into him.

She wanted him. More than she had ever wanted anything or anyone, she wanted to lose herself in him and forget everything. To believe for a few moments that they were a normal couple. If she shut her eyes, she almost believed it.

Beneath her skirts, Death's hand slipped between her and his thigh, only a thin layer of muslin between their skin.

I want you, too. The low husk of Death's voice had Signa's heart thundering. *Always.*

She rocked her hips into the fingers that pressed against her and let herself be lost to the pleasure. In that moment, Fate did not matter. Nothing did. She wound her arms around Death's neck and gasped quiet breaths against his shoulder as he whispered her name and curled his fists in her hair.

And as she tipped her head back and lost herself to him, she imagined that Death was there with her in the flesh and that, one day, they would build the life together they'd always wanted. A life in which they would never have to feel this way again.

TWENTY-FOUR

Blythe

BLYTHE HAD DREADED THIS MOMENT AS MUCH AS SHE'D ANTICIPATED IT. She sat in the carriage across from Byron, suffocated by the tight quarters and lack of conversation—and from the navy traveling dress she wore, laced to her neck to look as respectable as she could manage. Byron had already given her an earful about Signa's sudden departure the night before, and how it would only make things look worse for the Hawthornes, given how *helpful* Signa had been. Blythe had sat there in silence as he fumed, letting her uncle pace off his anger as she focused on a single speck on the wall behind him and refused to tell him anything more about why Signa left. She couldn't tell him what Signa had done, or that Percy wasn't coming back.

At least not yet. Not until she could make sense of that knowledge herself.

Signa Farrow was a traitor who did not belong at Thorn Grove. She was a liar. A *murderer.* And something even worse than all those things—something impossible that had the power to both take and give life with her own hands.

The weight of this knowledge hadn't hit Blythe quite so hard as it perhaps should have, and she'd spent the full night tossing in her bed, wondering if some small part of her had known the truth all along. She'd caught glimpses of shadows and seen flickers of impossible things. Things that were sure to get her sent to an institution if ever she spoke of them.

But Signa had seen them, too. Whatever strange world Blythe had dipped her toes into since knocking on Death's door, Signa was fully living within it.

Maybe someone wiser would have kept Signa around for answers, but the last thing Blythe wanted was for whatever Signa was involved in to affect her father. Especially on the very day when, weeks after he'd been taken from her, she'd finally see him again thanks to her bargain with the prince.

They'd arrived before dawn, while the streets were still quiet. The carriage pulled close to a towering, ruined castle with a foundation that was cracking at the seams. When Blythe had first heard that an abandoned castle had been turned into a men's prison, she'd imagined prisoners living in comfort, some of them getting more food and better quarters than they'd had previously. But there was not a lick of comfort to boast of at the prison where Elijah was confined, and Blythe had to turn herself to stone as they approached, not allowing even a hint of emotion to betray how she felt.

The prison lawn was surrounded by thick iron bars too sleek and tall to climb but open enough that passersby could watch the prisoners work and be reminded of the life that awaited them should they fail to be law-abiding citizens. Blythe kept her expression flat as she watched a row of men take step after step on an ever-spinning wheel. Each man had his own small compartment, with walls on either side so that no prisoner could glimpse another. Each man was chained to a bar before him, which he gripped for balance while walking upon a wheel.

"They'll be at that all day," Byron noted without remorse. Blythe wondered whether it was a Hawthorne trait to be able to turn into seemingly unfeeling stone when the need arose, or whether he truly felt no pity. "They'll have the appropriate breaks, of course, but they'll be churning grain until dusk."

Just like that, she had her answer. "The *appropriate* breaks?" As much as she tried to withhold some of her bitterness, the words were sharp. There were more men toiling across the lawn, loosening and separating strands of rope. They didn't look at one another. Didn't speak. Even if they wanted to, masks obscured their faces, with only the tiniest slits cut for eyes.

The very thought of her father in such a place—made to walk on a never-ending wheel from dawn to dusk or to spend his days stripping rope or whatever else they had the men do—was enough to turn Blythe's blood cold. If she could have, she'd have burned the prison to the ground.

"I fail to see which part of this is appropriate."

The look Byron flashed her was nothing short of scathing. "Don't be soft, girl. Every man within those walls is a criminal. The hard labor will help them better themselves enough to reenter society and, hopefully, keep them from making the same mistakes twice."

"My father doesn't need to *better* himself. He's already better than any man I know." Only then did Blythe meet Byron's simmering glare as she turned and let herself out of the carriage.

Byron followed, having waited for William to clamber down from the drivers seat and open his door. "You'd best reel yourself in now," he warned. "Should I feel that your being here is a mistake, I'll have you taken back to Thorn Grove. Do you understand? Mind your tongue before it's our ruin."

It seemed there was little other choice. If Blythe had to play the role of a respectable young lady, so be it. She'd certainly had enough training.

A pale man with a severe face and splotchy red cheeks met them at the gate. He held out his hand as they approached. "Perhaps the young miss would prefer to wait in the carriage." His voice was low and thick, as if he had a perpetual sinus issue.

Blythe clenched her fists, biting back bitter thoughts about how *he'd* be the one wanting to hide in a carriage once she gave him a piece of her mind.

Before she could do so, Byron pressed two coins flat into the man's palm. "She stays," was all he said. The man grunted and pocketed the coins before he drew the gate open and stepped aside. His eyes lingered on Blythe for a beat too long, and it was an effort to restrain herself from flashing the man her most diabolical glare. Every inch of her skin was angry and prickling, as it had been since she'd last spoken with Signa. She *wanted* an excuse to be angry. But for her father's sake she bit back that roiling emotion and clenched her shaking fists at her sides. She hoped that anyone who saw them would think she was nervous.

"You'll have an hour," drolled the splotchy-faced warden, his steps brisk as he led them through the prison and down a stone staircase so cracked and steep that Blythe had to brace her palm against the wall to steady herself. The air grew more frigid with each step, and soon enough she realized exactly where this man was leading her. They had her father in an ancient, freezing dungeon.

"It's only for the visit," Byron whispered, as if he were able to feel Blythe's simmering rage. "He'll be back upstairs with the rest of them once we leave."

Blythe didn't like that notion any better. She braced herself as the door opened and she prepared to see her father for the first time in a month. But there was nothing to prepare her for who waited behind the door.

Elijah Hawthorne was a husk of the man he once was. He'd lost too much weight too quickly, and he had skin that hung loosely around his neck to show for it. His face was gaunt and his frame so withered that he looked as though one solid breeze might topple him. The skin beneath his eyes was corded with lines of deep purple, and he was even more disheveled than he'd been the year prior, when he'd been grieving the death of Blythe's mother. There was a cut on his lip, too, red and raw—and so obviously someone else's doing that Blythe gripped the bars of the cell door to steady her rage.

She hardly recognized her father like this, made small and drab in his dingy gray uniform, his legs chained to a chair and his wrists in shackles. It was his eyes alone that kept Blythe from despair—not as bright or mischievous as they once were, but not so forlorn as those of a doomed man, either. The spark of fire within them had dimmed, certainly, though she was glad to see that it had yet to be extinguished.

The cell door groaned shut behind them, and Blythe's breath caught when her father glanced up at her, his face softening.

"You are truly a sight for sore eyes." He leaned back in his chair, the manacles clanking. " How are you, my girl?"

Heat surged in Blythe's eyes, tears she had no intention of letting him see threatening. She wished so deeply that she could hug him without getting thrown back into the carriage.

"I'm better now that I've seen you," she told him. "But you're most certainly not. What happened to your face?"

When Elijah adjusted to try to discreetly cover his cut with his hand, Blythe turned her attention to the guard outside the cell. If he was the one who did this, she'd burn him at the stake. Before she could ask, Byron took hold of her shoulder and squeezed tight.

"Enough," he hissed under his breath. "This is not the place nor the time." There was no overlooking the scrutiny in Byron's eyes as he assessed Elijah, who tilted his head back with the most vicious scoff.

"I suppose it pleases you to see me like this?" His bitterness was so unexpected that Blythe hesitated to take one of the seats across from her father, looking between the two men as Byron sat. Given the force of the guard's scrutiny, she had no choice but to follow suit.

"There is a week left until your trial, Elijah. We have other matters to discuss."

Panic lodged itself in Blythe's throat. A *week*. She'd been so distracted with Signa that she hadn't realized the trial was so close.

"Are you keeping up with Grey's?" Elijah sneered. Blythe again looked between him and her uncle, wondering what she'd missed.

"Of course I am." If there was anything for which Byron could be counted on, it was keeping up the family business. "Not that it matters. Given everything that's happened and a year of your efforts to soil its reputation, we haven't a single patron."

Elijah scratched his fingernails along his pants, his leg jittery. "There's a waiting list in the drawer in my study. Extend an invitation to those on it—they'll want to stake their claim while they have the opportunity. This will blow over soon enough."

This was the last sentiment Blythe wanted to hear from her father. He wasn't asking because he was concerned about Grey's but because he was concerned about *them*. Elijah wanted his family to be taken care of if he was found guilty, and the very thought of it had bile rising to Blythe's throat. "Invite them yourself once you're out of here in a week," she said.

Elijah reached out as if to squeeze her hand before the manacles stopped him. Blythe's face fell; she wished nothing more than to tear them free.

"Why hasn't Signa come?" he asked as the silence dragged, his jaw tensing. Though it was Blythe he turned to for an explanation, Byron answered. "Miss Farrow returned to Foxglove manor this morning."

Elijah's shackles clanked against the chair. "Does she intend to come back to Thorn Grove?"

"Considering she took her lady's maid with her, I have my doubts."

Elijah wilted before their eyes, skin sallow and sickly. His shoulders caved inward. "If she's decided to abandon us, then I fear we may have a harder time than we thought."

Blythe hated the resentment in his voice. She hated how the fire in his eyes had dimmed so much that she pounded a fist on the table to get his attention. Behind her, a warden shouted a warning until she settled back in her seat, still seething.

"You have no right to say that." Her words were tight, each as enraged as the next. "We're all trying to clear your name. Signa's odds of that were no better than mine."

So what if Signa could do the impossible? So could Blythe, even if she wasn't sure how. She'd make a deal with the devil himself if that's what it took to free her father.

"Are you certain that finding the late Lord Wakefield's murderer is what we should be focused on?"

A chill ran down Blythe's spine at her uncle's question. Yet it was her father who asked pointedly, "Is there a reason you think we *shouldn't?*"

Byron stared his brother dead in the eyes. "I'm saying that perhaps we will not find a culprit, Elijah, and that it might be time to look at alternative strategies for getting you out of prison or at the very least lessening your sentence."

Oh, how she wanted to strangle her uncle. So did Elijah if the rage on his face was any indicator. Perhaps it was fortunate that his hands were shackled.

"Are you suggesting that I killed Lord Wakefield?" For all his anger, Elijah's voice was remarkably measured. "What reason would I have to do something so foolish?"

Byron gave no indication of backing down. It was as though he couldn't even hear the ridiculousness of his own words. "I'm not suggesting anything. I'm only trying to get you out of here, Elijah, and we're running out of options."

Elijah leaned in as close as he could and hissed under his breath, "I didn't kill him. I will always be the first to admit my past failures, of which there are many. But do you truly think my mind so weak that if I *were* to have killed the duke, I would do it under my own roof, with a drink fed to him by my own hand? My manner would be much less conspicuous, I assure you."

Growing up in Thorn Grove, Blythe was entirely too used to her father and uncle's bickering. It didn't seem there was a single gathering where the two did not butt heads, for her father was far too lewd for Byron's taste, and Byron too rigid for Elijah's. Nevertheless, Blythe fixed her father with a glare.

"Do you think it's wise to admit that aloud while you're shackled in a cell and awaiting trial?" Elijah's grin slipped, and when Blythe was satisfied with his embarrassment, she turned to her uncle. "And *you.* If you kept your opinions to yourself long enough to think rationally and not let some silly competition color your thoughts, perhaps you would not be wasting time with baseless accusations."

Redness flooded Byron's skin from the neck up, but she ignored his sputtering.

"I haven't a doubt in my mind that you're innocent." Blythe kept her voice low enough for the warden not to pry. "We're not going to think of alternatives—we're going to find the killer. I promise you both that I will not rest until my father walks free and the culprit is hanging from a noose. Now, everyone stop bickering, and let's make a list of suspects."

They had a week left, and God help her, Blythe needed to make it count.

PART TWO

TWENTY-FIVE

FOXGLOVE MANOR SAT UPON THE EDGE OF A WEATHERWORN cliffside.

No one who saw the sloping porch or shattered windows would call it a "proud" estate, nor was it the warm and welcoming seaside manor that Signa had once envisioned establishing a proper life in. As it stood, Foxglove was as dreary a gray as the skies behind it and the thrashing water below, and was shielded by overgrown ferns and dampened jasmine that clawed its way up the towering structure.

Signa had felt the land's bitter chill before she'd even stepped out of the carriage, Gundry looping circles at her muddied heels. Elaine followed, clutching her bonnet tight as the wind gnashed against them. Her small face was pinched as she watched the storm circle like a starved predator, waiting to strike.

This close to the cliff's edge, Signa couldn't help but wonder whether such a storm might whisk them away and toss their bodies into the fervent sea. She peered down at the scuttling crabs that huddled on jagged rocks covered with sea-foam and frowned, for such curiosity did nothing to ease her troubled mind. She would have of course preferred for the home to have been readied and staffed prior to her arrival so that Foxglove at least wouldn't *look* as precarious as it felt, but they'd have to make do. She and Elaine had come with only their belongings and enough supplies to get settled, which was fortunate. Considering the storm poised to strike at any moment, there was no saying when they'd be able to head into town.

Still, Foxglove couldn't all be doom and gloom. Signa's parents had lived here once, after all, and were rumored to have hosted dozens of extravagant soirees during their years. Perhaps the gloom was rare, then. Or, better yet, perhaps there was beauty in the midst of the gloom, and she needed only to squint to find it. She tried—very hard, in fact—until her temples pulsed and her eyes grew sore.

"It has potential." Signa tried to sound hopeful, more for herself than for Elaine, who looked very much like a woman who regretted every decision she'd made in the past twenty-four hours. If the tiny white parasol she clutched was any indication, Elaine had been thoroughly ready to leave the dreariness of Thorn Grove behind in favor of seaside living. Seeing her dread, Signa almost felt guilty for asking the woman to accompany her.

Almost.

"All it needs is a little elbow grease," Signa pressed on, determined not to let the woman turn back while she had the chance.

Elaine took one look at the slate-gray stones and exhaled. "I'm afraid I haven't got that many elbows, miss."

Only Gundry seemed to favor the estate. His paws were caked with mud and bits of grass, and his tail wagged as he sniffed at the heels of the carriage driver who clambered from his post, pressing one hand over his cap to keep the wind from snatching it as he carried the last of the luggage into the manor and then toddled back out. Signa had never seen someone in such haste, more eager to leave than even the horses, which were stomping and huffing their disapproval as the driver rushed back to his seat. He gave Signa no opportunity to invite him inside until the storm passed but instead snapped the reins and hurried off down the path.

A crow cawed down at them from the manor's tallest spire, and Elaine whispered a prayer.

Signa couldn't blame her. "I'll put an ad in the paper," she decided aloud, turning toward Elaine with the widest smile she could manage. "I'm certain we'll have a full staff to assist us in no time."

Elaine made a low noise in the back of her throat that was likely meant to be agreement but sounded more akin to agony. "Aye, miss."

Signa decided that if Elaine stuck around, the woman could have whatever position in the house she'd like. It wasn't as though there would be any shortage of them. Foxglove appeared every bit as large as Thorn Grove, though it was both taller and narrower, with towering gray spires she was certain the town probably found cheery and not at all unsettling. And while she hadn't gotten close enough to see what condition they were in beneath all the thriving greenery, there were stables, too, which would require a groom and stablemen once she gathered some horses. It was going to be more work than she ever imagined.

"We should hurry inside," Elaine said, following Signa's gaze. "We'll be caught in the rain if we wait any longer."

She was right, though Signa knew it was the cold clawing its way into her bones that Elaine truly wanted to get away from. While Signa had grown accustomed to such a chill, even her mortal body had its limits, and eventually there was no choice but to freeze or cross the last few steps into her new home.

Foxglove was where she was meant to make a new life for herself. One where she would live without the Hawthornes, Death, or anyone she loved. She tried not to let such bleak thoughts plague her mind and sought instead to think of all the possibilities waiting for her as she carefully stepped over broken shards of glass and into the manor.

Signa was glad to find that, aside from the dust, it wasn't nearly as dreary as it appeared on the outside. It was, however . . . unique.

The entryway itself was a long stretch of space lined with portraits that had been meticulously hung, the space between each one measured with the utmost precision. Yet they were not nearly as colorful or precise as the portraits Signa was used to. The angles were sharp and unrefined, and the artist had a tendency to exaggerate features like the whites of eyes, the reediness or fullness of a body, or a smile so wide it was unnerving.

Aside from an ashy table decorated with an odd vase holding flowers that had long since wilted, ready to crack apart at the tenderest touch, not everything felt quite so macabre. Entirely out of sync with the art, Foxglove's walls were all bright shades that almost tricked Signa into believing it truly was the cheerful seaside retreat she'd imagined—buttery yellows, delicate blues, and wallpaper adorned with imagery of birds. From the elegant carvings around the ceilings to the plush rugs she walked across, every detail had been lovely prior to the soot and grime that now coated them.

The climate was far from dry, and yet after twenty years of abandonment there was little to show for that. The porch was sloped, and several windows had been destroyed by vines and ivy that crawled their way in through broken glass. But there was nothing that couldn't be remedied.

Signa's pace was little more than a snail's crawl as she made her way into a sage-green parlor with the most exquisite tea set on the table. There were trays inlaid with gold, ruined by tacky outlines of whatever had once been ready to serve but had long since been stolen away by ants. Signa's skin crawled as she approached, not daring to touch this moment that felt stilled by time.

"Are you all right, miss?" Elaine's voice was shaky, and for her benefit Signa nodded.

"I am." She had trouble with her voice as she looked from the dusty marble busts to the rich leather sofa. She tried to imagine what this room might have looked like twenty years before, when her parents had been alive. There was still a deep imprint upon one of the cushions—had her father sat there? Had her mother, Rima Farrow, preferred the couch, or the beautiful green armchair across from it? Had they taken their tea here at this table?

How wonderful it would have been for Signa to have a single memory of her parents existing in this space. As it was, she had only remnants of what they'd left behind.

She turned toward more portraits that hung ready for her inspection, a few of them dispersed throughout the parlor. They all appeared to be done by the same hand, though it was a portrait of two women that drew Signa's eye. She recognized her mother immediately, with her dark hair that had been painted in fast, messy strokes, and severe eyes that were the same shape as Signa's. Beside her stood a young woman with thick ringlets the color of gingerbread. She was softer than Rima, a ghost of a smile playing upon rosy lips that were puckered like a heart. She had her arm draped around Rima's waist, pulling her in close for the portrait.

There was so much about her family that she still wanted to know, and yet walking these halls felt like she herself was a ghost infiltrating the memories of a stranger. It was impossible to take a single step without questioning whether her mother had decorated the room she stood in or if her father had ended his nights in here as Elijah so often did in his parlor. Letting her thoughts wander, Signa absently pressed a finger to the portrait, trailing it over the glazed paint. She stopped cold, however, when the lips of the woman standing beside Rima drooped into a frown.

Signa swallowed her gasp as she yanked her hand back, not wanting to alarm Elaine. It had only taken a second for the tip of her finger to go numb from the chill that shot through her spine like the crack of electricity.

There was a spirit watching them. And now it knew Signa could see it.

Wonderful.

"You'll have a room to yourself in the servants' quarters," Signa told Elaine, tucking her numbed finger into the folds of her coat and offering her most practiced smile. "Feel free to pick out whichever you'd like and get yourself settled."

Elaine had never moved so swiftly as when she bent to grab hold of her luggage. She nodded and hurried to find said quarters, casting furtive glances over her shoulder as if she expected someone to try to snatch her from behind.

Signa waited until Elaine was down the hall before she set her palm atop Gundry's head with a sigh. "Let's find ourselves a room of our own, shall we?" And perhaps a spirit, too, while they were at it.

She gathered her belongings and turned her attention to the stairs. They were far more standard than the ones at Thorn Grove, the banister a hefty mahogany wood. A small chunk seemed to have broken off, the wood around it stained dark. The farther into the home she ventured, the slower her steps became as anxiety crept into her bones.

She was trying to have a good outlook, truly. She was *trying* to stay positive. But now that she was alone for the first time all day, the nerves were settling in.

What if she opened her nursery by accident? Or worse, her parents' suite? Signa's mind warred with itself—half of it wanting nothing more than to find that suite and gather all the information she could about her parents' lives, while the other half warned that their belongings should remain untouched. What if there were things in there that her parents wouldn't have wanted her to find? What if there was something that made her view them differently than the pristine parents she'd finely crafted in her mind? Not to mention that there was a spirit somewhere nearby. She could feel eyes against her skin, raising goose bumps along the back of her neck. What if it was malicious, as Lillian had once been?

Gundry ran ahead of her, and while Signa had imagined that he might look at least a little menacing while hunting spirits, his lolling tongue hung sideways out of his mouth as he circled back every few minutes as if to say that their path was clear. Signa caught glimpses of a sudden light beneath the door of a room she passed, and flickers of the telltale pale blue of a spirit blinking in and out of the far corner of her vision. Whoever it was, Gundry seemed unconcerned. And if he wasn't worried, Signa told herself not to be, either. She was a reaper, after all.

It took several minutes of pacing the halls before Signa gathered her courage to try one of the doors. Fortunately, the first suite she came across had clearly been meant for a guest. It was so wonderfully plain that the moment Signa was inside, the unshakable itch in her bones and the roiling in her stomach settled. The tension in her shoulders eased as she dropped her luggage to the floor.

She decided that the first thing she should do was clean. Elaine didn't deserve to do such an arduous task alone, and the chore would help get her mind off things. And so Signa stripped the bed of its sheets—they might have been white once, though she couldn't tell through all the dust layered onto them. And that was as far as she got before all the dust made her think back to living with her aunt Magda, and how miserable she'd been before Thorn Grove. From there, it didn't take long until the dam of swelling emotion she'd been repressing since leaving finally burst open, reminding her once again just how alone she was.

Her stomach tight and her chest trembling, Signa kicked the bedding so that the dirty side lay flat on the floor and sank onto it. After sneezing several times from the dust, Gundry padded to her side to lie beside her, resting his chin on her leg with a gentle lick. Signa curled her fingers in his fur, tears coming hot and fast.

"It's just you and me, boy." She sank low enough to rest her head against Gundry's back and burrowed her face into his neck. He was one of the few slivers of normalcy left in her life, and he was a wolf in sheep's clothing—the thought was so ridiculous that she almost laughed, clutching him tighter until there came a crash of thunder outside the window.

Gundry burst to all fours, hackles raised as his fangs bared. Signa followed his pointed ears to an old vanity near the window, tense and holding her breath. Its mirror was hazy from dirt, but not so hazy that Signa couldn't see the billowing hem of a dress, there one moment and gone the next. Panic surged in her throat, but seconds later she saw the likely cause: not a spirit but a tiny gap in the windowsill that was causing the curtains to billow with the sharp wind. She hurried to shut the window before drawing back to Gundry's side.

"It's all right," she whispered as she brought the other side of the blankets over them like a cocoon. She had to say it a few more times, scratching him behind the ears before he wound his body protectively around hers. "We're going to be fine. This is our home now, and I won't let anything hurt us."

They fell into silence, and though Gundry's breathing soon deepened with sleep, every creaking floorboard and gust of wind kept Signa wide awake. For a while she debated forgoing sleep entirely, but Foxglove was her home now, and she refused to let anyone or anything make her fearful of it.

And so she tucked into Gundry, shut her eyes, and forced sleep to claim her.

TWENTY-SIX

LATE THAT EVENING, AS RAIN THRASHED AGAINST THE WINDOWS and the thunder raged, Signa woke to hands squeezing her throat.

She'd been lost in nostalgia, dreaming of eating sweets with Percy and taking lessons in the drawing room with Marjorie until the corners of her vision tunneled inward with darkness. Suddenly it was Percy's face she saw, eyes dark as a moonless night as he squeezed her throat. Blythe stood behind him, half turned and ignorant of what was happening. Signa reached toward her, trying to call out. Her scream rang silent in the night, vision fading. Yet even as Percy's image disappeared, the grip on her throat did not cease. It was then—as Signa gasped for breaths she could not find—that she realized her breathlessness was no dream and jolted herself awake.

Gundry stood across from her, at least three times his normal size. His fangs were bared, shadows dripping from his maw. He was snarling, though it was impossible for Signa to hear anything over the rushing of her blood.

She tried to lurch upright only to find that she couldn't move. Sitting on her chest was an older woman Signa had never seen, who beamed down at her with a watery smile that reminded Signa of her grandmother. The woman smoothed hair from Signa's forehead with one hand as she pressed down on her throat with the other.

"It's all right," crooned the spirit. *"Go back to sleep."*

Signa tried to reach into her pocket, panicking when she found it empty. She'd used the last of the belladonna while revealing her powers to Blythe. Her hands trembled as dread rolled over her. She bucked, desperate to free herself, but the spirit held tight, and the cold sank deeper into her.

It was like the time Thaddeus had possessed her all those months prior, back in Thorn Grove's library. Though this was no possession—Signa still had control of her body, even if she was having trouble using it—the spirit was wholly consuming, and it was a horrifying realization that she could very well be murdered.

But all Signa could think was that she had no right to die. Not with Elijah's fate hanging in the air, and certainly not before she was able to have a life with Death at her side. This wasn't the time to test whether her ability to evade death extended to suffocation, and so, as her heartbeat slowed and Signa stood on the threshold between life and death, she seized the short opportunity she had and let her powers flood in before she lost consciousness.

Signa? Death's voice was in her head at once, and if not for the spirit on top of her, she might have cried in relief. *Signa, what's happening?*

There was no time to tell him. The familiar frost of her reaper abilities settled into her veins, steadying her. Every shadow in the room consumed her, and she felt invincible. She pushed aside her doubts and the memory of the terror in Blythe's eyes as tendrils of darkness snaked around her fingertips. She drew it around her, letting it feel her desperation and need for escape. And then she pushed that darkness out like a weapon, and let the night do her bidding.

Signa couldn't say what happened in those final moments. She didn't know just how many shadows had gathered to her, and she had no awareness that all of Foxglove had stilled in awe of the power she'd commanded. She only knew that moments later she was rolled over on all fours and choking on the breaths her body demanded. Her throat was raw, aching, the skin around it bruised. Whether from the cold or the death that had nearly claimed her, Signa trembled so fiercely that it was impossible for her to move from the grimy sheets on which she'd fallen asleep.

Only then did Death arrive. He came in a gale that shook the windows, clashing against the manor as he pinned the spirit against the wall and shackled her with his shadows. Thunder crashed as he lifted his hand, the night pooling into a scythe in his palms.

Death did not speak nor give the cowering spirit so much as a moment before he struck. But the blade hovered against the woman's throat, stalled by the shadows Signa used to halt it in the final second. There was fury in Death's eyes as he whirled to face her.

"She was trying to *kill* you," he spat, pressing down harder and testing Signa's hold on him. "Do you realize how much energy it takes for a spirit to *touch* a living soul? For even daring to lift a finger against you, she should die."

"Gundry would have taken her," she argued, trying to keep her voice calm.

"You foolish girl. Gundry can't reap spirits!"

Signa steadied her hold as the hound whined. "Don't take her," she said, staring Death firmly in the eyes until his shoulders eased, his rage ebbing just enough for Signa to drop her shadows and trust that he wouldn't make any rash moves.

Her teeth were chattering as she forced herself onto shaky feet. While she would have loved to stand tall before the woman, she had to draw a blanket from the floor and wrap it around herself as she walked, desperate for the mere promise of warmth. She swayed, and while she wasn't coughing up blood this time, a glance out of the corner of her eye revealed that the color was leaching from her hair, once again turning it silver. She'd have to worry about that later.

Having been focused solely on trying to save her own life, Signa hadn't gotten the best look at the spirit. As she stood before her now, the woman wasn't quite as old as she'd thought, perhaps in her sixties. She had an intense widow's peak, and a permanent scowl that created deep crevices around her lips and forehead. Her shrewd lips were painted crimson, and the look in her eyes was nothing short of contempt as Signa approached and asked, "Who are you?"

"I have waited twenty years for you to walk through those doors." The spirit's voice was tight and cruel, and it reminded Signa so much of her late aunt Magda that her stomach flipped.

"You have two options," Signa began, allowing herself to lean in to how natural the words felt, riled by the threat and the powers coursing through her. "You will release your grip on this world and move on to the afterlife, or you can be removed by force. Should you choose the second option, know that your soul will come to a permanent end."

The spirit didn't drop her gaze from Signa's as she said, *"The moment he releases his hold on me, I will try to kill you again and again, until you join me on the other side."*

Signa was grateful for the blanket draped around her and for the fact that she was already shivering so that the spirit wouldn't know the effect those words had.

Perhaps she'd been a fool not to inspect the remainder of the manor before she slept. With the presence of her parents lingering in every inch of Foxglove, she'd wanted to crawl into a space of her own and settle. But it wasn't only herself she had to think about now, and with a start Signa thought of Elaine, alone in the servants' quarters without a soul to help her.

Right then Signa did not feel the stirrings of Life's powers within her. She felt every bit a reaper as she looked upon Death and commanded, "Take her," before she fled the room without waiting to see his scythe fall.

Signa dropped the blankets somewhere behind her and ran to the servants' quarters. With the storm raging outside, the sky was so dark that Signa hadn't the faintest clue what time it was as she raced down the stairs. The cold floor against her bare feet did little to ease her shivering, but nothing could slow her until, finally, she saw Elaine seated at a table near the kitchen, still in her nightgown as she sipped from a steaming cup of coffee. The woman half yelped when she noticed Signa.

Alone. Elaine was perfectly, wonderfully alone.

"Miss Farrow!" Elaine held one hand to her heart, the other nearly spilling her coffee. "You gave me a fright!" She must have noticed Signa's shivering then, for her eyes narrowed. "Has something happened? Heavens, what have you done to your hair?"

Signa tried to push silver strands back. "Yes," she answered slowly, not having thought this far ahead. She'd expected that if she were being harassed, then surely Elaine would be, too. Signa had to shake her head to right herself, worrying her bottom lip. "I apologize for barging in. I heard an awful noise and needed to check that you were well."

Elaine's face relaxed. "I'm sure it was only the wuthering that you heard." She started to reach for Signa's hand, but Signa flinched back. She had been using her powers only moments before—if any effect of them remained, the last thing she wanted was to harm Elaine.

"The manor is large," Elaine began gently, not seeming at all offended. "And it's new to us both. I admit that I didn't sleep as well as I should have, either. But one day soon I'm certain we'll both feel comfortable here, especially once...Miss Farrow, do you hear a piano?"

Sure enough, there was most certainly the distinctive sound of an untuned piano playing above them.

Signa felt every bit like one of Fate's marionettes as she forced an unwilling smile to her lips. "As you said, I'm sure it's only the wuthering."

"Shall we investigate?" Elaine asked with grim severity, beginning to stand. Signa quickly waved her back down.

"I would much rather you begin breakfast once you're done with your coffee." It was far too early, and her stomach much too queasy for food. But she had to keep Elaine occupied while she sought out the source of the sound.

Fortunately, it didn't take much coercing. Elaine seemed more than happy to cup her coffee tight and pretend she heard nothing, leaving Signa to hurry back upstairs.

Three spirits had taken up occupancy in the drawing room. Two of them sat on furniture untouched by time—a mother and father, by the look of them. The woman was older, with generous curves and a face caked with makeup that Signa could see even on her translucent skin. Her hair had been piled almost comically high atop her head, and Signa found herself wondering how on earth it was keeping its hold.

The spirit beside her was a small, reedy man. He wore spectacles that sat low on the bridge of his aquiline nose, squinting through them as he watched the third spirit, who sat on the bench of a pianoforte, playing a dreary tune with a level of mastery Signa could never hope to reach. Physically, she appeared to be around Signa's age, with a long, slender neck and a small oval face that pinched as she focused on the piano. As she played, her translucent fingers never disturbed the thick caking of dust. A rat lay beneath the bench, long dead and little more than a skeleton that the spirit's ankle hovered beside.

The girl's mother and father watched proudly until the woman's head twisted to the side at the sound of a floorboard creaking beneath Signa's feet. She smacked the man Signa could only assume was her husband on the shoulder to get his attention. At once, the piano ceased.

"It's the girl," whispered the older woman as she shifted out of her seat to get a better look at Signa. *"That's her, isn't it?"*

"Is it that time already?" asked the man. *"Where's the husband?"*

The younger girl spun on the piano bench. In a nasally, high-pitched voice, she answered, *"It doesn't look like she's got one. There's no ring on her finger!"*

If they wanted to believe that Signa could neither see nor hear them, she'd let them. Without looking any of them in the eye, she drew closer to the piano bench as if inspecting it for the source of the music that'd been playing.

"No husband?" The man scoffed as he circled her, too close for Signa's comfort. *"You mean to tell me she's to inherit this house alone?"*

"Perhaps that's how they do it now, Father. It would certainly be a nice change."

"We should have been warned that she was coming." It was the woman who spoke now, her voice conveying just how greatly Signa's existence displeased her. *"She should have sent staff to prepare the home."*

Her lungs half clogged from the sheer amount of dust in Foxglove, Signa agreed.

"We always knew the day would come." The man removed his spectacles and puffed a breath upon them before he rubbed the glass and put them back on. Given that there was no air in his lungs, the effort made little difference. *"A home like this could only stay empty for so long."*

Behind him, the woman placed her hands on either side of her hair as if to balance it while she strolled closer. *"Even after all these years, you still give the Farrows too much credit for their taste. You were twice the architect that man could have ever hoped to be. Have you forgotten they're the reason we're stuck here to begin with?"*

"Mother's right," added the girl. *"Perhaps we should remind her of that. This home has been ours far longer than it's belonged to* her.*"* The girl spat the last word like it was a disease and rushed so close to Signa that it took everything in her not to flinch. *"All we'd have to do is slam a few windows and creak a few floorboards, and she'll go running."*

"We can haunt the mirrors," added the mother. *"Oh, I do love a good mirror haunting. The girl cannot remain here if she has no staff. We'll have to keep scaring them off."*

"I'm not going anywhere near that maid she brought," the younger girl hissed. *"Not when she looks like* that. *You'll have to be the one to haunt her, Mother."*

Signa bit the inside of her cheek, anger rising. It was one thing to toy with her, but to haunt Elaine?

"The only thing you will do is put an end to that music." Signa marched straight toward the piano and slammed it shut. "Dear God, can you imagine if someone heard you playing without a living soul sitting on the bench? And don't you dare even think of haunting anyone."

So stunned were the spirits that for a long moment no one spoke. The mother glanced at her husband, and quietly whispered, *"Is she talking to—"*

"To you?" Signa settled her hands on her hips. "Of course I am."

Silence hung heavy around them before the man cleared his throat and the daughter whispered in a shrill, disbelieving voice, *"You can* see *us?"*

"Do you think I'm talking to the walls?" Signa folded her arms. "Now listen to me, because this can be *our* home or *my* home, but this is certainly not *your* home. If you so much as creak the floorboards, I will have my hound dig up your buried bones so that I can burn them to cinders. Is that understood?"

"Are you the Farrows' girl?" asked the man. *"The baby, Signa?"*

"I am." There was the tiniest tremor in her voice when she answered. "And I'm trying to make a life here for myself, so there will be no more piano."

The girl frowned as she drew her bony hands from the keys. *"But we've been playing for years...."*

"I'm sure you have," Signa chided. "But I'll not have people thinking my home is haunted."

"But it is haunted," the man noted. Signa turned to him. Though he couldn't drink, he stirred a rusted spoon in an old teacup beside him, going through the motions. The liquid had evaporated long ago, leaving only a dark ring inside the cup.

"I *know* that." Signa slid a hand through her hair, exasperated. "But I don't need the rest of this town believing I'm a deranged spinster who dallies with ghosts."

The spirits shared a look, and Signa all but scowled at them again. "Never mind." She waved the girl from the piano bench. "Off of that. Off! I won't have any more of it."

"Then what do you propose we do?" the girl demanded, eyes flashing with such anger that for a moment Signa braced herself for the worst. *"We've few other options to entertain ourselves!"*

It was then that Signa felt the cold sting of Death settle against her skin. The spirits' eyes grew wide as they huddled together, away from the reaper that Signa could not see. Still, his presence alone was enough to bolster her spirit.

"You could always try passing on to the afterlife," she mused. "I'm sure there's plenty to do there. I hear you can even reincarnate if you'd like." Still in her nightgown with her hair strewn about, she was far from prepared for this conversation, let alone the situation at hand. Her throat remained raw, voice hoarse and rife with tension.

As she noticed the tremors racking Signa's body, the woman asked, *"What happened to you?"*

"That's what I'm trying to figure out." Again Signa cast a look down the hall, ensuring Elaine was still in the servants' quarters. She took a seat on a footstool across from them, arms wound around herself. The chill within her was easing some, not nearly as bad as if the woman had possessed her. At least she could be glad about something.

"Just how many spirits live in Foxglove?" Signa wished with everything in her for a lower answer. She was unprepared for the truth of it to roll from the man's tongue, his words spoken too quickly as he glanced between her and Death.

"Somewhere close to twenty, I imagine," he said. Signa's arms wrapped tighter as a wave of sickness overcame her, wishing she could look upon Death's face. *Twenty.* She had thought it odd enough to see a trio of spirits together. There were places she'd passed in her lifetime where spirits had roamed freely, certainly. Lands that had once been ancient battlefields and hospitals. But for twenty spirits to live under a single roof? It was preposterous.

"Where are they?" Signa pressed. "Why haven't I seen more of them?"

"Everyone has their favored spots." The spirit pushed his spectacles up the bridge of his nose. *"We like ours right here, away from all the riffraff. Most stay in the ballroom, though there are a few that roam the halls."*

Signa's blood went cold. Of course they'd be in the ballroom.

"They must know I'm here." She sounded as though she'd

swallowed a frog, the words a low rasp. "Why haven't more of them sought me out, and why have they left my maid alone?" It didn't seem wise to share with them that she'd been attacked only minutes earlier. She didn't want them getting any ideas.

What Signa didn't expect was for them to share another look.

"What is it?" She pulled the footstool closer to them. The two spirits on the couch leaned away as she neared, but rather than look *at* Signa, the older woman peered just over her head, toward the servants' quarters.

"I wouldn't go near that maid of yours even if you paid me to do it. There's something wrong with her skin. None of us have seen it before, and no one wants to be the first to find out what it means."

"What do you mean? There's nothing on her skin."

"It glows," the youngest added with such earnest vigor that she seemed more youthful than she was. *"You can't see it? It's all over her, and it brightens to silver whenever any of us get near."*

Signa forced herself to keep calm beneath the spirits' scrutiny, not wanting to give away her concern. Was it possible her powers had done something to Elaine without her realizing it?

Death must have shifted nearer, and oh what Signa wouldn't have given to be able to hear his voice in that moment. If he'd seen anything strange with Elaine, she had no doubt that he would have said something.

"We won't bother you," the man promised, though his eyes were trained to a spot just above Signa's shoulder, where Death must have stood. *"But we can't make any promises for the others."*

The windows in the sitting room flew open as a bitter gust blew in. Darkness crept through, and though she couldn't fully make out his individual shadows, she imagined they were closing in on the spirits as the darkness spread toward them, sucking all light from the room.

The man drew his family away, stepping in front of them like a shield.

"*We won't harm anyone!*" he promised this time, firmer.

Signa believed him. Still, she'd have to be cautious. All spirits who remained in the mortal world were held by an intense emotion or strong desire. For Thaddeus, he'd wanted to read all the books in the library, while Lillian had wanted to save her daughter and find her killer. Magda had remained because she was bitter and jealous and all-around terrible. It wasn't a surprise that some of those who had died here at Foxglove might be fueled by vengeance.

Signa had no belladonna left, and even if she did, the cost of slipping into her reaper form had become too great. Even now she could feel the weariness in her bones, as though she'd aged ten years within minutes. But the spirits didn't need to know that, let alone understand how her powers worked. They needed only to understand that she was a threat, and the weight of what she could do. She held her hand out, and at once the windows slammed shut, the darkness retreating.

"I am a reaper." Signa imagined that she was Blythe as she iced over her glare. "I am the night incarnate, the ferrier of souls." They were the same words that Death had spoken to her all those months ago, on the night of Percy's death. She'd held them within her for so long, languishing his words. It was time for them to ring true. "Death is at my command. You three would be wise to remember that, and to tell the other spirits as much. Should one try to raise a hand against me or any of my visitors or staff, I will not hesitate to strike. This is my home, and if anyone here does not wish to abide by my rules, they should leave now. Should they break my rules, they will leave without choice, and there will be no future for them. No afterlife. Do you understand?"

Not a single one of the spirits blinked their wide eyes. The younger girl even gripped her father by the sleeve before he nodded to Signa.

Only then did Signa allow herself to turn from them, and toward Death.

"Please give the others that same warning," she said, bowing her head in a silent thanks as she felt the cold slip away from her, understanding that Death had gone to do just that. Only then, as warmth slipped back into the room as the trio of spirits eased in the absence of Death's presence, did Signa feel the prickle of eyes along her skin and know there was another watching her even now. She tried to snatch a glance at it, though as she turned, Signa saw only the hem of a dress disappear.

It was the same dress she'd seen when she'd arrived. Not a curtain billowing in the wind as she'd hoped, nor the spirit that had tried to kill her, but someone entirely new. Someone who'd been watching her from the moment she'd entered Foxglove.

Signa didn't spare the trio another look as she crossed the floor to follow it toward a winding hall.

Though Signa knew better than to chase a spirit—though she had learned her lesson the night she'd followed Lillian into the garden and knew how foolish this was—it seemed that old habits died hard. Because at the end of the hall, Signa followed the faint flickers of blue that urged her forward, deeper and deeper into the bowels of Foxglove.

TWENTY-SEVEN

Blythe

IF ONE WANTED TO UNCOVER THE LATEST GOSSIP, THERE WERE TWO places to look:

First, the help. Not because they had any time for gossip, but because they were closest to a household's best-kept secrets. Considering that so much of Thorn Grove's staff was new, though, it didn't seem there was anyone Blythe might be able to con into gossiping with her about what rumors they might have heard in town. Unfortunately, that meant she had to rely solely on her second source—the ladies of the season, who had entirely *too* much time for gossip, and loved to share whatever tidbits they'd picked up even if they were little more than flaking crumbs.

The morning Signa had left Thorn Grove, Blythe woke to find a note on her desk with a single name written upon it—*Byron*. It was Signa's handwriting, and though no further explanation was given, she was certain it was a clue. And while it was better than trying to pluck leads for the duke's murder out of thin air, part of Blythe wanted to burn the note and cast it from her mind.

Her family was a disaster enough without one more matter to add to the equation, and yet she couldn't quit thinking about Byron's behavior when they'd met with Elijah. He certainly *seemed* frustrated by Elijah's position, though he also wasn't out advocating on his brother's behalf or trying to charm the prince as she had been.

It seemed that the weight of Elijah's future rested entirely on Blythe's shoulders, and so she would do what ladies of her age and status were expected to—invite others over for tea.

The only problem was that Blythe wasn't convinced anyone would show up. She'd spent the morning pacing around her room, then the halls, then the parlor. And when she wasn't pacing, she was sitting and stewing as nerves she hadn't anticipated roiled through her.

Sheer desperation had Blythe nearly tumbling over from relief as Warwick entered the parlor with Charlotte Killinger, Eliza Wakefield, and Diana Blackwater in tow. Though Warwick had always been entirely professional, Blythe didn't miss the extra pep in his step as he led the ladies to a table set for four. He looked as relieved for Blythe as she felt.

"I'm so glad you could make it!" Blythe put on her most practiced smile. Considering both her overwhelming relief and considerable amount of practice, no one could prove it wasn't genuine. "Warwick, could you please see that tea is brought up?"

He bowed his head and hurried off, leaving the ladies to settle into their seats. Piping hot tea was brought—as well as two trays of dainty sandwiches and sweet pastries—before they could even get out their greetings. Eliza was the first to grab a lemon scone, slathering it with blueberry preserves that Charlotte had brought to share, courtesy of a sudden abundance of berries near her home. Eliza dropped a copious number of sugar cubes into her tea and stirred, stiff and awkward as she brought the cup to her lips.

Charlotte, too, was rigid in her seat. Given the argument between them, Blythe couldn't blame her. Diana had yet to stir, watching the cup as though it might somehow leap from its saucer and attack her.

Blythe tried not to be offended. She supposed that since she had seen vines and ivy tear through the floor of her father's study only a few days prior, savage teacups might not be out of the question. Though if one *did* manage to sprout to life and spray Diana with tea, Blythe might think to thank it.

She'd invited Charlotte not only because she was close to Everett these days but also as an apology and out of a hope to mend their relationship. The woman was too good a friend for Blythe to let slip away due to her own stubbornness.

Eliza was invited because it seemed there was something going on between her and Byron. Diana, however, Blythe had invited for two reasons: the first being that if she wasn't, Diana would undoubtedly take offense and find something about the Hawthornes to spread gossip about, which was the last thing any of them needed. The second reason was that if Diana was there, news of this visit would spread throughout town by morning. Blythe figured it couldn't hurt to help salvage the Hawthorne name a little more before the trial.

"It's been ages," Eliza crooned, sipping her tea. "When was the last time the four of us were able to take tea together?"

It had been well over a year. A year of her mother's death, her own illness, and several months of a long, painful recovery that only Charlotte had cared enough to try to understand. Blythe had just begun feeling well enough to venture back into some semblance of her life the night the duke had passed.

"It's been too long," she said by way of answer, not caring to give them an exact number even if she had the months memorized. If she gave that number a voice, she feared it would somehow hold power over her. That she might suddenly fall back into the dark space she had clawed herself out of with every scrap of strength that she'd had.

"I'm surprised any of you were allowed to come," Blythe said with a casual grace that didn't match the way she scrutinized the group's every motion in response. She was certain her being seen with the prince at the investiture had something to do with their availability.

"Your father hasn't been tried." Charlotte's voice was as smooth as the springtime breeze, and just as calming. "And my father is wise enough to understand that the investigation is still ongoing, and that the papers will try to weave a story from anything these days."

At least someone among them believed in her father's innocence. Blythe hadn't realized how much tension she'd been holding in her shoulders until it ebbed. She looked to Charlotte then, offering the smallest nod to signal that she was relieved to have her friend return.

Eliza didn't need to explain her attendance—the duke had

overseen her, and now Everett had filled the role. As busy as he was with his new role and taking over the estate, Eliza could very likely get away with anything these days. And that was if Everett even cared that Eliza was at Thorn Grove at all.

As for Diana, she'd still not said a word and had just taken her first sip. It was tentative, testing it. She kept glancing behind each of the girls as well, as though expecting a ghost to pop out and frighten them.

Blythe had no doubt her family had forbade her from coming, and that Diana likely had to wriggle her way to tea. She would have clawed a path to Thorn Grove if it meant being at the very source of the town's latest scandal.

"Will Miss Farrow be joining us?" Eliza asked, scanning the place settings in search of a fifth.

"She will not," Blythe answered with every bit of composure she had. "Signa had to return to her own home rather unexpectedly."

Charlotte flashed her a curious look, smart enough to understand that after their discussion, this could be no coincidence.

"And what of Percy?" Eliza pressed. "Has there been any word from him?"

"I'm afraid not—"

"Not even a location?" Eliza seemed a touch strained, her grip tight on her teacup. "Certainly someone must know something."

Blythe left no room for rebuttal when she spoke again, "No one knows anything about Percy." She forged ahead, unwilling to linger on the topic. "Regarding my father, however, his trial will take place at the week's end." Saying the words aloud was like picking up a dagger and slamming it between her ribs. She wasn't above letting some desperation into her voice, nor was she above looking pathetically helpless as she set her teacup down and wrung her hands in her lap.

"I need to figure out who truly killed the duke, and my father will be released. Has"—she paused, her leg restless under the table—"has Everett mentioned any suspicions?"

Blythe hadn't anticipated being quite so bold, but there was no going back. Eliza's already fair skin paled until it was almost gray, purple shadows like bruises beneath her eyes.

"Heavens, Miss Hawthorne. If any of us had a suspicion, don't you think we'd have shared it?" Eliza's drew out her fan, fluttering it at herself until the pallor began to slip away from her skin. "No one has tried to reach out about money or the title. Everett has claimed everything without issue."

"And no one has tried to come after him," Blythe pressed, this time looking at Charlotte. "Right? You were there for him those first few weeks. Did you see anything odd?"

Blythe had been careful with her words, but even so, Charlotte nearly choked on her tea, splashing a drop on the collar of her dress.

Diana leaned toward Charlotte. "You're not still circling around Lord Wakefield, are you?" Blythe cared little for Diana's voice in general, though there was a knowing edge to it that made Blythe despise it more than ever. "I never thought you brave enough to try *that* again."

Again?

Charlotte's eyes flashed darker than Blythe had ever known them. "That is quite enough."

To her surprise, it wasn't Diana that Charlotte glared at but Eliza, whose expression was flat as she sipped from her porcelain cup. "This is hardly a conversation for tea."

On the contrary, it was exactly the sort of conversation that Blythe had hoped to have. Yet while Blythe wanted nothing more than to tear into the topic, Charlotte's fast, shallow breathing kept her from pushing.

"Forgive me," Blythe said for the sake of modesty. "It's just that I've been so concerned for him these days that I've hardly been sleeping."

"I've been feeling similarly." Charlotte reached out to clasp Blythe's hand and squeeze it gently. Blythe squeezed back, a silent apology that Charlotte answered with a smile. "Have the cook bring you some warm milk before bed. I'll bring you some dried lavender to put in it. It's not much, but it's helped me."

The thought of mixing anything into her drinks these days was something that Blythe wasn't able to stomach. Especially something purple. She didn't say as much aloud, however, not with Diana watching them from over the rim of her cup with skeptical eyes.

"Did you get that from an apothecary?" Diana's words were so sharp that Eliza flinched. Her tea leaked over her fingers and down onto the tiny saucer beneath her cup.

Charlotte cut Diana a scathing look, all but rolling her eyes.

"No, Miss Blackwater, I got it from picking lavender from my garden and letting it dry out. Imagine." It was perhaps the most snark that Blythe had ever heard from her friend. She sat up straighter, a little too proud. Even so, this conversation wasn't nearly as fruitful as she'd hoped, and she needed to make this tea party worth the time spent sleuthing.

While it perhaps would have been safer to dance around the topic, Blythe's fraying patience had her once again relying on the bold approach as she leaned toward Eliza and said, "I heard a rumor, Miss Wakefield, that my uncle has been seeking your favor."

Diana's cup stilled at her lips, eyes flicking toward Eliza. They *all* looked toward her, watching as the woman finished her sip and smoothed out her dress. She was a little flushed, but other than that and the tight press of her lips, she handled herself remarkably well.

"It seems you have good sources," Eliza answered. "He's been courting me for the past few months."

Blythe's palms burned with the memory of the emerald ring. It wasn't unheard of for a man Byron's age to marry someone in their early twenties, though someone of Eliza's status could have had anyone. And Byron . . . well. He was Byron.

"My uncle has never had much luck with women." Regardless of how she felt about the situation, Blythe did her best to keep any judgment from her voice. "If you're entertaining him, I do hope that you're serious."

Blythe couldn't be certain that she hadn't imagined Eliza's grip tightening on her teacup. "Byron is a good man, and I would never dare offend him. I am considering his interest the same as I'm considering every suitor's this season."

"Which is who, again?" Diana leaned in, her lips puckered as she took a bite of a tart that Blythe wouldn't have minded her choking on. "I heard that you haven't had a caller since you refused Sir Bennet."

Blythe tried not to make a face as she recalled the ancient man that Eliza had been forced to dance with the night of the duke's passing.

"He was an awful man," Eliza acknowledged with perhaps more calm than Blythe had ever seen her capable of. "Though I believe it's my uncle's death that's keeping everyone away, Miss Blackwater. Thank you for the reminder."

"You really ought to have taken the rest of the season off," Diana mused as Blythe leaned back in her seat, picking up her tea only because she didn't have a clue what else to do. It felt like an eternity of silence passed before Diana asked, as though she hadn't just been horribly offensive, "Have any of you heard from the prince, lately? It's been some time since I've had the opportunity to visit with him, though I do believe he's interested."

Charlotte's jaw hung ajar at the gall. Blythe, however, was not so well suited for letting things slide.

"Has he sent you flowers?" she asked, smiling innocently when Diana flashed a look in her direction.

"I don't need flowers to know that he's interested—"

"Perhaps you're right. I only asked because Signa received so many. They were the most luxurious I'd ever seen—the whole town was talking about it." As tart as Signa's name tasted, it was worth it to see Diana's face pinch.

Eliza's shoulders relaxed, as if grateful to have something else to discuss. "I believe the prince is joining us tomorrow, actually. Miss

Blackwater is right that hardly any men have approached me this season, given all that's happened. When I made note of that to Everett, he made a plan to invite all his top choices over. Little did I know that it would be for a fox hunt. However am I to flirt with men at a fox hunt?"

Charlotte soured her lips as she poured herself another cup of tea. "Hours of listening to the foxes cry out in agony . . . I don't understand how a person could witness it firsthand."

"Most women can't," Eliza said as she heaped butter onto a croissant, then some preserves. "That's why it's mostly a man's sport."

"'Mostly'?" Blythe perked up. "As in women are permitted to participate?"

Eliza looked her over, seeming surprised by Blythe's interest. "They are, though few choose to."

"Would you allow me to come?" Blythe pressed, ignoring Diana's upturned nose and Charlotte's long sigh. "Not to flirt, I promise."

"You would hate it, Blythe," Charlotte said. "You wouldn't have the stomach for such a distasteful sport."

"But Eliza does?" Charlotte was right that fox hunting was the last thing she cared to participate in; Blythe didn't have a lick of interest in the sport. Getting to the Wakefields' manor, however? She couldn't have asked for a better opportunity to get a closer eye on Everett or get Eliza alone, where she'd perhaps be more willing to explain exactly what that earlier look between her and Charlotte was all about.

"As a matter of fact, I've participated since I was a child." Eliza set down her croissant. "Come, if you'd like to try it. Though if you're in it for the men, they get far too competitive to pay us any mind. I've no idea what Everett was thinking when he thought this would help me."

"I'll be there," Blythe promised, biting back a grin. "If I'm going to be calling you my aunt soon, it's about time we start bonding."

While Diana spluttered on her tea and Charlotte covered her mouth midbite with a quiet choke, Eliza fixed Blythe with a fiery glare. "If you're not careful," she threatened, "then come tomorrow I'll see to it that *you're* the fox we're all hunting."

TWENTY-EIGHT

Foxglove's ballroom made up the entirety of the manor's top story. Signa stood outside it, several feet from double oak doors she'd watched the spirit slip beneath.

A single brush of her fingertips against the doors' delicately carved depictions of deer frolicking in a garden was all it took for her body to erupt in shivers. She couldn't control them, shaking so fiercely that she fell against the opposite wall, hands on her throat as she did everything she could to pull air into her lungs. It was as though she'd fallen headfirst into a frozen lake, held captive beneath the ice.

Never had she felt so many spirits lingering in one place. Wherever Death had ventured off to, he wasn't here, and every bone in Signa's body ached to flee. What if she couldn't defend herself? What if the spirits possessed her, and this awful chill within her never ceased?

It took a double take for her to notice that the severe-looking woman depicted on the portrait outside the ballroom doors was none other than a young Aunt Magda, and Signa could think of no worse omen.

Beneath the doors, pale light flickered. There was noise inside, too. Laughter, swishing skirts, the clattering of glasses, and words that Signa's swimming mind couldn't quite place. She didn't dare let the spirits see the effect that they had on her, and she had to clench her teeth tight and focus on settling the quivering of her body. She couldn't stop it entirely, but once she was steadier, she pressed her hand to the silver knob. Inside, the voices went silent.

It was not the ballroom's delicate blue archways or ivory paneling that Signa noticed first, nor was it the floral mural on the vaulted ceiling. If she'd had her wits about her, she might have noticed that the crystal chandelier rivaled the one from the queen's palace, or perhaps that her father's careful touch was upon every square inch of the grand estate. Instead, what she noticed were the dozen or so spirits that turned in unison to stare at her, and—only when she slipped on it in her surprise—that the floor was sleek beneath her boots.

Signa's feet flew out in front of her, and pain rocketed through her tailbone. Several of the spirits floated closer to investigate, and Signa promptly pushed herself across the marble.

"Stay where you are!" She wished she'd had the foresight to have brought a knife with her. It would be useless, of course, though having something sharp and solid in her grip would have been a great comfort.

"It's her," the spirit nearest to Signa whispered, though none of the others seemed to hear. The spirit was one of the loveliest that Signa had ever seen, and she recognized her as the woman from the

portrait. The one, Signa assumed, who had led her here. Her voice was like honeysuckle, so sticky-sweet that for a moment Signa forgot what she was doing.

Tentatively, as though she anticipated that Signa was little more than a skittish fawn who might dart away at the snap of a twig, the spirit drew a breath closer and leaned in so that her face hovered at Signa's level.

"Oh, I can't believe it's truly you!" The woman reached out as if to stroke Signa's cheek but remembered the impossibility at the last second. *"I've waited a long time to see your face again, Miss Signa. My, how beautiful you've become."* The woman bent closer, and Signa surprised herself by not flinching on pure instinct.

"Look at that." Her voice was awed. *"You have Rima's jaw. And that same sternness of your eyes, too. And oh! Yes, that's it exactly! I saw the very same look of aggravation on your mother's face more times than I could count. Your hands look soft, though. More like your father's. That pert little nose of yours is his, too. How marvelous!"*

Signa had planned for an impossible number of scenarios as she'd stood outside the ballroom doors. Turning into butter at sweet words had not been one of them. "My father?" she managed to echo, her voice raw. As little as she'd managed to glean about her mother over the years, she'd learned even less about her father. The most obvious trait she'd gathered was that he hadn't been nearly as social as Rima.

"Who are you?" Signa was annoyed with herself for how long it took to ask the question. All the fight she'd built up had vanished the moment she'd stepped into the ballroom.

"Your mother was my best friend, though I suppose I shouldn't be surprised you don't know that. Who would have told you, Magda?" She tipped her head back with a laugh so gentle that Signa couldn't believe she was talking to a spirit. *"My name is Amity."*

Before she could ask anything more, Signa's attention flashed to another spirit who'd drawn too close, lurking behind Amity. Her eyes were hollow and expressionless as she trailed from one table to the next, shuffling a dance card in and out of her pocket. Though the young woman's face had perhaps once been sweet, the right side of her skull was cracked open, dried blood caked in her hair from when she must have fallen to her death. Signa wondered if she'd tried to run from the ballroom, only to fall over the banister. God, she couldn't even imagine.

As Amity followed Signa's curious eyes, her shoulders drooped. *"That's Briar. I'm sorry, I should have realized she'd be too much for you to see. I've grown so used to her appearance that I didn't think—"*

"It's fine." Signa barely recognized her own words, not knowing what had come over her. Consoling a spirit? What on earth was she thinking? "Believe me, I've seen worse."

"Yes, I heard that you could see spirits! I suppose I'm glad that you can see me now, but how terrifying that must have been as a child to see things even worse than Briar. I wish I'd been there to help you."

"You have no reason to be sorry," Signa told her flatly. The words were strange in her mouth, like something she didn't quite know how to shape. "It's not as though you were responsible for me."

"Perhaps not entirely," Amity admitted. *"Though I* am *your godmother. Or was, I suppose."* Signa's mind went blank, and Amity gave

her no reprieve to consider this news before she rambled on, her excitement bursting with each word. *"We met at finishing school. Your mother hated the place. I was the perfect student until she arrived with her grand schemes. She always had us sneaking away in the middle of the night to visit whatever ballet or circus was performing in town. Or whoever she fancied at the time."* The spirit's eyes sparkled at the memory. And then they faded as she peered back down at Signa with a small, tired smile.

"I saw your parents with the reaper that night. They couldn't manage to stay in this world, but I could. I needed to make sure that someone found you, and that you'd be cared for. When I heard that Foxglove would be yours someday, I decided to stay so that I might see what kind of woman my friend's daughter became. It's lovely to be able to speak with you."

How strange it felt to learn of this woman only now. Signa would have given everything to have met Amity years ago, when all she wanted was to know that there was somebody in this world who thought of her, and who wanted her safe and well.

And yet she had no business getting chummy with a spirit, especially when another had just assaulted her. And so Signa avoided Amity's eyes as she tried to process the news that this woman was, allegedly, her godmother. She looked instead behind Amity, past a shuffling Briar, to where several spirits were dancing. There were two sets of both a man and woman spinning in an endless waltz, while three women sat gossiping at a table set with a cloth that had long aged to yellow.

Two more proud-looking young men—twins, by the look of them—argued in the corner. Every so often one would glance at a table of women. Each of the spirits was dressed in the most spectacular fashion. Though their attire was two decades outdated, the gowns billowed with the finest fabrics while fat jewels glittered from the ladies' ears and necks. No others were obviously injured like Briar, and even with their bluish glow, they were all marvelous.

At least a minute had passed since Signa had spoken, yet even as Amity stirred beside her, restless, Signa said nothing until she took another long sweep of the room, watching the spirits reenact the same movements and conversations once, twice, and then a third time before she finally asked, "Are they all like this?"

Amity sighed as she took a seat beside Signa. The floor grew colder with her nearness, and Signa tucked herself close, fisting her hands in her skirt to spare her fingers from frostbite. *"I've tried everything I could think of to get them out of their loops, but none of them will budge. They've been like this for twenty years."*

Signa didn't miss the longing in the woman's voice as Amity turned to watch Briar. If there was one thing in this world that she recognized, it was loneliness. Twenty years Amity had been trapped here, surrounded by familiar faces who showed not even a spark of acknowledgment that she existed.

Signa wanted to let herself be drawn to Amity but quickly reeled in such instincts. She forced herself to remember Thaddeus, and how he'd been the most charming man until his beloved books had been damaged by a fire. He'd lost control enough to possess her, and she would never shake the chill of that memory. With a spirit, sometimes it took only a pin dropping to set them off.

"A spirit tried to kill me this morning." Signa pressed back to her feet and stepped away from Amity. "Am I correct to assume that no one here poses a threat for the time being?"

"I should certainly hope not. I know there are some who blame your parents for what happened, but most are stuck in the same loop with no idea they're even dead. Should they ever free themselves, I imagine most would want to leave this place for good." She sighed, and while Signa knew better, it was hard not to trust a face so genuine, or eyes that lit with such excitement to finally have another soul to speak to.

"Not all of Foxglove is quite so depressing," Amity noted after a thoughtful moment, an intriguing inflection in her tone. *"There's actually something I'd like to show you. Something I think you'll love."* Her feet never moved as she glided to the door, batting gingerbread-colored ringlets over her shoulder as she checked that Signa was following.

Perhaps it was a mistake. A trap, set by a clever spirit. Signa knew what Death would say if he were to see her now, but so many years of hoping for family and wishing that someone had been there for her did not go away overnight. Signa's chest still panged with that desire, and she hurried to follow Amity from the ballroom, down the stairs, and out the front doors of Foxglove.

Fog dense as cotton swept in from the sea, shrouding the cliffside in a briny haze that salted Signa's tongue. So dark was the sky that it was impossible to see into the distance, forcing Signa to keep close to Amity. She wouldn't normally have minded the weather, though the howls of wind and a resting sun did little to settle her thoughts. Ahead, Amity wavered with the wind, wisps of her billowing away with each gust. The farther they ventured from the ballroom, the more she flickered in and out of the fog.

"This way." Her haunting voice was a beacon, leading the way anytime Signa lost sight of her. So damp was the soil that it tried to swallow Signa's boots with every step. She struggled to keep pace, wondering all the while if it was too late to escape back to the manor. Her mind raced, trying to figure out all the ways she might cross behind the veil of life to access her abilities—and whether doing so would be worth the risk—should Amity try anything.

She hadn't come up with a single reasonable idea by the time Amity stopped, hovering above ripe earth filled with yellow poppies and rosemary. Bushels of lavender snaked through fog-shrouded soil, twisting around flowers Signa didn't know the names of. She couldn't see how far the land stretched, only that it was massively overrun, with brightly hued windflowers struggling to find space to grow. It seemed there might be vegetables in this garden as well, and perhaps juniper shrubs, though it was difficult to tell, given that there were hardly any leaves and not a single berry growing on them.

"This place is far from what it once was." Amity crouched, running her fingers through the poppies. *"Your mother had an atrociously green thumb, but your father insisted on the garden. I think he wanted to give her something to care for before you arrived—something to settle her mind and ground her. He had the plans for it ready, though all they managed was to scatter some seeds before they passed. As you can see, many of them took root."*

Signa pried off her gloves and crouched to press a palm against the rich soil, fingers twirling around stems and petals. There were few things in life better than the feeling of earth against bare skin.

She didn't know what it said about her that the first thought in her head was whether the conditions here were right for belladonna to thrive. She cast the idea from her mind as soon as she'd had it, saving such things for a later time when Fate was gone and Death was no longer so worried about her abilities.

"My father had plans for it?" she found herself asking instead, forcing herself to a stand before she soiled her nightgown. She'd have to get a wardrobe better suited for gardening with as much time as she anticipated spending here. There was so much potential in this place; the excitement of it thrummed against her chest.

"There are sketches of what it was to become laid out in his study," Amity said, looking pleased by Signa's eagerness. *"Edward sketched everything, never without a plan."*

Signa's blood ran cold at the sound of her father's name. How long had it been since she'd last heard it? Five years? Ten? Had anyone spoken it aloud since she'd lived with her grandmother?

It was no secret that Signa had wanted to remain at Thorn Grove as long as possible. She'd dreaded her arrival to Foxglove, and yet now that she was here, finally in a home of her own, she realized that all she'd really needed was a moment to herself in a place where she was in full control. A place where she could focus on having a bit of earth between her fingers. A place where she could finally just… *be.* No hiding. No pretenses. No being looked at as though she were a monster.

Signa crossed the garden and pressed a tentative finger to the withered juniper shrub. Perhaps it was finally time that she gave her new powers their fair shot—not because anyone else expected it of her but because *she* wanted to. This garden could be her playground; here, she could do whatever she wished without judgment.

She tipped her head back, savoring the brine and the wind that snarled through her hair. She'd been wrong to fear change—wrong to fear Foxglove, for it was the perfect canvas. A strange, misunderstood place she could explore to her heart's content. Like, it seemed, had called to like. Here, she would grow roots of her own, and no one could ever force her to leave. Perhaps being alone wasn't always such a bad thing.

Signa decided it was worth the sacrifice of her nightgown as she lay down on the bed of poppies, shutting her eyes as the earth's chill sank into her bones.

Foxglove was going to be the perfect home.

TWENTY-NINE

Blythe

BLYTHE DIDN'T BOTHER TRYING TO PRETEND THAT SHE KNEW A LICK about what happened at a fox hunt. When she'd arrived, Eliza had taken care to ensure that Blythe was in suitable attire—which still required a corset, a horribly tight navy dress, and a proper black hat that fastened beneath her chin.

She'd been ushered from the Wakefields' manor immediately after arriving, taken to the surrounding forest with no chance to speak to Everett; she was hardly able to get a passing look at the new duke. He was surrounded by proud, entitled men Blythe recognized all too well.

As Eliza had predicted, none of them spared her or Miss Wakefield any attention. It seemed they cared only for Everett, and winning his ear as the new duke.

To his credit, Everett took the attention in stride, clasping shoulders and nodding whenever appropriate. Still, Blythe imagined it must have been a relief for him when his horse was brought over and another rider with golden hair moved beside him, face bored and stony.

Prince Aris may have been her best bet at helping her father, and yet resentment still curdled Blythe's stomach when she saw him. Eliza had no such qualms. When she was certain no one was looking, she tugged her corset so that it pushed her breasts up.

Blythe tried not to scrunch her nose at such an obvious display. So much for her interest in Byron.

As if able to feel her thoughts, Aris's eyes slid to Blythe's. She expected he would turn away, content to ignore her. But to the surprise of both Blythe and Eliza, he gave his beautiful dapple-white mare a gentle nudge toward her.

Though Blythe rode like a proper barbarian at home, with her legs on either side of the horse, in the public eye she sat in the appropriate sidesaddle fashion. It made her unsteady beneath the weight of Aris's stare, and for once she was grateful for the corset that kept her straight and unyielding as he approached.

"I assume your cousin is here, as well?" Aris gave no greeting, hardly sparing Blythe more than a glance before searching the distance for Signa.

Blythe hoped that she looked effectively disinterested as she picked at her cuticles. "No, she's not. I'm afraid you'll have to settle for having just me around for a while." She felt a little flutter of satisfaction when his eyes grew dark. Blythe didn't want Aris as her enemy, especially when she might very well need his help. Still, it was remarkably satisfying to see him riled.

"What do you mean by that?" His voice was a deep baritone that drew the attention of men several feet ahead of them. It was a commanding voice. One that oozed power, and that she had every intention of ignoring.

"Miss Farrow has left Celadon." It was Eliza who answered, keeping her own voice delectably sweet. She looked prim and innocent from where she sat atop a sleek chestnut stallion meticulously cared for and whose neck Eliza stroked absently.

Though she knew Eliza wanted only to make herself part of the conversation, Blythe was glad that she was the one who broke the news. While he did a fine job at masking it, the heat of Prince Aris's annoyance beat against Blythe like a current. She turned her attention to her borrowed horse, suddenly finding its coat remarkably fascinating.

"I see." Aris's tone held no inflection. "And when are you expecting her to return?"

"Not for a long while, I suspect." Eliza sat taller. "She moved back to her family's home. I imagine she'll be settling in. None of us had any idea she was leaving; it was all very sudden."

Eliza could barely manage to conceal her pleasure at reporting this, and Blythe was surprised at her own reaction of annoyance. She had to remind herself that it was good that there was someone else who didn't want Signa to return. Perhaps for a very different reason, but still.

Blythe shouldn't have been annoyed; she should have been glad. She should hate Signa with every fiber of her being and never want to see her cousin again, instead of being plagued by such stupid, frustrating worries about how Signa was faring in her new home.

She shouldn't *care*. She shouldn't keep thinking about how Signa had admitted things too easily, and that there were pieces to her story that didn't make sense.

What reason would she have had to kill Percy? She didn't need the money. And Signa certainly hadn't seemed *bad* by nature, just a little odd. So why, then?

Only when the horse twitched beneath her did Blythe stir, noticing that Prince Aris's eyes were practically boring into her. She adjusted her hat's strap and said nothing.

Ahead, a voice called out something indistinguishable and the hounds took off, riders on horseback keeping a close distance. Blythe's own mount didn't wait for the command before it followed suit. She gasped and held tightly on to the reins as it burst forward.

Everett was at the head of the group, leading the charge. Aris should have been up there with him and the other men, yet no one seemed to miss him when he ruined Blythe's plans to corner Eliza by keeping back with them. It was strange how easily he seemed to maneuver through society. A thousand people should have been clamoring to get at him, yet he navigated easily, unbothered by a single soul. Blythe wondered what he'd done—or how unapproachable everyone else must have found him—to earn such freedom.

With a snap of the reins, Eliza moved beside Aris. "Are there many fox hunts in Verena?"

Given how severe his face became at the question, one would believe she'd asked whether his mother was a woman of the streets. "Hardly. I have no taste for the sport. If it takes this many people and their hounds to catch a fox, it seems that everyone's time would be better spent elsewhere."

Blythe agreed, though she didn't voice her opinion or her surprise at how plainly he spoke of his distaste, especially in front of a Wakefield. Eliza cleared her throat, only a little thrown from her pursuit. "All the same, I'm glad you came. Perhaps you'll find that you enjoy it more than you expected. The Wakefield family has been breeding hounds for these hunts for generations."

It was certainly a lovely morning, early enough that even the birds were still rousing, with weather clear and mild enough to see endlessly ahead. Still, Blythe didn't have much of a taste for the hunt and preferred to keep at the back of the group and far from where she'd witness anything. Her entire purpose was to see what information she might glean, and while she had hoped to get Eliza alone before she started prying, it seemed there was no choice but to begin.

"I imagine it's been the furthest thing from his mind, but has Everett had his eye on anyone this season?" she asked. It was similar to the question she'd asked at tea, though this time Eliza sported a scowl so remarkably well practiced that Blythe couldn't feel that bad for being on the receiving end of it. It was rude to gossip, especially in such company, but Blythe didn't care what Aris thought. If anything, he looked as curious as Blythe.

“Please, don’t stop the conversation on my account.” So coy was the prince’s smile that even Blythe blushed. He looked every bit a natural atop his mount, seated perfectly straight and all too comfortable as he lorded above them. “I wouldn’t want to step on any toes.”

“Of course you wouldn’t,” Eliza acknowledged graciously. “On the contrary, finding a wife is very much a focus of my cousin’s. With my uncle gone, an heir is more important now than ever.” There was a grimace in her words, and Blythe had no choice but to push.

“Has Everett found someone?” she asked, praying for something—anything—that might help her father.

“There was almost a contender once, but my uncle did not approve the proposal. Everett was heartbroken; it took him a while before he was ready to resume courting. He seems happier now, though, so I imagine there must be someone.”

Blythe fisted the reins so tight that her leather gloves gave a squeak of protest. *Charlotte.* That’s what Diana had meant when she asked if Charlotte was still circling Everett.

“I’m glad to hear it,” Blythe said, trying to sound nonchalant even as her mind raced and her blood pulsed a manic rhythm in her ears. “Surely that must have been a while ago that he wanted to propose? I don’t remember him courting anyone other than Signa.” At this, Blythe couldn’t help but notice that Aris’s frown grew severe.

“Signa was my uncle’s choice for him,” Eliza said with a wave of her hand. “She has a fortune behind her. Everett liked her well enough to entertain his father, though Signa never showed an interest and Everett developed new desires."

Aris's frown smoothed. Blythe, however, was trying her best to quell her churning stomach.

She was perhaps one of the only ones who knew that Everett and Charlotte were still together. She had seen their happy glances, had seen the way they kissed with the excitement of young lovers.

The duke had forbidden Everett to marry Charlotte. And if he'd gone back to her as soon as the duke died...

Blythe could think of no better motive for murder.

She kept her mouth clamped shut and her focus pinpointed on the back of her mount's neck. If she dared to speak now, the words that slipped out would cause more trouble than they were worth.

So lost in her thoughts was she that Blythe barely heard Aris as he asked, "Are you well, Miss Wakefield?"

She stole a look just in time to see that Eliza's skin had gone pale, and she was swaying atop her mount.

"Forgive me, Your Highness." Eliza was as brisk as Blythe had ever heard her, and when she tried to smile her reassurance, it only made Eliza look even more ill. "I believe I've left something important back at the manor."

"Would you like us to accompany you?" Blythe asked, having to reel her focus back in as Eliza turned a faint shade of green.

If a look could kill, Eliza's would have had her in the grave within the second. "That's not necessary. I've held you hostage long enough as it is. Go and catch up with the others—I'll find you both as soon as I'm able."

Eliza snapped the reins, taking off in the direction they'd come from. Though Prince Aris should have ignored Eliza and accompanied her to safety, His Highness seemed content watching her race back toward the estate. His glinting eyes caught the rising sun, and for a moment they were so rich a gold that Blythe nearly scoffed. A beast as foul as him had no right to be handsome.

It was then that she realized just how quiet the forest had become. Though she'd seen Everett and his men in the distance only moments before, there was nothing of their red coats now. She could barely hear the hounds, either, and with a dawning horror realized the situation she'd gotten herself into.

All she wanted was to race back to Thorn Grove to figure out her next steps. She wished at once that Signa was still there to help her concoct a plan now that she suspected Everett. Yet she forced such thoughts from her mind as she instead found herself alone with Aris, unattended in the middle of the woods. One wrong rumor and she'd be as good as useless at helping free her father from prison. The last thing she needed was anyone suspecting she'd seduced the prince into speaking on his behalf.

"We ought to get back to the others," she urged, nudging her horse forward. "Anyone who sees us out here might think—"

"Be quiet." Aris slipped from his horse and tossed the reins to Blythe. She barely managed to catch them before they smacked her in the face. She very well almost throttled him with them before he whispered, "Something's nearby." Each of his steps was precise, trying to make as little noise as possible.

"You're probably hearing the hounds." Blythe scanned the forest for any hint of prying eyes. "We need to get back. There are things I have to take care of. . . ."

"Stop your muttering and *listen*."

She had half a mind to ignore his request and to take off with his own steed in tow, convinced he was toying with her. Yet Blythe gave him a single, begrudging chance, shut her eyes, and listened.

She heard the songs of the forest. A symphony of insect wings and chirping birds. The steady rhythm of a woodpecker high above, beating on the trees. A fluttering of the branches as birds flitted between them.

And somewhere beneath it all a quiet, chittering whine.

Blythe's eyes flew open. "What *is* that?"

Aris held out his hand, silencing her as he crouched and crept toward the direction of the noise. So deep into a thicket of trees did he venture that she nearly lost sight of him. Her horse blew a snort, as if sensing Blythe's unease and wanting no part of it. When the reservoir of her patience ran dry and she could no longer quell her curiosity, Blythe slid from the saddle and tied both horses to the sturdiest nearby branch.

She should have followed Eliza back to the manor. She should have used her illness as an excuse to try to speak with the staff and pry for more information about Everett. Instead, she was trotting after a prince through the woods, fully aware of what this would look like should anyone find them. She tried to be as mindful of her steps as he'd been, though, given the vast number of scattered twigs and bramble littering the ground, it was a more difficult task than she gave him credit for. She hiked her skirts to her knees, breathless and flushed with the effort by the time she found him several minutes later.

The last thing she expected to see was the prince on hands and knees in the dirt, his backside in the air as he reached into a tiny hole in the base of a tree.

"Brace me," Aris demanded.

Blythe flushed from head to neck. "I beg your pardon?"

"Believe me, love, if I was aiming to seduce you then you'd know it. Brace me so I can get hold of whatever's in there."

She opened her mouth, then pressed it shut with a huff. Checking once more that no one was near, Blythe moved behind him to settle her hands on his hips. Even if Aris himself appeared to have no shame, Blythe tried to keep her gaze averted from the trousers that fit around his thighs frustratingly well.

Aris grunted and dug around inside for a moment longer before he started to lean up, relying on her help to properly straighten. Only then did Blythe see the source of the noise—a tiny black fox, hardly even a kit. He held it out by the scruff, looking the poor creature over.

"There's blood on the ground," he said. "I'm surprised it managed to avoid the hounds."

Blythe's throat went tight. She had half a mind to push Aris aside and snatch the poor thing away from him, though what she'd do beyond that was a mystery. It wasn't as though she could take the creature back to Thorn Grove. Perhaps that would have been possible were her father still there, but Byron would have it thrown back into the forest the moment he saw it.

"Are you going to kill it?" she asked, unable to hide her unease. Though she understood that was the entire point of the day and that she had agreed to come, the whole thing felt hopelessly cruel.

Aris held the kit out toward her. "I hear some people like to wear them. Someone could make it into a scarf."

She blanched. "You wouldn't."

He drew the kit back into his chest, cradling it there as though it were a newborn child. "Of course I wouldn't. Do I look like a barbarian?" He brushed a hand down its dark fur, taking great care with his touch. "We can't just let the beast go. The hounds will find it in no time if it keeps making that awful noise. Besides, I don't think it's old enough to hunt for itself."

Blythe brushed a soft hand down the fox's back, careful to avoid touching the prince. "It's only making that noise because it's frightened. It can't help it."

"Frightened or not, it"—he paused and stretched the fox out again, inspecting its lower half—"excuse me, *she* is as good as dead if we leave her here."

Blythe's gaze flew upward, checking for any sign that he might be joking. Yet his too-bright eyes were as serious as ever, and already he was marching back to his horse. Blythe sighed and hiked up her skirts to follow him.

"You want to bring home a wild fox?" she asked.

"Would I be correct to assume that you've a carriage waiting for you at the Wakefields' manor?" He grimaced as the kit squirmed in his grip. "Be still and stop your fussing, you beastly thing." Despite the harshness of his words, Aris's voice was admiringly soft.

Blythe had to shake off her surprise before she could answer. "Of course. Though wouldn't you want to use yours—"

"And dirty it with a wild animal?" He looked back at her as though she'd sprouted a third eye. "I think not. Yours will do fine."

Blythe reeled in her temper, telling him only that he was horribly impolite for a prince, which he accepted as a compliment. She kept behind him with the horses in tow. The more she thought about his words, however, the more Blythe realized that she hadn't seen any carriage fine enough to belong to a prince when she'd arrived.

It made her wonder—where was the rest of the royal family? And why had she never heard of Prince Aris or the country of Verena before? She tried to remember whether she'd seen them the night of Aris's ball, though most of that night at Wisteria was a haze upon her memories. She remembered walking in. She remembered speaking with the prince and dancing with him... and then she remembered being back in the carriage with Signa, on their way home.

There were gaps in her memory she hadn't recognized before. Huge, glaring holes that filled her with unease.

"We can use my carriage," she said at last, forcing the words out. There wasn't enough time to muse over strange memory lapses and even stranger possibilities. Especially not when he might notice. "We'll drop the horses off with the groom and—" She cut off as she saw one of the Wakefields' stable boys bringing Eliza's horse into a stall. It seemed Eliza was too ill to continue her ride.

Perhaps it was because of everything she'd suffered through this past year, or because she knew that Eliza could very well be living with a killer, but something about the situation clawed at Blythe with a ferocity she couldn't ignore. She gripped the reins tight and hurried toward the manor, not waiting for Aris to protest as she called back to him, "Wait for me in the carriage! I'll be right behind you!"

THIRTY

Blythe

THE WAKEFIELD MANOR WAS NOT THE SORT OF PLACE ONE WOULD write home about. It was a stately building, well maintained and warmed by its rich tones and deep mahogany wood. Blythe had visited it several times over the years and was always underwhelmed by its simplicity. It had neither Thorn Grove's oddities nor the extravagant beauty of Wisteria Gardens. No fascinating art or scenery, or really anything to make it stand out or feel lived in. Disregarding its size, the manor was, simply put, a painfully ordinary home.

Blythe kept close to the walls as she slipped inside, walking on her toes so that the heels of her boots would not clack against the floor. Much of the staff was preparing for the men to return from the hunt. The butler barked orders, sending two young maids Blythe didn't recognize fleeing from the parlor with pillows in hand.

"Careful!" a feminine voice chided him. "We want to indoctrinate the poor girls, not send them running off in fear."

Blythe alerted at the voice as a short woman with rosy cheeks bustled out of the room with a serving tray in hand. It had been some time since Blythe had seen her, but she at once recognized her as Sorcha Lemonds, Eliza's lady's maid.

Blythe was halfway through deciding her next step when Sorcha spotted her and almost dropped her serving tray.

"Heavens, Miss Hawthorne! You're going to make an old woman catch her doom by skulking around in the corners like that. What are you doing here?" Her voice was sharp and abrupt, the words blending together in a uniquely northern accent that Blythe had always enjoyed listening to.

"Miss Wakefield and I were riding together when she took ill," Blythe said as she stepped away from the wall. "I came to check on her."

"No need to worry yourself. She's resting in her room. This bout will come and go like the rest of them."

"The rest of them?" Blythe stood a full head taller than the woman, and yet she was racing to keep up as the maid ascended the steps without spilling a drop of the tea she carried.

"Her headaches, dear. They're growing more frequent. I keep telling her to try and rest, but she only prattles on about needing to secure a good match her first year out. It's ridiculous, if you ask me. But does she listen? Of course not."

Only when the words were spoken aloud did Blythe realize that the past several times she'd seen Eliza, the young woman had been a sickly green or so ashen that she'd seemed ghostly, always complaining of a sour stomach. Her eyes immediately focused on the steam curling from the teapot.

They had never found the person responsible for poisoning Blythe. The staff had been culled, and eventually she was able to make a full recovery, but . . . what if the culprit had moved on to Eliza?

"She's still getting those?" Blythe was wading into unfamiliar waters, unused to this delicate extraction of information. She wanted to take Sorcha by the shoulders and demand answers, but the Wakefield family had always been so proper. One wrong move, and she was certain they'd enact some sort of polite protocol to toss her from the manor. "How long has she been having the headaches now? It seems like it's been ages."

"They started just before her uncle passed, though I swear on my late mother's grave that they've been worse since that night." The woman crossed herself. "I think it's the stress. I've never seen her in such a state."

Blythe pressed her trembling hands against her sides to keep them from being noticed. "Why don't I bring her the tea? If Eliza is feeling as down as you say, I'm sure she could use the company."

Sorcha's grip held tight as Blythe tried to pry the serving tray away. Though it was clear she wanted to deny Blythe's advance, a crash sounded from the kitchen. The maid squeezed her eyes shut, muttering words beneath her breath in a language Blythe didn't recognize before she handed over the tray.

"Very well, Miss Hawthorne. You remember where her room is?"

"Down the hall, third door on the right." Blythe flashed a smile she hoped was charming enough to keep Sorcha away before she hurried up the stairs. Only when certain she was alone did Blythe slump against the nearest corner, breathing in rasps. Her hands shook fiercely enough to clatter the teapot, and she had to sink down the wall and set it on the floor before the noise summoned anyone.

Blythe knew in her bones that she had no choice but to test the tea. Yet despite her efforts, her hammering heart had her pulling back each and every time she tried to pick up the teacup.

"Do you always hide in random halls of homes that are not yours, Miss Hawthorne?"

Blythe started at Aris's voice, jerking upright so quickly that she nearly knocked over the teapot and had to quickly grab it by the spout. She winced when its heat seared her palms. "What are you doing here? Where's the fox?"

"She's asleep in the carriage. The driver didn't wish to leave without you, so I waited ten minutes before I came to gather you myself. What are you doing?"

Blythe could see how badly she was shaking and knew there was no point in lying. If Aris had one redeeming quality, it was that he had not been in Celadon when she'd gotten sick, which meant that he couldn't have been the one behind the poisoning. If she was going to safely confide in anyone, it may as well be him.

"Not long ago, I was unknowingly poisoned." She curled in on herself, the very thought of poison resurfacing some forgotten trauma she'd buried deep in her body. "I'm worried the same thing is happening to Eliza."

Aris pursed his lips. "If it is, would you be able to recognize the taste? Or perhaps even the smell?"

The very thought of smelling belladonna turned her stomach.

She pressed a hand to it, fighting back her nausea. "I can't even pick up the pot to pour it."

"You'd be able to recognize it, though, if you tasted it?"

In any other moment, she might have laughed at the ridiculousness of such a question. "I don't think I could ever forget it."

Instead of a reply, the sound of pouring liquid had Blythe unfurling long enough to watch as Aris poured a swig's worth of tea into the cup. He was careful to keep it at a distance from Blythe as he swirled it.

"You want to try it," he whispered. "Don't you?"

Needed was more accurate. Because if it *was* poison, Blythe didn't want Eliza to suffer as she had. She tried again to reach for the cup, but still her hands refused to move. Observing her struggle, Aris asked, "If you didn't have to drink it from a cup, do you think you could do it?"

She swallowed, imagining the idea. When her mind didn't immediately reject it, she roused a little. "Perhaps? I'm not sure."

Again he swirled the cup, lips pressed into a thin line. "If I said I had an idea that might help you, would you wish to try it?"

She had no need to think before responding, "I would."

The answer had barely left her mouth before Aris tipped the cup to his lips and took the swig. Blythe bolted upright, about to demand that he spit it out when he took one side of her face in his hand and drew her into him. Blythe realized what was happening the second before he kissed her.

Her body drowned in the heat of him, tiny electric currents jolting up her spine as his tongue slipped between her lips.

Aris didn't taste of belladonna, but of warm ginger and honey. And good God was it delicious. It was a conscious effort to not let her tongue move against his, and to remember that this was no kiss. He was *helping* her. And yet, while she didn't mean for it to happen, she sighed against his mouth. The second she realized her slipup, Blythe jerked away, mortified.

She collected the teacup and the pot at once, settling everything back on the tray where it belonged.

"Thank you." Her voice was brisk as she stood, scooping up the tray. "I-it's only ginger." Though Blythe was doing her best to avoid looking at Aris, it was impossible not to see the smugness in his grin.

"I'm glad to hear it."

"Good," Blythe continued for no other reason than that she could not help herself. "And you should know that it's been a long time since anyone has kissed me. You took me by surprise, that's all."

Aris had no right to be so amused, and yet he was practically gleaming. "It wasn't a kiss, Miss Hawthorne."

She had to turn away from him, refusing to let him see that she was flushed from the chest up. "Of course not. I have been kissed before, Your Highness. I know they usually elicit a more rousing response."

Aris's laughter ceased. "Of course they do," he said with the utmost defensiveness. "That's because this was not a kiss."

Blythe only shrugged, hoping she didn't look like she was sweating as much as she was. "If you don't mind, I need to deliver this to Eliza."

"By all means, don't let me stop you."

She didn't intend to. Before she let herself get any more distracted, she shoved past him and hurried toward Eliza's room, knocking on the door once, then twice when no response came.

"Open up, Auntie!" she called, knocking again. Still there was no answer. Blythe's heart was racing, lodged in her throat as she opened the door and prepared herself for the worst.

Fortunately, Eliza had not suffocated, nor had she died in a mess of her own vomit like Blythe had once nearly done. Instead, she was asleep on her bed, above the sheets and still fully dressed. On the nightstand sat a small jar of laudanum.

Blythe let herself feel the weight of her exhale leaving her chest. Eliza wasn't dead or poisoned; the laudanum had just put her to sleep. Perhaps it truly was a passing illness; something entirely unrelated to poison. Blythe set the tea down on a table as something gave her pause.

Clutched in Eliza's hand, barely visible, was a tiny vial of half-consumed herbs. Not the kind prescribed by doctors, but the kind found in the very apothecaries that Eliza had always claimed to hate. Blythe reached for it, trying to get a better look. The moment her hand brushed against Eliza's, however, it was as though Blythe were thrust back weeks into the past, when she'd stared at Elaine's skeletal reflection in the mirror.

The Eliza before her was little more than a corpse of withered skin taut against sharpened bones. Blythe could do nothing but stare as a maggot curled over one of Eliza's hollow eye sockets, through her nose, then disappeared back into the corpse whose cheekbones were too gaunt and whose neck was twisted at an impossible angle.

There was something stirring within the depths of her body; a sickly and consuming presence that Blythe shut her eyes against.

It was a hallucination. It had to be. Eliza had been asleep, breathing contentedly only seconds before—

"Miss Hawthorne?" The prince's voice cut through her thoughts, and her eyes fluttered open. "Miss Hawthorne, are you well?"

Blythe forced herself to look at the bed, where Eliza was curled and resting peacefully. No bones. No hollow eyes or dark presence. Just a young woman in an enviously deep sleep.

Blythe gave herself fifteen seconds to memorize what the contents of the vial looked like, and then she stepped away from Eliza and took the prince by the wrist.

"Come on," she whispered, not daring to spare Eliza so much as another glance before hurrying from the room. "Let's get out of here."

THIRTY-ONE

EVEN WITH THE SKY AS GRIM AS IT WAS, THE TOWN AT THE BASE OF Foxglove's cliffs, Fiore, was busier than Celadon had ever been.

Men strolled the streets with faces less severe than those that Signa had grown accustomed to, untroubled by the business that awaited their return in the city. Courting couples out for a seaside promenade stopped to enjoy slices of sunshine that cut through the gray clouds, their voices jovial.

For all the doom and gloom of Signa's arrival, Fiore was truly lovely. Not even the unsettled sea was enough to dissuade those who hurried down the street to the pier, eager to soak up their trip for every ounce of its worth. Signa had spent a solid ten minutes standing on the pier herself, staring at the ocean but not daring to venture onto the sand for fear that a wave might whisk her away. Perhaps she'd visit the water in the summer calm; for now, though, she wasn't foolish enough to venture close.

Fishermen were coming in from the docks, their heads bowed as they spoke softly to one another. Signa caught snippets of their conversation.

"She's out there on the beach again..."

"... doesn't understand he's not coming back."

"Poor thing. My son knew him. I couldn't imagine..."

Signa pulled her attention away from the conversation as curiosity began to fester. She didn't need to muddy her mind with anything more than what was already going on. And so she focused her thoughts on how beautiful this beach would be come wintertime, so cold that the buildings themselves would quiver. A pleasant buzz warmed her skin as she pictured nights spent lounging by the hearth with a book and a mulled cider.

Her parents had been wise to put down roots in such a place—twenty years later the town was magnificent. She'd never been seaside before, and there was an indescribable charm to having one's hair tousled by the wind and every sound dampened by the rush of waves and the wind in her ears. Every moment she spent here, it felt more like home. So far that day, she'd managed to go an entire hour without thinking of Thorn Grove and wondering how Blythe was faring.

From the pier Signa had only to cross the street to arrive at her destination—a tiny printing press in a building of dark green, where a man was hard at work behind a window. Smoke from a cigar the man had tipped precariously in his mouth plumed the air, and she tried not to cough as she stepped inside.

The man's eyes barely lifted. "We're out of papers for the day, come back tomorrow." His voice was brisk as he rolled fresh ink over blocks of letters. Signa couldn't help but stare as he worked.

"I don't need a paper," she began, holding out her ad. "I live in the manor at the top of the hill. I'd like to place an advertisement to staff it."

The man arched a brow and took the sheet from Signa, skimming over it once. "Foxglove?" Surrounded by words as he was, the man didn't seem interested in speaking many of his own.

"I'm Signa Farrow," she said by way of answer, trying not to be put off by the way he huffed under his breath.

"Three pennies and it'll be in next week's paper."

Signa stilled. That was far too long to go without adding more living souls into Foxglove. "How much for tomorrow?"

The man paused to look her over, searching her left hand for a ring. He grunted when he didn't see one. "A half crown."

He turned back to his work then, and Signa tried not to bristle at his obvious dismissal. A half crown was a right and proper fraud, and yet Signa reached into her coin purse all the same and lay the coin flat on the table.

The man didn't reach for it right away, puffing on his cigar as he pulled a metal lever down, lifted it back up, rolled letters with ink, and repeated the process. "What happened up there changed this town forever. We lost parents. Grandparents. Daughters and sons. It's a damn miracle that someone hasn't burned that place to the ground. It's not meant to be lived in, girl. They say only ghosts live there, now."

Signa didn't expect to be hit by such a wave of resentment, or a fierce protectiveness over a place she was only now learning to call home. Still, it swelled within her, making her blood hot and her glare livid. As well as she'd been containing herself, she had half a mind to show this man what spirits were truly like. Fortunately, she had the wits to throw her attention elsewhere until she could de-escalate.

Across the street, two bickering children fisted sweets in their tiny hands as they followed a beautiful woman in an ivory gown and a wide-brimmed hat adorned with a blue ribbon. All three of them seemed entirely unaware of the young boy lingering behind them, to whom Signa's attention was drawn toward at once. He couldn't have been older than eleven and was drenched to the bone. His hair was plastered to his round cheeks, too bloated. His skin was gray, and his lips purple and quivering as he followed the family.

Signa's spine went rigid as the boy stopped. As if he felt her staring, he whipped to face her. His body faded from her view the second after their eyes met, and he flickered in and out of her vision until he was suddenly standing on the opposite side of the shop's window. Hollow eyes never straying from hers, the boy waved.

Signa had never seen a drowned spirit before. Had never seen bloated skin or water pooling from lips embedded with barnacles, made so much worse by the fact that he was a *child*. She clutched her reticule tight as the boy backed away, motioning for her to join him.

"Thank you for your concern," she hurried to tell the shopkeeper. "But I don't need anyone to tell me what a tragedy it was. I lost people that night, too. Now, if you'll excuse me."

Signa knew full well how odd she must have looked to anyone watching as she threw the door open and sprinted down the pier, following the boy. All the while the fishermen's words from earlier rang in her head—a woman looking at the tides and a boy who wasn't coming back. Not a sailor, as she'd thought at the time, but a child.

This close to the sea, wind lashed water and salt upon her, plastering Signa's hair to her neck. She barely caught herself from slipping on slick planks by grabbing hold of a splintered ledge. Farther and farther the spirit continued, and Signa ignored all curious looks as she followed him to the end, to where a woman sat alone, her bare feet dangling over the pier as she stared ahead without any obvious awareness of Signa approaching.

"You can see me.... But you're not like me, are you?"

Signa stilled at the sound of the boy's voice. He didn't *sound* waterlogged. He didn't sound bitter or frightening, or anything like how he looked. Signa forced herself to look back at him—to see past the horror and crouch to his level as she whispered, "I'm not."

The spirit exhaled, relieved. *"Then can you tell her something for me? I want her to know that she doesn't have to keep coming here. It wasn't her fault, and every time I see her here... I just don't want her to be sad."*

There was something about the boy's request that reminded Signa of the night Lillian had passed from this world. Through Signa, she'd been able to communicate with Elijah and let him know that she loved him, and that it was time for them to all move forward.

It hadn't been easy, but it was what they'd both needed. Only after that goodbye was Lillian able to pass on, and Elijah had finally been able to put the scrambled pieces of his life back together. If that was a gift that Signa could grant to someone else... how could she say no?

Squaring her shoulders, she crossed to the edge of the pier and took a seat beside the woman. "I know what I'm about to say may sound strange, but I have a message for you."

There was tremendous sadness in the woman's eyes. She didn't acknowledge that Signa had spoken.

Nerves crawled along Signa's skin, telling her to leave before she made this situation worse. But the moment she thought those nerves might get the best of her, a cool breeze settled over her. Death's arrival came as a kiss of wind against her cheek, bracing her. She tried to settle into the knowledge that he was with her as she worked up the confidence to tell the woman, "Your son doesn't want you coming here anymore. He wants you to know that this wasn't your fault, and that it hurts him to see you so upset."

"Tell her it was a riptide," said the spirit as Signa relayed. *"I know I shouldn't have been out. I'm sorry."*

Halfway through that final word, Signa careened back as the woman landed a sharp slap. The ocean thrashed around them, the wind howling its rage as Signa doubled over, cupping her stinging cheek as the woman gathered her boots and stood.

Signa drew her hand from her aching face, grateful for Death's chill as the wind soothed her skin. There were tears in her eyes from the sting of the slap, but one look at the boy's urgent expression had Signa pressing on. "Your son is wearing a white shirt and dark trousers. He doesn't have any shoes on, and there's a scar on the top of his left foot—"

"From when George and I tried to climb the rocks!"

"—from when he tried to climb the rocks with George." Signa wrapped her hand around the ledge and hauled herself to her feet. Across from her the woman trembled, boots slipping from her hands. One of them hit the ledge before slipping into the sea.

"If you think this is a joke—"

"I assure you I don't," Signa promised, watching as black tears rolled down Henry's waterlogged face and he smiled, skin pulling around the barnacles in his cheek.

"Tell her that I miss her."

Word for word, Signa did as the spirit instructed. She no longer had any awareness of her surroundings as she held the woman's hand and relayed every message, letting the woman cry until the words were gone and the skin around Henry's face began to smooth as the barnacles fell to the pier with a quiet clack.

"He's ready, now," Signa told the woman as the sky grew dark around them. "It's time to say goodbye." There was a sense of relief with those words. Relief that Henry wouldn't spend years haunting this beach, watching his mother grow old and pass on before he did. He wasn't yet caught in a loop of his death like the poor spirits of Foxglove, lost in a middle land between life and death where he would eventually lose all sense of self. He'd just needed a person who could help him, and now both he and his mother could finally be set free.

Signa held on to the woman as Death swept around them. And though she could not see him, she knew he was there when the child looked up and smiled, extending his hand.

Seconds later Henry was gone, and despite the night's chill and the woman who sobbed in her arms, Signa had never felt so warm.

THIRTY-TWO

Blythe

If it was discovered how Blythe spent the morning of her father's sentencing, Byron would have had her locked away in the bowels of Thorn Grove for all eternity.

"I may not be a gentleman," said William Crepsley as he opened the carriage door, "but I know a lady like you shouldn't be here alone."

"I'm not alone at all, Mr. Crepsley. I've got you here." Blythe wasn't permitted to attend the morning's trial, but she refused to spend hours holed away in her room, waiting for Byron to return with the verdict. Being alone didn't suit her these days; she found her mind too full for comfort.

Everett had motive, yet she needed more evidence if anyone was to believe he was involved. Eliza was ill enough that she was taking something from an apothecary she'd once loudly condemned. Signa suspected Byron and had made sure Blythe knew it before she left.

And Blythe was once again seeing things. There was no time to sort out any of it.

Blythe had already spent hours in the library this week, trying to identify what herbs Eliza was taking. She'd been able to make out only mugwort—usually used to alleviate cramping during a woman's cycle—and tansy, used for many things, including relieving headaches. Blythe had tried to research more the night prior, but each time she pulled the pages closer to the candlelight to read, the flame would wink out. It took several attempts at relighting it for Blythe to understand that the snuffed candle could be no coincidence, and to abandon everything as she fled the library.

Which led her to where she was now: in desperate need of a backup plan.

Wisteria Gardens loomed over her, massive and lovely. It looked even more elegant in the sunlight than the first time she'd seen it and seemed much more sprawling without the mass of bodies making their way inside.

Blythe hadn't allowed herself to think too long on her plan, for fear she might talk herself out of it. When Byron headed off to the hearing, she'd washed up, changed into a pretty gown of dusty rose, and snuck out of Thorn Grove. William hadn't given any protest. Even if he'd thought her destination strange, he didn't voice that opinion when she pressed three silver coins into his palm. Not until now, when it seemed he was realizing just what he'd gotten himself into.

Blythe faced him and said without the slightest hint of jest, "If my uncle finds out where you've taken me, he'll have you gone from

Thorn Grove by morning. So let's both play our parts and keep this adventure between you and I, yes?" William was a kind man, though kindness did her little good these days. She turned back to Wisteria without waiting for his response, ensuring that her dress and gloves were both smooth before she made her way toward the palace.

Blythe hadn't been to enough palaces to know how they operated, but it seemed that there should at least be a valet, or someone ready to greet her. As it was, no one approached as she climbed the stairs to the ornate golden doors and knocked.

A minute passed, then another. Blythe bit back her frustration. She hadn't spent all that time readying herself—and doing it alone, given she no longer had a lady's maid and was too stubborn to ask anyone else for help—nor had she paid Crepsley and forced him to risk his position just for Prince Aris not to be home.

She scowled and knocked again, harder this time, and longer. So long that she gave up on the knocker entirely and beat against the door until her knuckles ached. She was just about to pull her poor hand away when the door swung open.

Prince Aris didn't look nearly as surprised to see her as Blythe did him. She stumbled back as his hulking figure observed her from the threshold. "May I help you?"

The answer caught in her throat, so she asked instead, "Why are you opening your own door?"

Prince Aris leaned against the frame and crossed his arms. "Is a man not allowed to answer the door of his own home?"

"No," Blythe said hastily, then grimaced. "I mean yes, he is, of course. It's just that you're a *prince*. My father never even answers the door of Thorn Grove himself."

"Is that so?" Again, Blythe was struck by the oddity of his eyes, such an impossible shade of gold. They were as unnerving as Signa's. "I sent the staff back to Verena. So many people aren't needed to care for a single man."

"You sent all of them?" she pressed. She'd never heard anything so absurd.

When Prince Aris cocked his head, Blythe feared he would shut the door in her face. It wasn't as though she was making pleasant conversation by continually insulting him, but nerves were getting the best of her. To her surprise, it seemed that the corners of the prince's lips quirked. Then, as if deciding he didn't care for it, Aris abandoned the expression.

He was every bit a prince as he assessed her—like a predator before its prey. A boot ready to squish an insect beneath it. Blythe could imagine how many people had shrunk back from those eyes; there was a second when even she felt the urge to. But she would be damned before a prince made her feel less than, and so she squared her shoulders and stared right back at him.

He ran a hand down his jaw, smoothing out the tension of his clenched teeth. "I kept a cook, the butler, and someone to care for the horses."

Though Blythe couldn't place why, it felt as though she'd won some miniature battle that was warring between them, and victory had her puffing her chest as Prince Aris extended a hand into Wisteria.

"Shouldn't the butler be answering the door?"

"Have you come all this way to offend me," he asked, "or do you intend to come inside?"

All at once, Blythe's heart was in her throat. No matter how many scenarios she'd envisioned for today, none of them had been of Wisteria so empty, or the two of them so thoroughly *alone*. A single butler, a cook, and a groom she'd likely not see in a palace this large meant nothing. Anyone who discovered her whereabouts would surely assume that Blythe's visit could mean only one thing, though she couldn't let that sway her. Not with the stakes being what they were.

Aris was a *prince*. Blythe had seen firsthand the power he held over others, and the way people clung to his every word. He had gotten her and Byron a visit with her father on no notice. If he could do that, then she could only imagine what else he could manage.

"What's wrong, love?" Aris cast her a look from over his shoulder, eyes glittering. "Afraid I'll ruin you?"

She wasn't afraid. Not of him, at least. And so she clenched her fists, sent William a firm look to tell him to remain exactly where he was, and followed Prince Aris inside and to a parlor warmed by the largest hearth she'd ever seen, several times her height. He motioned for her to take a seat on a plush leather sofa and sat across from her.

A tray of tea was already on the table between them, filled with light sandwiches and pastries, and to her surprise, a second porcelain teacup.

Her skin prickled as he poured steaming tea into the cup and handed it to her. Blythe didn't drink it immediately but made a show of adding a splash of milk. She kept her eyes on him all the while, waiting until he took the first drink before she tested a small sip.

Black tea. Simple, and without a trace of belladonna. She exhaled a relieved breath as steaming tendrils spread across her skin. It wasn't that she expected the prince to try to poison her, but one could never be too careful with whom they trusted.

Aris cast her the most peculiar look before he leaned back on the couch and folded one leg over the other. The smallest sliver of his ankle was visible, and Blythe did her best not to pay it any attention. It was strange how scandalous such a small slice of skin could seem when it was just the two of them.

The tea was warm in her hands, and she used the heat of it to reel herself in as she straightened and began, "I apologize for an unprompted visit. I was hoping that I might speak to you about—"

"About your father." Blythe flinched as Prince Aris tapped his spoon along the side of the cup, the clanging too loud for such a quiet space. "I'm no fool, Miss Hawthorne. It can be no coincidence that you've decided to pay me a visit the day of his sentence."

She pressed her lips into a thin line and set her cup on its saucer. "I know you never had the opportunity to meet my father, but I believe you'd quite like him. He's had a rough year, but I assure you he's innocent. He just needs an advocate."

"You assure me, do you?" Prince Aris spoke with such amusement that Blythe had to dig a nail into her palm to remind herself not to react. "No offense, Miss Hawthorne, but I hardly know either of you. Even if your father is the wonderful man you claim, I'm sure you can see what inserting myself into this situation could do to my reputation should your *assurances* prove false."

She'd expected this was coming. What reason would a prince have to assist two strangers? It was a fool's errand to come to Wisteria, but she'd had to try.

She had seen Aris take only a sip or two, and yet he'd already poured more tea and stirred in another sugar cube. Blythe's world was crumbling around her, fraying and burning at the edges, and he was taking his tea without a care in the world.

"Reconsider," she said, not a question but a plea. "I know he means nothing to you, Your Highness, but he means everything to me. I beg you to reconsider."

The veins in his forearm pulsed as he took another sip from a teacup that was laughably small in his hands, looking this time as though he didn't care for its flavor. He opened his mouth to respond. To tell her no, surely. But Blythe didn't give him the chance. She stood, damning all embarrassment or propriety, and put everything she had on the line.

"You came here looking for a wife." She didn't dare allow her voice to break, even with the emotion churning within her. There'd be time for it later, once she was alone in her room and all her options had been explored. "In return for helping my father, take me."

It was as though the hearth itself stilled as the palace grew quiet, its crackling silenced for the single breath it took for Prince Aris to throw his head back and laugh. It wasn't a cruel sound so much as surprised, but Blythe could feel the heat of shame spreading through her all the same.

"I'm perfectly eligible," she defended. "My family has money and status, and I know how to maintain a household. I'm certain I could learn to maintain a palace as well. I'm not the best with stitching, I admit, but I can play the pianoforte and the harp, and I'm not at all bad with a paintbrush. I'm also great company for outings and can be immensely more charming than I've afforded you the luxury of experiencing."

Prince Aris let her speak until she was blue in the face, all but needing to gasp for air as she continued listing her merits. He propped his chin in his hand, making no motion for her to stop.

"I'm one of the season's most eligible. You can read about it in the papers. All you have to do is help clear my father's name," she said once she'd exhausted every good quality she could think of. Most of them, admittedly, were an overplay of the truth. While Marjorie *had* taught her the ins and outs of being a woman suitable to her status, Blythe had always believed she'd make a piss-poor wife. Not that he needed to know that.

"You do sound most impressive." The prince cleared his throat, and his amusement along with it. "Perhaps all that was true when those papers were written, but after the Lord Wakefield scandal, your eligibility is doubtful to say the least." His eyes trailed over her from head to toe, not so much leering as assessing. Yet when he spoke again, his voice sounded almost like a purr. "As flattered as I am, love, I cannot marry you. Though I might be willing to help you, for a price."

Blythe's blood ran cold, and she was unable to hide the sheer desperation stirring within her as she said, "Name it."

And so he did. "I cannot marry *you*, but I could marry your cousin."

Dread sank its claws into her. "Signa isn't an option."

"I understand you care for her—"

"You're wrong." Blythe hadn't intended for the words to be so harsh, yet she did not shy away from them. "I do not care one bit for Signa Farrow."

Aris leaned forward, elbows resting on his knees. "You two were thick as thieves the last time I saw you together."

Blythe knew she shouldn't give him the satisfaction of a response. Knew that if she tried to tell anyone the truth, they'd never believe her. She wanted to keep it tucked deep within her until she had sorted through her own feelings and knew what to do with them. She had every intention of doing just that and tried to tear her gaze from Aris. Yet her neck ached the moment she glanced away, her movements slow and stiff.

She set a hand against her neck, massaging it, but the stiffness refused to leave until she looked back at him. It was as though her gaze was being pinned forward. As though something demanded that her attention stay with the prince.

"What changed, Miss Hawthorne?" His words echoed, as though the two of them sat a great distance apart. Her eyes locked to his, mesmerized by the depth of their gold. She blinked, and the entire room filled with the color, casting Aris in a hazy glow.

"You'd never believe me if I told you." Blythe spoke without any sense of her lips moving.

She couldn't control herself, unable to look away as Aris whispered, "You've no idea the impossibilities I believe."

She couldn't say no. Blythe sat rigid in her seat, mind numbed and with only a vague understanding that this conversation was happening. She was coherent. She was *there*. But she had no control over herself as the words were coaxed from her. "I watched her kill a foal... and then I watched as she brought it back to life. She did the same thing to my brother, though he was left for dead."

Only then did Blythe reclaim herself, the fog dissipating from her mind. She was sweating profusely and grabbed a handkerchief from the table. Slowly, carefully, she allowed herself to glance up to see that the fox kit they'd rescued earlier that week had jumped onto the chair beside Aris, and that the man's hand had stilled upon it. He didn't seem to be breathing.

She must have been feverish. That was the only way to explain the strange mistiness over her thoughts, or why she'd been foolish enough to let even a word slip, let alone the entire truth about Signa. Her hands clasped in her lap, a leg bouncing beneath her skirts as her mind worked to unravel what to do next. What to say.

"You're certain you saw her do that?" Never had she heard Aris speak as quietly as he did then, nor seen his eyes so gentle.

"I was only joking," she tried, hoping her voice sounded even half as amused as she tried to make it. "It was nothing as serious as that, it was just time for her to leave—"

His entire body had gone rigid, and Blythe realized with a rush of terror that he knew the truth. She tried to make herself smaller beneath the weight of a stare that frightened her to her core. Around Aris the golden haze flickered once more, gone one moment only to reappear when she blinked.

"You believe me." Blythe whispered those words aloud several times before she could convince herself of that reality. "You believe me... because you're like her, aren't you?"

God, what a fool she'd been not to see it sooner. While Signa had been trailed by shadows and darkness, Aris radiated light. He wasn't surprised because he'd *expected* this. Blythe would never have offered up all her truths to him on her own accord. He'd drawn the words from her. Forced her to speak them into existence.

"Touch me, and I will kill you." It was a weak threat, given that she had not a single weapon on her, but Blythe poured as much belief into those words as she could. She'd take the pins from her hair and stab them into his throat if she had to. "What did you do to me?"

Aris started to lean even closer, only for Blythe to kick his knee, startling the fox awake. Aris hissed a breath, doubling over while Blythe leaped from her chair and circled behind it, plotting her next ten steps.

"Stay where you are." She assessed their shared space for anything she could use against him. A poker from the hearth. The shard of a broken teacup she could smash against his skull. "What is Signa, and what are you? And you'd better explain to me why in the bloody hell you're *glowing*."

"You can see that?" Aris sounded surprised enough that Blythe tensed, wondering if he was plotting something. "It's not a glow. They're threads, Miss Hawthorne. Look closer."

She didn't want to take her eyes from his again, every part of her tensed and ready to spring should he try anything. But Aris, to his credit, kept remarkably still. It took at least a full minute before Blythe listened, turning her attention back to the glow and staring.

Blinking. Staring again. Her vision swam if she looked at any one spot around him for long, yet she held her eyes open until they were dry, just barely able to see one of the threads, then two, before everything became hazy again.

"Three times you have knocked upon Death's door." The coolness of his whisper sent a long chill feathering down Blythe's spine. "Three times you have defied your fate. It would seem that each of those three times was not without lasting effect."

"I don't care for riddles." She decided that the moment he looked away, she would snag the poker. "Answer my question. Who *are* you?"

The way Aris watched her would have someone thinking he'd never seen a woman before. He scrutinized her face. Her hair. The way she shielded herself behind the chair, creating a barrier between them. It was as if he were seeing her for the first time.

"I am not a who so much as I am a *what*," he admitted, and already Blythe was cringing, unable to believe she'd allowed this man's lips to ever touch hers. "If I had to guess, it seems that after you died all those times, you earned the ability to catch glimpses behind the veil."

"More riddles." She no longer bothered to wait for him to turn away and made a grab for the poker. She held it into the flames, heating the metal without ever breaking eye contact. "What veil? And *what* are you, then?"

There was a grandness in the way he watched her, like a lord assessing his people. The look crawled over her skin, and in that moment Aris felt so much larger and more severe.

"The veil is what separates the world of the living from everything beyond."

His clipped response was not what Blythe had been expecting. Her stomach clenched, mind working to find words. "What do you mean by *beyond*? Do you mean to tell me that I'm seeing the dead?"

"Not at all. I mean that you're seeing things that living people cannot." Blythe had every urge to kick him again for his nonsense, though this time she managed to refrain. "If you could see the dead, you'd already know. Your cousin is followed by shadows because she is a reaper. When she wills it, her touch is lethal."

Blythe had already known this much from seeing Signa's power in action. It was the fact that Aris was the one answering that sent Blythe's heart spiraling, quickening her breath and making panic rise in her throat.

"Sometimes I see more than shadows beside Signa. I used to see her speak to them, and thought I was ridiculous and imagining things. But there's someone else, isn't there? Someone I can't see."

Aris's jaw tightened as the fox shifted out of his lap and moved instead to nestle beside him. "There is. But are you certain you want to know who it is?"

She had her suspicions, and though she wasn't certain that she wanted to hear the words aloud, Blythe forced herself to nod all the same.

"It's Death himself that you've seen," Aris said, his jaw flexing when Blythe stopped breathing.

Signa had spoken to that figure so tenderly. So *lovingly*.

"They're together, aren't they?" So light-headed was she that Blythe had to brace herself. "Is he why she's like this? Is he why she killed my brother?"

Aris stood so quickly that Blythe barely had time to brandish the poker, its white-hot tip a mere inch from his throat. He glared down at her, as still as marble.

"With Death, your cousin is a reaper. With him, she will take the very lives she was meant to create. But with me, she could be so much more. That's why I'm trying to save her, Miss Hawthorne." Aris held his hands up, placating Blythe when she drew back. "All we have to do is convince her of that truth."

"Can you do the same things she can?" Her voice was tight, and it took a great amount of will not to have it squeak. "Is that why you want to marry her?"

"It's the powers that gave life to the foal that I prefer. But no, I cannot do the same things she can. I can control fate. From the moment a person is born, I weave their fate onto a tapestry. I can alter them, too."

Signa must have known the truth. It's why she'd tried to keep Blythe from Wisteria and why she'd had such a severe reaction to Blythe being near Aris. Signa had known, and she'd never told her.

"So you *are* the one responsible for what happened to my father?" The question fractured in her throat, and Aris frowned at such a pathetic sound.

"That's like asking if I'm responsible for every time the earth quakes or a person catches a cold. Perhaps to some degree I am, but I didn't force this to happen, and I've no vendetta against you or your family. I do not meddle in the affairs of humans when I can avoid it."

"But you know what will happen to him. Don't you?" Never had she looked at someone so closely, as if trying to read his very soul for confirmation of her suspicions. Though he gave no answer, the pity in his eyes told her enough.

Blythe let the poker drop to the floor. She wound her arms around her stomach, fighting to hold herself in while the truth shattered around her.

"You're going to need my help, Miss Hawthorne." Blythe hated how desperately she clung to each of Aris's words, and she knew in that moment that should Aris ask for the sun, she would find a way to give it to him. For her father, Blythe would give everything.

"Today, your father will be sentenced to hang. He'll have two weeks to live before they come for him—two weeks for you to get me Miss Farrow's hand. If you do, I promise that Elijah Hawthorne will be spared." As if from thin air, Aris produced a small piece of what appeared to be a golden tapestry, which he handed to her. It was warm to the touch, and so uncomfortably strange—almost alive—that she had to fight the urge to drop it. The longer she stared at it, the brighter the threads became, a halo of gold surrounding them when she squinted.

"What is this?" She stroked her thumb across the threads, tensing when she noticed that Aris shuddered. He reached forward to touch her gloved hand, stilling it around the tapestry.

"The deal will be made when Miss Farrow places a drop of her blood upon those threads. It will bind her as my wife, though the offer must be made willingly."

Blythe wanted so badly to hate Signa for what she'd done to her family, and yet... maybe none of this was Signa's fault. Maybe she'd had no choice in taking Percy, and Death was to blame.

Blythe had lost a brother, but she would not lose her father. And perhaps... perhaps she did not have to lose her cousin, either.

Tucking the tapestry against her chest, Blythe took her first easy breath in months. And with her exhale she made a bargain with Fate.

THIRTY-THREE

TWO DAYS HAD PASSED SINCE SIGNA HAD HELPED HENRY MOVE ON to the afterlife.

She'd returned to Foxglove, unable to focus on anything but the comforting warmth spreading through her despite being windswept with her cheeks reddened from the thrashing gale.

Yet the happier and more settled she became in her new home, the guiltier she felt as the days continued to tick by without any reprieve for Elijah. Why should she feel at peace when he was still trapped in a cell, curled on the cold stone floor and alone in the darkness? Death had been watching over him, ensuring there was no more abuse and that Elijah at least received his meals, but it wasn't enough. With every passing day, she felt further from the truth than ever.

She had to *do* something, which was why she stood in the garden, her fingertips resting on the twig of a juniper bush.

"Are you sure you weren't simply imagining that you have other

powers?" Amity asked from where she lay on a blanket of poppies, her hair strewn about the flowers. *"You've been trying for an awfully long time."*

Considering that the sun was headed west and Signa had been out there well since dawn, that was an understatement. As she crouched before the dried juniper and gripped its naked branches, she willed the powers of Life to fill her. Yet every time she tried, the blood in her veins thrummed with longing for her reaper powers, instead. Her body was overly aware of all the souls that waited inside, pulled toward them now more than ever since that night with Henry. She tried to ignore their calls, for it was Life's powers that she needed, not the reaper's.

Elijah's verdict would be read any minute, and should the worst happen, she would be there. Forget finding the murderer—she would make whoever it was irrelevant. Should Elijah Hawthorne be sentenced to hang, Signa would use Life's powers to ensure he would not stay dead for long.

It was a secret hope, made of nothing but dying embers. But for Elijah Hawthorne, this was the least she could do.

"Grow," Signa urged the frail juniper bush. "Grow, you silly little thing." Her eyes bore into the branches for one minute. Two. By the third she groaned and fell back on her blanket, wishing to roll herself in it like a cocoon and mope in that very spot.

Amity propped herself onto her elbows, watching. *"You're just as dramatic as your mother."*

"Oh? Did you ever watch my mother try to bring the dead back to life?"

Amity pursed her heart-shaped lips, twirling a ringlet around one finger. *"I can't say that I did."*

"Then I don't want to hear it." Signa curled her fingers in the blanket for the sole purpose of not tearing them through her hair. "There has to be something I'm missing. There are conditions I must meet first if I'm to use my powers as a reaper. Perhaps there are conditions for Life's powers, too." Or perhaps she was simply too afraid of the pain to allow herself to access them, for every time she tricked her mind into believing she was close to unlocking them, she'd clam up in anticipation of the oncoming pain.

"What about when you've used them in the past?" Amity asked, wisps of her body fading and then resurfacing as a breeze blew by. *"Was there any constant?"*

It was a good thread, and one that Signa pulled on, sorting through the memories. Both times she'd used her powers, there had been heat. Sweltering, blistering heat that felt like she'd fallen into a furnace.

Signa stood at once. She gathered up her blanket and tucked it under her arm, wondering how close she could get to Foxglove's hearth without melting herself. Anything was worth trying at this point.

"Have you got another idea?" Amity hopped to her feet, shifting so close to Signa that had it been anyone else, the proximity would have been unnerving. Yet Amity had become her most favored company over the past few days. And though Signa tried to keep away and remind herself how unwise it was to get close to a spirit, Foxglove felt far too empty without Amity's happy chatter.

"I do. Follow me." Signa snapped two twigs from the juniper bush before she hurried into Foxglove, relieved to find that the maid had already tended to the hearth and that Gundry was curled beside it. Signa checked over her shoulder before she sat and scooted so close to the flames that they nearly licked the toes of her boots. Amity lingered behind, floating several inches higher than normal to get a good view. Signa leaned in and shuddered as the warmth devoured any last tendrils of cold flooding through her. Cupping one of the snapped twigs in her palms, she shut her eyes and focused with everything in her.

"Grow." As often as she'd said that word over the past two days, it was almost a chant at this point. "Grow, grow, grow, grow—"

"I'm a little confused... Are you trying to burn them?"

"I'm trying to burn *myself,* relatively speaking." Signa had to temper her annoyance, loosening her grip to avoid breaking the twig in half. "Haven't you anything better to do than watch me suffer? At this rate I'll be here all night."

Signa hadn't meant it cruelly, yet Amity's lips drew downward all the same.

"No," she whispered, voice fracturing. *"I do not have anything* better *to do."*

Immediately Signa regretted an entire lifetime of ever opening her mouth. Given that spirits operated on heightened emotions, Signa should have known better than to say anything. Amity had been alone just as many years as Signa had. Surely, she craved company, and what else was there for her to do?

As Amity's eyes pooled with bloody tears, Signa set the juniper twig aside and made her voice every bit as soft and placating as Death's.

"I didn't mean it like that. I'm glad for your company, Amity, truly."

Amity only sniffled, avoiding her stare.

"Who else would have waited twenty years just to make sure I was safe?" Signa pressed, trying not to consider how hard she was working to placate a spirit she'd sworn not to let herself get close to. "I appreciate you waiting, truly. But what would you have done if I'd never arrived?" *And what will you do now that I'm here?* was the question Signa didn't dare ask aloud. As much as Signa was growing to rely on the spirit's company, twenty years was a long time. Surely, Amity had to be curious about what came next.

"I never thought I'd have the chance to speak with you." Amity took a seat beside Signa on the edge of the hearth. *"I planned to leave once I saw you settled... though it wasn't only for you that I stayed. I'd hoped that the others would be out of their awful loops by now."* Amity's eyes lifted to the stairs, toward the ballroom.

Signa followed her gaze. "You care for that woman, don't you? For Briar?"

"More than words could ever describe." Amity's smile reminded Signa of the twig she held between her fingertips, poised to crack at the slightest pressure. *"But still she does not know it. I can't leave here without her."*

Signa had no question that, were she in Amity's position, she, too, would wander the halls for an eternity before she willingly left Death behind. What torture that would be—while Briar had no idea what was happening outside her loop, Amity spent her days aware of every moment. Signa's heart ached at the thought, and though she knew it was unwise to get involved, she couldn't help but think back to Henry.

Her mouth opened, and Signa was seconds away from making Amity a promise she wasn't sure she could keep when Death's chill frosted over the parlor, tamping the flames.

His presence was like none she was used to. This was no invitation to be swept away for a dance or to enjoy each other's company. This was the chill of a body buried six feet under—the chill of a Death she had met only once before, on the night he'd tried to take Blythe.

Though Signa could not see him, she knew in the marrow of her bones that something was horribly wrong.

"What is it?" The question sliced through her throat, because she already knew the answer. Even before Gundry pressed against her hip with a whimper and Amity's eyes turned to hollow, lifeless things, Signa knew.

"Elijah has been found guilty for the murder of Lord Julius Wakefield." Amity's voice rang as strong as a church bell, each word a strike that had Signa unsteady. *"He's set to hang in two weeks' time."* The spirit cast her eyes toward where Death's chill seeped into the earth. The floor beneath her was turning slick with frost.

Since the day she'd been banished to Foxglove, Signa had known this would happen. Still, she clung to the last piece of Death's news like it was a life raft—two weeks. She may not have made progress on summoning Life's powers yet, but she still had two weeks.

She needed only to ensure that they counted.

Signa almost missed the note tucked into Gundry's collar until the hound scratched at it, nails snagging against the parchment. Gently, she pried it from him. The note was not in Death's usual elegant font but in quickly scrawled letters.

Blythe has her eyes on the Wakefields. Charlotte and Everett have been courting for months—Lord Wakefield did not approve of an engagement.

Eliza has taken ill. I stayed with her overnight, though it doesn't appear that anyone is harming her.

Byron has kept to his study. He locked himself inside after the verdict was read and cried.

It was a relief that Death had kept his letter short and precise, for each of his facts struck like a blow to the stomach. There was one final line on the parchment, cleaner and more precise.

I love you, Little Bird. We're going to save him.

They would. They *had* to. Unfortunately, they could no longer do it alone.

Signa knew there was no getting around what came next. Knew there was no other choice as she told Death, "Find Fate, and bring him to me."

THIRTY-FOUR

Never had Foxglove felt so bright as it did in Fate's presence.

The sky was painted a brilliant cerulean as the sun bore down without a single cloud to shade its path. Gone were the cawing crows, replaced by seagulls whose squawking through the open windows had Signa trying not to flinch as she watched Fate saunter through her parlor, bending or crouching or lifting onto his toes to inspect every piece of art that he saw.

"What a peculiar style." It wasn't criticism, yet Signa bristled all the same. It didn't escape her notice that Fate was as well-groomed as the day she'd met him, looking every bit as regal as a prince. He was freshly barbered, his clothing pressed and his boots so glossy that Signa expected she'd be able to see her reflection in them.

Foxglove had never felt so much like the seaside summer manor she'd envisioned as it did with him roaming the halls, making the world so bright that Signa's temples throbbed. She'd grown used to dreary days when the hearth ran constant and found a familiar comfort within them; a peace that settled her bones and made her feel at home. She should have known Fate's arrival would destroy such a peace.

"Do you intend to give yourself a grand tour?" It was impossible to keep her hostility reined in. Signa hated the way he looked at Foxglove; hated how he inspected her family's belongings, just as she hated that every time she looked at him, Fate's face triggered the memory of a song she'd only recently managed to scrub from her mind.

"It *is* customary to show me around, though I suppose I can do without." He showed no awareness of Death, whose chill settled against Signa's skin, soothing her paranoia as Fate took a seat on a green velvet settee, crossing one leg over his knee and looking far more relaxed than Signa cared for. "I've wondered when you would reach out. I thought about visiting you myself, but knew it was only a matter of time before you'd decide to collect on our bargain."

Signa had always hoped that the person she fell in love with would have a family that she could call her own. When it came to Death's brother, however, she would have preferred to do without. "You knew I was at Foxglove all this time?"

"Not all of it, no." Signa had offered him no tea, and Fate's attention flicked down to the tea table in obvious offense. "Miss Hawthorne informed me rather recently. She told me other secrets, too, about the horse."

It was an effort to keep her face smooth of the surprise that stole her breath. Surely, Blythe wouldn't have told him such things; she barely knew Aris.

"I suppose this makes today's conversation easier, then." She fisted her dress when she caught herself picking at her cuticles. "I didn't invite you here to make good on our bargain. I called you here because I need a favor."

God, how she hated those words. Hated the gleam in his eyes as he tipped his chin to assess her.

"You know I don't give anything for free, Miss Farrow." He leaned against the cushion, propping his elbow on a pillow as Signa stepped from Death's comforting chill and crossed to him.

"I assure you that this is a bargain you'll like." She glanced once behind her, wishing more than ever that she could see Death's face in the shadows, needing his reassurance. Inviting Fate into Foxglove felt like slipping farther and farther from Death's reach, but what choice did she have? For Elijah—for Blythe—she had to try.

"I need you to teach me how to use Life's powers."

Signa expected his face to turn smug. Expected his grin to stretch, or for him to look toward his brother and say something that would turn the floor to ice. What she got instead was a man who straightened as she looked at him, wearing not a hint of smugness as he told her, "Nothing would make me happier."

Signa's rage had her holding her breath as she took in his tailored pants and strange billowing white top that didn't fit this era, and the earnestness on his face. She *wanted* him to be smug. Wanted a reason to despise him even while he was helping her. He was a bastard for giving her nothing.

"I may have Life's powers," she warned, "but nothing else has changed. I will not be made one of your toys, Fate. Do you understand?"

There was no nod. No argument. Fate only motioned to the cushion beside him and said, "Have a seat, Miss Farrow."

It took a moment before she did, pressed fully against the opposite end of the settee with her hands bundled in her lap.

"I can't promise to know everything about how it works." Fate's voice was smoother than ever and far more sincere than she'd been prepared for, each word echoed by the beat of the music Signa was trying to pry from her head. "I only know what you used to tell me—"

"*I* never used to tell you anything," she sniped. If he was looking for her to waver or to see what he might be able to get away with, she wouldn't allow him to find it so easily.

"*Life* told me." He plucked a withered rose from a vase on the tea table. "Unless you plan to argue with me through the evening, close your eyes and envision what you want this flower to turn into. Grow the vision like a seed in your mind, and then set your hand upon the stem."

She shut her eyes, opened one to confirm that he wasn't trying anything scandalous, then shut it again and filled her mind's eye with the image of a rose, its red petals plump and its thorns piercing enough to draw blood. She envisioned healthy green leaves and an unbendable stem. Once she was certain that the vision she wanted was at the forefront of her mind, she reached her hand out and let Fate press the rose into her palm. A thorn pressed against her skin, though it bent and flaked off without the slightest prick, not one drop of blood spilled.

Fate inhaled so sharply at their touch that for a moment Signa's vision splintered, though she gathered herself once more and curled her fingers around the rose. She waited. And waited. And waited until she could no longer take it and cracked one eye open.

"Nothing happened." Fate scratched at his jaw with one hand as he used the other to lift the rose up to investigate. "It hasn't grown one bit."

"I can see it just as well as you can." Signa opened her eyes fully. "If you weren't so noisy, perhaps I could have kept my concentration."

"*Noisy?* Explain to me how I could have possibly been noisy when all I did was hand you this emaciated rose. Why do you even *have* dead flowers in your home?"

"Do forgive me. I apologize that my mind has been preoccupied by the imminent death of my uncle when I should have instead been clipping fresh flowers in preparation of your arrival."

His scoff had enough force to carry through the room. Even the hearth's flames shuddered in his rage. "It's no wonder you and Miss Hawthorne were close. You're both barbaric. I cannot control my *breathing,* Miss Farrow, if that's what annoyed you. I may be immortal, but my body is still that of a living man's. I'm sorry to disappoint, but I am not like your precious Death."

Each of Signa's words was a blunt strike she knew she'd regret even before they were out of her mouth. "That *is* a disappointment. My night would be going so much better if you were."

"Oh? Then why don't you have him come and help you? He seems so useful, sulking in the corner."

Signa bristled. She should have known better than to ask Fate for his help. "If he knew, then I'm sure he'd teach me. Assuming you hadn't taken away our ability to speak, that is."

Fate's laughter was as cutting as Death's scythe as he bobbed his head, nodding along to her scorn. "Oh yes, *I'm* the villain. Tell me, Miss Farrow, do you not think it odd that you can only see him when you're nearly dead? Don't you find something inhumane about that? Your body is smart enough to know the danger, considering you're sick every time you touch him. Your hair is turning *silver,* for God's sake."

"Only because *you* decided to get involved in my love life!" She ignored the urge to tuck her silver strands out of sight. "How foolish I was to think you'd help me. Only someone truly horrible could create such a fate for Death and me. If you can control whether we can speak to each other, then surely you can also determine whether he and I *see* each other. If you truly cared about my happiness, then you would let me be with him. But you are a selfish man." This last part Signa spoke not with rage, but with defeat as she plucked the rose stem from his hand and brought it to her lap. In the quiet that spanned between them, Fate kept seated, drawing long breaths until he settled enough to speak.

"I will not deny such claims," he admitted, "nor do I have shame in them. I have waited far too long for the things I want; I will not pretend to be sorry when I take them." He was cracking like the finest china, and Signa wasn't sure whether to fear or pity the fire in his words.

"Do you know why I asked you here?" She looked at his hands as they folded and unfolded in his lap, seeking something to do. "I do not wish to learn these powers for *me.* I would be happy to live the rest of my life without ever using them, for the pain they cause is that severe. I brought you here because I am out of options. I wish to help Elijah, but I cannot be at Thorn Grove right now to find Lord Wakefield's murderer. The best thing I can do is be there if Elijah is hanged and learn how to bring him back from the grave."

Fate was not the only one to startle at this plan. Foxglove grew so cold that the hearth snuffed out entirely, and Gundry whined from his position curled near it. Fate glanced to the corner where Death stood, and for once it seemed it was not to fight him.

"Just as you cannot cheat Fate, you cannot steal from Death, Miss Farrow," he said. "Especially not those he has already claimed."

"But I will." It was not a threat so much as it was a promise. "Should Elijah be taken from me, I don't care what it takes. I've used Life's powers before, and I'll figure out how to do it again. If I cannot be at Thorn Grove—"

"What does it matter if you cannot *be* at Thorn Grove?" Fate waved a hand as he stood, and once again the flames of the hearth roared to life, if only to silence Gundry's protests. "You were barred from a *place,* not from its people. If that is the single obstacle you must overcome to keep yourself from doing something so remarkably foolish, then bring those people to you! A horse is one thing, but there will be repercussions beyond your wildest imagination should you bring a human life back from the grave."

"You've no idea how rampant my imagination can be."

His laugh was not one of humor, but one that had him throwing his hands into the air and spinning again to where Death stood.

Only this time as Signa followed his stare, she could see shadows writhing on the floor. Faintly at first, then darker, until she followed those shadows up to the frown that pulled Death's lips and the severity that lingered in his stare.

"Talk to her," Fate warned before he spun back to Signa. "I will not teach you to use your gifts if *this* is what you intend to use them for, you ridiculous girl. Unless you wish to bring Chaos upon us all, then learn the rules. They exist for a reason. I have no desire to see Elijah Hawthorne die, but if you plan to save him, you'll need to find another way."

"If you don't wish for him to die, then prove it," Signa challenged, and for a moment Fate stood still as if processing those words. "If you walk out of here now, I promise I will hate you forever. You said that you care for me, and if that's true, then *help* me. I cannot lose Elijah."

The man looked at war with himself, veins pulsing in his forearms as he clenched his hands. Eventually, he turned to Signa. "If you want my help, then throw a party." It was far from the response she expected, and Signa recoiled when Fate stepped so close that she could feel the warmth of his body press against her skin. "Do as I say and get everyone in the same room, Miss Farrow, and you will get your answers. Just don't be angry at me when they're not the ones you wished for."

Fate did not allow Signa time to ask the thousands of questions that burned her lips but turned on his heel and saw himself out of Foxglove.

"Do you think he's being sincere?" she asked Death instead, taking hold of his arm as he approached. She curled her fingers into him to steady herself, already finding that her breaths came easier simply because he was there beside her.

Death did not turn his face from the hall where Fate had disappeared, though his shadows shrank with the retreating threat. "I think that no matter what my brother says, it's safe to assume that he's always up to something."

That much was clear enough. If Fate wanted to, he could give her the answers she sought. Instead, she felt as though she was falling deeper and deeper into a cleverly spun web, waiting to be feasted on.

"Would it truly be so bad for me to revive Elijah?" She gripped him tight, unsure how much longer they'd have together. "It couldn't possibly be any worse than dealing with your brother."

Death's shadows swept toward Signa. He pulled her against him in a sudden rush, and oh how she wanted to kiss him. Yet Death kept his face at a distance, mindful of her bare skin. "Foolish as my brother may be, for once I agree with him. You have seen firsthand the cost of keeping someone alive, Little Bird. Imagine what the cost might be for bringing them back from the dead."

Truthfully, Signa never wanted to find out. Still, frustration ate at her, nerves bundling in her stomach. "What then? We continue to play his game?"

"We continue to play his game," Death echoed, tucking the silver strands behind her ear and cupping her face between his gloved palms. "Only this time, we play to the end."

THIRTY-FIVE

Blythe

TWO DAYS AFTER HER FATHER HAD BEEN SENTENCED TO HANG, Blythe received an invitation.

She held it tight, reading the words once, twice, then three times more before the reality of them settled over her.

Signa Farrow had invited her to a ball. The woman who had killed her brother—but who Blythe now understood was being influenced by Death himself—had invited both her and Byron to attend a soiree at Foxglove little more than a week before her father was set to hang.

For the first half hour Blythe spent staring at the invitation, she had done so while inwardly fuming at Signa's gall. The next half hour she brainstormed what ulterior motives could possibly be at play. Finally, she set the invitation down on the table and took to pacing around the drawing room. With every step she was all too aware of the small tapestry tucked beneath her corset.

During the weeks that Signa had been gone, Blythe had spent

every day filling her diary with theories while coming to terms with the fact that there would be no more social calls to scrounge up for herself. She could barely show her face in tea shops since her father's verdict, and following the gossip had become near impossible. As much time as she spent plotting ways to break the news about Everett's potential motive and cast a doubtful light upon him, she doubted there was a single person alive who'd believe her. Which meant that after everything she'd done, Blythe had nothing to show for sleuthing other than a horrifying skeletal hallucination of Eliza Wakefield burned into her brain and a tapestry that could change her fate.

It was warm against her skin, the threads around it more visible by the day. Blythe should have been surprised by all she'd learned or by the ease with which Aris had controlled her. Yet why should she be surprised when she herself had seen the shadows that trailed behind her cousin, and how both her lady's maid and Eliza had looked sickly and skeletal one moment only to be perfectly healthy the next? Blythe had seen threads of gold sewed into the air itself, and hands that could take a life as easily as they could give one. She believed everything Aris had told her.

He was a strange man, and while she didn't trust him as far as she could throw him, Blythe couldn't help but recall his determination as he'd stomped through the woods to save a fox he'd then held bundled in his arms. He couldn't be *that* bad. He was powerful, yes, but so was Signa. Besides, far less favorable marriages had been made before. Even if Signa was angry—even if Death's hold on her was so fierce that she retaliated—Blythe would be doing her a favor.

By the end of this mess, perhaps Signa would realize that. Perhaps things between them could someday return to normal, and Blythe wouldn't have to lose her, too.

Blythe clutched the tapestry against her chest a moment longer before she moved to the desk, confident in what she had to do as she took up a pen and parchment and wrote Aris a letter.

> *On June the first, Miss Farrow will be holding a ball at Foxglove. I will be there with the tapestry and hope that you will accompany me.*

She copied down the details, then tucked the letter into an envelope, sealed it with wax, and sent William to take it to Wisteria at once.

He returned three hours later with Aris's response.

I would not miss it for the world.

PART THREE

THIRTY-SIX

It was remarkable how quickly Foxglove took shape, shedding its dusty drabness in favor of a poised and proper seaside manor. Signa had hired more help than she knew what to do with, and they'd been working around the clock to scrub every wall and floor panel until the water bucket ran clear. The once dreary curtains were shaken out, brightening into a lighter color than she ever would have guessed them to be. The furniture had been dusted, and the piano tuned and polished. Gone were any hints of cobwebs or the skeletal remains of rats, and as Signa ran a white-gloved finger along a bookcase in the parlor, not even a speck of dust made it onto the fabric.

It'd taken even more elbow grease than she'd anticipated, but the Foxglove she stood in now was a home to take pride in, one all who entered would respect. With the ball mere hours away, they'd made it so just in time.

"Everything looks fabulous," Signa told the staff, all standing at attention as she paced from the parlor to the entryway, checking that everything was in place. "You've all done a better job than I could have hoped for." There was a quiet, collective sigh of relief within the group. Signa's eyes found Elaine's at once, and the young woman shot her an apologetic look. The staff had been in a tizzy since the night of Fate's visit, likely never having imagined their new mistress would be hosting company so prestigious as a prince, especially in a house that—until now—had looked a disaster. She didn't doubt that word had gotten out of how she'd refused to offer the prince any refreshments, and she heard whispers of how strange it was that Signa hadn't wanted to swap out the strange macabre art in favor of something livelier.

She waited for the staff to scurry off to give everything one final pass before she turned her attention to the trio of spirits that stared up at her from the couch. She'd learned their names in these past weeks—Tilly was the daughter, Victoria the mother, and Oliver the bespectacled father who observed everything with a keen eye. He had, Signa learned, spent years working with her father in architecture.

"*What dress will you wear tonight? Will it be marvelous?*" Tilly asked with a note of longing. "*You should choose carefully in case you die. Imagine being stuck in a corset every moment for the rest of your life.*"

"There are far more important things to worry about tonight. Though, if you must know, yes. My dress will be marvelous." Though Signa admittedly hadn't considered the potential tragedy of dying in it, she certainly was now. "And if I die, it will hardly matter because I would never remain here with all of you. The afterlife isn't so bad, you know."

"You've seen it?" Tilly's eyes bulged so wide that Signa feared they might burst from her skull. If that was a possibility with spirits, she had no desire to find out.

"Only the entrance, but it's beautiful." Signa had grown used to keeping her voice low for the spirits, but she glanced cautiously around all the same before she added, "Unless you want to see it tonight, I need you all to be on your best behavior."

They only rolled their eyes. Had it not been for the fact that this was likely the twentieth time Signa had warned them to behave—as well as the fact that she still needed to get dressed for the evening—she might have lingered to ensure they were planning to listen.

As it was, Amity was waiting as Signa hurried up the stairs. The spirit hovered over Signa's bed, where a gilded gown was spread across the mattress. Signa ran her hand along the gold fabric, her fingertips buzzing.

Back at Thorn Grove she had worn a crimson dress as bold as blood to conquer Death. And now at Foxglove—to conquer Fate and put an end to this mess with Elijah once and for all— it only made sense that she wore a burnished gold befitting the royalty he played.

Elaine didn't linger after fastening her into the gown, instead heading out to check that everything was prepared for the guests' arrival and giving Signa time to inspect herself. The gown hugged her body tight, sweeping up to ensnare her throat with the most luxurious collar. It was heavier than she was used to, embroidered with gorgeous floral detailing along the bodice and bustle. Her hair was pulled back to show off as much of the dress as possible, pinned in loose waves.

Signa may have told Tilly that it didn't matter what she wore, but that was a lie. In this dress, she felt powerful enough to best Fate. So much so that she smiled back at her reflection, a warm calm settling upon her.

"You look beautiful." Amity hadn't so much as blinked while Signa readied herself, though she'd covered her mouth the moment Signa slid the dress over her skin. *"You and your mother could have been twins."*

Signa smoothed the collar into position. She was used to hearing such things from the few people who had known her mother, though she still savored the words, tucking them away for safekeeping. She'd been thinking about her parents a lot these days and couldn't help when the question slipped out: "Amity... I know the constable never found who killed them, but you were there. Do you know what happened to them the night they died?"

Shadows darkened her face, and for the first time since meeting Amity, fear struck a chord deep within Signa's chest. She'd gotten so comfortable that she'd become lax with her words, but as lively as Amity may have been, she was still a spirit. And if there was one thing spirits hated, it was being reminded of their own demise.

In that moment, Amity was like one of Fate's marionettes, hunched and lifeless in the eyes. Signa could only watch, one hand on her doorknob, as a range of emotions flashed through her in quick bursts before freezing upon a deep, festering rage that lasted only seconds before Amity's face smoothed suddenly. She frowned.

"Some things are better left unspoken, Signa." The spirit's voice rang as soft as snowfall, speaking as though nothing had happened. *"And*

some mysteries are better left unsolved. We should be going, now. Your guests are due to arrive any minute."

"Of course." Fearing that one wrong move would break Amity, Signa quickly altered course. "Though there's one last thing I need to do before I venture down to see them. Would you be able to show me where my parents' room is?"

Only then did the deep furrow and sharp planes of the spirit's face soften. *"It would be my pleasure."*

Stepping into Rima and Edward Farrow's room felt like slipping into the past. While the rest of Foxglove had been scrubbed and polished to perfection, the bedroom remained untouched, layers of dust that caked the floor and baseboards the only sign that time had passed since they'd last set foot inside.

"I'll wait for you outside," Amity whispered before she slipped out, leaving Signa to this moment—the final room she'd yet to explore.

She'd banned the staff until she could bring herself to see it exactly as it had been the night that the Farrows had left this earth. If she had all the time in the world, she might never step inside. But Signa refused to allow anyone else the chance to enter this room before she did, and now that Foxglove was filling with people, she didn't dare take that risk.

She took her first step past the threshold, the weight of a thousand questions heavy upon her chest as she forced herself forward. Her parents' bed was made, each corner tucked and smooth. There were still ashes in the fireplace and bottles of perfume on a vanity. Signa walked to them and lifted one of the elegant bottles to her nose. The smell was so foul that it had Signa tearing up at the first scent of soured amber and notes of something probably meant to be floral that she could no longer decipher. She wondered what it had smelled like twenty years ago when it had been new. She would have given anything to know what her mother had smelled like, and to spritz herself with that same scent to sit in the ghost of an imagined memory.

It was an effort to peel herself away and move to the wardrobe next, riffling through silk fabrics and taffeta gowns embellished with great flare. Signa let her fingertips slide across them, wishing she had the time to try them on. They were the colors she loved—plummy purples, navy as rich as freshly poured ink, and even a brilliant sage green—all without a hint of frill. She lifted the green satin gown, brushing away the corpse of a moth. Several more lay motionless at the bottom of the wardrobe. They had chewed holes in several of the gowns, though it seemed most were still salvageable. She shut the wardrobe, then shifted her attention to an ornate ivory jewelry box sitting upon a chest of drawers. The contents had Signa gasping—hefty gemstones fastened into rings, and diamond necklaces so dazzling that Signa was left with no choice but to fasten one upon her neck. There was a smaller one, too. A thin golden chain inlaid with an amethyst.

A necklace for a child, Signa realized. *Her* necklace. It was a wonder they hadn't been looted. Signa supposed she must have had the spirits to thank for that.

"Your taste was impeccable, Mother," she whispered to the room, skimming a finger across one of the diamonds before returning it to the safety of the jewelry box. There was so much more to investigate, though for now Signa shut the lid and let her eyes fall to a snuff box nearby. There was nothing in it but a mother-of-pearl inlay, nor did it look like it had seen much use. It was carved of solid horn and had her father's initials engraved into the bottom. She smiled as she examined it, realizing that her father's fondness for beautiful, curious things extended well beyond architecture.

It seemed she had her mother's sense of style, and her father's taste for the obscure. She held the snuff box against her chest, feeling close to them for the first time. If she shut her eyes and let herself believe, she imagined her mother coming in to scold Signa for wearing her jewelry without permission while her father explained all the details she'd never thought to learn about a simple snuff box.

One day she would see them again. One day she would learn what sort of people they truly were. Until then, she had Foxglove to fill in the gaps. Though it had been difficult—for things were new and strange and far from perfect—Signa hadn't the slightest doubt that this was where she was meant to spend the rest of her life.

She set down the snuff box and moved to the sitting room. It was filled with journals that, just as Amity had promised, contained her father's drawings. She thumbed through the original designs for Foxglove, then of the garden. Some were done in a strange, scratchy style similar to the portraits throughout the manor, and her chest warmed at the realization that they'd all been done by his hand.

There were sketches of Rima, too, and one of them with Signa as a baby curled in her mother's arms.

Signa stared at it for a long while, convinced that her heart had stopped. She'd never seen anything with them together. There were probably more portraits, somewhere. Perhaps one with all three of them.

She leaned against the desk, leafing through sketches when the music of the ballroom swelled from above. There were voices, too. Guests making their way inside, likely searching for a host who wasn't there to greet them.

Signa was so lost in her own thoughts that she didn't notice the bitter cold leaching into the room. Only when she heard his stirring did she turn to see that Death stood behind her in his human form. Her fingers slipped from the sketchbook, and when she turned to him fully, it was with tears in her eyes.

"Are you all right?" His voice wasn't in her head. It was spoken aloud, and that was enough for Signa's tears to come faster. Her body ached to run to him, and this time she did not hesitate to give in to that desire. Death went still as she locked her arms around his waist and pressed in.

"Signa..."

"I'm tired of goodbyes." Signa burrowed her face into his chest. "I won't say another one. We have to put an end to this. We need to stop—" She snapped her mouth shut with sudden realization.

It wasn't unheard of for Death to appear. Large crowds were one of the best chances she had to see him, and tonight she'd not only invited the entire town but also guests from Celadon.

Tonight she had invited almost every single person in this world that she cared for.

Signa drew back, ice in her veins. She held on to the edge of the nightstand, her stomach sick. "Who is it? Who are you here for?"

Death took her gloved hand tight. Not lovingly, Signa realized, but to steady her as he answered, "I've come for Eliza Wakefield."

THIRTY-SEVEN

Blythe

Foxglove was maze of a manor, where every room felt like its own story.

The bottom floor portrayed an unassuming seaside home decorated with gentle blues and lattice trim, yet as one made their way upward, the home shifted into themes of flora and fauna with darkening wallpaper that grew wilder the closer one got to the grand ballroom.

Byron gave no sign of his own opinions of the manor. He'd hardly spoken two words to Blythe since Elijah's verdict, and the gloom upon his face had grown increasingly darker by the day.

She'd separated from him the moment they'd arrived at Foxglove, and Byron had seemed relieved for it. Left to her own devices, Blythe searched for shadows as she scoured the manor's lowest floor, careful to keep herself beneath the glittering glow of the chandelier. She cast paranoid glances over her shoulders, expecting Death to be waiting for her.

How many times had she escaped him now? Was he angry? Would he try to take her again the first chance he got?

Blythe remembered his cold claws around her throat and the way the chill had seeped through her skin and settled within her bones, stealing the breath she'd fought so hard for. She remembered Signa standing before him, pleading for Blythe's life.

If Signa was a killer, why would she have fought so hard to save her? If she was out to get the Hawthorne family, she could have let Death take Blythe several times over. Instead, she and Percy together had brought Blythe the Calabar bean that spared her. It didn't make sense that Signa would harm Percy; it had to have been Death's hand pulling the strings.

Though Blythe knew nothing about the reaper and his powers, she felt safest beneath the light's warm glow. When someone offered her a glass of champagne, she took it with a smile, only to set it down on a table the moment the staff turned away, not about to end up like the late Lord Wakefield. She'd managed to get this far without letting Death get hold of her, and she had no intention of that changing tonight.

"Why do you look like that?" The voice came from behind her, and Blythe turned to see Aris pick up her discarded champagne and take a long sip from the flute. Blythe stilled when he swallowed, silently counting the seconds to see whether he would keel over and die. It wouldn't be without precedent, after all. Blythe had done enough investigating of the manor's history to know that a plague of deaths would not be a new occurrence for Foxglove. Still, she let herself relax when Aris remained standing.

"Look like what?" she asked.

Aris twirled his champagne, taking his time to respond. "Like a fawn readying itself to flee." He took two more sips and set down the empty flute. "It's difficult not to notice. Your dress isn't very discreet."

Blythe flushed. She'd packed quickly, choosing gowns she thought would suit a seaside aesthetic. She hadn't expected Foxglove to be quite so gloomy, though it seemed fitting that Signa would live in such a beautifully dreary place. As it was, Blythe had chosen a blush ballgown that skewed on the side of pink. It had pleated frills along the bottom, and collapsed sleeves laced with ivory. The crinoline she wore beneath her skirts was so full that it made it difficult to sleuth about. She hadn't even thought to consider that issue.

"I was looking for *him*." Blythe's eyes flickered to the corners of the room yet again. Aris followed her gaze with a frown.

"I don't think you'll find him on the ceiling, love. And he's not going to swoop down and kidnap you. Relax, little fawn, and tell me—have you got the tapestry?"

Blythe wasn't at all convinced by Aris. Still, she answered, "I do."

Aris squinted. "Where?"

"Don't worry about that." Blythe shot him an incredulous look. She distracted herself from the embarrassment of admitting it was pressed beneath her corset by taking in the sights of Foxglove.

While Blythe was no stranger to living in homes with unusual design aesthetics, there was something unsettling about Foxglove. Its interior was almost *too* bright and cheery against the encroaching rain clouds. It was a strange manor. Quaint and beautiful, but taller than it was wide and full of twisting turns she watched people disappear into. Most guests were making their way toward the ballroom, and Blythe's eyes darted from one face to the next, each of them unfamiliar. It was as if she'd stepped off a train into a world where she did not belong, and into a house that had her so paranoid that she kept eyeing the strange portraits, half expecting them to blink back. Never had she felt so disoriented.

She was about to turn and head to the lawn for fresh air, unconvinced that she'd made the right decision by coming here, when a haze of darkness floated past the corner of her vision. Blythe stilled.

"Is that him?" she asked through a feigned smile, not wanting Death to realize that she could see him.

If Aris was faking his surprise, he was a better actor than she gave him credit for. "You truly can see him, then."

"Did you think I was lying?" Blythe fought the urge to stare down the shadows. "If I couldn't, then why would I have believed your ridiculous story?"

Aris pressed his lips together, considering. "You shouldn't be able to see him so easily. I thought it possible that you had heard whispers somewhere along the way, though I suppose nearly dying several times did more of a number on you than I thought."

"It's not *easy*," Blythe argued. If anything, it was a constant and mounting frustration. She didn't know whether he had a face, or if he was nothing more than a bundle of shadows. She could see him only as shadowy haze and couldn't fathom how Signa could have fallen for such a being. He wasn't truly even a man... was he?

She blushed as soon as she considered the question, deciding it was best if she didn't give that too much thought.

"What is he doing?" Blythe stood closer to the prince than she had any right to, and if anyone were to see them, they would certainly think Signa's soiree most scandalous.

"He's watching us," Aris whispered. "Hurry and act like I'm seducing you."

She smacked his hand away when he teasingly brushed his fingers across hers, hating that she could feel heat rushing to her cheeks.

"Have I ever told you that my favorite color is the very shade of red you turn when you're flustered?" He was so close that Blythe could feel his breath against her cheeks, and she thought immediately of the intimate moment they'd shared at the Wakefield manor.

"You intend to marry my cousin," she admonished. "You should mind your tongue."

Aris took another glass of champagne as it passed, and if Blythe had to guess, she'd say it wasn't his second. "I have no interest in you, Miss Hawthorne, though getting you riled up isn't without its appeal. You should see my brother's face right now."

Blythe huffed and adjusted her gown, patting down the crinoline. Only when she was certain that she wouldn't flush again did she turn back to him, her retort ready. But all at once Aris was a prince again, poised with such confidence and pride that he seemed like the tallest man in the room. Blythe realized why a moment later when she saw Eliza and Everett Wakefield enter Foxglove. It took her a moment to notice that Charlotte was at his side, their arms linked.

Upon Charlotte's left hand was a sapphire ring, the sight of which had Blythe's vision spiraling.

It was official, then. They were engaged.

Charlotte's smile was as radiant as the moon. Everett's matched it as he leaned down to whisper something that had her giggling. He looked like the happiest man alive to have earned such a sound, and while Blythe wanted to let herself fill with warm butterflies and celebrate her friend, she wondered whether that ring had come at the cost of a duke's life, and if her father was going to be the one to pay its price.

Eliza, unlike the others, looked as though she'd been caught out at sea in a storm. She was haggard and weary, and while fashionable in a pleasant blue gown, she seemed too queasy to be here. Her hair was too long, pinned meticulously at the nape of her neck, but as stringy as the kelp Blythe had seen while looking over the precarious cliffside Foxglove sat upon. No cramps were this bad for this long; something was truly wrong.

Only then did Blythe notice her uncle standing behind the Wakefields. His frown was so severe that Blythe's anxiety spiked as she thought of the note Signa had left her. As Byron made a beeline for Eliza, so did she. He stilled when he spotted her, then turned on his heel. Whatever he had to say to Eliza, it seemed it was not worth it while in Blythe's vicinity.

Eliza didn't appear to have noticed Byron. She was too focused on the space between Blythe and Aris. "Did the two of you arrive together?" Eliza asked without so much as a greeting. No matter how ill she appeared, it was a relief that she was still behaving as herself. She attempted a wobbling curtsy to the prince, and Blythe was clearly not alone in her concern, given that Aris took hold of Eliza's arm and helped her straighten.

"You don't look well." Blythe didn't mince her words, for vanity would do Eliza no favors. "We should find you a room to lie down in."

Eliza stood as tall as she could manage. "I assure you that I am fine, Miss Hawthorne. Don't you dare rob me of this opportunity when the season is nearly at its end."

Blythe hadn't expected the spite in her tone and was about to chastise Eliza for her foolery when the shadow trailing them jerked to the side. Blythe tracked it, watching as it slipped up the stairs just as Signa was descending.

Blythe's knees buckled as though someone had pulled the rug from beneath her. She had half a mind to escape behind Aris and hide among the crowd but, given how Signa missed a step and had to catch herself on the banister when her eyes caught Blythe's, it seemed she'd lost her opportunity to hide.

With Byron acting suspicious and Eliza looking ready to fall over at any moment, Blythe knew there was no choice but for her to face Signa, needing all the assistance she could get. For the sake of her father she dipped her head, and it was enough of an acknowledgment that Signa's chest sank with visible relief as she hurried down the remaining stairs.

"Blythe." Signa's voice was winded, and her eyes flicked once behind the group, casting a furtive look toward the shadow—toward *Death*. Blythe tried not to shiver at how distracted Signa seemed. "I didn't expect to see you here."

"I didn't expect to come. Yet given my father's position, I had no choice but to see what you wanted."

Signa's throat bobbed as she stepped closer, letting her lips curl into a false smile to greet the crowd around them. "I understand your lack of trust in me, but I'm glad you came. Rest assured that tonight we will save Elijah."

That much, at least, was certain. Though as Blythe watched her cousin step away, greeting Everett and Eliza as a shadow trailed her every step, she hoped that Elijah was not the only soul that Blythe would save tonight.

Signa thanked the others for coming all this way, her eyes never leaving Eliza while Blythe stood there, numb. The tapestry warmed her skin, and Blythe absently pressed a hand against it as her eyes found Aris's. He watched Signa with a predatory gleam, assessing her every movement as if to decide when to strike. The shadow in the corner stood across from him. Blythe tried not to look at Death so obviously, though she was beginning to make out a face in those shadows.

"Why don't we head up to the ballroom?" Blythe forced her attention away from all of them. "Signa, could you show us the way?"

Signa's smile wavered, and she looped her arm through Eliza's.

Blythe tried not to let that bother her. Tried not to stare as she told herself that this wasn't Signa's way of saying she'd already found a replacement for Blythe, but because Eliza looked one strong breeze away from a collapse. Still, Blythe longed for the days when she would be the one beside Signa, gossiping and chatting about the most recent book they'd read.

"Is something wrong with Eliza?" Blythe stuck with Charlotte and Everett, speaking too quietly for the others to hear. "She's remarkably pale."

"I'm certain there is, but she won't tell us what." Everett didn't bother to conceal his contempt as he glared at Blythe, widening their berth. She was so taken aback by his ferocity that for a second she stopped walking. The Everett she'd known had always been so *polite.* She liked him a little better with his scowl, though would have preferred that it not be aimed at her.

"I understand if you're not the biggest fan of my family," Blythe began, "but my father is innocent. The wrong man is set to hang." With each word, Blythe searched Everett for any sign of nerves. Any sign that he was worried Blythe suspected his involvement. And yet he only cut her a scathing look, jaw clenched.

"I've no idea how to act around you, Miss Hawthorne, for I do not wish anyone else to suffer as I have. I am sorry that you're to lose your father, but I cannot be upset by justice." Everett turned then, hurrying the rest of the way up the steps without any regard for Blythe.

Charlotte stared after him, her lips pressed into a small frown. "We can't change the verdict, Blythe. Your father was found guilty."

So ragged was Blythe's breathing that she'd begun to shake. She folded her hands, pressing them against herself and biting her tongue until she tasted blood. She wanted to tell Charlotte exactly how suspicious she was of each of them but focused instead on the warmth from the tapestry that pulsed against her skin.

She would not give them the time to form clever excuses by giving away her suspicions. Not yet.

Blythe hadn't noticed they'd arrived inside the ballroom until Charlotte hurried away, leaving her surrounded by strangers in bustling gowns and servants passing gilded trays of dainty sweets and fizzing drinks. Behind her, Eliza was speaking to Signa in low, hushed tones, though her cousin hardly seemed to be paying attention. Signa's jaw was clenched, and Blythe followed her eyes to one corner of the ballroom, where Death's shadows were erratic as he moved toward Signa and back again, faster than Blythe's eyes could keep up with.

Blythe's heart leaped to her throat when a champagne flute swept from the table beside her and shattered onto the floor. Not even Death had been standing near enough to knock it aside.

Signa's hands were suddenly gripping her shoulders tight.

"Keep an eye on Eliza," she said at once. "Promise me you won't let her out of your sight."

"What's going on?" Blythe ducked out of her hold, still looking at the broken glass that was hurriedly swept away. No sooner had the staff finished than another glass fell.

"There's something I need to take care of. Just keep close to her!"

Before Blythe had the chance to form a single coherent thought, Signa hiked up her skirts and hurried across the ballroom floor.

THIRTY-EIGHT

God, what a fool she'd been. Signa *knew* spirits were fickle beings, just as she knew what happened when they were reminded of their deaths. Perhaps this was why Fate had suggested a party; not to help her, but to damn her further. She should have anticipated what it would mean to bring so many people into Foxglove, filling it with crinoline and dance cards.

She had re-created the night of these spirits' deaths, and now all of Foxglove was to pay the price.

Everywhere she looked, spirits were rousing from their daze. One of the twins who'd been stuck in a loop of eyeing a group of ladies now crossed the floor to offer his hand to one. She accepted it, and the two swept into a waltz alongside the living. The other twin's neck twisted to one side, twitching as his brother slipped away from their loop. Signa's palms went clammy as she watched. Had the man not already been dead, he seemed prone to snapping his own neck.

Behind him, a woman walked straight through Briar, who whipped toward the nearest table, sending a rush of cold air through the room that knocked over more empty champagne flutes and had guests squealing as they scurried away. One older woman went as far as to scream her surprise, and Signa's skin crawled from the sound.

"Briar?" Amity's eyes glowed red as she raced toward the spirit, only for Briar to look through her.

"Amity," Signa whispered as the spirit's face darkened, having to pause every few steps to smile at guests who murmured their alarm. "Amity, get control of yourself."

It was no use. Amity was circling Briar, trying to pry the restless spirit from her disillusions. Briar's body spasmed in response, while tears as black as tar rolled down Amity's cheeks.

Signa remembered the way Lillian had lost control back in the garden; remembered the way that frogs had marred the trees, their blood spilling down onto the soil. Once a spirit lost control, there was no going back. And the more living bodies that filled Foxglove's ballroom, the greater that threat became.

Signa had to weave around the second twin as he strayed from his table, following a silver serving tray of petit fours. He blinked when his hand went straight through the tray, then tried again with more focus until he was able to seize a cake for himself. His edges dimmed with the effort, and when he tried to devour the sweet—only for it to fall through him and land on the floor—the spirit's eyes flashed red. Behind him, Amity screamed at Death, backing away as he held out his hand in offering. She cared only for Briar, who was tugging her hair out by the ends in a fit of distress.

Something needed to be done, and fast. Not only for the sake of the spirits—whose pain Signa felt as though it were her own, eating her alive—but for Elijah, too. She needed to help the spirits before they sent her guests sprinting from the party and the Wakefields alongside them. Already they huddled in corners, hungry for sightings of the paranormal. Signa was certain that was why they'd come after all. Not to meet her, but to investigate the notorious Foxglove manor and see whether its rumors were true.

For once she didn't care. If it gave her a way to gather the Hawthornes and Wakefields into her home and force everyone to reckon with the false blame laid on Elijah, then the residents of this town could believe whatever they wanted. And yet the moment that Signa started toward Amity, a woman blocked her path.

"It seems that I didn't imagine you, then." Dressed in her finery, coiled hair twisted into pins, it took Signa a moment to place her as the woman she'd met on the pier—Henry's mother. She looked like an entirely different person, her skin refreshed and eyes no longer so angry or bloodshot.

"When I received the invitation, I was hoping it was you who was the new owner of Foxglove," the woman continued. "Is it true what they say about this place?"

"That it's haunted?" Signa asked through a wince, only half paying attention as Amity begged Briar to snap out of her haze. Across the room, Death's offered hand was once again refused, this time by a spirit whose body crackled like an approaching storm.

Foxglove was haunted indeed, and as plates and glasses fell from the tables and the chill in the air grew so intense that Signa's breath plumed, it seemed more people were taking notice.

"Well, yes." The woman dropped her voice. "You can see them, can't you? Don't worry, I won't tell anyone. After what you did for Henry, I owe you the world, Miss Farrow. That's why you're here at Foxglove, isn't it? To help the rest of them?"

The question was an innocent one, spoken with the casualness of friends. And yet Signa's response caught in her throat. Both the fervent whispers of her guests as well as the laughter of the spirits drowned away as her own world tunneled into focus. She looked once more to Amity, who was beginning to fret at her hair just as Briar was, tearing at strands she'd wound tight around her fists.

For twenty years these spirits had been unable to move on with their lives. It made her think of Henry and the smile he'd worn when he'd taken Death's hand. She thought of Lillian, too, and how her poisoned body had restored itself before she left the living world behind.

Death may have preferred to never take a soul until they were ready, but how could he know whether someone was ready if spirits could not pull themselves from a loop? Signa could not reap souls, nor did she know whether she'd ever have the capability of leading them to the afterlife as Death could. But she *could* ensure that none of these spirits had to spend one more day trapped in Foxglove.

"That's why I'm here," Signa confirmed, and the words tasted like the most decadent chocolate, warm and rich as they slipped past her lips. Her vision swayed a little, chest tight with a spreading warmth. "Yes. Of *course* it's why I'm here."

There wasn't a bone in Signa's body that could wait one moment longer. "It was lovely to see you, though if you'll excuse me..." She hurried away in search not of Death or the spirits, but for a man with sunlight upon his skin. Fate was a beacon on the ballroom floor, dazzling beneath the light that warmed his complexion as he spun from the arms of a beautiful woman to a man who laughed as Fate drew him into a waltz, a flute of champagne balanced between two nimble fingers.

Signa's body knew what needed to be done before her mind could catch up. She knew it in her heart of hearts, with such ferocity that she could not rest until she crossed the floor to steal Fate from the man he danced with. His golden eyes slid to her, and he extended a hand.

"Hello, Miss Farrow. Would you care to dance?"

She plucked the glass from between his fingers, setting it onto the nearest table before she slipped her palm into one of his. Signa didn't pull away as his other hand settled on the small of her back, nor did she care even remotely for the curious stares that lingered upon them, alarmed by the closeness in which Fate reeled her in. His chest was hot as a raging fire against hers.

"You look as radiant as the sun in that dress," Fate told her.

She smiled, recalling Death's words to her all those months ago. *You are bolder than the sun, Signa Farrow. And it's time that you burn.* Fueled by them, she tilted her head toward Fate. "I need your help."

Somewhere across the ballroom came a gasp as a wandering spirit tried to take the hand of an older woman. The woman promptly lost her breath to surprise, shivered once, and then fainted on the spot. Hovering over her fallen frame, the spirit screamed.

"It's happening again!" she cried, fumbling from the dance floor as she yelled those words over and over again.

The night wasn't going remotely as Signa had hoped. She focused on the heat from Fate's touch, searing her skin even through the fabric of her gown. "You seem to require my help a lot, lately. Tell me, have you remembered me yet?"

With the question came an unprompted memory of laughter that had once made her feel so alive. The pulse of a heart that had once beat for her alone, just as hers had for him. Signa missed a step, nearly tripping over her boots as the song he'd asked her to remember once again flooded her thoughts.

"No." She forced the lie out, throwing those thoughts as far as she could get them. "I remember nothing."

Fate sighed, so close that his breath brushed her cheek. "I know I'm asking you to consider possibilities that you don't wish to believe in, but did you expect a year ago that you'd be where you are now? Did you expect to be a reaper, or the lover of Death himself?"

He already knew the answer from the look of it, but still he waited for Signa to admit, "Of course I didn't."

Necks twisted to watch as she and Fate danced. She felt the buzz of every curious stare upon her skin as he leaned in and whispered, "If you came to live with me, I think it might help you remember who you really are."

For a moment, Signa lost her breath. Perhaps because of the

spirit that passed too closely behind her, or perhaps from the suggestion itself. "You know I can't do that."

"Can't?" he echoed. "Or you won't? When you look at me, do you truly feel nothing?"

It was a question made to break a person, and Signa felt its weight settle over her. The answer was so plain upon her face that she felt Fate's resentment before she saw it curl his lips. Step-by-step their dance hastened until the musicians were red in the face and the guests were gasping for air as they tried to keep up. If not for Fate's vise grip on her, Signa surely would have spun out of control.

"If you haven't remembered, then I have no reason to help you." Though he held his jaw high, Fate was as stiff as a rod beneath her touch. More and more she found herself wondering just how much of his bravado was an act. A shield. She wondered what he might be like beneath it, once the layers had been stripped back.

"Surely there's a part of you that must care, no matter how callous you make yourself seem."

His laugh was steady, as ominous as rainfall on a cloudless night. "Do you think me enough of a fool to get attached to a life so fragile as a human's? Why should I weep for the fates I weave when Death will take even the most magnificent of them from me?"

It was perhaps that moment in which Signa saw Fate for who he was—a man as tired of people dying around him as Signa had once been. A man who was willing to do anything for the life he wanted, just as she was.

"Then care for them because I do." She did not pull from Fate but instead pressed closer. She squeezed his hand tight, trying to ignore the way his touch burned into her like a branding. "Care because everything I love is at stake tonight, and because I'm asking for help that only you can give. You control the living. Freeze them as you did at Wisteria Gardens, so that I can take care of the spirits. Give me a chance to learn the truth of Lord Wakefield's death, and for once do not ask for anything in exchange. If you're not the villain, prove it to me."

Already the waltz was waning, and the quieter the music became, the more intense Fate's stare grew until the gold in his eyes was all but glowing. He peeled from Signa the moment the song had finished, as though she herself was a plague.

"Do not toy with me," he spat. "Do not say soft words in the hope that I'll go weak. You will have your truth, Miss Farrow—I've already promised you as much. I will give you twenty minutes to placate your spirits. After that, the rest is up to you."

He looked as angry at her as he was with himself, as if hating that she'd pulled this from him freely. There was no reward, no deal struck. It was an opportunity Signa wouldn't waste, the timer beginning the moment bodies froze around her, faces stilling amid laughter and couples stopped mid-twirl.

"Thank you," Signa said, though Fate had already turned to seek solace in another flute of champagne. She let him go, noticing then how still Death stood in the corner, watching. She could only imagine what he could be thinking. Though her heart ached, there was no time to console him.

"Later," she whispered, wishing for nothing more than the ability to reach out and take his hand. "Help me get them out of here."

Signa made her way across the ballroom toward her godmother, nearly drawing back as the spirit hissed at her.

"Amity." Signa dared not let one ounce of her fear seep into her voice, even as Amity loomed closer. Her head tilted to inspect Signa, who focused on deep breaths to steady her hammering heart. The moment she started toward Briar, though, it was as though Amity burst open. She glowed brighter than Signa had ever seen, more monster than spirit as she bared her teeth. Signa stumbled back, bracing herself on the edge of the nearest table to keep from falling.

But she would not turn away. There was too much riding on the night, and Amity deserved better. They all did.

"Amity!" Signa wished she had her berries so that she might pool her shadows around her, if only to settle into their protective embrace. "I want to *help*! You've waited for me all this time. You've helped me settle into Foxglove when I never thought I could call this place home. *Please,* let me help Briar. Let me help *you*!"

The words seemed to break something within Amity, whose body shook with a sob. In that moment, Signa felt herself drawn to the spirits the same way she'd been to Henry.

She'd *always* been pulled toward them. And perhaps she finally understood why.

Only when Amity stepped aside, eyes brimming with tears as dark as dried blood, did Signa close the remaining space between her and Briar. Her face was even worse than Signa had realized from afar, the left side so swollen that one of her eyes seemed ready to slip from its socket. A gaping wound on her right temple had splinters of wood still stuck inside. That, at least, explained the stain on the banister.

"Briar?" Signa kept still and measured, and when Death drew forward, she held out a hand to halt him, not wanting to spook the spirit who blinked at her, forehead pinched.

As horrifying as it was to have the spirit's attention, it was a good sign to have finally earned her awareness. Only, Signa wasn't sure how she felt about having earned the attention of the others, too.

Several spirits had twisted to observe the only moving body in a ballroom that had gone still. In the corner of her vision, Death stood poised to strike.

There are too many of them, he warned. *Be careful, Signa. One wrong move, and you could set off an avalanche.*

Signa needed no warning. Her bones ached with the memory of possession, making each of her movements more cautious than the next. There was no guidebook for this. All her life, Signa had relied on instructions. She'd memorized *The Lady's Guide to Etiquette and Beauty* from front to back. Had branded every rule of society and propriety into her mind and had been overly aware of every expectation placed upon her. Now she had only her own instincts to command her.

"There's a reason that no one here looks familiar." Though she stood face-to-face with Briar, the words were for all spirits listening. "Twenty years ago, you died here in Foxglove."

Signa tensed as Death threw his shadows toward her, but there was no need. The spirits shifted but did not attack.

"I'm here to help you." Signa exhaled a breath through barely parted lips as she stretched a hand to Briar. "You've been reliving the night of your deaths over and over again. But you don't have to spend your days roaming these halls any longer. There's so much more waiting for you, and if you let me, I'll show you that this is only the beginning of your story."

Although Briar remained still, Signa straightened in surprise as one of the twins stepped forward in her place. His eyes flitted from Signa to Death before he looked to where his twin stood. There was no mistaking the recognition that sparked in his eyes, and with a voice tired and cracked from disuse, he asked simply, *"Alexander?"*

The young man across from him flickered out of view, body spasming before he reappeared at his brother's side. His lips were dry and peeling as he opened his mouth once, twice, then shut it promptly when no sound came out. Already his eyes were becoming a strange milky white, growing vacant again as his focus began to stray.

You can do this. Death's words slipped through Signa's mind, the very encouragement she needed to approach Alexander.

"Look at my skin." She held her arm out to him. "Look at mine, then compare it to your own. Do you ever remember seeing such a glow upon yourself?" She could only wait, heart in her throat, as the spirit dropped his gaze. He turned his hand every which way, lips twisting downward.

"You are no longer meant for this place," she urged. "You're struggling because you're clinging to the world of the living when you've already died."

"Died," Alexander echoed, slumping forward as he glanced at his brother. *"We . . . died?"*

Signa shared a look with Death, bracing herself. "You did. But that doesn't mean you're at your end. There's more to come—would you like to see it?"

The spirit peered down at Signa's offered hand, tensing when his twin approached and clasped him on the shoulder. It took a long moment until he relaxed beneath the touch, relief pouring over him as he turned to his brother. *"Enough of this place,"* said the first, the blue of his skin beginning to fade. *"Let us take our leave."*

Color was blossoming on their once-translucent skin, and Signa nearly cried with relief as Alexander's peeling lips and the sores around them healed.

One glance at Death was all that was needed for him to sweep forward. He had told Signa that his appearance often changed to give the spirits the face of whoever they most needed in their final moments. Though she could not see what the brothers did, neither spirit recoiled as Death approached. Rather, they softened as they took hold of Death's hands, setting off a chain reaction of two more spirits who drew toward Death like he was a lighthouse in a storming sea, the haze from their eyes lifting.

"Hurry back," she whispered, the spreading warmth in her body all the confirmation she needed to know that she had been right. This was *exactly* what she was meant to do.

Amid the spirits, Death glanced from Signa to Briar. His jaw clenched once before he nodded. "I will."

He gathered the spirits who flocked toward him and was gone.

Several remained on the outskirts, curious but afraid to commit just yet. Briar was among them.

Second by second it seemed that the reality of her death was settling over her, though unlike the others, she had no desire to accept it. Her bottom lip trembled, and Signa knew the instant before a scream tore through the woman's throat that Briar wouldn't go so easily. Signa barely had time to shield her ears as the sound came, so piercing that every crystal flute near them shattered. Wind tore through the windows, and shards of glass flew from the tables, marring the skin of guests who were slowly rousing back to reality, jaws clenching and fingers twitching as they held their partners.

Twenty minutes had passed in the blink of an eye. They were almost out of time.

Amity recognized it, too. She pressed closer to Briar.

"We're out of options," Signa warned Amity, whose eyes flashed red in warning as Death's chill marked his return. "She's going to hurt someone."

"She's scared." Never had Amity's voice held such venom, and Signa knew without hesitation that should she try anything, Amity would become the most terrifying spirit she'd ever encountered. Amity cut across Signa, ignoring Death entirely as she grabbed hold of Briar's hand. When the spirit snarled and tried to pull back, Amity clutched her tighter.

"Come back to me." Amity held her even as bloodied black tears rolled down Briar's cheeks and neck. *"Come back to me,"* she said again, lifting onto her toes to press the softest kiss onto Briar's temple, just below the wound. *"I've waited too long for you to hear*

me say that I love you. Come back to me, Briar, so that I might tell you properly."

Briar stilled beneath the kiss, blinking the last of the tears free to focus on Amity, whose fingers were curled tight into Briar's as she held her. Though she said nothing for a long while, the sharpness of the wind died down and she laid one trembling hand upon Amity's.

"Is it really you?" So soft was Briar's voice that Signa thought she'd imagined it until Amity's laughter broke with the happiest sob Signa had ever heard. Amity wound her arms around the spirit, fingers smoothing over Briar's hair as she kissed her once more.

"It's me. And I'm not going anywhere."

Amity bowed her head against Briar's and whispered words that Signa turned from, knowing they weren't meant for her ears. She wished she could give them all the time in the world. Wished that she was not so worried about Briar losing control once more the moment the bodies unfroze.

"It's time for you to go," Signa whispered.

Amity lifted her head, offering the tiniest smile on those heart-shaped lips. *"I believe you're right."* Signa hadn't anticipated how badly those words would sting, though even amid so much sadness, she felt relief for her friend. Finally, Amity would have what she wanted. *"Your parents will be so proud when I tell them about the woman their daughter has become. These twenty years were worth the wait. I am happy to have known you, Signa, if only for a moment."*

Signa couldn't say with certainty when her tears came, only that they flowed with abandon. "I'm glad to have known you, too. Tell my parents that I look forward to meeting them one day, would you? It'll be the most beautiful reunion."

"It will." As Death drew closer, pieces of Amity wisped away with the breeze that slipped in through the still-open windows. *"Though I do hope you make us wait for a long while. Enjoy this life, Signa. Enjoy it freely, and do not let anyone keep you from who or what you love. When I see you again, I hope you'll have the most magnificent stories to share."*

Briar's wounds were healing fast, and Signa knew there was no time for more words. She bit back her tears as Briar and Amity followed Death's call hand in hand, eager to explore all that awaited them.

There was barely a moment for Signa to wipe her eyes as the ballroom surged into motion once more.

There were more spirits still, some of them even likely wandering rooms of the manor that Signa hadn't yet explored. The trio she'd met on her first night at Foxglove had poked their heads in and were watching while several others panicked from the surge of bodies that had kicked back into motion as golden threads spun around the ballroom.

Signa ignored them, as the worst of it had settled and, for the time being, all seemed to be in control. The music picked up mid-song, but laughter was quickly shifting to whispers as people noticed the thin cuts along their bodies and shattered glass that several maids were already hurrying to clean up. Signa caught sight of Byron and followed his gaze across the floor, to where Eliza Wakefield was gathering her skirts. She'd been far enough from the tables to avoid injuries, though she appeared more sickly than ever seen, with ashen skin and eyes as hollow as a spirit's as she stumbled toward the doors.

Behind her, Fate wore a grave expression and Signa understood that the moment Death returned, he would have someone else to claim.

Blythe's eyes found Signa's from across the ballroom, and without a word between them, they pushed through the crowd and followed Eliza down the stairs, out of Foxglove, and into the night.

THIRTY-NINE

Eliza was on her knees in the garden, throwing up in the poppies by the time they found her. She held her stomach, a sloshing vial of oiled herbs clutched tight in her fist.

Signa crouched beside her while Blythe seized hold of Eliza's hand.

"Give that to me," Blythe demanded with the chill of a wintertime storm. "Open your hand and give that to me now. How much have you taken?"

Though Eliza looked a breath away from death, she didn't ease her grip on the vial and instead tried to obscure it from view.

"Leave me alone," she seethed, every bit as lethal as Signa knew she could be. What Signa didn't expect, however, was the edge of fear in Eliza's voice as she clamped her eyes shut and curled into the dirt. "This is retribution. I'll come back inside once I—" She cut off with a choke as she doubled over again, bile trailing down her lips.

"She's delirious." Blythe shifted so that she was behind Eliza, loosening the laces of her corset as Eliza cried in relief.

"She's *dying,*" Signa clarified, not needing to look up to know that Death had arrived at last. The dirt was ice beneath her fingertips, and Eliza curled into herself, unable to stop her shivering. When the shadows pooled around her, Signa bared her teeth.

I will not make the same choice I did with Blythe, she told him. *I will not demand the same sacrifice from you. But all the same, I will not let you have her. Not until I try everything.*

Her clock is ticking, Little Bird, Death warned. *There are battles even you cannot win.*

Perhaps, though it would not be from a lack of effort. Signa pried off her gloves and took hold of Eliza's hand, plucking her fingers from the glass one by one.

"I need it," Eliza cried, fighting Signa to squeeze the vial. "You don't understand—"

"Mugwort." Blythe straightened from her crouch, fingers curling into the bark of the tree she braced herself against. "There's mugwort and tansy in that thing. You can help her, can't you?"

"Tansy?" It was a common enough herb, often used to aid with stomach pain or headaches. But Signa had to scan her brain over the mugwort, thinking through everything she'd ever heard about it. Everything she'd ever read. Its uses, its dangers...

She froze, face gaunt as she peered down to where Eliza clutched her stomach. Not around the middle, but lower, right on the swell of her belly. Blythe must have recognized the moment that Signa understood, for she leaned closer as Signa lifted Eliza's dress over her knees and saw exactly what she'd feared—blood. Too much of it, soaking through her undergarments.

"You're pregnant." Signa was breathless. How had she not realized it before? The obsession with finding a husband. Her nausea... Eliza had been pregnant all this time. Though neither she nor the baby would survive if Signa didn't act soon.

She looked to Blythe, who had already tossed her gloves aside and was pushing up her sleeves. There was no question in the look she slid Signa, only a demand—*fix this.*

"If you're going to do it, then it needs to be now." Death's voice was no soft thing. It was every bit as powerful as he was as it cracked through the night, awakening a fervor of determination within her. "It needs to be before she dies, otherwise I cannot allow you to claim her."

Fate's warning from days ago echoed in her head, causing Signa to hesitate before she set her bare hands onto Eliza. She needed to heal not just one life, but two, and she hadn't a clue where to begin.

She shut her eyes, focusing with everything in her on helping these two. On making them well and healthy. She envisioned it in her mind's eye, just as Fate had instructed. She pictured Eliza with full and glowing cheeks, and a child who would live to see this world. Yet as she pressed her palms against Eliza, Signa could not escape intrusive thoughts that warned her of the burn that was to come.

It was too painful. She couldn't do it. She couldn't—

"Don't you dare give up." Blythe took hold of Signa's hand and pressed it down. "Help them, Signa."

This time as the heat crept in, Signa threw the doors open and let it consume her. She didn't stop when it felt like fire licking up her skin. Didn't move even when she was convinced that this magic was melting her alive, or when her eyes stung so much that she worried she'd never see again.

She let the heat consume her until she saw only an abyss of pure white. There was nothing but endless space ahead until she heard a gentle, jovial laugh. A face took shape then—Fate's face, though more relaxed as he laughed, holding someone. Holding *her*, she realized.

Only, Signa wasn't herself, but another woman entirely. One with sweeping white hair as pure as snow, who laughed as she eased onto her toes to kiss him.

Vaguely, Signa understood that she was seeing another memory, this one of a time long ago, where the woman in her mind's eye had burned for Fate's touch, and his kiss alone could make her heart soar. It was a time when she saw Death sitting alone, watching beneath the shade of a wisteria tree, and she felt nothing for him.

As quickly as it came, the memory slipped away as Signa fell from Eliza. She took her head in her hands, aching with a pain so consuming that she wished she would faint. Yet her mind wouldn't allow such an escape, not after all she'd just seen. The memory was short and vague, nothing more than passing glimpses. But she could no longer claim it as coincidence. Life's memories were real, and as Death whispered words she could not focus enough to hear, Signa curled into herself.

Despite Life's powers and all the proof she'd had so far, she'd been clinging to the hope that Fate was wrong. That everything she'd done thus far had been a fluke, and that they'd one day find the true reincarnation of his wife and be done with this mess. Signa could ignore a song, but she couldn't deny these memories.

"Breathe, Little Bird," Death whispered as he bent beside her. Signa was trying her best to save face, though she nearly lost herself at those words because *this* was the man she loved. *This* was the man she wanted to kiss, and whose presence alone put her body at ease. But Signa could feel that more memories were waiting, biding their time to surface when she least wanted them.

Eliza came to seconds later. Her clammy skin had begun to dry, and her bleeding had halted. But considering that Signa could still see Death hovering nearby, Eliza must not have been fully out of the woods yet.

Blythe hadn't moved an inch, alert only when Eliza tried to peel her dress from her thighs, the dried blood clinging to her skin. "Careful," Blythe whispered, her voice dazed. "You should move slowly."

Eliza's thin brows pinched toward her nose. She looked from the poppies to the trees surrounding her as she pried herself from the dirt. "What on earth happened?"

It seemed that Blythe could barely contain her snort. "That's what you're supposed to tell us."

"You're pregnant," Signa added at Eliza's apparent confusion. This time when she said it, Eliza was coherent enough to look her in the eye. Signa had to try to block Life's memories out a little longer, instead gathering the scattered puzzle pieces of this mystery and speaking her thoughts aloud as she pieced them together.

"The night your uncle died, Everett told me that the duke was trying to marry you off—"

"To a man with one foot in the grave." Blythe, it seemed, was creeping toward the same conclusion as Signa.

"And one who wouldn't ask questions," Signa noted, her teeth still chattering every few words. "The late duke knew about the pregnancy, didn't he?"

There was no escaping the truth of the situation now, and Eliza seemed to realize as much. Her mouth opened and shut several times before defeat claimed her and she released the tension in her shoulders. "All Sir Bennet ever discussed was how much he needed an heir. Perhaps he was a good fit on paper, but can you imagine letting someone old enough to be your grandfather put his hands all over you?" She shuddered. All three of the women did.

One look at the discarded vial of herbs told Signa all she needed to know about the next piece of the puzzle, and so she pressed, "You didn't want to marry him. So you went to the apothecary for a solution." Signa remembered her own visit there months prior, when the shopkeeper had suspected Percy was up to something and had offered Signa the means to take care of him. Perhaps that, too, had been cyanide.

Eliza's answer came in words so sharp that each one was spoken like its own sentence. "I never, *ever* meant to cause my uncle any harm." She made a fist in her skirts, taking a moment to still the quiver of her bottom lip. "I read about cyanide in the papers. There were cases of poisonings where the men did not die but briefly took ill. I only needed to make my uncle believe that Sir Bennet was no longer a viable option. I wanted him to find someone else, so I slipped some cyanide into a drink that a servant was meant to bring to Sir Bennet. But Mr. Hawthorne stopped him on his way and grabbed the laced drink." For as long as she'd held in her secrets, they now flowed from Eliza's lips like a rushing river.

"I must have checked the dose a hundred times. No one should have died that night, I swear it." Eliza brought her knees to her chest, hugging them tight. "I never—God, I never meant for my uncle to die. I loved him."

Blythe crumpled into herself at the confession. Signa, too, wished they could sew Eliza's mouth shut and drag her to the constable to free Elijah before she said another word. Yet both she and Blythe held their tongues because, despite everything, there was a truth that hung between them—in Eliza's place, either of them might have been just as desperate.

It was no wonder Eliza had gone to Fate's ball only a week after Lord Wakefield's death; she'd been desperate to find a husband. If Eliza had known of her pregnancy before the duke's death, that meant she was at least several months pregnant. Signa peered down at Eliza's stomach; she was doing a remarkable job concealing it. She wouldn't be able to for much longer, though.

Signa picked up the vial of herbs and examined it closer. "Who gave this to you?"

Eliza stiffened at Signa's brevity. "My lady's maid, Sorcha. I've been ill since the start of my pregnancy, and it's impossible to conceal it from the one who helps dress you. Once she found out, she started to bring me herbs to ease the pain and cramping."

It was probably an innocent mistake, but still Signa couldn't rule out foul play without saying, "In low amounts, these herbs are safe. But they have another use, Eliza. Were you aware that these are popular among women with unwanted pregnancies?" They were potent and dangerous, and could bring as much harm to the mother as the baby. Still, that rarely stopped a desperate woman from using them.

Too often the world did not consider women as people but as stepping stones for men. A woman was ostracized the moment she strayed from the prescribed path, left to fend for herself in a world with too few opportunities. Signa wished there was a safer option than these herbs, but she couldn't fault Eliza for her choice.

"I only ever took the herbs to ease the pain." So great was Eliza's conviction that Blythe stirred. "I knew what they could do, though, and I wanted the option. I never meant for my uncle to die, but I couldn't marry the man he chose for me. God, I never meant for it to happen like this."

"What did you do with the cyanide after?" Signa pressed. "Did anyone see you with it?"

"No one," Eliza swore. "I panicked and threw it out."

While Blythe had kept quiet, sorrow knit itself into fine lines of her forehead as she asked in a whisper, "Where does my uncle play into this? Is Byron the father?"

This earned a blush so fierce that, at any other time, Signa might have teased the woman. "Byron knows of my condition, but the father isn't involved. He doesn't even know I'm pregnant."

"Don't you think it might be a good idea to tell him?" Blythe pressed. "Perhaps he'll be willing to help."

“What a *genius* idea,” Eliza all but spat. “Do you not think I would have told him if I could? I thought he and I would be married by now, yet I’ve not been able to contact him. Byron has been helping me search, and he offered to marry me himself, should I need the option. He’s a good man.”

With lead in her belly, Signa thought of the papers in Byron’s study; of the maps with crossed-out towns and scrawled notes. Months ago, Eliza had fawned over Percy, and he’d been more than receptive to her interest.

Five months ago… That timing checked out, and as Signa turned to steal a look at Blythe, it was clear from the glossing of her eyes that she’d realized it, too.

“Percy is the father,” she whispered. “That’s why Byron offered his hand.”

It was those words that caused Eliza’s resolve to shatter as she bent at the waist and clutched Blythe’s hand, sobs racking her body. “Why doesn’t anyone know where he is? Why would he run off unless he wanted no part of me or this child?”

Signa stared down at the vial between them. She thought of Percy’s pride and propriety, and wondered what he would have thought of the situation, had he known. Would it have reminded him too much of Marjorie to bear? Or would he have married Eliza, and been awaiting the birth of his child?

Whatever the answer, she’d never learn it. Eliza would never find Percy, and he would never be this child’s father. All because of her.

"Signa." She turned from Death as his shadows slipped behind her. "You are not the guilty party. Do not think of Percy or the life you took," Death urged. "Look instead at the one you gave life to. Had you done nothing, he would have killed Blythe."

There was barely a second in which Signa could have sworn that Blythe's attention whipped toward Death. She thought she saw the girl's eyes widen, but soon enough Blythe was bent toward Eliza, squeezing her hand.

Signa's chest felt as though it had been struck by a hot iron. They'd been seconds away from having an alibi to save her uncle. But they couldn't turn Eliza in; not when she was the mother of Percy's child and the last part of him that still existed in this world. Signa couldn't take that from the Hawthornes, too.

"You're going to be fine." Signa tried to imitate the familiar tone Death used to placate restless spirits, though she was doing a lousy job with her wavering voice. "If you choose to keep the child, tell Everett. He's a good man. But if for some reason he chooses not to be, you and your child will have a home here at Foxglove should you need it. And if you choose not to have the child, then we'll find a safer way to help you without those herbs."

Signa stood, seizing hold of Eliza's wrist and helping the girl to her feet. Eliza's body was as light as a feather, and though she seemed remarkably improved, she still swayed with each step.

"We'll make sure Everett knows not to worry about you," Signa promised as she wiped some of the dirt away from Eliza's brow, thinking through an inconspicuous way to get her safely into a guest suite. "Know that you will be fine, Eliza, and so will your child. You won't be left alone."

"Why would you protect me?" Eliza asked, more a demand than a question, with each word tense and clipped. "As much as we may pretend, we are not friends. I'm the reason your uncle is in prison."

It was fair to ask, though Signa had no answer to give. Had the father of this child been anyone else, would she still protect Eliza? Blythe would have probably thrown her to the wolves to save her father, and wouldn't that have been fair, too?

"You did everything to protect yourself and your child. I can't fault you for that." There was no true and correct path that she could see, but this one felt the most right.

Eliza stared at her for a long moment, eventually reaching forward to clasp Signa by the hand. "Thank you," she whispered, looking as though she was about to say more when a heavy thudding sounded behind them.

Signa recognized Byron's footsteps before she saw him, his walking stick clutched tight as he looked to Eliza with such a rawness that Signa worried she'd mistaken him for someone else. He hurried through the garden, poppies crushing beneath his boots as he took hold of her shoulders. Byron was no fool; one look at the blood and mud on her gown was enough for his eyes to mist. His lips trembled, opening to try to find words when Eliza steadied her hand over the one that fisted his walking stick.

"We're fine," she whispered, shifting her free hand to her belly. "Both of us."

Thank God they were near a tree, for Byron had to reach out to balance himself, threatening to crumble beneath the weight of his relief.

"They're aware?" he asked coolly, to which Eliza nodded.

"They are. And it's because of them that I am well, so do mind your tongue, Byron."

Blythe and Signa shared a look, though Blythe was quick to turn away. Already he was shrugging out of his coat to drape it around Eliza.

"I'll fetch a maid to help clean you up," he promised, voice low with sincerity. "No one will know anything about this."

It seemed even a man as severe as Byron could be undone by a baby.

"Find Miss Bartley," Signa noted. "She won't tell anyone what she's seen."

He nodded, waiting until Eliza gained her footing enough to loop her arm through his before making the short trek back to Foxglove. The fog enveloped them like a wanting maw, and any hope Signa had left faded as it swallowed their figures whole.

This was truly the end, then. Without anyone to pin the blame on, Elijah would hang.

Blythe seemed to be thinking the same thing, for she stepped forward. "My father can't be made to take the fall." Any trace of emotion had disappeared beneath her mask of stone. She reached into her corset and pulled out a small swath of gold fabric, which she held out to Signa with the utmost severity. "We only have one way to fix this."

Around them, Death turned the world to ice as Blythe held her cousin's stare.

It couldn't be what she thought it was…and yet when Signa took the tapestry, the heat of it stung so sharply that she dropped it and clutched her hand to her chest to nurse an invisible wound. "What is that?"

Blythe drew a breath, and with her exhale she seemed to morph into someone else entirely. Someone so cold and unfeeling that when her eyes narrowed on Signa's, Blythe almost didn't seem human.

"This is how you fix your mess," Blythe told her. "You're going to marry Aris."

FORTY

Signa's heart had never felt so heavy as it did with the tapestry laid before her, Blythe's hand still atop it. There was a challenge in her cousin's eyes. One that Signa could not dismiss, regardless of the weariness that settled over her.

"How long have you known what he is?" she whispered.

"Not quite so long as I've known what *you* are." Blythe drew her hand back, face set with grave severity. She didn't blink as her eyes bore into Signa's, waiting for her next move as though this were a game of chess.

Behind Blythe, Death bristled enough to quake the trees, and Signa had to risk shooting him a glare before a storm broke overhead.

"This isn't the way," he all but raged, words striking like a lance. "We will find another."

Perhaps, though with Fate's warning about bringing a soul back from the dead, Signa could not see that path, nor did they have the time to find it. Blythe was right to call this Signa's mess, and she had a responsibility to protect this family.

Go, she told Death, for it would do neither of them any good to have him here for this conversation. Signa squared her shoulders, unflinching beneath the intensity of her cousin's stare. *I need to talk to her alone.*

Signa—

Go. Please.

Death seemed at war with himself, thunder cracking as the shadows of the night flickered, irate. It was only as his attention strayed toward Foxglove that the pressure in the air eased. *Don't do anything foolish* was all he said before he disappeared toward it, and Signa knew without a sliver of a doubt that he and his brother were to have a conversation of their own.

Alone now, Blythe kept a careful distance that Signa felt like a knife to her side. Gone was the girl she'd laughed with in the snow and spent late nights gossiping with over tea. Gone was the friend she'd viewed as a sister, and in her place stood a woman Signa didn't recognize.

"I don't know what Aris has told you about me," Signa began, praying that she could find the right words. "I don't know what he's told you about himself, either, but it's not safe to trust him."

"I don't care whether it's *safe*." Blythe cradled the tapestry against her stomach. Her voice was surprisingly calm, lacking the bite that Signa expected. "You're not safe, either, Signa. I watched you take a life with a single touch. You took my brother's, too. He was going to have a child! Now that child has no father, we have no alibi, and my father is withering away in a cell and set to hang in a week. I won't let him die for this." The tapestry's warmth radiated toward Signa as Blythe extended it to her. It took everything in her not to draw back.

"I know Aris is no prince," Blythe continued. "But whatever he is, he has power. In return for you marrying him, he's agreed to free my father."

The warmth was seeping into Signa's skin now, and inch by inch it felt as though she were being set aflame. Her breaths were as thin as the memories from earlier pressed against her mind.

"Don't you think that's odd?" Signa could barely form the words as she stared down at the golden haze that surrounded the tapestry, so bright that it was painful. "He shows up out of nowhere and wants to marry *me*? And he won't help us unless we agree?"

"He knows about the shadows that follow you. He doesn't want you near them."

Only then did Signa reach forward to snatch the tapestry from Blythe's hands. It took everything in her not to drop to her knees as the burn tore through her.

"I'm sure he doesn't," Signa hissed, double-checking that her hand hadn't turned to char. "Do you even know what those shadows are?"

For the shortest moment, Signa could have sworn that Blythe's face softened, her gaze gone watery. Such tenderness, however, was fleeting, there and gone in seconds.

"Even his name is dangerous," Blythe said. "I don't dare speak it out loud."

Signa hadn't expected her to know the truth. Hadn't expected her to believe it. Her mouth was numb, words a struggle to form let alone speak. "He saved your life," was all she could manage. "Multiple times, he protected you. He let me *save* you."

Wrinkles marred Blythe's forehead. Whatever Fate had told her, it certainly wasn't this.

"I don't care." Blythe drew back, angry and mourning and looking every bit like her mother in that moment. "I *can't* care, Signa. This is the only option. It's the only way we have to save him, and you know it."

As Signa let the tapestry seep into her skin, she knew with everything in her that Blythe was right. She may have been able to use Life's powers, but was relying on them worth the risk of Elijah's life? Was it worth the risk of whatever chaos Fate promised she would bring upon them?

He'd said that he would do whatever was necessary to get Signa away from Death, and now he'd finally made good on that promise. Because to save Elijah, there was no choice but for Signa to accept Fate's deal.

Fate was lounging near the dance floor, feasting on a glittering petit four in one hand and champagne in the other as the balcony window shattered, Death descending in a tempest of shadows. Fate was midbite, barely having caught sight of his brother when the lights in Foxglove flickered off and Death wound his hand around Fate's throat.

Fate's champagne flute hit the wall, shattering as Death wrenched it from his hand. He choked on the cake, grappling for a hold as Death shoved him into the wall and pressed a forearm against Fate's windpipe.

"You may start wars, brother, but I am *always* the one who ends them." Death's hand stretched to summon his scythe. Yet it seemed he either *could* not or *would* not raise it against his brother, for in the end that hand remained empty.

"Get off me," Fate spat, freeing himself from Death's hold as Signa and Blythe raced into the ballroom. "God, you're covered with dirt. This is a party, brother. Show some decorum." He brushed himself off, and only then did Signa notice that the bodies around them had stilled once more, some of their mouths open midscream. Beside her, Blythe covered her own mouth as Death took his brother by the collar.

"You cannot force someone to be with you," he snarled, the air around him so tight that Fate was wheezing, face turning blue. "She'll hate you forever, and so will I."

"I'm not *forcing* anyone," Fate barely managed to hiss, threads of gold glinting throughout the ballroom, brighter and brighter until Death eased his hold enough for Fate to draw a sharp breath. Fate had no need for words to make his threat clear; his threads were attached to everything, and Signa had seen once already just how easily he could manipulate them. "Whatever oath we enter into will be one that Signa makes of her own free will."

"Is this why you told me to throw a party?" Signa cut across the ballroom to stand before the two men. "Not to help me, but so

I would discover that I have no way to save Elijah other than to rely on you?"

"I have merely laid the pieces to watch the story unfold." Fate's expression darkened as he clawed himself free from Death's grasp. "Did I not make myself clear when I said that I was willing to do whatever it took? Did I not give you the answers I promised?"

She'd known all along how unwise it was to trust Fate, though there had been no other options. She was free to accept his offer or not, but as she stole a look at Blythe and saw just how ashen she looked and how tightly she hugged her arms around herself, Signa knew there was no other choice. At least not one that would protect Eliza *and* the Hawthorne family.

Death had once promised he'd burn this world down for Signa. And yet it seemed she could not do the same for him, for the Hawthornes had staked their own claim on her heart, and she would do what she could to protect them. When Signa died, she would have however long she wanted with Death at her side. But for now, she looked Fate square in the eyes and said the only thing she could.

"I'll do it."

The moment the words had passed her lips, it felt like her world had ended. "This will be no happy union, Fate, I assure you. Every day for the rest of my life, I will fight to rid myself of you. But if you promise to free Elijah and allow the Hawthornes to live their lives in peace, I will make this deal willingly."

"Signa..." Death sought her stare, but she refused to give it to him for fear of changing her mind. She could look only at Blythe, staring down the reason for this promise. The reason she was ready to give up everything she loved, to protect the family that had taken her in and loved her when no one else had.

"Please don't do this. You promised me no more bargains," Death whispered, and oh how she wished she didn't have to. How she wished she could curl up into his arms and pretend that the sound of his heart breaking did not cleave her own in two. Every day for the rest of her living years, this decision would destroy her.

"I want one more night with him," she told Fate, who at least had the decency to look uncertain as she approached, as if he, too, was fearful that Signa might slip from his grasp at any moment. "Give me one more night. Not to plot or to find a way out of this, but to say goodbye. Come tomorrow morning, I will pour my blood upon that tapestry and bind myself to you. But first, give me one night without sickness. Without a time limit."

Fate's jaw clenched. "I will not share you—"

"I am not yours!" She didn't care about the memories. Didn't care about what he may or may not have meant to her in another lifetime. Right now, Fate was the villain he'd sworn never to be. "You and I are not bound, and we never will be unless you agree to my terms. I want one more night."

From his expression to his posturing, everything about Fate bristled with agitation. Still, he must have sensed that Signa meant every word. "It is more than he deserves, but I will give you your night. Only one, to say goodbye."

It wasn't enough. It would *never* be enough. Still, she crouched to pick up a shard of broken glass and pressed it into her thumb, waiting for the blood to swell before extending it to him. "Until the moment

I bind myself to you, you must agree that you will allow me not only to see Death whenever, but to touch him without harm. Swear this to me, and that you will free Elijah the moment an oath is made, and you'll have yourself a bride."

"Signa—" Death reached for her, and her heart nearly shattered when she sidestepped him.

Fate did not smile but looked plainly upon her as he withdrew a needle from his vest pocket, pricking it into his thumb and pressing it to hers to seal the blood oath. "I agree to your terms."

Fate was a fool if he thought this was how he was going to win. She didn't know how long it would take, but eventually she would escape him. Eventually she'd find Death again, whether in this life or the next.

Signa turned to him, not caring that Fate and Blythe were watching. Not caring that they were in the middle of a dark ballroom surrounded by curious spirits and Fate's marionettes as she took Death's face in her hands and pressed a kiss onto his lips.

Signa hated that her first thought wasn't of the kiss itself, but that she should commit the way his lips fit against hers to memory. That she should memorize every dip and curve of his bare skin beneath her fingertips, and the wash of coolness that settled over her. The tension in her body eased as Death drew her into his chest, winding his arms around her.

"Come," Signa whispered as her fingers closed around his. She pressed onto her toes, kissing him once more. "Let's get out of here."

Music resumed the moment Signa stepped out of the ballroom, hand in hand with Death. Voices trilled from within once more, laughter floating in the air as the ball swept back into action. No one seemed to remember that the lights had gone out, or anything of two immortals fighting beside them.

Signa paid no mind to the guests in her home; let Fate and Blythe see to them. What did it matter anyway, when she would soon be leaving Foxglove as quickly as she'd settled in?

There was an overwhelming sadness in such thoughts; one that would consume her if she let them. And so she had no choice but to cast them from her mind as she glided down the stairs with Death in tow. No choice but to cast *all* thoughts from her mind, considering the emotion that threatened to overwhelm her at any minute. If this was to be her last living night with Death, she refused to spend it crying.

Death whispered her name, calling to her, but she didn't still. Signa hurried to the second level and the room that she'd made her own.

"*Signa*," Death called again, urgent this time. "Stop whatever this nonsense is and *talk* to me." His grip on her hand tightened, and he pulled her to him as he leaned against the wall in a hallway. Empty as the hall was, Signa couldn't help but feel like there were eyes upon her, watching. But what did that matter now? If people saw her talking to the shadows, what repercussions could there be? Come tomorrow, Foxglove would no longer be her home and nosy neighbors would be of no concern.

"There's no time," she whispered, wishing that he would hurry and follow her. Wishing that he would stop fighting. But Death held tight as he bent to rest his forehead against hers. He was in his human form, dark eyes blazing. Signa's eyes fluttered shut at the touch of his cool skin, her own still warmed by her beating heart.

"We could have all the time in the world, Little Bird," he whispered. "You don't have to do this."

There was nothing more that Signa wished than for that to be true. She would spend an eternity with Death, would their circumstances allow it. And oh, how happy she would be.

Signa tilted her face up, pressing a kiss onto lips that had been made to fit hers. "You know I do," she whispered, taking his bottom lip between hers and kissing him again.

Death held her in both arms, dragging her body into his with no sign of letting go. "Then we'll find a way to break the oath once Elijah is free."

She cupped his face in her palms, unable to stop her tears. Once her blood was on that tapestry, there was no saying how long it would take to break her deal with Fate or how he might retaliate.

"Listen to me." Signa settled her palms against either side of his face. "I love you. You have made me happier and more myself than I have ever been. If we're only to have one more night, then I want it to be something that we can always think back to." Her hands slid down his body, fingers intertwining through his. She brought one of Death's hands to her lips, kissing his knuckles. He was still and silent, but he gave no argument as he let her peel away and start back toward the suite she had hoped to one day share with him.

It'd been little more than a child's fantasy, really. With something so big as life and death between them, she should have known it would never be her reality.

She didn't let go of his hand even as they stepped inside and she bolted the door behind him. The moment she let go, she feared he would disappear entirely and that would be the end of their story. And so she held him close, facing him as she backed toward the bed.

There was no mirth in his eyes. None of the smoky coolness she had come to expect. Instead, only sorrow filled his stare as he sat on the bed and drew her into his lap.

"You are my world, Signa Farrow." The tenderness in his voice threatened to break her resolve. Signa had to turn away, shutting her eyes against the feather-soft kisses he peppered down her neck. "Whatever happens tomorrow, know that this will not be our final night together. I swear that nothing could ever stop me from fighting for you."

"I know you won't." His words were the most beautiful song, and she held to them like a promise. Let Fate believe he'd won; neither she nor Death would ever stop fighting.

Signa slid her legs on either side of him and wound her hands around his neck as he kissed her, lips lingering from her neck to her mouth, then down to her chest. Her eyes fell shut, body suffocating beneath the layers of her gown even despite Death's perpetual chill. She shivered as his hands found its laces, as if reading her mind. He'd always had that way about him; that uncanny ability to know what she was thinking or what she wanted.

God, she was going to miss that.

Signa slipped off her dress, helping him slide it to the floor. Death took his time to brush his hand down the shape of her, thumb tracing patterns across her hips. Signa tipped her head back, savoring every touch. She helped free him of his shirt, then his pants as the shadows he summoned followed his hands to trail along her skin, carving a path of ice that seared within her.

Death took his time tasting her, lips rolling over her breasts, her navel, and traveling lower to the most sensitive part of her as he laid her on her back.

His name tasted like honeyed wine as she whispered it into the night. Her hips rocked against him, but when she shut her eyes to savor the tension rising with her, the shadows were behind her neck, tipping her head back up to him.

"Look at me." His voice was no whisper, but a command that seized her attention. "I want you looking at me when I touch you."

It was a privilege, she realized, to be able to look upon him after so long and see him as he held her. As he consumed her. Her hands twisted in the bedsheets, and it was the hunger in his eyes that struck her core, her body shuddering with the release that rolled over her.

Death leaned back then, and Signa took a moment to appreciate the sheer sight of him before her, hips tangled in the sheets, gaze never straying from hers. She'd have given almost anything to spend the rest of her life with him here like this. Eyes locked with his, Signa drew herself into his lap, wanting to taste and feel every inch of him tonight, while she still could.

Death groaned with a desire that rippled over her. She wanted to earn that sound. Wanted to draw it from his lips again and again. She wound her arms around his neck, holding him as their bodies connected and she rolled her hips against his. One of Death's hands came around her neck, steadying her against him as the other settled on her thigh, thumbs pressing into her skin.

"You are mine." The words were not possession, but a promise. "For as long as you'll have me, you are *mine,* Signa Farrow. I will burn this world to cinders before I let anyone take you from me."

When the sun rose, their time together would be over. But for tonight, they would make the most of this goodbye. She would explore all that there was of him, and hoped that when dawn came and left them with only their memories, they would think of this night forevermore.

FORTY-ONE

Blythe

BLYTHE WAS BREATHLESS WHEN SHE RETURNED TO THE BALLROOM, flushed and clutching her chest.

She couldn't say what drove her to follow Signa, or what she might have done if her cousin had noticed her in the hall, watching as Signa spoke to the murky haze that was becoming more visible by the second.

Maybe Blythe had gone to talk to her. Maybe she'd gone to try to quell the raging guilt that was bubbling and festering within her.

Or maybe she'd gone for answers.

He would have killed her. He would have killed her....

She'd heard Death when he spoke those words to Signa back in the garden, his voice like smoke and honey. She couldn't seem to scrub the sound of it from her mind.

He would have killed her.

Surely Death hadn't been referring to who she thought he was. It wasn't possible. And yet... Blythe still had not cried. Weeks of knowing that her brother was dead, and still she could not bring herself to mourn him.

It wasn't so different than when she'd found out about Signa. The truth had stared her in the face since the beginning; it was only a matter of believing it.

She missed Percy more than she could put into words, and yet for some ridiculous reason she felt only guilt clawing at her throat, fighting to suffocate her. Not for losing her brother or for her lack of tears, but for being unable to wipe away the memory of Signa's heartbreak and the tenderness of her touch as she held Death.

Signa Farrow was in love with the reaper. She was in *love,* and yet she was willing to give up her own happiness all because Blythe had asked.

Signa deserved it, though, didn't she? For all the harm that she'd brought to the Hawthorne family? Besides, women married near strangers all the time, and surely Aris was better than death incarnate... wasn't he?

The ballroom was too hot, cramped with dancing bodies ignorant of what was happening around them. Why were they still here, twirling in their ridiculous gowns and laughing while Blythe's world fell apart?

Her father was to be hanged. Her dead brother had left an unborn child behind. Signa, the cousin she wanted so desperately to hate but couldn't no matter how hard she tried, was going to marry a man Blythe could not even begin to trust. And if her head didn't stop its pounding soon, she had half a mind to tear it from her neck.

Each breath that Blythe took felt like someone was dragging

nails down her throat. All she wanted was for the party to end and for these people to leave. Byron had gathered Charlotte and Everett to watch over Eliza, and the only person Blythe still recognized was Aris. Even the way he sipped his champagne was too smug for her liking, and before she knew what she was doing, she was storming over to him.

"Are you certain that he has foul intentions?" Blythe didn't know the question was on her mind until it spilled out of her, earning immediate scrutiny from Aris as he set down his drink. He didn't need to ask who she was talking about.

"He is Death, Miss Hawthorne. I'm sure you can answer that question yourself."

That was the problem, she couldn't. Signa had always seemed like a relatively sound judge of character, and her love for him was undeniable. She'd claimed that Death had saved Blythe, too. If all that was true and both she and Death really were on Blythe's side . . .

She took the half-full flute that Aris had set down and finished it in one swig, grimacing. "You'll take care of her, won't you?" God, it would be so much easier if she could dismiss Signa from her mind and think of her only as the killer who had pried Blythe's family apart.

"Of course I will." Aris extended his hand, and Blythe took it on instinct. He led her to the dance floor, one hand slipping to her waist. "She will want for nothing, I assure you. At the very least, you can rest easy knowing that your cousin will no longer be surrounded by death every waking moment of her life."

That was precisely what was bothering her. Whether Blythe understood it or not, it was difficult to ignore that being with Death at every moment seemed to be *precisely* what her cousin wanted. Never had Blythe seen Signa with such tenderness or adoration upon her face. It wasn't infatuation or a morbid curiosity, but real love that Blythe was going to rip from her. All because of Aris. All because of *Fate*.

"I know what you are." The words were too soft, too timid, and Blythe despised them. "And I know that you are aware of things that no one should be aware of. I want you to tell me the truth—do you know what happened to my brother?"

His severity was like a punch to the throat as he squeezed her hand. "Your cousin killed him—"

"I know that part." It had been a while since she'd danced, and yet her body moved effortlessly with his just as it had the night of his ball, the dance ingrained in her bones. "I want to know *why*. The truth, Aris. Please."

When his eyes flickered over her, seemingly searching for an escape, Blythe wanted to curl into herself and never unfurl. Because in that moment she knew why she hadn't cried, knew why Signa had taken Percy, and that what Death had said in the garden was the truth.

Percy had been the one who had tried to kill her. Which meant that Percy had killed their mother.

Blythe shoved away as the music crescendoed into a crashing finale. Her head throbbed harder, and the world continued to spin even as she stopped moving. Aris watched her with narrowed interest as she staggered away from the dance floor.

She'd made a mistake. An awful, horrible mistake.

"Miss Hawthorne?" Aris closed the space between them, taking her by the elbow. "Miss Hawthorne, what's wrong?"

Heat lanced through her body at that touch, and she ripped her arm from him. She needed to get out of there. Needed to give her mind room to breathe, to think, and... God, what had she done?

"Get them out of here," she all but gasped. The words sounded like a distant echo, as though they hadn't even come from her lips. "Get everyone out."

And before Aris could argue, Blythe fled the ballroom.

FORTY-TWO

Morning came too quickly. Signa watched as dawn crept through her curtains, slices of dusky orange cutting across the room.

She was wound in Death's arms, head against his chest and entirely at home in the cocoon of sheets they'd drawn over them. She and Death kept to their silence, neither daring to shatter the peaceful lie they'd built around themselves. Yet as birds sang and the sunlight had them burrowing deeper into the sheets to shield their eyes, Signa knew there was no other choice. If they didn't get up, Fate would find them soon enough. She pressed kisses down the length of Death's neck and chest before she forced herself from him to get dressed.

Perhaps it was foolish of her, but the dress she grabbed from the armoire was stark black mourning wear, and neither she nor Death made any comment of it as she slipped it over her body.

Shadows slid up Death's neck as he stood, shrouding himself in a mantle of darkness. He brushed a finger down Signa's neck as she pinned her hair up, then let his hand slip to her waist.

"There is another option." His voice was as sweet as ambrosia, and so divine that all Signa wanted was to lose herself within it. She didn't want to hope, fearing she would only be disappointed. And yet she peered up at him, praying for words that could save them.

Death curled his hand around her waist, his hips pressed against her low back as he drew her close. "We could find a way to kill my brother."

She should have known it was a fool's hope.

"And what of Elijah?" she asked, not unkindly. "We leave him to hang?"

"We can find someone else to frame—"

"And doom another?" It would be a lie to say that she hadn't considered it, but . . . No. There was a way out of this that would affect no one but her and Death. She'd brought enough people into her mess. "You and I are not confined to the rules of time, Death, and Fate is too vain a man to be bound to someone who despises him." It didn't matter what memories returned to her; Fate would always be the villain who had forced her hand.

"Is Blythe truly worth such a sacrifice?" Death countered. "Fate is as stubborn as he is vain. He will do anything to spite me, Signa. You cannot count on him to end your bargain so easily."

Despite its bluntness, the question was fair. In the grand scheme, Signa hadn't known the Hawthornes long. And yet she felt bound to them, forever woven into the folds of this family that had inherited her. The last thing she wanted was to spend her years seeing Blythe's fire snuffed out, or to know that she could have prevented Elijah's death when he was only just beginning to truly live.

The Hawthornes were her family, and with everything in her, Signa loved them. And so she took Death's hand in hers, brushing her thumb across his skin as she answered, "I wish that she wasn't. Truly I do, because I know what I'm losing and that I'll spend every moment away from you wishing that it didn't have to be this way. But we will have our time, and when we do I swear that I will never leave your side again.

"My love for you is not confined to time, nor fate," she continued. "It is a love that I will hold with me for an eternity, which is why I am not afraid. I swear to you that I will always be yours, even when I am not."

Death's reflection grew hazy upon the mirror, wisps of shadows smearing the glass. "You are a fool to think that I could so easily let you go." He clenched his jaw tight, curling a finger around the loose baby hairs at her neck. He slid that same finger down her arm until his fingers laced through hers. Death's expression had hardened, a new resolve settling over him as he ushered her toward the door. "Come, Little Bird. It's time for us to visit my brother one last time."

Though she knew nothing good could come of it, there was little choice but to let Death lead the way.

Foxglove was still in disarray from the ball the night prior, champagne flutes abandoned on the mahogany banister and rugs strewn about, their edges folded over. She and her staff had put so much into Foxglove this past month, and for what? To let some strangers disrespect her home just so she could lose it? Signa gritted her teeth at the thought.

Everything within her hardened at the sight of Fate waiting for her at the bottom of the stairs. He didn't once acknowledge his brother's presence even as Death's rage turned the floor to sleet. "It's past dawn," was all Fate said, his face severe as he took in her choice of dress. "You're late."

Death answered before she could. "We were busy."

Signa gave his hand a squeeze of reproach, but holding back Death was no better than fighting a storm. The clouds darkened with each step they took toward the parlor, and when they came close enough to see the tapestry laid out on the table, Signa knew that the best thing she could do was to release her hold on the reaper.

Fate was ready, a golden light emitting from his skin as Death threw him against the wall. The light cleaved Death's shadows as Fate matched his brother and took him by the throat.

"I gave you your night." Though Fate spoke with a remarkable calm, every word was lethal. "Signa and I made a blood oath, brother, and you've gotten more from it than you deserve."

The stairs creaked behind them, and Signa stilled when she caught sight of Blythe peeking around the corner, still dressed in her evening wear from the prior night. The sight of her had Signa's throat swelling. She was about to turn away in the hope that her cousin would return to her room when Signa saw that Blythe's eyes were bloodshot. Blythe hurried down the stairs before Signa could stop her and grabbed hold of her cousin's hands.

"I'm so sorry," Blythe whispered at once, mindful of her uncle and the Wakefields still sleeping upstairs. "I never should have put this on you. I never should have let Aris give me that tapestry." She turned to glare at the thing, breathing so hard that Signa tightened her grip to steady her.

"It's all right," Signa said, and she meant it. For the Hawthornes, this was a sacrifice worth making.

Fate had taken care with the tapestry, laying parchment paper beneath the threads to catch her blood. Signa stilled at the sight of a small switchblade that rested beside it, able to smell the alcohol that he'd used to clean it.

Death and Fate still had each other by the throat, and Signa knew there was no time to wait. If she hurried, Death wouldn't be able to stop her. He wouldn't have to watch.

"I need you to know that I only ever wanted what was best for your family." Signa pushed the words out, forcing herself to command Blythe's attention. "I never wanted to hurt Percy. I loved him, Blythe, I truly did. I wanted him to be my family, too."

Blythe held Signa tighter as she asked, "Then why did you do it?"

Signa forced herself to smile as she let Blythe's hand slip from hers. "Because you deserved to live. You deserve the world, Blythe, and I hope that you take it." Plain and simple, that was the truth. Signa turned before she could see Blythe's eyes swell with tears, crossing to the table to take hold of the switchblade. It was smooth and cold beneath her hands, and she flipped it open with a shudder, remembering the night of Percy's death and that he'd tried to attack her with a blade just like this one.

She clasped the knife tight in her hands, shaking the memory from her mind. From somewhere behind her, the men seemed to notice her new position. Death yelled something inaudible as he hurried toward her, his words drowned out by the rushing of her blood as she lifted the sharpest point of the blade to her finger and pricked the skin.

The world fell silent as the blood welled up, and all Signa could think about was how odd it was that one drop could change everything. One drop, and her life would be forever changed.

Yet change, it seemed, was not in her cards that day.

Signa fell to the floor, the wind knocked from her lungs and her blood smearing the wood as someone threw her aside. Blythe stood over her, wild-eyed as she looked not at Signa but at the tapestry in front of her. Blythe ripped it from the table, clutching it to her chest.

"Miss Hawthorne." Fate did not speak loudly, but with a grave severity a thousand times more threatening as he took a step forward and told Blythe, "I need you to put that down."

Never could Signa have imagined Blythe fearless enough to turn her simmering eyes toward Fate. "No."

Signa fisted the switchblade tight, keeping it ready in case he dared to make a move against her cousin. Unlike Death, Fate was not made up of shadows but had a human body that needed to eat and breathe. Perhaps he would not be so immune to a blade as Death was.

"Put that *down*," Fate repeated, spitting the words through his teeth. "There is an oath in place."

"You don't need to remind me of the oath, Aris. I was there when you made it." Blythe didn't look away from Fate as she ran her finger down the length of the tapestry's threads. Fate froze midstep.

"Until the moment Signa pours her blood upon the tapestry and willingly binds herself to you, you will allow her not only to see Death, but to touch him without harm," Blythe spoke the words slowly as she raised the tapestry to eye level. "You also promised to free my father the moment an oath is made and you have yourself a bride. Did I get it all right?"

"You did," he agreed. "Now put the tapestry down and we'll still have our deal."

Signa knew she should move. Knew she should rip the tapestry from Blythe's hands and spare her cousin from any more of Fate's threats. Yet there was an electricity in the air that kept Signa rooted to the floor, clutching the knife. She whipped her head to Death, only to find that he was inching toward her, careful not to draw his brother's attention.

Don't move, he whispered, the words inside her mind.

Even Fate was hesitant with the steps he drew toward Blythe. For each one he took forward, she stepped back toward the roaring flames in the hearth.

"You used me," Blythe began. "You made me believe the worst of my cousin. But I know the truth now, Aris, and I could never live with myself if I let her make this deal."

"Miss Hawthorne," Fate seethed, "if you take one more step—"

"Then you'll what?" Blythe held the tapestry out, nearly letting the flames taste the fabric. "What will you do to me, Aris? As clever as you are, I expected more from you."

Fate's chest heaved with slow, measured breaths as he looked between her and the fire. It was clear he was debating making a dive for the tapestry. Anytime he drew a breath closer, however, Blythe lowered it toward the flames until Fate backed away, tearing his hands through his hair in frustration.

"Come now," she urged, as merciless as Signa had ever seen. "Aren't you going to ask me why I expected more?"

Exasperated as he was, Fate had no choice but to play along. "Why, Miss Hawthorne?" If words could kill, his would have severed her five times over. "Why did you expect more from me?"

Blythe gave no warning as she sliced her palm across the iron poker near the hearth and turned to stare Fate dead in the eyes. "Because you never specified who had to be your bride."

Blythe smiled as she spilled her blood upon the tapestry's golden threads.

FORTY-THREE

Blythe Hawthorne had bested Fate four separate times.

Signa allowed Death to grab hold of her, dragging her to the opposite side of the room as Fate clutched his left hand to his chest, a glowing band igniting upon his ring finger. Blythe wore a matching one that she paid little mind to as a thread shone bright between them, binding them.

"We have to help her," Signa whispered as Fate crossed toward Blythe in three long strides, looking poised to wrap his hands around her throat. And yet Death held Signa tight.

He made an oath with you. Death's voice was lighter than she'd heard in ages. *For as long as he lives, he cannot bring harm upon Blythe Hawthorne.*

Only then did Signa's body ease, tears of relief spilling from her even as Fate closed the space between himself and Blythe.

"You have no idea what you've just done," he snarled, poised to kill.

Blythe did not back away, but instead pressed against his chest as she tipped her head to sneer at him. "On the contrary, I believe I've just fulfilled an oath. Are you not proud of your wife's cleverness?"

Fate's nostrils flared. "You are *not* my wife."

"I believe this says otherwise." She held up her finger, wiggling it. Fate looked as though he were seeing red. He pushed from her and whirled toward Death and Signa. Death had his shadows around her in a second, shielding her, but there was no need. It wasn't Signa that Fate looked to with murder in his eyes, but Death. Fate's golden eyes glinted, the barely visible threads around him shifting. Whatever he tried, however, didn't work. The golden band of light on his finger flared bright and he gasped, the vein in his neck bulging as he doubled over and clutched his hand tight.

Blythe's footsteps were as light as a dancer's as she closed the space between them and wound her fingers into his blond hair. She bent toward his ear, speaking the words as softly as a lover, "I want my father freed this afternoon."

When Fate laughed, the sound was manic. "You're going to regret this." There was no masking his rage. His sorrow. Yet Signa could not pity him. He had laid this trap; he shouldn't have been surprised to have ended up caught in it.

Just like during their game of croquet, he should have known better than to underestimate Blythe. They all should have.

"Don't worry, darling." Blythe laid a kiss upon his cheek, leaving a press of rouge. "You'll have the rest of your life to make it up to me."

Never had Signa seen such anger. Such a promise of destruction in one's eyes as she did when Fate turned, storming into the threads of light that disappeared his body within seconds. To where, Signa didn't care to know.

With only the three of them left, the parlor fell silent. Signa couldn't say whether seconds or minutes passed before Blythe sighed and perched herself on the edge of a leather chair, inspecting the band around her finger.

"Is it horribly noticeable?"

Signa took her first breath in who knew how long. She hadn't realized how tight her body had become, chest so constricted that it felt on the verge of collapsing. Peeling from Death's grip, she moved toward Blythe for a closer inspection.

"No, actually." Signa's words were loosened with a breath. The band on Blythe's finger was cleverly masked—little more than a dim shimmer one had to squint to see, like white ink on fair skin. It reminded Signa vaguely of a scar, and she clutched her chest when it became even tighter with guilt.

"I was going to take care of this, Blythe. You never should have gotten involved."

Blythe dropped her hand, inspecting Signa now. "And yet I did."

And yet she did.

Signa stared at her cousin, uncertain whether she was meant to shake her or hug her or tell her how much of a fool she'd been to make a bargain with someone as powerful as Fate. Though Blythe must have had some sense of the power he wielded, not even Signa knew the extent of it.

"He is Fate." Signa kept her voice soft, desperate to know that her cousin understood the gravity of her situation. "You cannot break an oath with him."

"Why not?" Blythe sat straighter, calm as she looked at Signa. "Have I not bested him before?"

Death and Signa shared a look as she wondered whether Blythe had any idea just how true that was.

"Regardless, I'm not certain I'd want to break it." Blythe hopped down from the chair, and before Signa could ask what she meant, said, "There are no false pretenses between us. I may live my life however I'd like, and all pressure of courting will be gone. Everyone will even believe I'm a princess." Blythe may have dazzled with her smile, yet the corners of it wavered. Still, she reached to take hold of Signa's hand with the same softness she'd shown earlier.

"Don't worry about me. I appreciate you being so willing to save my father, but I'll take it from here." Signa's chest nearly broke when Blythe placed a gentle kiss on her hand.

"After all that I did," Signa whispered, "why would you help me?"

"Because you were willing to help *me*." The answer came too easily, in a voice that was too light. "You deserve to live, too, Signa. I may not understand everything, but I know Percy was the reason I was dying. I know that you saved me from him."

The unexpected words brought immediate tears to Signa's eyes and had her stomach so sick that she bowed at the waist. She hugged herself tight, trying to keep herself together.

"You were never supposed to find out."

"I know," Blythe whispered. "But I needed to. Now, leave it to me to take care of Byron and the others. It's time that I go pack. I don't want my father coming home to an empty house."

Elijah, home. Never had there been words more magnificent.

"I'll be on a train first thing tomorrow morning," Signa said, only to stumble over herself as she realized her misstep. "I mean . . . if that's all right with you."

Blythe's smile was like birdsong on a warm spring day. "It is," she whispered, and Signa's heart softened when Blythe squeezed her hand once more. "I'm sure my father would want you there, too."

Death had given them some space after Fate had left, but he slowly drew back to Signa's side. He pressed a kiss onto the top of her head, and Signa nearly wept when it didn't steal her breath or still her heart. She eased into Death's arms as Blythe started toward the door. At the threshold, however, Blythe turned to look back not at her cousin but at Death, whose shadows had slipped from him.

He didn't notice at first because it was impossible. A fluke. And yet he stilled as Blythe continued to stare, observing his human form with narrowed interest.

"Take care of her." Blythe's words were not a kindness, but a threat. "My cousin seems to see the good in you, and I'll trust her judgment. But if you so much as bring a single tear to her eye, I'll have your head on a pike. Do you understand me?"

Both Signa and Death were at a loss for words as they stared at Blythe's retreating figure. They listened to the soft clacking of her boots against the stairs before they turned to each other, and Signa could not help herself as her sob gave way to laughter.

They had won. They'd conquered Fate. They'd saved Elijah, her relationship with Blythe was on the mend, and now Signa could *see* Death. She could *hold* him.

"Blythe can see you."

"A side effect from nearly dying, perhaps," Death said, though he sounded distant as he continued to stare at the door. It took Signa laughing again and cupping his face in her bare hands to steal his attention, which he was more than happy to offer as he bent to her touch.

"You're so warm," he whispered, "I can feel it." The crack in his voice was enough for the emotion to swell within her once more. Signa threw her arms around him, kissing him through hot, happy tears. She wound her legs around him as Death all but tackled her to the ground, squeezing her tight. Signa savored each one of her breaths as she tucked herself against his chest. They had won, and for the rest of their eternity she would never let go.

"So I take it that you're staying, then?" Tilly stood at the edge of the parlor, her head poking inside. The disappointment in her voice had Signa cackling as she clasped Death's hand in hers and raised it toward the spirit.

"Yes, I'm afraid we are."

The other two spirits approached then, timid as they glanced around the room. Eventually Tilly's mother, Victoria, looked to Signa with a disapproving pucker of her lips. *"We would appreciate if you at least kept better company. The man was far too bright for my taste."*

"There was another who glowed, too, just like the lady's maid," Tilly

added, voice conspiratorial. *"I do wish you'd stop bringing them. The light is bothersome on my eyes."*

Signa felt her grin slip. "There was someone else with a glow? Who was it?"

"She's asleep upstairs now." Oliver was once again trying to wipe away the smudge he could never seem to clean from his glasses. *"The one everyone's making such a fuss about."*

"As they should!" Victoria piped. *"She's pregnant and unmarried! They were up all night scheming up ways to conceal it. How tasteless it is to—"*

"They speak of Eliza," Signa interrupted, ignoring Victoria's huffing as she spun toward Death, who didn't look nearly as concerned as she felt.

"You healed her, Signa." He tucked a strand of hair behind her ear, no longer silver. "Perhaps the glow is a side effect of that."

"Perhaps," she echoed, though the words didn't sit right in her gut. "But I've never done anything for Elaine."

It was then that her eye caught sight of something behind Death. Or rather a *lack* of something. Signa's spine went rigid as she looked to where the tapestry had once lain. Blythe had torn open her palm in that spot, and yet despite all the blood she'd spilled, there was not a drop of it on the wood.

Cold dread swept over Signa as she thought to the ring of light Blythe had showed her, upon the finger of an unblemished hand.

"Death," Signa spoke his name slowly, testing each word before allowing it into existence. "Amity once asked me whether there was a constant to Life's magic. Something present whenever I used it."

From the vines in Elijah's study, to the foal in the stables, and again with Eliza... *Blythe* had been a constant. "What if it's not me who caused that glow?" She picked up the poker Blythe had slashed her hand on—uncomfortably warm from being near the hearth—only to find that there wasn't a speck of blood upon it. Death took it from her, and the moment the iron fell upon his fingers he jolted back, dropping it with a clang.

He clutched his hand to his chest as the skin hissed and smoked, shadows swathing over it. Immediately Death crouched for a better look at the poker, and though there was a long moment in which he wore no expression, in the end his face broke into the most joyous laughter Signa had ever heard as tears rolled over his beaming cheeks.

"You found her." He scooped up the poker once more, laughing as it sizzled against his palm. With his free hand he grabbed Signa, pulling her into his embrace. His tears were cold as they fell onto her shoulder, his voice soft as snowfall as he whispered, "After all these years, you truly found her. It would seem, Little Bird, that fate always has a way of working itself out in the end."

Signa's body numbed with disbelief, her mind a whirlwind of thoughts. It couldn't be true... and yet it was the only explanation that made sense.

Signa had seen Life's memories, but every time they came to her, Blythe had been there. The realization brought such a great relief that Signa had no words.

This was why her body burned, and why she had such trouble accessing those powers. They'd never belonged to her, but to Blythe.

Blythe was the reincarnation of Life.

"Do we tell her?" Signa whispered as she stared at the poker, unsure what to feel. For as much as she could understand Fate, Signa hated him for what he'd tried to do. But if Fate were to find out who Blythe truly was...

"No." There wasn't an ounce of hesitation in Death's words. He squeezed Signa close, pressing a kiss against her temple with no care for the spirits who stirred uncomfortably behind them. "Let them figure it out on their own time. Theirs is a story in which we should not interfere."

Signa wasn't certain she agreed. Part of her wanted little more than to hurry up the stairs and tell Blythe then and there. But Death's joy kept her in place, wound tight in his arms.

Perhaps she would tell Blythe soon. For now though, she would trust that Death knew what he was saying.

"They may try to kill each other," Signa noted, though her voice held no argument.

"You once tried to kill me, and look where that got us." Death's eyes beamed brighter than ever as he rose to his feet and pulled her up alongside him. "Now, Little Bird, why don't you show me around this house of ours?" He offered his hand, and with a heart so full it could burst, Signa took it.

EPILOGUE

Blythe

Everett Wakefield and Charlotte Killinger married two months later with the midsummer sun beaming down upon them.

It seemed that happiness was everywhere these days. Blythe watched it blossom between the bride and groom as he drew her in for a kiss. It was in the tender touch that Eliza pressed upon her swollen belly, and the way that Elijah laughed when she jolted from the baby's kick. Eliza was only weeks away from meeting her child, and Elijah had welcomed her into the family without a second thought.

Signa, too, had unfurled like a flower, sighing as she threaded her fingers through Death's as he embraced her.

Blythe supposed she should be happy, too, now that she had her father back and knew that neither Everett nor Charlotte was the duke's killer. Even so, no matter how grateful Blythe was for the way things had turned out, there was no ridding herself of the deep unease that coiled like a spring within her.

Whatever Signa had done that night in the garden, it hadn't just affected Eliza and the child. Blythe hadn't told a soul of the things she'd seen, or how in the moment their lives were saved, Blythe had fallen into a sea of white light. The warmth of it had coaxed her, easing her worries and stealing her thoughts for seconds that'd felt like hours. And in that sea, she'd dreamed of velvet laughter. Of a faceless man who spun her in his arms, dancing to unfamiliar music that she somehow recognized. Music she knew every step to.

It was ridiculous, and yet Blythe couldn't rid herself of the memories. They scratched against her mind as she watched Everett cup his hand around Charlotte's face, reminding Blythe of a time when a faceless someone had held her like that. A time when the heat of his kiss had blazed through her body, and she wanted nothing more than to drown herself in his touch.

Memories was the wrong word for what these images in her head really were, because they didn't belong to her. Surely Blythe wouldn't forget falling in love. Especially not with someone whose hands felt so strong against her cheek, or so powerful as they slid down her hips and lifted—

She shook away the image, hoping no one noticed that she was blushing. If she could take a shovel and dig the thoughts out, she would have by now, for they were doing her and her late-night fantasies no favors. She threw her attention instead to the happy couple, clapping with the others as the newlyweds kissed.

After everything that had happened over the past year, the Wakefield manor felt too beautiful for comfort. Its glassware and gilded cakes were too glittering, and the audience too opulent in their suits and gowns. Blythe kept expecting something to break, or perhaps for fire to rain from the sky, which wasn't at all helping her to focus. That spring within her coiled even tighter, and she wanted to turn around and follow her unease. It felt like someone was watching her, yet she couldn't sense where those curious eyes were coming from.

"It's a beautiful wedding, isn't it?"

Blythe flinched, recognizing the voice as Signa's a moment too late. She took in Signa's dark navy gown, a sharp contrast to her own, which was a shade of blue so icy that it almost looked silver. Elijah stood a short distance behind Signa, animated as he spoke to a laughing Eliza.

"He's going to make a fantastic grandfather," Signa continued when Blythe didn't say anything, eyes narrowing on her cousin.

"He will," Blythe agreed, turning her attention to the bride and groom. "And I daresay Charlotte has never looked happier."

Blythe's chest swelled as the couple held each other in tender arms. It was good to see Everett with a light in his eyes, again. The death of his father had been labeled a natural cause. The rumor was that the alleged poison was nothing more than a mistake made by a hasty coroner, thrown off by the body belonging to such a high-profile figure. A lie, of course, but one Blythe knew she and Signa would take to their graves.

Or at least she would. She wasn't certain whether Signa would even *have* a grave.

"Has a name been chosen for the baby?" Signa asked a touch louder, earning the attention of the other Hawthornes, Eliza included.

She and Byron had announced their marriage days after Elijah's return to Thorn Grove. They claimed to have been married months prior, citing Elijah's imprisonment and Lord Wakefield's death as the reason they'd kept the news from the public. There were whispers, of course, given the prominence of Eliza's belly. But there would be no way to disprove anything; the two planned to take an extended trip to the countryside for the birth so that no one would know when the child came.

It may not have been the marriage that Eliza envisioned for herself, though it was one that had saved her. There was no romance between her and Byron, and as Eliza had told the girls already, Byron expected nothing that she was not inclined to offer. He had loved Percy, and all he wanted was to be there for the child.

"Cyril for a boy," Eliza said with tender eagerness, grinning as she looked to Byron. "We're still deciding for a girl."

"It's a strong name," Elijah said before excusing himself to congratulate Charlotte's father. All the while his grin was so wide that Blythe feared his face might split in two.

The excitement in Byron's eyes, too, was undeniable. Signa prodded at it, her voice teasing, "Are you ready for their arrival? I imagine it feels like the child will be here any day."

Byron placed a hand on the small of Eliza's back. "It'll be a relief to have them here." He tried to sound casual about it, though casual for Byron meant that he might as well have been shouting from the rooftops.

"The day cannot come soon enough." Eliza's voice softened, ensuring no curious ears were paying them any mind. "I fear I will not know peace until this child is delivered safely."

“They will be.” There was an edge of hardness to Byron’s posture. “There is no one to threaten the child’s life anymore, Eliza. You may sleep easy.”

The severity of Signa’s darkening eyes straightened Blythe’s spine.

“Did someone want the child gone?” Signa asked, not the least bit taken aback when Eliza puckered her lips at such a brazen question. Even Byron tensed further.

“My uncle did.” Eliza kept her voice soft, meant only for the four of them. “He gave me two options the night before his death—get rid of the baby or be engaged to Sir Bennet by the week’s end.”

Byron didn’t bother trying to conceal his bitterness. “The child deserves better than someone with one foot already in his grave. The baby is a *Hawthorne* and should be raised as one.”

Blythe felt Signa’s eyes slide to her and understood the look at once. Byron had not necessarily said anything damning…and yet one could not help but wonder at his tone while remembering how adamant Eliza had been about the dose of cyanide. Blythe had thought it little more than the ramblings of a guilty woman, and yet as she looked upon the possessiveness of Byron’s touch as he held Eliza, sweat trailed a line down her back.

Eliza claimed to have rid herself of the cyanide in a panic that night. And if that was true, it was possible that Eliza had not been the last person to touch the poison or the drink that had made its way to Lord Wakefield.

Byron was one of the few who’d known about Elijah’s sobriety. He was one of the few who could have ensured that it wasn’t Elijah who drank the poison, but Lord Wakefield. Because had Lord Wakefield lived, Percy's child would have been lost to them, either never born, or made the secret bastard of a father Byron believed was unsuited to raise a Hawthorne.

Looking at Byron now—at the pride in his eyes and the possessiveness of his touch—Blythe realized one thing: Byron never would have allowed either of those scenarios to happen.

Blythe knew that her cousin had come to the same understanding as they watched the two retreat toward a shaded table, Byron taking great care to help Eliza into a seat.

For the sake of Percy's child, it was Byron who'd poisoned the duke. And though the truth of it weighed upon her chest like a brick, there was nothing to be done. It wasn't as though they'd ever get a confirmation out of Byron, and even if they did, what would it matter? They'd chosen to protect Eliza. Now they'd have to do the same for him.

So lost in her own thoughts was Blythe that she didn't hear the clinking against crystal until she noticed several heads swivel toward it. There wasn't so much as a moment to check in with Signa about this new information, for her cousin's attention had already been stolen away by the sound. Only when Signa blanched did Blythe follow her gaze.

Prince Aris did not wear black as the other men did but had outfitted himself in a frock coat the color of autumn moss. He looked every bit a prince as he smiled upon the crowd and raised his champagne into the air, waiting for others to mirror him.

"I'd like to extend my congratulations to the new husband and wife, and to propose a toast to the joys of marriage!" He'd cleaned up nicely since Blythe had last seen him, no longer wild and haggard or raging like a rabid dog. His golden hair had been freshly barbered and his shoes polished, though it was the ring of golden light around his finger that Blythe struggled to peel her eyes from. She wondered whether anyone else could see it.

"You've made the commitment to honor one person, for better or worse. Richer or poorer. To cherish and be faithful to them until Death himself comes for you." He kept his voice jovial even as he scanned the crowd, one corner of his lips twisting upward as his gaze settled upon Blythe. "It's an admirable commitment, and I can only hope that, one day, my future bride and I will be half as happy as the two of you. Isn't that right, Miss Hawthorne?"

Several ladies gasped and looked toward Diana, who had undoubtedly still been proclaiming herself the future princess of the imaginary Verena. In the end though, it was Blythe that all eyes sought out, including her father's. Elijah had gone pale as a ghost, and in that moment, Blythe wanted nothing more than to cross the floor and pluck Aris's eyeballs from his skull. Then she'd shove them back into their sockets just so she could pluck them again.

She didn't though, as a better, more vicious plan had entered her mind, refusing to let her shy away from his challenge. It was a decision that would warrant a discussion she *really* didn't want to have with her father, but there was no way Blythe could allow Aris to win the war he'd waged.

She lifted her own flute of champagne and threw on her brightest smile as she twirled around the crowd. "You two are an inspiration to us all!" Someone ought to have given her an award for the joy she managed to slip into her own voice. "Let us toast to your brilliant future, and to your many years ahead. I hope that His Highness and I will soon be as happy." She tipped the flute back among polite clapping, swallowing the drink in a single swig.

Blythe could have sworn she heard Death's laughter in the rustling trees, though she didn't glance back to confirm it. Instead, she tossed her hair, nearly laughing aloud when Aris caught sight of her father, the smug grin sinking from his lips as Elijah brushed past Blythe, heading for the prince himself. Even a deity was no match for a father scorned, and as Aris braced himself, Blythe offered her condolences with a sweet wave.

If this man believed that he would be her ruin, she would show him just how wrong he was. There was nothing in this world that would make Blythe happier than spending the rest of her life making *Prince* Aris Dryden regret his very existence.

Again the rustle of laughter sounded, and this time Blythe saw Death's shadows ensnare Signa as he whispered, "And now the show begins."

ACKNOWLEDGMENTS

Writing a book may be a solitary endeavor, but the act of putting one out into the world requires a village. Fortunately, I get to work with the best village imaginable.

Thank you to the fantastic team at Hachette Book Group for giving these books the perfect home at Little, Brown Books for Young Readers. A special shout out to:

Deirdre Jones, for being the loveliest editor and the best partner I could have asked for to help shepherd this series into the world. I'm very lucky to get to work with such a fabulous mind!

Shivani Annirood, for your publicity prowess and helping get as many eyes on these books as possible.

Jenny Kimura, for your stunning designs and for making every edition of this book absolutely breathtaking.

Robin Cruise, Chandra Wohleber, and Logan Hill, for scouring for every typo and weird line that made no sense to ensure that the book reads as smoothly as possible.

Stefanie Hoffman, Emilie Polster, Savannah Kennelly, Christie Michel, Victoria Stapleton, Shawn Foster, Danielle Cantarella, Sasha Illingworth, Jessica Levine, Alvina Ling, Megan Tingley, Jackie

Engel, Marisa Finkelstein, and Virginia Lawther. You all have my endless gratitude for the things you have done for this series. Thank you so much for being such a wonderful and supportive team. I feel very fortunate to be working with you.

Across the pond at Hodderscape, thank you to Molly Powell, for your editorial eye and giving this series such a brilliant home in the UK.

Kate Keehan, Sophie Judge, Callie Robertson, and Matthew Everett, for all of your support and work with this book.

Lydia Blagden, for the most stunning UK cover design I could ever have asked for. I get goose bumps every time I look at it.

Ellie Wheeldon, for creating an audiobook I could not possibly be happier with.

Kristin Atherton, for bringing the characters to life with your incredible voice and acting. You are the perfect audiobook narrator for this project, and have captured this story and its characters beautifully.

All my thanks to the incredible team at Park & Fine Literary and Media:

Peter Knapp, for being my absolute dream agent. Thank you, as always, for being the most amazing advocate and business partner. I continue to be beyond thrilled to get to work with you and this absolute rock-star team.

Emily Sweet and Andrea Mai, for such amazing support of both me and this series.

Kathryn Toolan, for making my day every time you send me an email. Thank you so much for being phenomenal and getting this series into the hands of readers all across the globe.

Stuti Telidevara, for so much help in keeping everything on track and being so supportive.

At APA, thank you to Debbie Deuble-Hill for endlessly pushing to ensure that this series gets the most perfect on-screen home and for introducing me to my new favorite place to get a cannoli in LA.

Elena Masci and Teagan White, thank you for the loveliest covers I have ever seen in both the US and UK. You both truly outdid yourselves for *Foxglove,* and I couldn't be more in love with your spectacular art.

To my Round Table friends, for putting up with my many schemes and being the best support system in this truly wild industry. I am very grateful to have you. A special shout-out to Lady Lancelot herself, Rachel Griffin. May our publishers continue to have us on the same publishing schedule forevermore, otherwise I fear we may perish.

Bri Renae, for being one of the very first readers, and for loving Death more than anyone.

Josh, for always being supportive, even when I randomly turn into a zombie gremlin with a spontaneous need to travel somewhere or hole myself away in a dungeon.

Mom and Dad, for a lifetime of support and believing I'm way cooler and more impressive than I am, and for letting everyone else know it.

The most incredible street team, for making the process of bringing this series into the world so much more enjoyable than I ever imagined it could be. I am so lucky and grateful to have met such an amazing and supportive group.

Haley Marshall, because of course this book is dedicated to you. Thank you for over a decade of friendship, laughter, and for always being the first person to read and let me know that things (usually) are not as dogshit as I think they are.

God, for getting me here.

And finally, to every reader who has made it this far. Thank you for every kind message, review, and for every bit of cosplay, fanart, tattoos, or amazing crafts you have shared for this series. You all are so ridiculously talented and just plain incredible, and I'm so happy to have you as readers. Thank you for loving this book as much as I do. It's because of all your support that the next page is possible.

Turn the page for a sneak preview of

AVAILABLE AUGUST 2024

ONE

IT'S SAID THAT THE WISTERIA VINE IS A SYMBOL OF IMMORTALITY.

Blythe Hawthorne had often admired the flower—as deadly as it was beautiful, and resilient enough to thrive for centuries even if left forgotten. Yet as she crushed a petal between her fingers from the looming vines and let its color bleed onto her skin, she pitied the wisteria for the fate that she and the flower shared. How tragic that they were to forever remain rooted in Aris's garden, their splendor wasted on the likes of him.

Blythe, at least, had one advantage over the wisteria—she had thorns. And when it came to Aris Dryden, she had every intention of using them.

Blythe trailed a look across the garden to where dozens of guests stood in wait. Sunlight cut through the wisteria canopied above them, bathing the courtyard in a golden haze of light that had people squinting as they chatted, their breath pluming the air.

Blythe envied their fine coats. Her skin was chilled from

autumn's dampness, and the gossamer sleeves of her gown did little to stave it off. November was an unusual time for a wedding, though with Aris, she supposed she should always expect the unusual. If the alleged prince decided he wanted to get married on an autumn morning at an hour when the sun hadn't yet dried the dew upon the moss, who was society to question him?

Aris Dryden was a man who got what he wanted. This day just happened to be a rare exception, for he was being forced to marry a woman he could not stand.

And to be fair, the feeling was mutual.

"You don't have to do this." It was Blythe's father, Elijah Hawthorne, who spoke. "Say the word, and I'll get you out of here."

In any other world, Blythe would have taken him up on the offer to flee Wisteria Gardens. But to secure Elijah's safety after he was falsely accused of murder, Blythe Hawthorne had spilled her blood upon a golden tapestry and bound herself to Aris—to *Fate*—for the remainder of her years. She even had a glowing band of light on her ring finger to show for it, the golden hue so faint that it was nearly invisible to the eye.

"I'll be all right," she told her father at last. It was no use to try to sway him with sweet words about how much she loved Aris or how happy she was to be marrying the brute. As it was, she was shivering in the damp air and itchy from what felt like a hundred layers of taffeta, and she had to keep fighting off a sneeze every time her veil brushed near her nose. She had no patience left within her to lie, and Elijah was no fool; he knew that Blythe had never intended to marry.

"You'll make a beautiful princess," he whispered, and Blythe surely would have agreed, had Aris *actually* been royalty. "But I want you to remember that Thorn Grove will always be open to you. No matter the day or the hour, you can always return home."

"I know that," Blythe promised, for she understood that truth better than anything.

Only when Elijah seemed certain that there would be no talking her out of this wedding did he bend to kiss her head. He adjusted Blythe's veil to shroud her face as he eased away. She scrunched her nose, turning to the side to sneeze.

When the lilting pings of a harp began a sauntering melody, Elijah extended his arm. "Are you ready?"

Never. A million years would need to pass before Blythe could even consider being *ready*. But instead of the truth, she told her father, "I am," for if this was what it took to keep him from being hanged, it was more than worth the sacrifice.

As much as Blythe tried to focus, the world spun as she stepped into the courtyard. The ground was a pathway of stepping stones with vibrant clovers that curved around each one; Elijah steadied her as she nearly slipped upon them, her choice of shoe providing little grip.

Blythe's heart beat against her chest like a torrent, drowning out the pinging of the harp that slowed its tune to match her careful footsteps. She looked to the crowd, to faces that blurred into sharpened slivers of too-white teeth and hungry eyes that devoured her with every step, as if readying to pluck the skin from her bones. Blythe held her chin sharp even as her hands fought to tremble, refusing to let anyone scent her fear.

It wasn't until she saw her bridesmaid, Signa, standing near the front of the crowd in a beautiful lace gown that the pressure in Blythe's chest deflated. Death loomed behind Signa, his shadows winding around her own fretting hands.

Tiny shocks pulsed up Blythe's spine at the sight of his touch upon her cousin's skin. Everything in her body ached to flee from Death's presence, and yet... he was the one Signa had chosen. Blythe would never understand *why*, but if Signa was happy and Elijah was free, then all was well in the world.

As Blythe passed her cousin, the harp song faded, and her father drew to a halt. Blythe was left with no choice but to finally turn her attention to the golden-haired man who stood before them in a coat as richly hued as a sapphire. *Handsome,* she supposed others might think him, and yet all Blythe could see was the resentment that festered within Aris Dryden like a poison. He masked it with a cleaving smile, as if ready to join the fray of predators set to devour her.

Aris stepped forward, offering Blythe his hand. Had Elijah not tensed beneath her grip, reminding Blythe of his presence, she may not have taken it.

"Hello, love." Aris may have whispered the words, but his voice was a weapon that slipped through Blythe's skin and struck to the hilt. "I hoped you wouldn't make it."

She squeezed his hand, forcing her own smile onto a face she hoped looked half as vicious as his. "I wouldn't have missed this for the world, my darling. Though do feel free to divorce me tomorrow." The thread between their fingers shone bright, searing into their skin so intensely that Aris laughed to cover his grimace.

"And spare you from a lifetime of misery? I think not. You have no idea how much I intend to—" He froze, having been speaking so quietly that their heads were bowed, nearly touching each other, when he demanded in a dangerous tone, "What on earth are you wearing?"

Blythe didn't need to follow his gaze down to her feet to know that he was referring to her velvet green slippers. Her favorite pair, in fact. She'd adjusted her dress just enough to allow him a glimpse. As buttoned-up as Aris was, Blythe hadn't had any doubts that he'd notice.

So, it seemed, had their guests. A quiet tittering sounded from the audience, and though Blythe paid it little mind, Aris's jaw tensed. He squeezed her hands, hissing words through a false smile. "You are not marrying me in *slippers*. Go and change."

Blythe curled her toes into the velvet. "And stop the wedding? I wouldn't dream of it."

If she weren't already so aware of Aris's power, she would have realized the full extent of it as his eyes flashed gold and the world fell still. Elijah's foot stopped mid-step on his way back toward the guests, and Blythe reached out to stroke her finger along the belly of a hummingbird that had frozen beside her, its wings unmoving. Some of the guests had their mouths ajar, bodies bent in stilled whispers, and not a single eye blinked in awareness. Only Signa and Death continued to move, swathed in the shadows. Signa drew a step closer, though Aris halted her with a scowl that seared like a melting sun.

"Go and put on shoes." Aris bowed his head to Blythe's level, holding back none of his contempt now that their guests were frozen. "This is ridiculous. I refuse to play your games."

Blythe had earned every bit the reaction she'd hoped to from such a proud man, and the grin she sported said as much. "It seems you haven't noticed, my love, but you're already playing."

The millions of golden threads surrounding them glimmered. Several wound around her wrist, and as Aris made a motion as if to tug her forward, Blythe braced herself. Yet it was Aris who stumbled back, clutching his own wrist with a hiss of pain. He looked not at Blythe but to Signa, whose face was stony.

Had her cousin also struck a bargain with Fate? It seemed that he was unable to harm her, and Blythe's realization came in the form of a baleful laugh as she drew chest-to-chest with Aris. Or chest-to-stomach, really, given that he was a good head taller.

"I will wait out the rest of my life rooted in this spot if it means beating you," she told him, meaning each and every word. "Free the others from whatever spell you placed upon them and let's get on with this charade."

A long moment passed in which Aris did nothing. So long, in fact, that Death began to stir. Though she knew the reaper meant to help, Blythe tensed when his shadows inched closer. It was all she could do to keep her eyes on Aris, trying to ignore Death's presence by putting as much heat into her glare as she could summon. She couldn't say how long Aris matched that stare until, eventually, he gritted his teeth and grabbed hold of her skirts, tossing them over her slippers. Only then did Elijah's foot hit the ground with a slap and the quiet whispers resume. The hummingbird darted over Aris's head as the minister approached.

"Wilt thou have this woman to be thy wedded wife . . . ," he began, and no sooner had the words left his mouth did Blythe's world sway. She dug her heels into the earth, rooting deeper with each vow that passed his lips. "Wilt thou love her . . . forsaking all others . . . so long as you both shall live?" Though she missed most of what the minister said, her world came crashing to a halt with his last question. Blythe glanced sideways at Aris, who kept his head down and his jaw so tight that she thought his teeth might snap.

"For as long as she lives," he agreed, so curt that the minister flinched before turning his attention to Blythe.

"And wilt thou have this man to be thy wedded husband, to live together after God's ordinance in the holy estate of Matrimony? Wilt thou obey him, serve him, love, honor, and keep him in sickness and in health; and, forsaking all others, keep thee only unto him, so long as you both shall live?"

Aris shot Blythe a dark look that halted her laughter before it could escape. She cleared it from her throat. "I will marry him, and I will love him even more when he is sick." She said it so sincerely and with such a disarming smile that, though the minister was thrown off, he brought forward a golden ring designed to resemble a snake, set with eyes of jade.

"Repeat after me. With this ring I thee wed, with my body I thee worship . . ."

Each word was acid in Blythe's mouth, the ring burning as Aris shoved it down her finger while reciting the vows. Blythe bit her tongue as he pressed it so deeply toward her knuckle that she'd have to oil the blasted thing to get it off. Which she certainly would be doing the moment they were out of the public eye.

"Hello, *wife*," Aris spat, voice too low for anyone else's ears.

Blythe smiled through the pain, curling her hands around his so that she could dig her nails into his palms. "Hello, husband."

Neither looked away as the minister motioned them to their knees for the ceremonial prayer, and the rest of his words fell away as Blythe's ring finger seared beneath her golden band.

It was not a ring but a shackle. One, it seemed, that neither she nor Aris would be escaping any time soon.

Adalyn Grace

ADALYN GRACE

is the #1 *New York Times, USA Today,* and internationally bestselling author of the Belladonna series and the All the Stars and Teeth duology. Prior to becoming a writer, Adalyn studied storytelling as an intern on Nickelodeon Animation's popular series *The Legend of Korra*. Local to San Diego, she spends her nonwriting days watching too much anime and playing video games with her two dorky dogs. She invites you to visit her on Instagram @authoradalyngrace or her website, AdalynGraceAuthor.com.

A DEADLY GOOD SERIES
FROM *NEW YORK TIMES*
BESTSELLING AUTHOR
ADALYN GRACE

thenovl.com

BOB1151